A PROMISING FUTURE

Walking along the secluded beach, Christina was drawn to the crashing sound of the surf. The air, damp and salty, was enveloping. And the soft sand clung to her calves, blending with the subtle tan of her skin. She paused to brush it away, and, leaning down, looked back to see the house in the distance shrouded by the early morning fog.

Slowly, Christina removed her clothes, leaving them in a neat pile in a grove of palm trees, and ran into the foamy surf. Ten minutes later, refreshed, she returned for her clothes.

"Here, I brought you this," a man's voice said.

Christina turned to see Ash Young holding a towel out to her. He had been hidden by the trees as she approached. Now, standing before him, Christina realized she was completely naked.

Ash himself was surprised that he'd appeared, but something about Christina was beckoning him. She smiled hesitantly and came forward to take the towel from his hand. And in that moment, she was overcome by the undeniable sense that Ash Young—a stranger to her now—was prevailing over her future....

EXCITING BESTSELLERS FROM ZEBRA

PASSION'S REIGN by Karen Harper   (1177, $3.95)

Golden-haired Mary Bullen was wealthy, lovely and refined—and lusty King Henry VIII's prize gem! But her passion for the handsome Lord William Stafford put her at odds with the Royal Court. Mary and Stafford lived by a lovers' vow: one day they would be ruled by only the crown of PASSION'S REIGN.

HEIRLOOM by Eleanora Brownleigh   (1200, $3.95)

The surge of desire Thea felt for Charles was powerful enough to convince her that, even though they were strangers and their marriage was a fake, fate was playing a most subtle trick on them both: Were they on a mission for President Teddy Roosevelt—or on a crusade to realize their own passionate desire?

LOVESTONE by Deanna James   (1202, $3.50)

After just one night of torrid passion and tender need, the dark-haired, rugged lord could not deny that Moira, with her precious beauty, was born to be a princess. But how could he grant her freedom when he himself was a prisoner of her love?

DEBORAH'S LEGACY by Stephen Marlowe   (1153, $3.75)

Deborah was young and innocent. Benton was worldly and experienced. And while the world rumbled with the thunder of battle, together they rose on a whirlwind of passion—daring fate, fear and fury to keep them apart!

Available wherever paperbacks are sold, or order direct from the Publisher. Send cover price plus 50¢ per copy for mailing and handling to Zebra Books, 475 Park Avenue South, New York, N.Y. 10016 DO NOT SEND CASH.

Pay THE Price

IGOR CASSINI

ZEBRA BOOKS
KENSINGTON PUBLISHING CORP.

ZEBRA BOOKS

are published by

KENSINGTON PUBLISHING CORP.
475 Park Avenue South
New York, N.Y. 10016

Printed in the United States of America

To the surviving members of the Cassini Clan—Oleg, my brother, Brenda, my wife, Marina, Alexander, and Nicholas, my children—with love.

My thanks to Sarah Gallick, for invaluable help, generously given.

Prologue

Palm Beach
December 1977

Ash Young sat in the studio of his home staring out at the beach. His Palm Beach mansion was aptly called Belvedere, for it had a most pleasing view of the Atlantic. This time of the morning the view was at its best, almost completely unsullied by people.

He kept staring at the rough ocean. The waves beat angrily against the shore while the sun tried in vain to peek through the huge, gray clouds. He could see a fishing boat far out at sea. The people in it were probably tourists after swordfish or marlin. Perhaps the boat would capsize and they would die, stupidly.

What about his own death? Would it be any less stupid? He wondered for a minute how he would die. In bed clutching at all the gold he had accumulated so that his greedy heirs, his relieved employees, his triumphant enemies, could not take possession of it? Driven insane by the ghosts of all the men he had ruined, beginning with his own father? Or buried like a pharaoh, with all the treasures he had won for himself?

And what about after? Would the pearly gates of heaven open to him, Ashley Rodman Young, richest of the rich, and would he be given a proper seat, worthy of his ranking on Earth, at the table of the Almighty?

Or would he be led down into the bowels of hell to be greeted by the Lord of Darkness for the destruction and grief he had caused in his lifetime?

Jesus! He was beginning to sound like his mother. Hellfire and damnation had been her department. As far as he was concerned there was no afterlife, no eternal paradise or punishment, just nothingness, void, silence, emptiness. It was here and now that counted. And you got nothing for free. You had to pay for it.

He had paid for everything he owned, he thought, as he looked around the studio. Like the rest of Belvedere it was furnished with priceless antiques. His desk was an original Louis XV, a jewel of craftsmanship made of the finest mahogany and kept shining by his butler's expert hand—he would never allow any of the maids to touch it. It was small and rested elegantly on four slender legs shaped like columns and adorned with golden bronze fittings. The knobs of two drawers were also golden and the whole effect was one of beauty and expense. And expensive it had been. It had cost him one hundred and fifty thousand dollars.

He reached into the right hand drawer and brought out a modest wooden box. From it he removed a big, brown Davidoff Dom Perignon cigar, clipped the end and lit it, drawing on it with pleasure. Davidoff of Geneva was an institution, the Harry Winston of tobacco, handling the finest of them all. Old Monsieur Davidoff had a special contract with the Castro government to manufacture his cigars in Cuba and Ashley Young had an arrangement with Davidoff to ship him a box of fifty twice a month.

Young leaned back in his chair and continued to stare out at the water. On top of the desk was a copy of the latest issue of Alex Mercati's magazine, *The Reporter*. The cover story was "Ashley Rodman Young, Tycoon with a Social Conscience." There was a photograph of him surrounded by replicas of his various newspaper, broadcasting, cosmetic, shipping, airlines, banking and oil interests as well as his philanthropies. The photograph showed a handsome man of fifty with silver hair, gray eyes and a weather-beaten complexion.

In a way it had all been easy. After that first confrontation with his father in 1949, when fresh out of Princeton, he had taken over Young Oil and Gas and his success had snowballed into an avalanche. He had enlarged the oil empire tenfold, acquired a string of banks, a fleet of tankers, two airlines merged into one, a cosmetic company, a chain of small newspapers, and two TV broadcasting stations, in Texas and California.

He had attained all his goals. He ruled an empire and had achieved wealth and power beyond his boyhood dreams. His fleet of ships rivalled Ludwig, Onassis, Niarchos and Pateras. He was a key business advisor to the king of Saudi Arabia, the emir of Kuwait and the Shah of Iran. He entertained royalty and presidents at Belvedere and at his exquisite Fifth Avenue apartment. He was feared and respected. He had reached the pinnacle. He had access to everything money could buy.

Money had not helped his family though. He glanced at the silver framed photographs of his wife and daughter. *The Reporter* only briefly referred to "the fun-loving, exuberant Stephanie Young." That was putting it kindly. The truth was that his daughter was a nympho and a stupid one at that. He had raised her with the best that money could buy, yet instead of growing up as a princess she behaved like a tramp.

Jessica was another problem. *The Reporter*

called her "elegant and remote." Stoned and frigid was more like it. When he married her she had been no Marilyn Monroe, but she had been warm and attractive, meek and obedient. Sex between them had never been anything wild but at least in the beginning it had been adequate. Now it had frozen into a distant and polite arrangement. They had separate rooms and separate lives. Lately she seemed like a robot, repeating the proper phrases, making the right gestures, but totally without feeling. Those pills she took all the time seemed to have deadened her to everything.

He shook himself out of his reverie. The cigar was a mere stub now and the fishing boat was only a dot on the horizon. The sun had come out and he decided to go down to the pool for a swim.

August was waiting for him in the hall. Tall and gray-haired, the butler looked far more elegant and well-bred than many of the honored guests who came to Belvedere. He had served for twenty years with the Duke of Marlborough until Ash wooed him away ten years ago by doubling his salary. His Grace had been furious but Ash calculated it had been worth it to lose the duke as a friend in order to acquire August as a butler. It always came down to that. Analyze the price and decide whether you were prepared to pay it.

"Sir," August intoned. "Will you have refreshments by the pool?"

"Yes, August, after my swim."

"Sir, Mrs. Young wishes me to tell you that she went out shopping this morning and that Lord and Lady Duncan and Mr. and Mrs. Frazier will be coming for lunch."

Damn. He had forgotten about lunch. Duncan was a pain in the ass. He would want to talk about the good old days when they had been friendly rivals on the polo field and his own mind would be elsewhere. The party for the Saudi Arabian oil minister tonight was far more important. How could Jessica have invited them on the same day? Was even the simple matter of scheduling beyond her?

Angrily, he dove into the water and swam the length of the white marble pool. It was Olympic size and the water, siphoned from the sea, was purified and heated and kept at an even temperature of sixty-eight degrees. The marble patio surrounding the pool was shaded by huge palm trees which had twice been replanted after devastating hurricanes.

Finished with his four laps, he practiced a few leg kicks. It was good to keep in shape.

After twenty minutes of this he emerged from his swim refreshed and in better spirits. While August wrapped him in a thick, white towel, Ash smiled to himself. What was he worried about anyway? The hell with it. If you could pay the price, anything was yours for the taking. Wasn't that what life was all about?

Part One

1

Ardmore, Oklahoma
August 1924

It was the end of Chatauqua week in Ardmore, and in spite of the late August heat a great crowd had turned out. The huge, canvas tents had been set up on the fairgrounds and culture-thirsty Sooners were filing in for the last day's events. Drew Young bought a single ticket and filed in with them.

The audience was a mixed group of Mennonite farmers, Ardmore businessmen and Choctaw Indians who mostly huddled in the rear. A smiling, young usher wearing a button that read "Keep Cool with Coolidge" led him to one of the front benches where he would have a good view of the stage.

Across the aisle, he noticed the boy seating a

15

pretty, blond girl of about twenty. She was fanning herself, trying to get some relief from the heat. The skirt of her high necked, white poplin dress was a little too long to be fashionable, even in Ardmore. She wore no wedding ring and she had placid, blue eyes and long, black lashes which she lowered, blushing, when she realized he was smiling at her.

"Who is that girl?" he asked, as the young usher handed him a program.

The boy smiled. "Pretty, ain't she?"

"Yes," Drew agreed. "But who is she?"

"That's Mildred Rodman. Her father's got a revival tent on the other side of the fairgrounds. He's a preacher, here to save the Choctaws. They got a farm in east Texas, I hear, but he got the call." The boy's tone was ironic.

"It looks like every soul in Ardmore is here tonight," Drew remarked as he looked around the crowded, steamy tent.

"Oh, the Reverend just closed down for this week. He knows he can't compete with this."

The show began quickly with a welcoming address by the mayor. Then a barbershop quartet sang, followed by an orator in the style of William Jennings Bryan and an Indian maiden who sang and demonstrated tribal rituals.

Drew barely paid attention. He was busy watching the pretty, blond girl.

At intermission a man came through selling

small paper cups of lemonade. He saw his chance, paid for two and walked over to the girl who was still fanning herself.

"Will this help?" He offered her a cup.

She looked at him, puzzled and obviously embarrassed. Mildred Rodman did not consider herself the kind of girl who would take gifts, even a cup of lemonade, from a stranger.

"You're very kind," she assured him. "But—"

"Please," he insisted.

Flustered, she took the paper cup and smiled up at him. "Thank you." She sipped it delicately and stared at the stranger.

At twenty-eight, Drew Young was tall and rugged, with thick, black hair and piercing, Irish blue eyes. He had grown up on a Wisconsin farm and graduated from the University of Wisconsin with a law degree. He had gone to Chicago to seek his fortune, but in 1922 he was almost caught in a raid on a speakeasy. Deciding it was an appropriate time to head west, he moved on to Oklahoma and got a job with the Office of Indian Affairs. He did not plan on staying long; he was sure he was meant for greater things.

Now, as he smiled at the blond girl, he thought wistfully of the flappers in Chicago. This girl was more the Mary Pickford type. Sweet and innocent. And a lady.

After the second act and the grand finale, a

brass band playing "I'll See You in My Dreams," Miss Rodman consented to let him walk her home. They talked of the coming election as they strolled through the quiet town. Miss Rodman was convinced that John Davis would win, the country would never elect Mr. Coolidge, who had succeeded that awful Mr. Harding. She told Drew proudly that she was a Fundamentalist and a great supporter of William Jennings Bryan in his brave stand against evolution.

Drew explained that he was working with the Choctaws, supervising the leasing of their tribal lands to farmers and Miss Rodman thought that was a noble occupation.

She told him that she was twenty and committed to the Lord's work. She and her father, the Reverend James Paul Rodman, had come to Ardmore to bring religion to the Choctaws. She would much rather be back on the farm in Overton, she sighed, but Daddy had a call. All she could do was hope that come fall they would go home.

He suggested they stop in at the town hall dance, but she looked shocked. Dancing was not respectable. He asked if she would like to come to the picture show some night. Her eyes lit up and she said yes. But first, she insisted, he must come hear her daddy preach. He promised to come the following night, when the Reverend Rodman would be resuming his mission.

It was a revelation. The tent was more packed than the Chatauqua and the crowd was mostly Choctaws, men, women and children. They all stared at the star of the show, the Reverend James Paul Rodman.

He was a tall, ascetic man, but his eyes had the wild look of a fanatic. His three-piece black wool suit was relieved only by a gold watch chain stretched across his lean middle. He thundered on for an hour against the evolutionists, wets, Catholics and all other godless infidels, and if Drew had not been told the Reverend was a man of God, he might have thought he was an envoy of the devil. But he seemed to be the only one in the tent who thought so. As he gazed around the hot, steaming tent, he saw the Choctaws were listening in awe.

Mildred stood on the stage beside her father. She was wearing a blue voile dress that matched her eyes. She was as rapt as any Indian and occasionally she would emphasize one of her father's points by hitting a beribboned tambourine.

After the show, during which twenty-five Choctaws had been "saved" and the collection basket overflowed, Drew went around behind the tent to call on Mildred and her father. They were living in a small trailer parked in back.

Mildred answered the door. She looked a little nervous.

"How did you like it?" she asked.

"I'm saved, Miss Rodman, totally and completely," he answered, blue eyes twinkling. "And I'll know I've made it to heaven if you'll just come into town with me for an ice cream soda."

"Please don't joke about our work," she winced. "But I would like a soda. Just come in and meet Daddy first."

She led him into the tiny, tidy trailer where the Reverend was counting the evening's take at the kitchen table. He put it away hastily as she introduced them. Then she disappeared for a few minutes, leaving them alone. The radio was on and Drew recognized the voice of the revivalist Gypsy Smith.

The Reverend was unimpressed. "My daughter tells me you met her at the Chatauqua," he began.

"Yes, sir," Drew agreed, leaning forward in his chair. "I asked her to the dance afterward but she refused."

"Quite rightly," Rodman assured him. "Dancing is the devil's invention, made to tempt Christians into sin. It's a practice almost as evil as fornication."

"I see," Drew said and, as Mildred hurried him out of the trailer, he made a mental note to limit his further contacts with the Reverend.

As it happened, that night would mark his last meeting with the Reverend, for when he and Mildred returned from their ice cream soda they lingered for a few minutes near the doorstep.

"Thank you, Mr. Young," she told him. "I enjoyed talking with you."

"Please don't go," he said as she put her hand on the door.

She turned to him, slightly surprised. She had not had much experience with men and, with only the teachings of her father to go by, she was not sure what happened next. She need not have worried, for Drew Young had taken her in his arms and was kissing her on the mouth and pressing his body against hers. She stiffened and would have pushed the presumptuous Young away, but at that moment they were suddenly pulled apart with a force as strong as the one that had just held her.

"Get out of here," the Reverend Rodman screamed. He had been hiding behind the bushes, waiting for them for nearly an hour, and he leaped out as soon as he saw the cad take his daughter in his arms. "I knew what you were up to the minute I saw you."

He grabbed Drew by the lapels of his jacket and stood almost eye to eye so that as he ranted occasional spittle splashed on Young's face.

"Daddy," Mildred pleaded. "You don't understand. Mr. Young behaved like a perfect gentleman."

"Don't lie for him, daughter," he answered,

then turned back to Drew. "So, you even try to turn my child against me!"

"You're crazy," Drew said. By now shock had been replaced by disgust.

"Crazy am I?" Rodman roared. "I'll show you who's crazy!"

With that he released Drew. Discretion being the better part of valor in this case, Drew began to beat a hasty retreat from the campground, but not before the Reverend had administered one good swift kick in his pants.

As Drew Young vanished out of sight, Mildred turned to her father. "Daddy, how could you?" she said as they entered the trailer. "He didn't mean any harm."

"How do you know?" Rodman answered. "You know nothing of the evils of men. When the time is right, I'll find you a God-fearing man."

Chastened, Mildred bid her father good night and left him alone in the kitchen to finish his bookkeeping.

The truth was that James Paul Rodman had no intention of losing his pretty daughter to anyone. Smallpox had already taken his long-suffering wife and his younger daughter in 1920. Now there was only Mildred to care for him and do the chores on the farm. As he finished counting the evening's donations, he realized that he had about exhausted the financial possibilities of Ardmore for the season. It was time to return to Overton.

"Mildred," he shouted. "Pack up your things, girl. We're going home."

Mildred sighed drowsily and began to pack. Watching her father and Drew Young argue had set her to shaking, but she was not dissatisfied with the outcome. Drew Young had everything a girl could want in a beau; he was handsome and kind and ambitious. In spite of what her father thought, he had treated her with respect. She could easily imagine them courting and, following the natural order of things, marrying.

Marriage.

The word sent chills down her spine, for Mildred Rodman lived in dread of the time she would marry. The sexual education administered by her father had succeeded in crushing any natural passion she might have felt. The thought of the sexual act made her gag and, although she was far from vain, the idea that she might actually become swollen with child disgusted her. Still, she was not stupid enough to believe that Kilgore offered much of a life for an unmarried woman who was not getting any younger.

She imagined that she would just go on keeping house for her father. They would grow old together and when Daddy passed on, perhaps she would marry an older man, someone looking more for a housekeeper (and she was a good one) than an object for his lust.

So, relieved at her narrow escape, Mildred Rodman followed her father back home to Texas.

*   *   *

The next morning, when Drew Young came to his senses, he decided to visit the Reverend again. After all, what would it cost to apologize to the old bigot? He disliked making an enemy of anyone and he had charmed plenty of people, from cynical oilmen to naive Choctaws, and he could surely charm the Reverend. There were not so many pretty young women in Ardmore that he could afford to let Miss Mildred Rodman slip away.

But when he arrived at the fairgrounds, he found to his dismay that the Rodmans' tent and trailer were gone. They had left during the night and it was with sadness that he realized he might never see Mildred again.

In the year and a half that followed, Drew Young almost forgot about Mildred Rodman and her father. The country was booming and so was Ardmore, and Drew, as an ambitious young man, had every intention of making the best of it.

Through a Louisiana woman married to a Choctaw and living on the reservation, Drew had met her brother, Columbus Joiner. A youthful sixty, "Dad" Joiner was a local character, best known for having purchased leases for 320 acres of farmland in Rusk County, Texas, sight unseen. He planned to sell them at a profit and went down to take a look at just what he had. But once Joiner saw the scrubby east Texas fields something clicked.

"I took one look at that land and I just knew there was oil," he told Drew.

Drew only laughed. "That's not what the big boys say." It was well known that the major oil companies, including Humble and Standard Oil, had already written off east Texas just as most folks in Ardmore had written off Dad Joiner's schemes.

That did not phase Joiner, though, and by 1926 he had leases on over four thousand acres. None of them, according to the major oil companies and their sophisticated geologists, had a prayer of yielding oil.

"The only way Dad Joiner is going to get rich in east Texas is by selling those leases to other suckers," his detractors used to say.

In spite of that, Drew Young liked the older man and was convinced he was no fool. He enjoyed his stories, so when Joiner's sister invited him for supper one evening, he accepted the invitation. He was tired of boardinghouse food anyway and Dad Joiner was always an entertaining companion.

They ate in the cozy kitchen of Joiner's brother-in-law's cabin on the reservation. Dad had just returned from one of his frequent trips to east Texas. Once again the subject was the alleged oil in Rusk County. Aware that Drew had saved his money and was looking for investment opportunities, Joiner was trying to convince him to invest in some of his leases.

Joiner was no fool and no dreamer, and in spite of himself Young was almost convinced that he should join the man on his next trip to east Texas. After all, Joiner had been right before, but he'd had to quit drilling and others had reaped the oil. This time, he assured Drew, he was going to hang on.

Dinner finished, Joiner's sister rose and began to clear away the dishes. Joiner explained that his sister and her husband disapproved of smoking and suggested Drew join him on the enclosed porch for some of the weed. It soon turned out that Dad Joiner had a story he did not want to tell in front of his sister.

Between guffaws, he managed to tell Drew about a Rusk County preacher who had called at a bordello in Shreveport. He had revelled all night, according to Joiner, using not one but three of the madam's favorite girls. Unfortunately, when it came time to pay the bill, the saintly man was outraged. He invoked the wrath of God on the ungrateful sinners whose souls he had come to save. Contact with him had purified these creatures of lust and debauchery, he assured them, and on that high note he left the place.

He was found the next morning, a few yards from the bordello, sprawled in the mud, his throat cut from ear to ear. They took their brothel debts seriously in Shreveport.

"I'm afraid the only one who was sorry to see him go was his daughter," Joiner concluded.

"Mildred Rodman," Drew said softly. His mind was forming a picture from the past, a picture of a sweet, pretty, blond girl. Then he recalled the last time he had seen her father, his face twisted with rage. Of course he should have recognized the hypocrisy in the old faker. He wondered how Mildred was doing now that she was alone.

Joiner shook his head. "That little lady's sitting on a gold mine and she won't even talk to me. I offered her good money to lease her farm, just for the oil rights, but she won't even talk to me."

"There's oil on the Rodman farm?" Drew asked.

"Of course there's oil," Joiner boomed. "I haven't tapped it yet, but it's there, the way it's all over Rusk County."

Suddenly Young saw where his future lay. It

27

lay on an oil-rich farm in east Texas in the arms of a pretty, blond girl who was all alone in the world.

"I used to know Mildred Rodman," he said casually.

"Well, son," Joiner smiled. "That girl's about the only reason I could understand if you told me you didn't want to come in with me. Whoever marries that sweet thing is going to be a rich man."

"Thank you, Dad," Young said. "I think I'll be heading for east Texas myself."

2

Kilgore, Texas
February 1926

It took three days for Drew Young to wrap up his affairs in Ardmore, resign from the Office of Indian Affairs and turn his Chevrolet toward Texas. He drove all night and, following a map that Dad Joiner had drawn for him, he headed straight for the Rodman farm. The last paved road was the interstate highway. After that he followed dirt roads that became bumpier and muddier as he neared Overton, a mere whistle stop just outside Kilgore.

Dawn was breaking as he drove the Chevy up a narrow icy path lined with pine trees straight to the door of the farm. Snow had covered a good part of the land but it did not hide the scrubby, barren look of it. He caught sight of the late Reverend's trailer parked outside the house, near a faded red barn. The house itself was a small, white bungalow with a front porch, and on that porch two rather sad-looking wicker armchairs.

Mildred answered the door. She was as pretty as ever, even in her black mourning.

"Oh, my goodness," she fluttered. "I was just going out for groceries."

"Is that any way to greet an old friend?" he grinned.

She relented. "No, I suppose not. Come in."

She was mourning her father, she explained. He had died of a heart attack after preaching the gospel to a gathering of the faithful in Shreveport.

Drew said nothing about what he had heard, only that he was sorry. She showed him around the farm, explaining how they had managed to eke out a meager existence from the land by raising cotton, corn and sweet potatoes.

"It doesn't look like much now," she said. "But come spring, when the bluebonnets and mountain pinks are out, it gets real pretty. Of course if people like Dad Joiner had their way this whole country would be covered with oil wells."

"An oil well can buy a lot of flowers, Mildred," Drew answered as he gazed around the scrubby farm. He realized it was going to take some convincing to get her to allow him to start drilling.

He gave her a lift into Kilgore in the Chevy and when he invited her to dinner that night she said she could not accept but he could share her meal in her home. By the time he left he had managed to persuade her that they should marry.

They were married a few days later, on March 21, 1926, by the preacher who had replaced the late Reverend Rodman. Dad Joiner was Drew's best man.

Their first night together was a disaster. Mildred refused to take off her long, white flannel nightgown, and when he kissed her she kept her lips tightly closed. She never responded to his caresses but endured them in silence, clenching her teeth and praying to God and her father that she might be forgiven. He told himself that she was inexperienced, it would take time for her to get used to him, but in the months that followed it never got any better than that first night.

In fact, things got worse, for it began to dawn on Mildred Rodman Young that she had made a terrible mistake. The fact that she hated sex did not surprise her. She had never expected to like it. But she had at least believed that Drew Young was an honest, respectable man. True, their courtship had been brief, but she had been sure that Drew understood how she felt about oil men. She did not care how much oil lay beneath her farm. She did not want to see it covered with ugly oil derricks. Even if they brought in millions of dollars. Love of money was the root of all evil, the Bible said.

But to her chagrin, they had only been married a few days when Drew began to put in a well only a hundred feet from the house. For months he labored there, drilling deep into the earth.

It came up dry.

He rapidly dissipated all the money he had saved in Ardmore on his derrick and, broke, was forced to shut down and return to working for Dad Joiner. Dad had not struck oil yet either, but his various leasing arrangements could sure use Drew's legal expertise.

Meanwhile, Mildred became pregnant almost immediately and after that she would not allow him to touch her at all. He did not know whether he was angry or relieved. They shared the same large bed for a while, but night after night he would just turn his back to her and go to sleep dreaming of black gold.

In the morning he always seemed to wake up to another dry well.

Mildred got a bittersweet satisfaction out of their money troubles.

"God is punishing you," she assured him. "You'll never find peace until you heed the word of the Lord."

She became more involved in the local church her father had founded, the Haven of Christ. Because the new pastor, Reverend

Reede Whitby, was a bachelor, she continued with the same duties she had carried out for her father. She headed the Women's Guild, and played the organ for Sunday services and the Wednesday night Temperance rally. Drew himself never returned to the Church after their wedding day.

"You should try to come, at least once in a while," she pleaded with him. "People notice these things."

"Tell them I'm sick," he snapped.

"I can't tell them you're sick every Sunday morning," she wailed. "They'll start saying it's because you were out drinking all Saturday night like Lou Seals and Harlan Henderson."

"Don't you understand, Mildred, that I don't care what people think? Especially that sanctimonious bunch of churchgoing hypocrites you spend your time with? And you'd be a lot happier too, if you stopped paying attention to what they think."

But Mildred sought solace in her church, doubling her activities in spite of her pregnancy, so that, as Drew pointed out, she was spending more time with Reverend Whitby than with him.

"So what if I stayed home," she'd scream shrilly. "You'd never be here!"

He had to admit that was so. He had turned the Reverend's old trailer into a small office and spent days there poring over maps and geologists' reports, planning where he would drill next. Other times he was travelling with Joiner to Dallas and Fort Worth, always trying to raise money for more drills.

In the late fall of 1927, Drew was away so much that Mildred began to fear she'd be alone when her time came. She confided her fear to Reverend Whitby who suggested his maid's sister, Maria Gomez. The girl was a recent widow and had just suffered a miscarriage. "A blessing in disguise," the Reverend opined. "There's so many of them already."

Maria was big and strong and she'd delivered several babies herself already. Although Mildred and Drew could hardly feed themselves, much less a servant, Mildred asked Maria to help her in return for free room and board. She also promised to teach Maria to read and write.

Although she suspected that Drew had begun to see other women, Mildred was confident that Maria Gomez was too big and plain to appeal to her husband.

As she had feared, however, he was away with Dad Joiner when her pains began to come. It was Maria who helped her through her long and difficult twenty-seven hours of labor. There were many times when Maria was sure they were going to lose Mildred's baby, but by the time the infant emerged, a lustily bawling boy, there was no doubt in the mind of Maria or of his mother that the boy was there to stay.

A few days later, Drew returned to find he was the father of a son, born November 30, 1927 and already christened by the Reverend Whitby as Ashley Rodman Young.

Drew's new responsibilities did not encourage him to give up his dream. If anything, the fact that he now had a son compelled him to stick to searching for oil. When his well came in—and he knew it would—it would be the foundation of a dynasty. But Mildred soon set him straight about the dynasty part. One day he returned from Houston to find she had moved all his clothes into the old trailer. The cot where her father, the Reverend Rodman, had once slept was now made up for him.

"What's this all about?" he demanded.

"I'm not a well woman," she insisted, tears welling up in her eyes. "Dr. Franklin says I have to rest. And the Reverend Whitby says a good man would understand."

He didn't fight it because he was honestly relieved. The less he had to see of her the better. All the soft sweetness that had so enchanted him in Oklahoma had dried up under the Texas sun or frozen in the bitter cold of the east Texas winters. Sometimes, during their three years of hardship, Drew told himself that Mildred would change when he struck oil. Poverty didn't agree with her. . . . She was meant for a more gentle life. . . . When his well came in, his old girl would come back.

To her credit, Mildred kept their household going during those lean three years. Mornings, she set out lines for catfish and perch in the little creek that bounded the east end of her farm. Evenings, they ate whatever she'd caught. When it got too cold even for the catfish at the muddy bottom of the creek, they ate the vegetables she'd managed to put up that summer. When the winter winds howled outside their drafty bungalow, she stuffed the cracks with newspaper.

As she had suspected, her own milk was too skimpy and so Maria, breasts still heavy with milk, nursed baby Ash. In spite of Mildred's efforts as a teacher, Maria never learned to read or write, but she was devoted to the boy, so Mildred kept her on. But the nurse's warmth and affection didn't counteract the steady stream of thwarted hopes and hatred that Mildred poured into her son.

*   *   *

On October 3, 1930, Dad Joiner brought in the Daisy Bradford 3 at nearby Henderson. Soon she was yielding 300 barrels of oil a day. And on December 28, the Lou Della Crim came in thirteen miles north. It was all part of what came to be called the East Texas Field or the Black Giant, a great pool of oil beneath the earth.

The Rodman farm lay between the two finds and Drew was more convinced than ever that he too was going to hit oil. He drove himself at a furious pace, determined to succeed.

After October everything in east Texas seemed to change. Farming and pastures were forgotten overnight. Everyone was drilling for oil or preying on those who did. After all, they reasoned, Dad Joiner had struck it rich just by blind luck, surely they could too.

To Mildred's horror, an armada of ten thousand boomers, gamblers and desperadoes descended on the tiny hamlet of Kilgore making it the center of the oil boom. Speculators arrived with armloads of cash, ready to buy up the oil rights to the farms. The town became a bedlam overrun by violence and crime. Even the small Baptist church was ravaged. Pistol Hill nearby became notorious for the desperadoes who congregated there. Shacks and tents sprang up everywhere. Suddenly the country roads were choked with traffic, streets filled with people. A new telephone exchange was put in and hotels and rooming houses were crowding three to a bed.

She began to dread the trip into town. Kilgore had never been much, just one main street, but now most of that had been torn up. They had even put an oil derrick in the Church of Christ churchyard. She could remember when the town was so quiet at night that the occasional stray coyote could wander unmolested through the streets. Now those same streets were lined with dusty cars from God knew where, while brazen whores in silk pajamas paraded around, soliciting customers. Most of the houses and buildings remained unpainted because no one had the time. Any able-bodied man was looking to make his fortune in the oil business.

She avoided looking out her window these days. Her farm had been ruined by Drew's unsuccessful derricks and now it looked like every other farm in Rusk County. Any tiny space that could support a derrick was being leased; she had heard that lease hounds were offering two thousand dollars an acre. She would have taken it, just to get out of Overton, but Drew refused to allow her. He insisted that he was going to hit oil.

She sniffed at the thought. Even if he brought in oil now, she didn't see what good it was going to do him. Not the way the oil business was heading.

Something had gone badly wrong with the oil boom. As more oil was produced, prices fell. The oil men simply produced more oil to make up for it in volume. They had to, because under the rule of capture oil belonged to whomever brought it to the surface. Every well in east Texas was working off the same pool, and if Drew Young did not capture a piece of it, one of his neighbors—or more likely one of the major oil companies—would.

Beginning late in 1930, the state of Texas had tried to limit oil production and prop up the price but the east Texas wildcatters would have none of that. They continued to flood the market with cheap oil and the price per barrel dropped from $2.29 in 1926 to $1.10 in 1930 to $ .50 by 1931. It could not go on and so, on August 17, in the midst of one of the worst heat waves east Texas had ever seen, Brig. Gen. Jacob F. Wolters led ninety-nine officers and more than a thousand enlisted men into the area. He set up headquarters at the new Kilgore city hall and the order went out that all wells must be shut down by noon.

When they told Drew Young, he just grinned. "I saw that order and I read the governor's proclamation," he said dryly. "Neither one says one word about drilling, only producing oil. So long as my wells come in dry I guess the law don't apply to me."

Young had already seen in Chicago what happened when all the forces of government attempted to enforce an unpopular law, and he fully expected his fellow oil men would be as resourceful as the Chicago bootleggers. He was no Al Capone, but then who had oil ever killed?

Still, the decision cut back on oil production. All of a sudden Kilgore was rife with jobless roughnecks. Things were worse than ever because the population of the area had swollen so.

"I guess we're safe, anyhow, the place is crawling with National Guard, Texas Rangers and sheriff's men," Drew observed wryly. But in spite of that, he and his friends quickly discovered how to produce "hot oil."

"I guess those Boy Scouts of Wolters' don't understand us," he assured his confederates.

All that summer and fall Drew Young staggered home at night, dead tired after working all day under the boiling sun. The drilling had been difficult, and for a while there was nothing but mud, sand, and water. They drilled nearly thirty-five hundred feet and still nothing. Those were days of discouragement and despair. He took to carrying a pearl-handled revolver to protect himself against roving bandits.

Mildred assured him he had as good a chance at striking oil as he did at winning the Irish Sweepstakes. He was desperate for money. It cost between $30,000 and $35,000 to drill a well, and that well most likely would come up dry. All of his had. Yet he steadfastly refused to sell his mineral rights to any of the majors like Humble or Texaco who were all over the place.

One night over a lean dinner of thin hominy and thick coffee Mildred mentioned that a man had been looking for him. He owed so many so much that at first he was sure it was a bill collector.

"No," Mildred assured him calmly. "He's interested in buying my farm. He's offered me $10 an acre."

Of course, he told himself. That was why she was giving him her mean little smile. She'd said she'd never leave the land, but the minute some city slicker came in offering $10 an acre she was ready to sign on the dotted line.

"What'd you tell him?" he demanded.

"I told him to come back tonight and talk to my husband," she answered, pouring him another cup of coffee.

"Good. Then I'll have the pleasure of telling him 'no thanks' to his face."

"Are you crazy?" she screamed, slamming the coffee pot down so hard on the table that coffee slopped from the cups onto the faded tablecloth. "Maybe you don't mind if I starve to death, but what about your son?"

"He's not starving now and he never will be, 'cause his daddy knows better than to swallow the line of some front-man for Humble Oil!"

Suddenly there was a soft rap on the front door. They stopped their arguing.

"I reckon that's Mr. Ainsley," Mildred said.

"I'll handle this," Drew answered and headed for the door.

Standing in the doorway, Arness Ainsley radiated the same plump, sleek prosperity Drew had seen in the used car dealers and lawyers thriving in Dallas and Houston. He appeared well dressed in a dark suit and Stetson, and he

41

carried a heavy leather Gladstone bag. He grinned broadly at Drew.

"Evenin'," he said, tipping his hat to Mildred who was standing behind Drew. "I guess the little woman's told you why I'm here."

"Yes, sir," Drew acknowledged and—to Mildred's surprise—escorted their caller into the living room. "Mildred, let's get some coffee for Mr. Ainsley."

More surprises were in store that night. When she returned with a fresh pot of coffee, the two men were deep in conversation and it was clear that Mr. Ainsley had moved beyond his original price of $10 an acre, he was up to $20. By the time she'd finished pouring the coffee, he was up to $40. Her hand was trembling so with excitement that she could hardly hold the cups as she passed them around. She had to leave the room for fear she would faint, but she watched through a keyhole as the man opened his Gladstone, filled to the brim with one hundred dollar bills.

"Sir," Mr. Ainsley said firmly. "I'm prepared to offer you $50 an acre for all 300 acres of your wife's farm. That's $15,000 cash money right now."

Drew stood up. "And I, sir, am prepared to chase you off my land with a rifle if you're not out of here in five minutes."

The look in his eyes proved he was serious.

Plump Mr. Ainsley scurried out into the night so fast poor Mildred didn't have a chance to grab him and explain that her husband had suddenly lost his mind. Instead she was left to confront Drew alone.

"Are you insane?" she screamed. "$15,000 is more money than you'll ever see in your life. How could you let him get away?"

"Don't you understand anything Mildred? Don't you see that if our Mr. Ainsley—or whoever's behind him—is willing to pay us $50 an acre it's because he knows it's worth a lot more. They know as well as I do that we're sitting on black gold."

"Black gold, black gold," she sneered. "Don't talk to me about black gold while you destroy my farm. This land was beautiful once. There were oak and pecan trees, and pines and redbuds. Now all I see is your derricks. This farm is mine, and I'm going to sell it and live like a lady in Houston!" She pulled her shawl tightly around her and headed for the door, still hoping to capture Mr. Ainsley.

"Where do you think you're going?" Drew demanded, grabbing her by the shoulder and spinning her around.

Hatred flared in her eyes. "I'm going after Ainsley and getting my money tonight."

"You're not going anywhere," he said and in a sudden flash cracked her across the face with his hand. Dazed, she reeled, then fell in a heap at his feet, staring up at him, her eyes pools of fear mixed with loathing.

He'd never hit a woman before, but, Drew told himself, she had asked for it. Now all the anger that had festered within him came raging out of his mouth.

"Listen to this, Mildred. This farm belongs to you on paper only. I've earned it. Sleeping with you and not sleeping with you, putting up with your nagging and your hatred these last three years. Do you think I did it because I loved you? Maybe a little in the beginning, but you took care of that."

"I always knew you didn't love me," she whispered. "But I thought you stayed on for the boy."

"No, Mildred, not even him. He's your son, and I see your poison in his eyes every day. No, I stayed for this farm, because I know there's oil here and someday it's going to make the three of us rich. Yes, Mildred, the three of us, because there's plenty to go around. But if you don't like it, leave. But I'm not going to."

"I could get a divorce," she insisted. The very word was anathema to her, but it was her only hope. "I'll divorce you for adultery—you know I've got grounds. And I'll get my farm back."

"No, Mildred, there'll be no divorce. I'd kill you first."

Their arguing was cut short when they saw

their small son standing in the doorway, his eyes wide with fear.

"Mama," he said, rushing to Mildred as she struggled to her feet. Drew did not help her.

"Now see what you've done," she said. "You've frightened the boy."

"Don't worry about him," Drew insisted. "He's too young to understand."

But the three-year-old did understand. He saw that his parents hated each other and that neither one was interested in him.

Drew Young saw Ainsley once more, when one afternoon he came across his body being carried out of a local saloon. The wheeler dealer had been shot dead in a quarrel over leases with another promoter.

Although Drew would never have admitted it to Mildred, there were many times during that summer of 1930 when he thought he'd made a mistake. Maybe he should have grabbed Ainsley's money when he had the chance. He seemed to have no luck scraping even a thousand dollars toward the $35,000 he was going to need for another well.

Then fortune smiled on Drew Young and brought him money and love in one package— at least for a time.

Not even a man as obsessed with oil as Drew Young could spend all his time looking for it. Spurned by Mildred, he had found many pretty women in towns like Dallas and Houston who were willing to share their favors for a price. He preferred it that way. When a woman was bought and paid for there were no complications. And since he had no intention of leaving Mildred and her land, he wanted no complications. That was another reason for confining his affairs to the road and not getting involved with a woman near home, although the flock of beautiful, flashy young whores who moved into town after the oil boom were a tempting lot. All that changed, however, when he met, or rather renewed his acquaintance with, Laurette Mayfield.

He was walking out of Houston's Fielding Bank where he'd been struggling to get a $35,000 loan. They'd told him they'd have to think about it. He was a worried man, with his mind on his impending ruin, when he walked right into her.

"Oh, excuse me, ma'am," he said automatically, then looked into the bluest eyes he'd ever seen. They seemed somehow strangely familiar, as did the young woman they belonged to. She was a pale blonde, with curly hair cut fashionably short and set to emphasize her resemblance to Jean Harlow. Her eyebrows were plucked and drawn in a thin arch to give a perpetual surprised look to her face, and the heavy red lipstick that outlined her mouth seemed begging to be kissed. She was wearing a fashionable light blue suit and a large straw hat that shielded her pale skin from the sun.

"Why, Drew Young," she laughed. "Don't you remember me?"

He stared at her for a few seconds more. He could have stared at her all afternoon, but people kept pushing them aside to get in and out of the bank.

"Laurette," she prompted.

"Laurette Mayfield, of course," he said, embarrassed now. But the last time he'd seen her she'd been a skinny fifteen-year-old bringing sandwich lunches to her two older brothers in the Oklahoma oil fields. She'd had a crush on him then. That had been almost . . .

"Seven years ago," she said, as if reading his thoughts. "A lot of water under the bridge since then."

They went to lunch at the elegant Rice Hotel where she was staying. He got a certain pleasure at the way heads turned to look at her as they walked through the lobby. She was a beautiful woman, and she was with him. He might not have more than two dollars in his pocket, but he knew he was the envy of every man in Houston.

"I heard about your brothers," he started awkwardly. There'd been an accident, a derrick collapsed, a fire started and both men were killed.

She shrugged. "Accidents happen. They were roughnecks. They knew the risks."

He was surprised at the callousness, but he knew that life could not have been easy for her after losing her brothers. Her parents had died long before. He quickly dismissed her coldness. He was too curious about how she had become the sophisticated, worldly woman he beheld.

"After my brothers died, I knew I had to support myself, but I wasn't going to do it in Oklahoma. I headed for New Orleans and got a job as a maid with a rich Creole family. You should see their house, Drew. It's right in the heart of the French quarter. You'd love it."

She prated on, telling him about how the childless couple she worked for had taken an interest in her. They sent her to school, as she'd only reached the third grade in Oklahoma, and when her French was good enough, they took her to Paris. Now, after four years in France, she was back in the United States.

"But why Houston?" he asked.

She demurred, talking about how exciting Houston was, how the oil-fueled building fever that swept the city made it so different from New Orleans.

"And those men selling oil leases on the street corners like newspaper vendors . . ." she continued.

But he knew that there was more to her story than that. Finally she admitted the truth, her eyes lowered as she spoke softly. "My friends are divorcing."

Instinctively he read the situation. Mr. New Orleans had been caught dallying with Laurette.

Now Mrs. New Orleans was divorcing him and Laurette had been sent to wait it out in Houston, the nearest big city where a girl like her could be amused but safe. Sooner or later, he told himself, Mr. New Orleans would call her back. Until that day, however, she would be his.

He sneaked up to her room that afternoon and they made love until dawn. She yielded the soft pink curves of her body to him in a different way than the other women he had known. She had made great strides since Oklahoma.

That summer he saw her every weekend. No one worked the oil fields on Saturday and Sunday, so it gave him a chance to drive his aging Chevrolet all the way to Houston for those sweet hours with her. She moved out of the Rice Hotel—which discouraged irregular relationships like theirs—and set herself up in a discreet boardinghouse where the proprietor was broad-minded. When Drew offered to take care of her rent she refused, indicating that the New Orleans friend was supporting her.

By August, when everyone in east Texas seemed to be striking oil but him, they had become so close that she knew everything about his dreams of oil. And, to his intense pleasure, she even shared them, suffering with him each time his well came in dry. But the night he admitted he was a man at the end of his rope, a man who couldn't scrape up enough money to take her to a decent place to eat, much less build yet another derrick, she took him totally by surprise.

They were at her boardinghouse where she was letting two rooms, a sitting room with a tiny adjoining bedroom. It was small and pretty and cozy, but he was never comfortable there because he sensed the presence of his weekday rival.

During dinner at a small restaurant nearby, she had told him that she'd be leaving Houston in a few days. Her friend in New Orleans was free now, and she wanted to return. Still, she asked him back to her room, where she made tea for the two of them on the little hotplate behind a Chinese screen.

As they sipped their tea, he poured out the story of all his disappointments. All the wells that had come in dry.

Suddenly she put down her cup. "How much do you need?" she demanded.

"About $35,000 and chances are three to one it'll come in dry."

She said nothing, just went into the other room and returned with a rope of pearls. The clasp was one large cabochon ruby.

"Now wait a second," he protested. "I can't take that from you."

She laughed. "I'm not giving it away. I know you Drew Young. You'll get that oil, and when you do I'll get my share."

They shook hands on it. The next day they sold the pearls for $40,000. Three days later he drove her to the train that would take her back to her lover in New Orleans while he headed back to Overton.

He knew this money was lucky and he built the next derrick with supreme care. The roughnecks he hired to work on this had to be the best men in east Texas. This time, he knew, it was right. Mildred, of course, had long ago discovered that he "had some woman in Houston," as she put it. She could be surprisingly perceptive at times, but there was nothing she could do about it except rail against him for wasting their money. He never told her how he got this $40,000. And even she would never guess that Drew Young had sunk so low with oil fever that he would take money from a woman.

It was a warm November day when Drew stood next to the giant Texas Christmas tree and heard that special sound of oil rushing up and out and uncontrolled into the air. It rained black gold all over Mildred's precious white bungalow and it poured so hard that she came running out of the house to see what was happening. She carried their young son in her arms and the frightened nurse Maria hurried close behind her. By the time they reached Drew, they were soaked black with raw petroleum.

Drew Young took his four-year-old son in his

51

arms and carried him to the well. A big jet of black oil was sprouting in the air, arcing against the clouds and spraying the four of them as it fell to the earth.

"See that beautiful sight, sonny!" Drew screamed above the roar of the well. "That's gonna make us rich!"

Years later the boy would remember it as the only time he ever felt close to his father.

*　　　*　　　*

When the money started to come in, Drew Young began to look around him. He was generous enough to advance some money to neighbors who hadn't been so lucky—yet. By then, most of them had leased their land to the big independents like Humble or Texaco. All Drew asked in return was a piece of the potential royalties—when and if there were any. By the mid-1930's Drew had accumulated mineral rights to more than a quarter of a million acres of east Texas. The rest of the country might be singing "Brother, Can You Spare a Dime," but Drew Young preferred "Makin' Whoopee."

Drew also began to take an active role in politics and helped lead John Nance Garner's campaign for the Democratic presidential nomination in Chicago. When that battle seemed lost, he convinced Garner to run as

Franklin Delano Roosevelt's vice president. And the ticket won by a landslide in 1932.

At home, Drew's son was treated like a young prince. After the Lindbergh baby was kidnapped, Mildred insisted that young Ash be guarded day and night. When he wasn't with Maria, he was with one of the two bodyguards, ex-fieldhands. Drew himself avoided being alone with the boy and left most of the responsibility for rearing him to Mildred.

Their new-found prosperity did little to change Mildred. She still dressed in the Sears Roebuck housedresses that made Drew remember wistfully the exotic silk pajamas Laurette favored for entertaining in her boardinghouse rooms. Mildred barely talked to him anymore. She spent most of her days at church. If she was at home she would be glued to the radio. She had become a devoted listener to F.D.R.'s Sunday evening fireside chats. As the boy grew older she would force him to listen to her cultural programs, like Walter Damrosch's *Music Appreciation Hour*.

In fact, it was Mildred's love of "the finer things in life," especially music, that led indirectly to their leaving Kilgore and moving to Houston in 1938. That was the year, spurred on by her devotion to the Haven of Christ Church and the Reverend Whitby, that Mildred decided she was going to form a choir. Whitby himself was grateful for all the help he could get in his small parish. He thought the idea of a choir was just great. He and Mildred spent long hours planning the musical selections which would include parts for male and female voices. Once more, Mildred tried to interest Drew in joining but he was adamantly opposed.

Among the members of the new choir was a local widow, Claire Austin, who operated a dry-goods store in Kilgore. She was dark haired and pretty. But Mildred considered her too flashy to be attractive. Mildred was quite astonished at Reverend Whitby's interest in the woman—which quickly led to friendship. Mildred chose to ignore Whitby's rather heavy-handed hints that she should turn over her duties as choir leader and organist to Mrs. Austin who was, after all, a childless widow and therefore free of Mildred's God-given responsibilities. Of course, Mildred refused to step aside. In fact, she gradually came to see it as her sacred duty to keep an eye on Whitby and Mrs. Austin lest the widow lead the innocent churchman into temptation—or worse.

But Mildred could not be on guard twenty-four hours a day. She did, after all, have a household of her own to run, a son to raise, and a husband to look after. She tried her best, but she came to suspect that all was for naught and that her beloved Whitby was flirting with the sins of the flesh. One hot August afternoon her worst fears were confirmed.

It was one of those days when nothing went right. To begin with, Drew was away on a business trip in New Orleans. She should have been used to going to Sunday morning services without him, but it always made her angry to see other women who had managed to drag their husbands to church while she had failed. She could hardly keep her mind on Whitby's sermon, something from Paul about it being better to marry than to burn. Fortunately, she had brought eleven-year-old Ash along and she could concentrate on policing his behavior, cracking him on the ear when his attention wandered.

After services they returned to the farm which was now a farm in name only. The bungalow was surrounded by Texas Christmas trees, the 30-foot-tall towers of steel and gadgets to control the constant flow of oil. The Youngs' new prosperity meant that the bungalow was freshly painted: white.

Waiting on the doorstep was a young neighbor girl, blond-haired Ella Rayburn. She smiled as she saw their new Packard approach.

"Howdy, Miz Young," she said cheerfully.

Mildred was coolly cordial. The girl's family were not churchgoers, and she was something of a tomboy, which Mildred also disapproved of. But she seemed decent enough. And because the farm was so isolated, little Ella was the only child for Ash to play with.

"Can I go play with Ella, Ma?" asked Ash.

"Yes, son," she agreed. "But don't forget, we eat dinner at two." The new cook, another blessing of oil riches, was working over chicken fricassee, boiled potatoes and corn. The warm rich smells drifted from the kitchen out to the front porch.

The boy scurried off with Ella, and Mildred went about her business inside. Although Sunday was not the day for cleaning or washing or other domestic chores, she did not consider needlework a duty. She spent the afternoon embroidering a new tablecloth for Reverend Whitby's dining room and daydreaming about what her life would be if only Drew would die and make her a rich widow. She'd be free to marry Whitby at last—and heaven knew the man was smitten with her. Why, it was *disgraceful* how that Austin woman had thrown herself at him and *pathetic* how the Reverend, always a gentleman, had allowed it.

Lost in her fantasies, Mildred lost track of the hour as well. Twice, the stout, German cook—anxious to move on to Sunday supper with her own family—had to remind Mildred of the time.

"My goodness, where does the time go?" Mildred muttered as the cook shook her gently. "And where's that rascal Ash?"

"I don't know, ma'am," the cook replied, putting on her hat and moving toward the door.

Though Mrs. Young paid her well—and on time—the cook didn't relish spending extra time with her.

"Last time I saw that boy," the cook added, "he was heading for the barn with Ella." With that she slipped out the door.

Mildred waited until the cook's battered Model A had disappeared down the rutted drive toward the main road, then she stormed out of the house and headed angrily toward the barn. Hogs and chickens scattered to give her room as she moved swiftly toward her quarry. The barn door was shut, but she tore it open in one angry gesture, then stood in the doorway and screamed.

"I know you're in there, come down this minute!"

From up in the hayloft, Ash watched his mother, unsure of what to do next. He could not make out her face, for she was blocking the sun. All he could see was the outline of her thin form. Her voice raged furiously while, behind him, an impatient and half nude Ella Rayburn whispered.

"Come back here Ash, let me show you something. Don't pay her no mind. She's just guessing we're here."

"No," he answered. "She's looking right up here. She sees us, I tell you."

"What do you care, Ash?"

That was a good question. Ash pondered the

answer. Until his mother so rudely interrupted, he had been enjoying Ella's short course in anatomy. Unfortunately, she had just reached the part about which he was most curious and had begun to remove her white cotton bloomers when his mother stormed in.

"What is it, Mama?" he shouted down obediently. Beside him, Ella made an angry, pouty face.

"I know you're up there with that slut. Both of you come down here this minute!" She was in the barn now, standing at the foot of the ladder.

"What're you talkin' about, Mama?" Ash had decided to feign innocence a few minutes longer.

"Don't sass me, boy!" she shouted. Whipped into a fury, she began to climb the trembling ladder. Ella only giggled stupidly and leaned back in the hay.

Suddenly, Mildred's head appeared at the top of the ladder. Her eyes were wild with rage and her face so twisted with anger and fury that a frightened Ash leaped off the loft to escape her and landed in another pile of hay on the floor of the barn. Ignoring the girl, Mildred looked down on her son.

"Don't you move, you devil," she screamed.

He could not have moved if he'd wanted to. He was riveted by the unreal mask that his mother's face had become. He was accustomed to her tirades, especially about fornicators, but she had never actually lost her temper with him—until now. Caught in a fever all her own, she moved swiftly down the ladder and caught Ash by an ear, dragging him along with her, out of the barn and toward the Packard. He had never seen his mother drive as fast as she did that Sunday, tearing down the road back to town, lecturing him on the sins of the flesh, of the evil women sent by Satan to lure men.

She confused Ash when she carried on about raven-haired temptresses, since Ella was definitely a blonde. And why did she talk about men of God, when she had never called him that before?

"Your father should have had this talk with you a long time ago, but he's never home—too busy with his business in Houston and New Orleans. Thank God we have a friend in the Reverend Whitby," she went on.

So that was it, Ash told himself. At last he understood. She was bringing him to the Reverend for a talking to. He sank down in the front seat, having learned at a young age that that was the only response to one of his mother's moods.

By the time they pulled up in front of the Reverend's house, much of Mildred's anger had abated. It was almost 3:30 p.m. The streets of Kilgore were deserted. Almost everyone in town was inside escaping the summer heat and enjoying Sunday dinner.

No one in Kilgore locked his door, and the

Reverend was no exception. Mildred was familiar with the house because so many church meetings were held there. She knocked on the screen door, then walked right in, followed by a sulky Ash.

"Yoo, hoo, Reverend Whitby," Mildred chirped as they moved down the hallway. Ash noticed the chirpy tone his mother's voice always took on when she was talking to the Reverend.

There was no answer but silence. Yet the house did not have the feel of being deserted. In fact, they soon noticed that the remains of Whitby's Sunday dinner were still on the dining room table. It looked like he had been entertaining a visitor. If Mildred noticed the second plate, however, she said nothing.

The quiet spell was broken by the sound of the Reverend's voice trilling from the upstairs landing.

"Is that you, Mrs. Young?" he called out.

Who else, Ash thought, would have the nerve to barge into someone's house uninvited?

"Yes, Reverend," she answered. "Are you all right?"

"Oh, yes, I just felt a bit tired," he said. "I felt the need for a midday nap."

"No wonder, the way you work. But I was hoping you could have a talk with my boy here."

Up until that moment, they had been

carrying on this dialogue rooms apart, for Mildred and Ash were still in the dining room, and the Reverend's voice was coming from the upstairs landing. When Mildred moved to the foot of the stairs, her total attention was on the Reverend. At first, she didn't notice anything amiss. Suddenly, her eyes fell on the stream of lady's garments and undergarments that had been strewn from the foot of the stairs to the top landing where the Reverend stood in his robe. And from behind him she glimpsed the dark-haired temptress, Mrs. Austin.

Was nothing sacred? She looked several times from the lacy undergarments to the blanching face of the Reverend. She resisted the urge to pick up one of them, just to fondle the silk and lace. Never in her life had she seen such delicate items, except in pictures. Yet she knew they were the tools of the devil and she suppressed her curiosity. Instead she glared at the Reverend, who was unmasked in her eyes as another false prophet, another Pharisee, another Judas.

Frozen with fear, the Reverend stood rooted in one spot at the head of the stairs. He did not move. Mrs. Austin, however, was capable of motion and eased in front of him.

"Why, Mrs. Young," she purred. "How nice of you to call. You can be the first to hear the good news. The Reverend and I are engaged. We'll be married next month."

Mildred felt the room spin, but she willed

herself not to faint in this house of depravity. She searched around her for Ash and, catching sight of him again, took him by the arm.

"Jezebel," she hissed, as she moved grandly out of the house. She fancied she heard laughter behind her, but she would not dignify the two sinners by turning around. Instead she marched Ash back to the Packard and home where they ate a dinner of cold chicken fricassee in silence.

That night, when Drew Young returned from his business trip to New Orleans, Mildred announced that for once she agreed with him: they should have moved to Houston long ago.

Two weeks later they packed up their worldly goods, including Ash and his nurse Maria, and moved down to the elegant and booming part of Houston known as River Oaks.

3

Houston, Texas
October 1940

The young boy, now nearly thirteen years old, crouched by the staircase, terror in his eyes and his body trembling. Ash Young was supposed to be sleeping but the screams downstairs had awakened him, and he had tiptoed to the top of the stairs where, hidden in the darkness, he could view the scene below.

"You've been drinking again with your whores," his mother was screaming. "May God strike you dead."

He watched his father take a few unsteady steps toward her.

"Shut up, you ugly bitch!" he growled. He was a big man and at the moment he looked like an angry bear.

The two of them were standing in the center of the luxurious River Oaks house his father had purchased shortly after he struck it rich. The house was decorated with the best that Houston had to offer. There was bone-colored wall-to-wall carpeting in the living room and a magnificent stone fireplace that took up one whole wall. With the aid of the Marquis D'Oyley Mildred had furnished the house with French antiques and paintings. Still she was unhappy.

Drew Young stared blankly as his wife, dressed in a faded housedress and slippers, stood there, screaming at him. Her blond hair had faded to a drab brown and the innocent, blue eyes that so appealed to him when he first saw her had taken on the glazed look of a religious fanatic. She had obviously waited up for this, gradually building her hatred as she reviewed all his sins in her mind.

"How dare you talk to me that way!" she shrieked as she reached for the iron poker by the fireplace and swiped at him.

He saw the blow coming and ducked. At the same time he grabbed the weapon, wrenching it from her hand and raising it in a big arc before bringing it back down on her head.

From his hiding place at the top of the stairs, Ash winced at the sickening sound and watched his mother fall without a cry, blood oozing from the wound in her head.

His father dropped the heavy poker and kneeled by her body. He looked bewildered as he reached for a handkerchief and clumsily tried to stop the blood. Failing that, he staggered back to his feet and, leaning on the fireplace mantel, took a silver flask from his pocket. Mildred never allowed spirits in her house, but there was nothing she could do about it now.

He took several gulps from the flask, then he went back to the body and, lifting her head, tried to make her swallow some of it. There was no response. For the first time he seemed to realize that she was dead. Suddenly he panicked, grabbed the poker and ran out into the darkness of the night.

Ash waited awhile to be sure his father was gone, then came down the stairs and approached his mother's body. She lay on her side, her eyes still open and angry, blood oozing from the ugly wound and soaking into the light-colored carpet. Her arms were outstretched as if she were trying to push her husband away.

Now that his father was gone, Ash viewed the scene with total detachment. He had not loved his mother. In fact, he hated her for constantly invoking her cruel God who was supposed to punish him and everyone else for their deadly sins. If there was a God—and he doubted it— he preferred his father's devil.

He felt no sorrow. Perhaps a touch of pity

mixed with contempt. Pity for the miserable life she had led and contempt for the way she had forced that life on his father and himself.

Most of all, he felt relief. She would no longer force him to kneel and pray six times a day. There would be no one to whip him every time he committed the smallest infraction. She had never shown him love, only fear, the fear of hell and damnation. He and his father could be friends now. They could be close.

He struggled to organize his thoughts and decide what to do. Wake up the servants? Call the police? Suddenly he heard a noise behind him.

He turned around and saw Maria Gomez, his plump Mexican nanny, standing near the door. Her dark eyes were wide with fear.

"Did you see?" he asked her in Spanish.

She nodded.

He placed a finger across his mouth in a gesture of silence. "Nana, not a word to anyone."

"But *chiquillo*," she protested. "Police will come and ask questions."

"You just tell them you heard screams and saw a man—you don't know who—run out of here," he commanded. "If you tell more, Nana, we'll all be in trouble. They'll take me away from you. Now, go call the police."

He knew she would do as he said. She always did.

He carefully picked up the monogrammed handkerchief, soaked with his mother's blood, and ran upstairs to his room. A few minutes later, composed, he came back down to await the police with Maria.

*   *   *

By dawn, the police were swarming over the Young house, looking everywhere, questioning Maria and the other servants. They told them nothing. When they talked to the murdered woman's sleepy-eyed young son, he told them he had heard a noise and screams but he had been too scared to come out of his room.

The dead woman's husband said he had been at the ranch, had only come down from Kilgore a half hour ago, just in time to hear this terrible news. Had anyone at the airport seen him arrive? No, he hadn't taken his private plane: he'd driven down in the Cadillac. Alone.

Everyone in Houston knew Drew Young, the legendary wildcatter who'd struck it rich in east Texas only days before the Supreme Court declared Governor Sterling's martial law invalid. They patted him on the back and offered their condolences. Sorrow was all over his weather-beaten face as he swore that he could not fathom who could have done such an evil deed.

Mildred was such a good woman, he assured

them, a pious churchgoing woman. She had no enemies. It could not have been a robber because nothing had been taken except for the fireplace poker. He could not imagine who in the devil's name could have killed her. Unless—

Unless?

Wiping away a tear, he mentioned that Mildred had fired their simple-minded old handyman, Bill Perry, only a few days before.

The police were immediately interested. Why had she fired him?

Well, it seemed that Mildred had caught the old man planting a cross on top of the small grave he had dug for his pet rabbit. She could not stand for such sacrilege.

"What the hell," said one of the officers. "There's your motive. Revenge."

Poor Bill Perry furnished the evidence himself the next day when he brought the poker to the house. He tried to tell them that he had found it in some azalea bushes in the garden, but the officers were more concerned with the fact that his fingerprints were all over it. The fact that there were other prints including Mildred's and Drew's was considered irrelevant. Everyone was only too happy to have found the culprit.

The rest was terribly simple. Drew Young had many friends in the Harris County District

Attorney's office and at the trial they swiftly proved beyond the shadow of a doubt that Bill Perry had murdered Mildred Young. He was sentenced to be hung.

The entire trial made a tremendous impression on Ash Young. He felt sorry for Bill Perry, but the old man was probably better off dead. There was no place in the world for anyone that dumb.

As for Ash's hope that his mother's death would bring him closer to his father, he was sadly disappointed. Drew Young, who had never devoted much time to Ash, now avoided his son like the plague. The boy made him uncomfortable. Those gray eyes were just like Mildred's, cold and unblinking. They gave him the shivers.

Drew had come to dread those dinners, alone with his son, endless evenings in which they would sit at opposite ends of the long oak dinner table, unable to exchange even a few words. Ash would stare at his father. He wanted so much to cry out to his father that he loved him, that now that Mother was gone they could finally be friends, that he would keep forever the secret of her murder. Instead he sat there, mute, confused by his father's coldness.

Now Ash had only Maria Gomez to share his loneliness. His father wasted little or no time around the house, choosing to spend most of his nights in his suite at the State Hotel, preferably in the company of an expensive whore. So the old Mexican nanny tried to be mother and father to the distant and lonely boy she had practically raised since birth.

Maria was the only person to shed a tear when Ash, at fourteen, was sent east to Choate, the fashionable prep school. He had been there only a few months when Japan attacked Pearl Harbor and Congress declared war. Shortly thereafter, Germany and Italy declared war on the United States. Patriotic fervor swept through Choate but Ash resisted it. Still bitter and angry because his father had sent him away, he resented all those silly boys proudly playing soldier and waving the flag.

He enjoyed shocking his schoolmates by telling them he admired Adolf Hitler and Benito Mussolini and that he couldn't see why Americans wanted to fight them and be allied with Uncle Joe Stalin.

"The world would be much better off if Germany dominated Europe," he would argue, "than if Communist Russia overran it."

When a classmate pointed out that Hitler was persecuting the Jews, Ash dismissed the matter with a shrug. "You and I aren't Jews. What do you care?" was his answer.

Needless to say, he made few friends. It didn't matter. At home his father had been a fervent supporter of Roosevelt and the New Deal. In adopting such contrary opinions, he was beginning to experience the first pleasures of rebellion.

Although his father had campaigned vigorously for Roosevelt in four presidential elections, Ash knew it was not the man or his New Deal that Drew Young admired. His father expected to gain from any war and long before Pearl Harbor he had acquired two small companies, one manufacturing airplane parts, the other weapons. By the time war broke out, he was in a position to lean on Texas congressmen for lucrative defense contracts.

Disgusted by his father's profiteering, Ash grew inhibited and secretive, with no place in his heart for sentiment or pity. He was devoured by one ambition: to be rich, far richer than the father he had grown to hate.

Ash was a fair student, remarkably good in any subject which had to do with numbers and precise equations, though below mediocrity when it came to the humanities. Latin was a dead language, therefore a dead issue. Foreign languages were a waste of effort.

"English is the universal language of business," was his comment. "Even in China and Africa they understand the word dollar."

At vacation time Ash had no choice but to return to Houston. But even on those occasions, father and son saw little of each other. Ash spent much of his time riding, which he enjoyed, or visiting the various oil properties his father owned. The oil wells fascinated him.

They were, after all, the source of energy for the modern world, an unending source of power and riches.

"One day soon, all this will be mine. And then the world will know who Ash Young is," he would think as he looked at the hundreds of oil wells, skeletal giants, that dotted the horizon for miles on end.

* * *

Ash was eighteen when he had his first woman. Sex filled his thoughts, as with any healthy young man, but his feelings were mixed and confused. He had felt the need of a woman, yet he was afraid to admit it to himself; he was almost ashamed.

The harsh sermons of his mother warning him of the sins of the flesh still rang in his ears, and the hate and fear he had felt for her were now reflected on all females. As a teenager at Choate he had often envied his classmates who hung pictures of sexy pin-up girls in their lockers. He had never dared to and when, alone in his bunk, he had inevitably succumbed to the need to masturbate, immediately afterward he had felt dirty and ashamed.

The woman who took Ash's virginity was the mother of the only boy he had befriended at Choate. Robert I. Osgood Jr. was an intelligent boy. His father was a prominent New York surgeon, an exemplary prototype of WASP dignity, and his mother, Martha Tilwell Osgood, was a voluptuous, dark-haired woman of forty.

Ash had been a guest at the Osgoods' Oyster Bay estate several times before, but on this weekend in late June, Dr. Osgood was away on a trip and Mrs. Osgood spent most of her time with the two boys. That Saturday night, the three of them attended a small dinner dance at a neighbor's home.

She was wearing a tight, gold lamé gown, cut very low in front and showing her sensuous figure to great advantage. For the first time Ash was conscious that his friend's mother was also a remarkably attractive woman. When the orchestra began to play "I'll Be Seeing You" and she asked him to dance, he leaped to his feet so quickly that he almost knocked over their champagne glasses.

He was an awkward dancer and he muttered an apology as he placed his arm tentatively around her waist, still trying to keep an honest distance between their bodies.

She smiled and whispered in his ear, "Don't worry, Ash, just hold me tight," pushing herself against him.

They danced, or rather held each other in a tight embrace. His embarrassment disappeared as her hips rubbed against him to the tempo of the music. The scent of her perfume, the sensation of those hard and generous breasts pressing him, and the unusual amount of champagne he had drunk, made him lose all his inhibitions and he felt his entire being stir with desire. As the music changed to a faster tempo, she loosened her grip on him, giving him a soft kiss on the ear while whispering, "Tonight."

It was almost 2:00 a.m. when the Osgood chauffeur brought the threesome home. Bob had imbibed so much champagne he had to be carried to bed by the chauffeur. Ash wasn't sure of his next step and he stood awkwardly at the foot of the stairs waiting for a signal from Mrs. Osgood. She gave his hand a squeeze and whispered, "Later," then turned and walked upstairs to her room. He stood there admiring the gentle sway of her hips until she was out of sight, totally confused.

What was he supposed to do? He decided to head for his own room. She was, after all, his hostess and she knew exactly where his room was. He sat on his bed and tried to decide whether he should wait there awhile and then go to her room. Was that what she had meant when she whispered, "Later"? Or was he just being presumptuous; would she laugh, or perhaps scream in anger, if he walked into her room? And what if she was waiting for him? What was he supposed to do? He had never made love to a woman and he dreaded looking like a perfect fool.

The situation was resolved for him when he heard the door open and Mrs. Osgood enter. She was wearing a sheer negligee and in the dim light he could see that she had nothing on underneath.

He gasped involuntarily and remained frozen on the bed. She approached him slowly, sat beside him and said softly, "Let me help you undress."

Fascinated, he was unable to move for awhile, but gradually, as she loosened his tie and unbuttoned his shirt, he relaxed and leaned back on the bed, obeying her commands and watching her efficient hands unbutton, unzip and finally strip him completely. Then hands and mouth moved over his entire body, and he closed his eyes, abandoning himself to this delicious torture.

He was about to come to a violent climax when Mrs. Osgood suddenly stopped. She smiled at him as she moved on top of him, straddling him. She rode him slowly at first, then her tempo increased until she screamed and they both climaxed.

He fell asleep soon after, and when a uniformed maid woke him for breakfast the next morning he was alone. At the table downstairs she smiled at him but otherwise acted as if nothing had happened. They were alone, Bob was still upstairs nursing his hangover, but she made no reference to the night before except to insist that from now on he must call her "Martha."

He wanted to make love to her again, but it was impossible. Dr. Osgood returned later that afternoon, and by evening he and Bob were on the train back to Choate. He was never invited back and he didn't know how he could go about seeing her again.

Although he never saw Martha Osgood again, his one night stand with her had a profound effect on him. It confirmed his idea that all women were whores, but it also made him recognize that he could accept sex as a pleasurable necessity.

By the time he started at Princeton that fall, sex and polo had become his favorite pastimes. But as much as he pursued these trivialities and frivolities in college he never lost sight of his real purpose, the main reason that made him run: to destroy his father and replace him as head of the Young empire.

Part Two

4

Houston, Texas
December 1948

Houston was in the middle of a postwar boom that would be the greatest in its history. Only most Houstonians, including Drew Young, disliked calling it that. To them it was part of the natural order of things. Natural that the Houston channel was now processing twenty-four million tons of shipping into the city, natural that half a billion dollars worth of buildings were going up downtown, natural that Houston had the largest population in the entire South and was now its major industrial center.

Drew Young was proud of the part he had played in carving out a major city from a steamy bayou. He could take his place right up there with Hugh Roy Cullen and Jesse Jones when it came to philanthropy, too. He had given money to the symphony orchestra, the Fine Arts Museum, St. Luke's Methodist Hospital and Rice University. He had even set up the Mildred Rodman Young Foundation, endowing it with forty million dollars in memory of his dear departed wife.

Right now a lot of the old boys were taking sides behind Mr. Jones or H.R. in one of the biggest controversies to hit Houston since they dug the channel. Mr. Jones wanted zoning, but H.R. was fighting it. He called it "un-American and German," but as Drew looked out his window he had to admit the city needed it.

He hadn't been as smart as old Jesse Jones, though. In 1917, Mr. Jones had built three ten-story office buildings, but he built them on foundations that could support twenty-two stories. Sure enough, twenty years later he put up the rest. He was all prepared for Houston's boom. Now everyone else was trying to catch up.

In spite of all the tall buildings, the world's largest Baptist church, the world's largest Woolworth's, you still did not need to drive more than twenty miles from downtown Houston before you were out in the open prairie. That was where Drew would have liked to be, or at least swapping lies with the old boys at the Esperson Drugstore or in the lobby of the State Hotel.

Anywhere but here in his office with his strange, young son. Reluctantly, he turned away from the window and faced him.

Ash had been looking the office over appraisingly. His father's office fit the man. The desk was large and solid, and the chairs and sofas, all sturdy and comfortable, were covered with dark brown leather. The thick carpet was dark green. On a mahogany commode behind Drew's desk were three silver framed photographs. One was of Sam Rayburn, inscribed to his friend Drew Young, the second showed Drew as a young wildcatter carrying his son in his arms and beaming with joy beside his first oil well at Rodman Farm. The third photograph was of Ash scoring a goal for the Princeton polo team last year.

Drew eyed his son with suspicion. He was wearing a gray flannel Brooks Brothers suit that matched his eyes, a white, button-down shirt and a dark blue tie. He was a head shorter than his father and had inherited not only his mother's size but her features. Something about the way the boy watched him made him uncomfortable.

With his stylish Eastern clothes, his trim, little moustache and brown hair parted in the middle and sleeked down with Brilliantine, he looked like some kind of Eastern dandy, not like the flesh and blood of Drew Tucker Young.

He had never been able to understand the boy, so quiet, so secretive. Mildred used to say that it was all his fault, that he had no way with children, as if she had. Then after Mildred died there had been practically no communication between them. He sent the boy to boarding school in the East and when he came home from Choate on vacations he avoided him. To tell the truth, he was always relieved when he left.

Now Ash was no longer a boy. He had graduated from Princeton months ago and returned to Houston, but Drew had seen little of him until this day. Ash had insisted that they meet.

Drew took the bottle of Jack Daniel's he kept in his desk and poured each of them a generous glass.

"What was so important, son," he said, "that you had to see me right away?"

Ash smiled at his father but his cold, gray eyes did not smile.

"Yesterday was my birthday," he said. "I'm twenty-one and I thought that you'd want to make me a present."

"Of course, I should have remembered," Drew said, relieved. He extracted a few hundred dollar bills from his tooled leather billfold and threw them across the desk. "Take these and buy yourself something nice."

Ash laughed. "That's not exactly what I had in mind."

His son's arrogant attitude grated on Drew's nerves. "What exactly did you have in mind?" he asked.

"I want the old Rodman farm."

"Who in the hell would want that old house?" It was Drew's turn to laugh. "You couldn't live in it. We use it for the roughnecks on the derricks. It's a wreck."

"Apparently I'm not making myself clear, Father dear," Ash's voice was heavy with sarcasm. "I want the old house and all the land around it. Everything that constituted Mother's farm."

Drew was indignant and he smashed his big, red hand down so hard that the papers on the desk jumped. "What the hell are you talking about boy? Are you plumb crazy? There's no farm anymore, just oil wells."

"Eureka!" Ash exclaimed. "You finally get the point. Oil wells. That's why I want Rodman farm. Remember when you said we'd all be rich?"

"But we are rich," Drew responded. "One day all this will go to you."

"I want it now," Ash snapped.

"The hell you do!" an enraged Drew Young

thundered as he jumped to his feet. "Now get out of here before I throw you out!"

Ash did not move. He leaned back in the chair and lit a Lucky Strike, taking long puffs and exhaling slowly. He was going to take his time before answering. He had waited eight years for this moment.

"Oh, no you won't, old man," he said at last, his gray eyes hard. "Because if you do, I'll have you arrested for killing Mother." He watched with pleasure as the color drained from his father's face.

"You're crazy as a coon," the older man hissed.

"Not at all," Ash said evenly. "I saw you kill her. You were so drunk that night you didn't even notice me but I saw it all. I saw Mother grab the poker and come at you and I saw how you wrenched it from her and hit her. You killed her all right."

"They'll never believe you," the older man said, but there was fear in his eyes as he sank back in his chair.

"But they will," Ash insisted. He was enjoying his father's discomfort. He proceeded to open his leather briefcase and remove a child's composition book. He passed it across the desk to his father.

Drew opened the book. Inside was a description of that terrible night in 1940. It was obviously a child's description which made it all the more believable. Ash had written it down the very night it happened, and folded neatly in the back like an old pressed flower was the bloodstained handkerchief with his initials.

"And that's not all," Ash assured him. "Remember Maria Gomez? She saw everything. She didn't admit it to the police because I asked her not to. She only cared about how the whole thing would affect me. But she dictated a letter and it describes everything that happened that night."

"Why didn't you tell all this to the police then?" Drew muttered.

"Why? Because I loved you. You were my father and I was afraid they would hang you or put you in jail where I'd never see you again." He took another drag on the Lucky Strike. "I was glad you killed her, you know. She was a bitch and she made our lives miserable."

"It was an accident!" Drew insisted.

"Then why did you let an innocent man hang for it?" Ash said. "You see, Dad, I hold all the cards."

"And now?" Drew asked weakly.

"Obviously my feelings about you have changed," he laughed. "I think it must have been the first year at Choate. After Mother's death, I wanted so much for us to be together. But, you couldn't wait for Mother's body to be cold before you shipped me off to boarding school so I'd be out of your way. It began to dawn on me that I was going to be seeing even less of you than before."

"Why didn't you say something?"

"Would you have changed?"

They both knew the answer to that.

"So I decided to take a lesson from you, Dad," Ash continued as he took back the copybook and handkerchief and put them in the briefcase. "I made the best of a bad bargain. You got rich off poor Mother's land and I decided that while I was locked up in your school I'd let you continue to make money for me. When the right time came, I would claim it. Now that time has come."

Drew Young said nothing, but Ash could tell from the beads of sweat on his brow that he was fighting fear and impotent rage.

"You don't know anything about the oil business, Ash. I'll give you a good job in the company and train you for a few years," Drew said between clenched teeth.

Ash laughed. "You don't understand, Daddy dear. I don't want a job in your company. I want my own company, to run it the way I want, and I want my own money right now."

Drew was at the end of patience. "You're a fool, sonny. The Rodman farm is the heart of the Young Oil company. If I gave it to you, it would destroy the entire organization, which took me all these years to build."

Ash smiled mockingly at his father. "Just as I thought, Dad."

"You really hate me, Ash, don't you?" the older man said heavily.

Ash rose from the leather chair. "I'll be back tomorrow to pick up the deed to the Rodman farm," he said. "I'll need some cash, too. A half a million dollars should do it. I guess you'll agree there is no need to shake hands on this," he chuckled, walking toward the door.

Young stared at his son. "Now I understand why your mother lived in fear of the devil," he whispered. "She gave birth to him!"

Ash responded with a short laugh as he slammed the door behind him.

Young lingered behind his desk for a few minutes after his son had gone, then he poured himself another tall glass of bourbon. He unlocked the center drawer of the desk and removed a pearl-handled revolver, a souvenir of his wildcatter days. He hadn't used it in years but it was in excellent shape, a fine piece of machinery. He finished the bourbon, put the barrel of the gun to his right temple and fired.

5

Houston, Texas
December 1948

Drew Young's suicide made the front pages of newspapers coast to coast. The press speculated wide and high on the cause of the suicide, and it was hinted that perhaps there were cracks in the financial structure of the Young empire, or perhaps the great tycoon had been ravaged by a mysterious illness and preferred a quick death.

Financial columnists wondered who would succeed Young as the head of the large company since the heir apparent, his son, was only just out of Princeton with no business experience. But the day after Drew Young's impressive funeral, Ash himself put all speculation to rest when he called a special press conference in the offices of the Young Co.

Sitting at his father's desk, and flanked by the executives who ran the various elements of the Young empire—oil, shipping, aircraft parts, armaments—he announced to the startled gathering that he was taking over the reins of the Young organization. In fact, he said, he had made concrete plans to further expand the empire by making new acquisitions.

When the representative of the *New York Times* stood up to ask him when he had had time to formulate these plans, since his father had died only three days before, Ash answered, "Six months ago at Princeton."

Surprise showed on the face of the reporter. "Mr. Young, how did you know six months ago that you were going to replace your father so soon?" he asked.

"My father told me a year ago he wished to retire and wanted me to take his place," Ash replied calmly.

"One more question, Mr. Young," said the *New York Times* man. "Why did your father want to retire? Was he in ill health? And with all due respect, are you not very young, twenty-one I believe, and inexperienced, to take over such an organization? It would seem that a businessman like your father would have wanted to train you for a few years before abdicating in your favor."

Ash was prepared for the question. Smiling easily, he replied, "Age has never been a handicap to success. Alexander the Great succeeded his father, King Philip of Macedon, when he was about my age, and he was not yet thirty when he had conquered half the world."

A Houston reporter raised his hand. "Why did your father commit suicide?" he asked.

"I don't know," Ash replied coolly.

"But surely a man like your father wouldn't kill himself unless he was pushed to do so," the reporter insisted. "Was he in financial trouble or ill?"

"He was neither, to my knowledge," Ash said, his voice calm and steady. "The Young empire, as you call it in your newspapers, is healthy and strong. These gentlemen next to me, who have worked with my father for years, can attest to that. As to my father's health, I believe it was excellent."

Helen Potter, the syndicated columnist for the *Los Angeles Times*, stood up. "That confirms the coroner's report, Mr. Young," she said. "But surely you must have formed some opinion as to why your father shot himself. I understand you visited him in his office shortly before this occurred. Did you and he have an argument?"

Ash lifted his hands to the sky in a deprecating gesture. "Miss Potter," he said. "I often read your column, which I enjoy, and I would be happy to reply at length, if I could. I did visit my father and we did discuss some business and private matters. He seemed somewhat preoccupied but not unduly, and nothing in his behavior could have made me suspect that he contemplated taking his life. My father's death may very well have been an accident."

"A man doesn't shoot himself in the head by accident. The police seem to have ruled that out," Miss Potter continued.

"I know, I know. But my father often played with guns. He loved the feel of them," Ash said, his eyes steady. "The gun could have gone off by accident. At least that's what I prefer to believe, Miss Potter. And now, if you will excuse me, ladies and gentlemen, I thank you all for coming here."

Thus said, he stood up and walked past the stunned assembly and out of the room.

*   *   *

The press conference held by Ash Young established at least this much in the Houston community: Drew Young's little boy had grown up. He might have been sent to a stylish Eastern school and look like an Eastern dandy, but underneath he was still as tough as any red-blooded Texan. And people even said with some pride that "the boy won't be a pushover." What remained to be seen, however, was how resourceful and smart the boy really was.

Ash proved that he was both in a matter of

months. He had anticipated that the "police action" in Korea would become a full-scale war, so he worked hard to assemble and refurbish the old fleet of Liberty ships and tankers his father had bought at the end of World War II for a song. Now he was ready with his ships to transport the much-needed oil to the war zone. In fact, he was one of the first, and the competition had to take notice.

Ships were a good thing. But if he wanted to become a really powerful man he needed an instrument that would give him control over money. He had to own a bank.

Being a banker gave you liquidity, one of the main requisites if a man wanted to be sure to remain in business. He had read and been told about successful businessmen who had gone to their downfall because banks would not extend them a loan when they ran short of cash in a moment of crisis. This was especially true in Texas, where most oil men were heavy borrowers. They always needed cash to finance their next drilling operations.

He vowed he would not end up like Glenn McCarthy, building a lavish twenty-seven-million-dollar hotel one year and then watching the Shamrock go to his creditors the next.

Besides, the most respectable men in Houston were bankers. Houston was still a small town in many ways and folks talked of visiting Jesse Jones' bank, the National Bank of

Commerce, and of Judge Elkins' bank, City National. Ash bought control of the Fidelity Bank, and for a long time they never called it anything but Drew Young's boy's bank.

Ash enjoyed the power and the recognition the bank brought him. The only thing he didn't like about banking was the people who came to borrow money.

*   *   *

One afternoon a young woman came to see him in the office that had been his father's. He hadn't changed it much except to add a large painting of Drew Young.

At first he didn't know why she was there. His secretary was out to lunch and the woman must have sneaked in. He watched her carefully. She was in her late twenties, pretty with blond hair sleeked back in a chignon. She seemed to have taken great pains with her makeup, but it didn't hide the lines of worry etched in her face. She was very nervous. She was wearing a blue gabardine suit and a red-and-white-striped blouse that was meant to be gay though her sad face defeated it. She took off her white gloves when she sat down on one of the leather chairs.

"I'm Carol Mason," she told him. Her east Texas twang reminded him of his mother. "Larry Mason is my husband."

He knew who Larry Mason was. One of hundreds of would-be wildcatters who didn't know when to stop, who kept coming back to the bank to borrow more money on their land, all the time talking about how they were going to strike it rich and buy up the whole bank. But Larry Mason, like most of the others, would never be able to pay those loans back and Ash had just given him notice that Fidelity would be foreclosing.

"Sure, I know Larry," he said. He was still not sure why she was here. Had that loser sent his wife to beg for an extension?

"Larry doesn't know I'm here," she said as she nervously wrung a flowered handkerchief in her hand. "But Mr. Young, I just had to talk to you. I can't believe you'd foreclose on us if you knew our story."

"Oh, and what is that?" He was already bored with her and made no attempt to hide it.

"I'm worried about our children," she said. Her eyes began to fill with tears. "We have three and Andrea, our youngest, has a rheumatic heart. She's supposed to have an operation but if you foreclose we'll never be able to pay for it." She started to tremble and wiped her eyes with the handkerchief.

Ash was unmoved. He explained to her that her husband had contracted the debt fair and square. He had never come looking to lend money to Larry Mason and he had never begged him to put up his land as collateral. It was a well-known fact that most banks would not even lend money to wildcatters. It just wasn't his problem that Larry was a bad businessman.

The woman stood up and looked directly at him, her eyes still filled with tears. Slowly she took off the suit jacket, then she began to fumble with the buttons on the striped blouse. She opened it and he could see her breasts. She had pale skin and large, dark brown nipples he could see through the thin, cotton brassiere. She seemed to think that the sight of her breasts, or maybe her whole body, could repay him for the loan. All the while she kept smiling at him. It made him sick. When it came to whoring this girl was strictly an amateur. An amateur whore married to an amateur oil man.

"Not interested!" he snapped, standing up to signal that her time was up. "But I'm sure you'll have no trouble finding other buyers. Try some of the bars on Elysian Street."

The girl broke down and left his office in tears. That afternoon he foreclosed on the farm and never saw them again. He heard they moved to California or something and that the little girl had died. It only convinced him that he had been right about Larry Mason. He was irresponsible and a loser.

That sort of thing didn't bother him. He had

no great need to be liked. He wasn't in a popularity contest. He was out for money and power, tons of it. The end justified the means.

*　　*　　*

When he was still at Princeton, Ash studied the life and career of John D. Rockefeller and how he waged a relentless war against his competitors. A war with no holds barred. It brought many men to ruin but it made Rockefeller's Standard Oil company the biggest of the big. The end justified the means. Machiavelli had coined the phrase; Ash lived the philosophy. All the great rulers and conquerors, even the great American robber barons had lived by that motto. The end justifies the means.

If it worked for them, it was going to work for him. The end was to be rich and powerful and the means was to cut the throat of anyone who stood in his way. He had done it to his father and he would do it to anyone else. He was someone to be reckoned with and it was about time the world knew it. In Houston the word had already spread that Drew Young's stylishly dressed boy was as tough as nails.

Ash always managed to make a profit, even on his failures. There was the time when the Young Oil & Gas Co. tried to take over the Overton Oil Co. It was a small and not terribly profitable operation but the owner simply would not sell. It had actually gone to court where the Young Co.'s team of seasoned old-timers was up against the Overton Co.'s one lawyer, a tall, lanky country boy who looked like Gary Cooper. His name was Tom Patterson and he turned out to be as hard as nails in the courtroom. He blocked the Young Co.'s every move and finally even Ash had to concede defeat.

He admired a man who had brains and guts and this young Patterson had plenty of both. He wanted him on the Young team and in the months that followed he courted Tom Patterson over lunch and golf dates at the Bayou Club. But if Patterson was impressed that Ash belonged to the exclusive 130-member country club, he never showed it.

He was only a year older than Ash but he was a tough customer. He wasn't interested, he told Ash. He didn't even particularly like him and made no attempt to hide it. That only made Ash want him more. Every man had his price and it was only a matter of time until he found Tom Patterson's.

When he did it turned out to be one hundred thousand dollars a year, five percent of the Young Oil & Gas Co. and the title of executive vice president. Patterson became second in command. He was to help Ash mold and expand the Young Co. into one of the largest conglomerates in the country. Ash already controlled oil, shipping, airplane spare parts, arms and banking companies. But there was still another world to conquer.

The spare-part company Drew had bought before World War II was servicing airlines and Ash decided it was time he got into the wide open field himself. Texas Airlines, a small, well-managed company which covered western routes, was exactly what he had in mind. If he could buy control and merge it with Transair, an ailing company in spite of its lucrative charter to preferred routes across the country, he would have a major airline on his hands.

Buying Transair was a simple exercise, but Texas Airlines was another matter. It was a solid, profitable company, headed by a tough president, James Coudair, a wartime ace. Neither Coudair, who owned ten percent of the company, nor its major stockholder and founder, Chairman Allen Caldwell, had any intention of selling.

Undiscouraged, Ash managed through intricate maneuvers to acquire twenty-five percent of the outstanding shares of Texas Airlines. With that voting clout, he was able to place two of his men on the board, but he still did not control it. The more Caldwell and Coudair resisted the takeover, the more it became a matter of life and death for Ash to achieve it.

If fair means did not succeed he would find another way. He hired the two best detective agencies in the country to investigate the private lives of his two antagonists.

Two months later he had in his hands the trump card he needed. Caldwell, a widower, had a twenty-one-year-old daughter he adored. Six months before she had been involved in drug smuggling with a boyfriend. Her father had barely managed to suppress a scandal by committing her to a clinic, from which she had just emerged. She was staying at her father's house in Dallas.

"What about the boyfriend?" Ash asked.

"He went back where he came from." The detective shrugged.

"Find him," Ash ordered.

Soon word came back that Carlos Montero was living in a dirty walk-up in the barrio. Ash quickly sent two emissaries to make him an offer. All he had to do was contact Margaret, take her out once, and he would receive five thousand dollars.

"Her father said he'd kill me if I came near her again," Montero said dubiously.

"What do you care what an old man says?" one of the men insisted.

A glimmer of suspicion flashed in Montero's glassy eyes. "What do you two get out of this?"

"We like to help people in trouble, Carlos," answered the first.

"And we believe in love," added his companion with a smirk.

But Carlos' mind was already struggling to

calculate how much smack five thousand dollars would buy him. "Am I really going to get five grand for this?" he asked.

"Here's one grand to prove it, and that's only on account," said the taller man, putting ten hundred-dollar bills on Carlos' bed. "There's forty more of those if you do as we say."

Carlos fondled the bills and then quickly put them under a pillow. But he was still suspicious. "I don't know if I can get in to see her. Her old man's got people watching her all the time."

"They can't arrest a man for trying to see the girl he loves," the shorter man encouraged. "You just call her, tell her you love her and you've got to see her. That little girl's probably pining by the phone right now."

The man was right, for to Carlos' pleasure, Margaret agreed immediately to sneak out of her house, fooling the nurse who had been hired to watch her and racing to meet him at the seedy little apartment where they had spent so many stoned but happy hours.

By the time the police, alerted by an anonymous tipster, broke into the apartment, they found the two young lovers stoned into unconsciousness, surrounded by enough heroin and drug paraphernalia to convince even Margaret's father that she was back on junk again.

The press had also been duly tipped and the next day the papers carried details of the sordid story, complete with pictures of Margaret Caldwell and her companion being carried away by the police.

The scandal broke just a few days before a Texas Airlines stockholders' meeting. Caldwell was so shaken by his daughter's arrest that he could not concentrate on the proxy fight. Coudair alone was no match for Ash Young, who managed to get himself and three other cohorts elected to the board, making it six for Young and giving him control. Two weeks later Caldwell resigned as chairman and Young replaced him. He managed to convince Coudair to remain as president, then he merged Texas Airlines with Transair.

Still Ash Young's ambition was not satisfied. If he really wanted to become a man of consequence and national recognition he needed more than just money. He could no longer spend all his time working. He didn't go to parties, had never been interested in becoming part of the Houston social set, had abandoned polo since Princeton, and, although he had inherited his father's membership in the exclusive Bayou Club, he rarely played golf.

He had to start getting out, meeting people, maybe getting involved with a woman. It was time.

He was engaged in such thoughts late one evening in his office, when Tom Patterson barged in. Patterson was the only man at the

Young Co. who would have dared enter his office without knocking or previous permission. But he was more than an employee, he had become a friend. It was nine o'clock and they were the only two people left in the office.

"Any problem?" Ash asked as he looked up.

"No problem, Ash. But it's time you stopped working. Come on to my office, I've got a surprise for you."

Tom was grinning from ear to ear and his blue eyes twinkled. He looked more like Gary Cooper than ever.

"What is it?"

"Follow me and you'll see. I promise you won't be disappointed."

He was through for the night anyway and his curiosity was aroused. Tom did not usually play games. He followed him into his office next door. It was slightly smaller than his own and it was decorated exactly the same except that Ash didn't have two beautiful young women sitting on his leather sofa.

One of the girls was a blue-eyed blonde with creamy pink magnolia skin who Tom introduced as Mary Eaton. She was pretty, but it was her dark-haired companion in the red dress who interested Ash. Tom introduced her as Teresa Martinez.

"Ladies," Tom announced. "This is my boss, the infamous Ashley Young."

"He doesn't seem like such a monster,"

Teresa Martinez purred as Ash noticed her slight accent, dreamy eyes and breathtaking figure.

"Thank you," he bowed.

"But he's a monster if he doesn't come to dinner with us," Mary Eaton added.

"Touché," Ash laughed. "What are we waiting for?"

The four of them went for steaks at Madeline's. Everyone in Houston knew how Madeline Pollard had started out as a dancing teacher, then opened the most elegant restaurant in town. From there they went on to the Shamrock.

Glenn McCarthy's famous hotel was situated just outside Houston on seven acres of grounds. It had only been open four years and had already changed hands three times, passing from McCarthy to the Equitable Life Insurance Society when he defaulted on a thirty-four-million-dollar loan. It had just been sold to the Hilton chain for eighteen million dollars.

Ash parked his white Cadillac convertible in the underground parking lot and they took an elevator directly up to the Emerald room, the huge nightclub that held a thousand people. The maitre d' recognized Ash, although he was not a regular customer, and brought them down front to hear the Dick Haymes Show.

He hadn't been nightclubbing since Princeton and it felt good to be out with a friend and two beautiful women. It felt good to be dancing and laughing, especially with Teresa Martinez.

They hardly minded that even at the elegant Emerald Room they had to bring their own bottles or that at midnight all liquor had to disappear from the tables. That was Texas law.

At one o'clock the club closed. They went on to the 2-K Sandwich Shop, an unimpressive luncheonette filled with people in evening clothes who, like themselves, were having too good a time to go home.

For the first time in his life he did not feel awkward with a woman. Teresa was tall, almost as tall as he, and when they danced he could feel the warmth of her body next to his. It was a beautiful body. She was slim with long legs, generous breasts and a small waist. Those soft brown eyes reminded him of Maria Gomez. Maybe it was just that she was so unaffected and plain lovely, but he had never had such a marvelous time before.

He took her home and left her at her door but not before extracting a promise that they would meet again the next night. It was almost four o'clock when he went to bed.

Four hours later he was at his desk. His first order of business was to call his secretary and tell her to send six dozen roses to Miss Teresa Martinez.

Rona Gibson calmly took down the address in shorthand but she could hardly wait to tell the other girls the news. In the four years she had been working for Ashley Young he had never once asked her to call a lady and now he was sending this one flowers. She found herself wondering what Teresa Martinez looked like.

The next thing Ash did was drop in on Tom Patterson.

"That Teresa Martinez is a delightful girl," he said casually, but his friend knew him too well to be fooled.

"She's a knockout," Patterson agreed. "I just met her last night when Mary brought her over. Frankly, if it wasn't for Mary I'd be chasing her myself."

"Know anything about her?"

"She works with Mary at Foley's. Just broke up with a guy she's been involved with for awhile and she seems nice enough. But go easy, Ash," he warned. "Teresa is a chicana and the Mexican girls aren't like our girls."

"Find out anything you can about her, will you Tom?"

Patterson promised to look into the background of Teresa Martinez. He looked thoughtful after Ash left. Could it be that the heartless Ash Young had a soft spot after all?

6

Houston, Texas
1935-1954

Hector and Carmelita Martinez came to Houston in 1935 to find a better life. Their son, Luis, was born at home the following year and a daughter, Teresa, came two years later. The four of them shared a cramped apartment in the barrio, but years later when Teresa Martinez recalled her childhood she only remembered the happy times.

She remembered the way they celebrated their First Holy Communions and Saints' Days with all the neighborhood coming to their apartment for Mama's chicken molé and enchiladas. Mama would roll out tortillas with her rolling pin and stand at the stove while the others ate. All the time she would be chatting with her family and friends. That was before Mama got sick.

Things began to change when Teresa was thirteen. Mama fell ill with tuberculosis, the scourge of the barrio, and Teresa dropped out of school to care for her. Papa struggled to pay for her doctors and medicine, as well as to feed and clothe them all, but it was a losing battle. It hurt her to see her proud father unable to care for his family. Teresa tried to help, but Luis rebelled. He too stopped going to school and soon stopped coming home at all.

Teresa and her father learned from neighbors that Luis had become a *cholo*. He was running with a local gang, Los Apaches, that battled other gangs with names like Los Asesinos and Companeros de la Muerte for control of barrio turf. At first she couldn't believe that her gentle brother could be a *cholo* but when news went out that Mama had taken a turn for the worse, Luis showed up.

His black hair was short and slicked back and he wore a white shirt and tight, pegged, khaki pants. On his right biceps was a crude tattoo that read, *"Mi Vida Loca."* Hector somehow blamed the boy for his wife's illness. When he saw his son standing in the doorway he went to hit him, but to his surprise Luis pulled out a switchblade knife and held it to his neck.

Teresa screamed.

"Don't ever do that, Papa," Luis said. "Or

I'll cut your throat." He turned and left the apartment and Teresa never saw him alive again. They brought him back two months later, his body riddled with bullets. The Apaches had lost a battle and Luis was dead at sixteen.

Perhaps because of that tragedy, Carmelita died a few months later and Hector followed soon after. In a year and a half, Teresa Martinez had lost everyone she had in the world. Even her godparents, chosen with such care by Hector, had returned to Mexico. She was not yet seventeen years old and from now on she would be on her own.

She had already blossomed into a beauty with large, dark brown eyes that were almost as dark as her black hair. She had long legs for a chicana and a voluptuous body that she hid modestly the way the sisters at school had taught her. No short skirts, no sleeveless blouses.

But what could she do to earn a living? Some of the girls she had gone to school with were already getting married and others were working only until they did. Chicana girls did not work in the downtown stores and offices. Then she heard that some of the girls from her neighborhood were working at the Leeds Petrochemical factory, getting forty dollars a week.

Modestly dressed in the same black cotton

dress she had worn to her parents' funerals she applied for a job at Leeds. A Senor Machado examined her application and then Teresa and laughed. He was a large fat man and when he laughed his whole body shook.

"Chica," he said when he managed to get control of himself. "A girl with your looks deserves better than this." He scribbled something on a note pad, tore it off and handed it to her. "The White Horse is a classy joint and the owner's a friend of mine. He'll give you a job and you'll make some real money."

Terry took the paper nervously and hurried out the door before Senor Machado tried to take it back.

Ricardo Videla's White Horse was a small but popular cabaret on Elysian Street on the east side of Houston. It catered to rich locals and travelling businessmen. The bar provided set-ups for those who brought their own bottles, but it was best known as a place where a lonely traveller might find a pretty companion for the night. Ricardo prided himself on having the best-looking waitresses in Houston.

The waitresses were in fact the only reason why customers flocked to the White Horse. The place itself was dingy, smoke-filled and poorly lit. The tunes coming from the piano over the boisterous sound of the hard-drinking crowd were more noise than melody.

The club was deserted when Teresa arrived

late that afternoon. She found Videla sitting at an empty table, going over some accounts. Hesitatingly she gave him Machado's note and as he took it he looked her up and down. Suddenly his dark face broke into a smile.

"*Siete*," he told her as he got up and grabbed a chair. "If you're looking for a job you've come to the right place."

Videla was tall and broad shouldered. His hips were small but too much indulgence in oily Mexican food had given him a paunch. His slicked-down black hair and his long, thin sideburns made him look like a retired bullfighter. He had been one, though not one of the greats, and he still wore the mementoes of where an impatient bull had gored him in the groin ten years before. He had spent months recuperating and it had ended his career as a torero. He didn't have the heart for it anymore.

When Teresa told him her age, he whistled. Hiring a seventeen-year-old girl was asking for trouble but since she was only a chicana he could probably handle it. Besides, the big, brown eyes and that gorgeous figure, even hidden under that potato sack of a dress she was wearing, made the risk worth taking.

"You get fifty dollars a week plus tips," he barked. "And with those knockers the tips should be great."

Teresa blushed.

"Don't be embarrassed, *chiquita*," he

laughed. "If you want to do well you'll have to use those tits. When do you want to start?"

She hesitated, explaining that she was still looking for a place to stay. She was staying with neighbors but the apartment was crowded and they couldn't offer their hospitality much longer.

"No problem, there are rooms upstairs," Videla assured her. "You can stay here. No charge."

She had given away most of what had belonged to her parents, so she carried all her worldly goods across town in one trip. The little room Videla assigned her on the second floor was more like a closet, really, with barely enough room for a cot and a table and a chair. The narrow, curtainless window looked out on an alley below.

She put her small statue of the Madonna on the table and quickly changed into the costume Videla gave her. It was a little embarrassing, it was so bare, and she was glad that the sisters and her parents couldn't see her. She tried to concentrate on the money she would be making which she would save so that when she married her husband could buy a house or start a business. Just because she was alone now didn't mean she wouldn't have a dowry.

That night Videla introduced her to the other waitresses. They were all anglos, mostly girls from the South, drawn to Houston by the lure of a boom town. There was Betty Jo from Oklahoma and Dixie Carter from Alabama and a girl they called Pinky. They were all friendly even though they used words that would have shocked even her poor brother. Sometimes they gave her advice.

"Not like that," Dixie yelled at her when she saw her lean over to serve a table of six men. "This way," and she jiggled her shoulders a little to give them a quick flash of her nipples.

"More tits mean more tips," Dixie said as she walked away.

Even without Dixie and the other girls, Terry was a sensation that first night. She got more tips than all the other girls together, but since they pooled their money no one minded. By the time the club closed at one in the morning she was exhausted. Her feet ached from the high heels and she felt humiliated by some of the remarks and propositions that the men made to her. They talked about her breasts, her legs, her eyes as if she was a cow in a meat market.

She was glad to get to her room, bare and dismal as it was. It was a relief to climb on the cot, say her prayers and close her eyes. She had almost fallen asleep when she heard the knock at her door.

"Who is it?" She realized that she had not even looked to see if there was a lock on the door.

"It's me, Ricardo." He didn't hesitate but walked right in and stood over her, smiling drunkenly.

"What do you want, Senor Videla?" She was frightened and pulled the thin top sheet up to cover herself.

He ripped the sheet from her hand and pulled it down to the edge of the bed. All she was wearing was a thin, cotton nightgown.

"You've got great knockers," he said as he leered at her.

She didn't know what to do. She was frozen with fear. "Please, Senor Videla," she pleaded. "Go away."

But he didn't seem to hear her. He was in a world of his own as he stepped onto the narrow cot, which creaked under his weight. She shrank away but he took her in his arms, his large hands groping her breasts through the nightgown. She tried to push him away but that only seemed to excite him more. He began to kiss her face and when she opened her mouth to scream he stuck in his tongue, probing her mouth. No one had ever kissed her that way.

His hand was on her legs now, lifting the nightgown, caressing her thighs. Then he was on top of her. She was crying by this time and as she struggled, sobbing, he entered her and she screamed in pain.

When it was over he stayed with her, holding her in her arms, trying to comfort her. He was ashamed of himself. It hadn't occurred to him that she might be a virgin. She kept crying that she wanted to die and he kept trying to explain to her that she was not ruined.

"No man will want me now," she sobbed. "I'm a *puta.*"

"That's not true," he insisted. "I love you. I'd do anything for you. Why I'd even marry you myself if I didn't have a wife already."

Teresa began to sob again as Ricardo rocked her in his arms.

"If losing your virginity made you a *puta,*" he said, "most of the girls in Houston would be whores."

She stopped crying for a minute and stared at him.

"You think only anglo girls sleep around?" he said. "Believe me, the chicanas do it too."

Gradually Ricardo brought her around. After all, the damage was done. She couldn't bring it back. The next night she went back downstairs and from then on she was the most popular waitress at the White Horse. She went out with the customers, but only if she liked them, not for the amount of money they offered.

She learned the art of pleasing a man and after a year at Ricardo's she knew there was no man she couldn't satisfy. There was only one thing she wouldn't do. The lessons of her mother and the sisters still hung over her and she wouldn't go with a married man. Not even Ricardo. Especially not Ricardo.

Poor Videla was so mad about her that he made her the hostess of the White Horse, which was only right since she was drawing most of his business.

*   *   *

One night Sam Rosen came in. He was a tall, handsome New Yorker in his early forties and she could see he was a big spender. He was with a party of four men, all looking rich and successful. He ordered champagne all around and she learned that he was a dress manufacturer in New York. She recognized the name of his company; she had seen it on the labels of expensive dresses at Foley's. He left a one-hundred-dollar tip.

The next morning he called her and invited her to lunch with him at the Rice Hotel. Over broiled lamb chops and avocados he told her about his business and his wife.

"Your wife?" Teresa could feel herself stiffen.

"Oh, we've been separated for years," he assured her. "We're working on the divorce right now."

Sam was different from the other men who came into the White Horse. He was more sophisticated and he treated her like a lady.

115

Even after they went to bed together two nights later he still seemed to respect her. Maybe, she dared to hope, he would be the man who would marry her. She could leave the White Horse and live like a decent woman. She prayed that it would work out.

And for a while it seemed to do just that. Sam stayed in town a week, and he told her he came in from New York one week a month. He took her to clubs, nice clubs like the Last Concert, a night spot that was popular with anglos and affluent Mexicans. He couldn't believe that she had never been to a Mexican nightclub before.

He convinced her to leave the White Horse. He got her a job at Foley's and he found her an apartment. Ricardo Videla could not believe that she was leaving, and begged and threatened, but she told him she was going to a better life. When she moved out, he stood screaming at the door but she ignored him and stepped into Sam's waiting taxi. That part of her life was over, and she was beginning again with Sam.

With her dark good looks and natural style, Teresa fit right in at Foley's. She worked in the better dress department and nobody treated her as if she was different, a mere chicana. She even made a new friend, Mary Eaton, a pretty, blond anglo. They would have lunch together at the counter at Woolworth's.

Mary's boyfriend was a lawyer and he usually worked late into the night. Sometimes the two girls would go to the movies or dinner together. One night, after they had been to see *The Creature from the Black Lagoon,* Teresa invited Mary up to her apartment.

"How can you afford this on a Foley's salary?" Mary asked immediately.

She confided about Sam and how he had found her the job and helped her with the apartment. She never mentioned the White Horse.

"Are you sure he's separated?" Mary asked as she leaned back on the sofa.

"Of course. Why would he lie?"

Mary laughed. Underneath the Southern belle exterior she was as hard and calculating as any of the girls at the White Horse. "Maybe he lied because he knew he couldn't get you otherwise."

Teresa stared at her friend. Sam had told her he loved her. She couldn't believe he would lie.

"There's one way to find out. We could call him at home."

"Oh, no, I couldn't."

"If you don't, I will," Mary insisted. "I think it's stupid to waste your time with a married man when there are so many men in Houston who'd die to go out with you."

So Teresa sat there while Mary called Sam Rosen in New York. She could only hear one side of the conversation but it was enough.

"Hello? Mrs. Rosen? My name is Jean Smith

and I'm calling from the Rice Hotel in Houston." She sounded very official. "We're polling our customers and we'd like to ask you a few questions."

The other end must have agreed because Mary went on.

"You *are* Mrs. Sam Rosen?" She looked at Teresa and nodded her head. Affirmative. "I see. And how long have you been married." Pause. "Oh, I see. And how many children?" Pause. "Oh, I see. Well, thank you very much Mrs. Rosen and I hope you'll come to Houston yourself someday."

Mary hung up the telephone in disgust. "He's married, for sixteen years and he has three children. And if there's any separation or divorce in the works, she knows less about it than you do."

*   *   *

Sam called her a few nights later, blissfully unaware that the party was over.

"How could you lie to me Sam?" she cried. "You had no intention of divorcing your wife!"

He told her he loved her—that even if he couldn't get a divorce immediately he could get a legal separation, and they could be together. He pleaded, begged, and finally threatened to have her fired, but she had made up her mind. She still clung to a few remnants of her upbringing; a good girl didn't go with married men. And no matter what had happened at the White Horse, she wanted desperately to be a good girl.

The next morning Sam Rosen flew in from New York, and showed unannounced at her apartment. He looked haggard from a sleepless night. He offered her money, a lot of money for Teresa, if she reconsidered.

She remained adamant.

Then he turned ugly. "You lousy bitch," he screamed. "I found you in that pick-up joint when you were selling your ass to the highest bidder, and now you assume this sanctimonious attitude of the misunderstood virgin. Face up, Teresa. You're nothing but a pretty whore! Now you can go back to that beautiful life."

He threw a $100 bill on the bed and walked out.

Teresa did not move. For a while she just stood there, frozen. Then she broke down in uncontrollable sobs. She did care about Rosen. He had been kind and generous with her, had treated her like a lady. But what he had just said to her was awful and unfair. She was not a whore. She had been with men, and they had given her money and gifts, but she had never asked for them. The men she had slept with were those she had chosen. She still had a code. She was not going to be the mistress of a married man. She would not destroy another man's family and, perhaps, herself.

The next day at lunch she told Mary what she had done.

"That's great news," Mary cheered, unconcerned about the pain in her friend's face. "Tom's after me all the time to come up with a date for his boss. He's supposed to be real good-looking and all he does is work."

"Oh great," Teresa managed a smile. "When do we meet?"

"Tonight. I'll call Tom and we'll drop by his office tonight."

So she wore her favorite red dress and went with Mary. It was only when the cab let them out at the Young building that Teresa thought to ask the boss's name. That was when she realized that her date owned the building as well as a good chunk of Houston. She was going to meet the famous Ashley Young.

7

Houston, Texas
March 1954

It was Sunday morning and they had just
finished making love. Ash leaned back in the
pillows of Teresa's bed. She leaned against his
shoulder, clutching his arm around her. In his
hand he held a Lucky Strike and occasionally
he would take long, deep drags on it. He had
never considered himself much in the erotic
department, but maybe that was because he had
taken other women more out of need than
desire. With Teresa it was all different. In bed
she was a wonder, sensuous yet gentle, giving
herself to him completely.

"Would you like some breakfast?" she
asked, slipping out of bed and standing beside
him. Her black hair was loose and fell to her

shoulders. "I'll fix you some ham and eggs."

"Great." There was no doubt about it. He was a happy man.

Last night he had taken her to the Bayou Club for dinner and as they danced she told him she loved him. The truth was he felt the same way about her. It was strange to use the word "love." He had never used it before except with his parents, as if either one of them knew anything about it. Teresa, he was sure, knew about love.

Teresa was also thinking about love as she prepared their breakfast in the tiny kitchen. She had fallen in love with Ash from the start, and last night, after a few glasses of champagne, she had told him so. He asked her to marry him and she consented.

As the eggs sizzled in the frying pan, she measured out coffee for the percolator and thought about their future together.

Ash Young was different from other men, shyer and not so brutally aggressive. He was rich but he was also a good man and he loved her. When they were married she would be a good wife, make a good home, have children.

She thought about the wedding. It was too bad she wouldn't be able to go back to her little church in the barrio but Ash had told her about his mother, how she had been a religious fanatic who turned him against churchgoing forever. Maybe, in time, he would come around. Meanwhile she would be married and that was the most important thing.

The coffee was ready and she fixed a little tray and brought it to Ash. He was still in bed.

"Thank you, my darling," he said as she laid the tray beside him. "And your reward is in my jacket."

She took the jacket off the back of the chair and giggled as she went through the pockets. In one she found a small blue box. She looked at Ash, puzzled.

"Well," he said impatiently. "Open it."

She opened it slowly. Inside was a huge, pear-shaped diamond ring. She had never seen a diamond so big in her life.

"Oh, darling, it's beautiful!" she said, rushing to his side of the bed. She kissed him. "I love it."

"Now we're officially engaged."

"I love you, I love you, I love you."

"At twenty carats, you'd better."

He watched her as she played with the ring like a child. He was still a little surprised himself at the way things had happened. He knew he would eventually marry but he had somehow expected his bride would be the daughter of one of Houston's leading citizens, not the daughter of a Mexican laborer who worked as a salesgirl at Foley's.

But Teresa was a woman of quality in spite of her background. She was a lady and with a little education and polish, things that he could buy for her, she would be a princess. With her beauty and demeanor she would outshine any other woman, not just in Texas, but the world.

"I want you to move out of here," he told her. "I have another place for you, at least until we're married. And I want you to quit your job. The future Mrs. Ashley Young can't be a salesgirl. You've got to learn to live in style."

"OK, master," she told him happily. At that moment she would have done anything for him. After all, he was going to be her husband.

She gave her notice the next day. Mary was devastated, but she insisted they would always be friends. She began to plan the wedding. It would be a small affair with Mary as her maid of honor and Tom Patterson as Ash's best man. She picked out a white wedding gown at Sackowitz's.

Just before Ash left for a business trip to New York, she told him she was pregnant.

"I'm sure we can arrange an abortion," he told her. A child so soon was not part of his plan.

"Abortion is murder," she told him, horrified. The worst *puta* in the barrio would not kill a baby. Besides, they were getting married anyway, all they had to do was move up the wedding.

"All right," he said reluctantly. "When I

return from New York we'll get married immediately."

＊　　　＊　　　＊

Ash had come to New York to discuss
building two supertankers to carry oil from the
Middle East to the United States. For two days
he had been in meetings with engineers and
shipbuilders and he was bored stiff, but at last
they had finally agreed to terms.

To celebrate completion of the deal they had
come to Romeo Salta on West 56th Street for
dinner, all eight men, and he was more bored
than ever.

As it always is with men drinking together,
they talked about women, boasting of their
conquests and regaling each other with lewd
stories. Some of the lewdest were coming from
the American seated next to Ash.

He was an engineer in one of the shipyards, a
rugged, fairly handsome man in his late
thirties, which made him about ten years older
than Ash. He had lived in every city in the
world and seemed to have a dirty story about all
of them. Ash found him crude and boring and
was about to cut him off when he got on the
subject of Houston.

"A great place, Houston. Best cocksuckers
anywhere, especially those Mexican girls on

Elysian Street. Ever been to the White Horse?"

All Ash knew about the White Horse was that it was a dive and a haven for low life. He wasn't surprised that the engineer knew it well.

"No, I haven't," he told him dryly, hoping to discourage him, but the engineer was oblivious to insults.

"Well, be sure to go. Ask for Teresa. You can't miss her," he went on, not noticing the boredom in Ash's gray eyes. "What a piece." The man laughed and gulped another glass of red wine. "Tall, brunette, with brown eyes and a pair of knockers you won't believe."

"When was this?" Ash's voice was tight.

"Couple of years ago."

Ash excused himself and went directly to the phone. There must be hundreds of Mexican girls named Teresa in Houston and all of them were dark. Still, the description of the girl bothered him. He had to know. He placed a call to Houston. Teresa answered on the first ring.

"Darling," she sounded happy. "I was just thinking of you. Do you miss me as much as I miss you?"

Ash ignored her. He had no time for small talk. "Did you ever work at a place called the White Horse?" he barked.

There was a long pause before she answered. "Yes," she said and her voice was very soft.

"That's all I wanted to know." He slammed

the phone down and returned to the table. The travelling engineer had moved on to his memories of San Francisco.

*   *   *

When Teresa hung up the receiver, she was shaking and she felt as though she was going to collapse. The White Horse seemed so long ago that she had almost managed to forget it. She never thought about it at all anymore. Now suddenly Ash knew everything.

She tried to reach him at the Pierre but he was out. He must have called her from a restaurant, but no one knew where he was or at least no one would admit to knowing. It was already nine o'clock. She called an hour later but by then Mr. Young had left word he must not be disturbed.

She tried Mary Eaton but there was no answer. She called Tom Patterson. Between sobs she told him about Ash's call.

"Tell me about the White Horse," he said kindly.

She poured out her story over the telephone. She told him about Videla and the other girls and what it was like at the White Horse.

Tom listened patiently, and when she was finished he asked her if she had ever mentioned any of it to Ash.

127

"No, I didn't," she admitted. "I told him everything else, but I didn't want to lose him and now I have."

"Try to calm down, Teresa, and get some sleep," he said gently. "I'll see what I can do." He hung up the phone.

*   *   *

When Patterson finished with Teresa, he turned to Mary Eaton who was beside him in bed. She had only heard his side of the conversation but she had a pretty good idea what it was about.

"Jesus, Ash can be a cold sonofabitch." He shook his head. "I really feel for that girl."

The following morning, he picked up Ash at the Houston airport. As they drove back to the office in his air-conditioned Cadillac, Ash began to discuss the tanker deal as if nothing else had happened. Patterson cut him off.

"Teresa was in all states last night," he said. "She's gone to pieces."

Ash stared at the road ahead. "It seems to me I asked you to check her out months ago," he said. "Did you know about the White Horse?"

"Yes," Patterson admitted. "I knew she worked there. But Christ, Ash, she was a kid. She didn't do anything any other girl hasn't."

"She was a whore!"

"That's being a little dramatic."

"She's a whore and a liar," he snapped. "And I got the story from one of her boyfriends." That was what bothered him the most. Not just that she had misled him, but that he had almost faced marriage with a little whore whose drunken ex-boyfriends would be telling him stories about her wherever he went.

"But you asked her to marry you," Patterson insisted. "And she's expecting your child."

"I don't give a shit," he said bitterly. "For all I know it's not even mine. Pay her off and get her out of my life."

In spite of his close relationship with Young, Patterson was appalled. As they drew into the parking lot of the Young Building, he turned to his boss.

"This isn't fair, Ash. The girl loves you and you told me only a few days ago that you loved her. Whatever happened in the past, she's still a good girl."

"What do you call a good girl?" Young snapped. "Someone who's good in the hay? I give her top marks there, but I'm not marrying a whore." No, he had been willing to accept Teresa as a poor chicana, a salesgirl in a department store who had never gone beyond ninth grade. He had even accepted that she had been kept by Sam Rosen. He had actually been impressed with all her bullshit about leaving Rosen because he was a married man. And all the time she had been lying. That was what really got to him. He had compromised and accepted her, and all the time she was lying. She had betrayed him. And no one betrayed Ash Young.

"Give her a check for five thousand dollars, see that the rent on the apartment is paid through the end of the year, and then the hell with her," he concluded.

*   *   *

The first few weeks after Ash's phone call, Teresa tried again and again to reach him at his office or his house in River Oaks but he refused to come to the phone. She showed up at the Young Building and his mansion but she never got past the secretary or the housekeeper. She was distraught. Even her days at the White Horse now seemed better than the future ahead.

One thought began to dominate all others. She was pregnant and unmarried. She was not just a *puta*, she was going to have a bastard child. She was so ashamed, she wanted to die. She sat in her dark apartment sipping vodka and praying for death.

Then she realized what she had to do. It was a sin, but she had already sinned so much maybe God would finally forgive her. She dressed in the white, silk negligee she had bought for their honeymoon. She ran the water in the bathtub.

She wanted it as hot and steamy as she could bear. Next she poured in bath salts and the room began to fill with the scent of Blue Grass. She took a fresh razor blade and laid it on the shelf beside the tub.

She poured another glass of vodka as the bathtub filled. She wanted to be very drunk. Feeling no pain, as Dixie at the White Horse used to say. That was what she wanted, to feel no pain.

She finished the glass and went back to the kitchen for more. She decided to bring the whole bottle back. She was going to need it.

She stepped into the tub and let the fragrant water cover her body. She said a last prayer to the Virgin and then she took the razor blade and made two deep incisions in the sign of the cross on each wrist. They began to ooze blood. Numbed by the vodka, she closed her eyes and thought about how nice it would be to see Mama and Papa and Luis again.

8

New York, Teheran, London
1955

The break with Teresa was the final straw. He was tired of Houston. He would never be accepted there, the old-timers made it clear that they disapproved of him. He was not the man his father was and there was never going to be any invitation to join the Petroleum Club or any of the other bastions of Houston society.

Well, he didn't need it. If Houston thought it was too good for Ash Young, he knew he was too big for Houston. When Phil Stewart, his old Princeton polo buddy, invited him to spend a few days in New York, he seized the chance.

Of course Stewart turned out to have an ulterior motive. He was bored with his family's brokerage house and wanted to put together a polo team.

Ash was interested. An idea had been building in his head ever since he read in *Town & Country* about how Charles B. Wrightsman, another Texas oil man, had started his social climb on a polo pony, and had managed to become an international figure, hobnobbing with European titles and the cream of New York and Palm Beach society.

The cutthroat competition of the game had always excited Ash, but now he also saw the polo pony as a vehicle for meeting the right people.

Sometimes he regretted missing out on polo's golden era, during the 1930s. The mechanization of the cavalry and income tax had pretty much dealt twin death blows to the game and that was a tragedy. It now cost a high goal player about one hundred thousand dollars a year to play right. Indoor polo was less expensive and becoming more popular, but it couldn't compare with the real thing.

There was simply no thrill like galloping astride a fine pony, armed only with a whalebone whip in one hand and a long-handled mallet in the other. When he managed to knock the small, white wicker-root ball through the lath goalposts at the end of the field, the thrill he felt was almost sexual.

Putting together a polo team turned out to be more complicated than assembling a tanker fleet. First there was the matter of handicaps. A committee of the United States Polo Association rated players on overall ability once a year, assigning a handicap from one to ten. The better the player, the higher the handicap. It was useful because it allowed beginners to play with more experienced players, much like golf.

Phil Stewart was a five goal handicap and his friend Stephen "Laddie" Bosford was a four-goaler. Now they needed a fourth player and he had to be a crackerjack to counterbalance Ash. Try as he might, he would never be better than a two.

They were training at the Meadow Brook Club on Long Island every day but they had to have a fourth man before they could officially declare themselves a team. Then Laddie Bosford remembered Manolo Chavez.

"He played at the Gulf Stream Club last year," he told Ash. "I'd never seen anything like it. Chavez moves like lightning. Not even Tommy Hitchcock could match him."

Ash had heard about the wild off-field antics of the Argentine playboy but now he was only interested in how he played polo.

"Get him!" he said excitedly. "No matter what the price!"

They finally did get him, after dozens of phone calls and cables to Buenos Aires and the promise that he could fly over with two horses he had selected and that Ash would pay for.

Ash wanted to call his new team the Texas Rangers, but that name had already been used by Wrightsman. He settled for the Wildcats, and they would prove to be worthy of the name.

In their first game against the Meadow Brook Blues, Chavez proved to be an aggressive, speedy malletman. Astride one of his long-headed, big-boned Argentine thoroughbreds, it seemed at times as though man and horse were one. A true centaur. They went on to check the Brookville team 8-4, winning the Long Island Polo League outdoor title that season.

Bosford and Stewart were light and fast and, although not ten-goal players, they were high scorers. As forwards they made the crucial goals. Chavez was in the pivotal position and could easily turn the tide of a game, but he was reckless. In one game he set a record for fouls: twenty-five calls for roughness.

The Wildcats played on Long Island, in Florida and in California, winning most of the time because of Chavez's incredible play. After the games there were the parties, elegant affairs with the players at center stage. As the millionaire captain of the Wildcats, Ash was very much in demand and, to his surprise and delight, women sought him out.

Caught up in the enthusiasm, he decided to take the Wildcats on a tour of Europe. They flew over in his new Lear Star jet, and under the sponsorship of the Rothschilds in France, Prince Colonna in Italy and the Marques de Villaverde, Generalissimo Franco's son-in-law, in Spain, they played in Paris' Bois de Boulogne, in Deauville, in Biarritz, in Rome and Madrid.

In Biarritz he met the Shah of Iran and his beautiful green-eyed wife, Soraya. They insisted he bring the Wildcats to Iran where the game had been invented.

In Teheran, the shah gave them a memorable reception. Before a select crowd of diplomats, generals and dignitaries of all sorts, the Wildcats played an Iranian team captained by the shah's young half-brother Abdorezza. Chavez played a somewhat restrained game, peppering the Iranian goal line with only a few of his murderous hits, and to everyone's satisfaction the two teams ended in a draw.

Ash was quick to recognize that he and Mohammed Reza Pahlavi had much in common. Both were upstarts, sons of strong-willed and successful fathers whom they had ultimately deposed, and both were ambitious. Ash was trying to build himself a business empire and the shah wanted to make his country a mighty military and industrial power.

They even shared a weakness for titles. The shah kept around half of the deposed royalty of Europe. Vittorio Emanuel di Savoia, son of the last reigning King of Italy, was his favorite five-percenter and had already made millions of lira arranging for the sale of helicopters and other hardware to Iran.

The shah readily agreed to a long-term contract to ship oil on the Young fleet and he asked Ash for suggestions for investments in America. They also discussed at length the virtues of American fighter planes against the new model the French were producing. Ash had studied every new plane, commercial and military, in production. At the moment he was shopping for something bigger than the Lear Star.

As he was leaving, the shah presented him with a fine Persian enamel box. Inside was a beautifully inscribed excerpt from the great Persian poet Firdausi's epic about the first Persian international polo matches centuries before.

"I might be interested in your opinion in the future, Mr. Young," the shah told him. "If you don't mind."

"I'd be most honored, Your Majesty," Ash assured him. He sensed the beginning of a long and profitable arrangement.

*   *   *

From Iran, the Wildcats flew to London where they established headquarters for a month. They were fast becoming famous, or infamous, for wherever they went they left a long line of satisfied women and cuckolded men. Chavez was the leader, but Stewart and

Bosford, though more selective, were just as busy. Even the introverted Ash was beginning to enjoy himself.

Soon the London papers were full of stories of his imminent marriage to Lady Pamela Winship, the beautiful daughter of the Earl of Connair. Ash was well aware that marriage to the lady in question would have satisfied his vanity and secret social aspirations. After all, she was related to the noblest families of the realm, and in addition she was quite an erotic lady in bed. But Ash's dream of making a titled lady his wife was short-lived.

It happened in Deauville, a week before he was to return to the United States, and he would never forget the occasion. He and Pam had gone to the exclusive resort on the Normandy coast where the Wildcats were entered in a triangular polo tournament with French and English teams.

Their first night in Deauville, they had shared a cozy dinner at their hotel, the Normandie, and then visited the casino where they had dropped a few thousand dollars at the baccarat and roulette tables. They moved on to the nightclub below where a Negro band was playing American jazz.

After a few drinks Ash had suggested they leave, but Pam protested. "Darling, go if you're tired. I'll just stay awhile. I love this kind of music," she purred.

"But I can't let you stay here alone," he had answered, annoyed.

"Why not? It's not the first time. I can take care of myself."

He had stood up to go, but after a moment's hesitation he had sat down again.

"Don't be such a sourpuss, lovey," she had teased him. "Let me just hear a couple more tunes and we'll go home. I'll go over and ask for them myself." She ran over to the band leader, a big and handsome black, and began an animated conversation.

It occurred to Ash that it was taking Pam a bit too long just to ask for a couple of tunes, and he was shocked out of his wits when, as she was leaving, she planted a kiss on the man's lips. These English women, he thought angrily, had no sense of modesty or decorum.

He refused to discuss it with her as they drove home. But he was angry and deeply disturbed and that night he didn't make love to her. The next morning he left early to meet his teammates on the polo field. She was still sleeping when he walked out, unwilling to wake her.

It was raining on the field when he arrived and after a few hours he agreed to cut short the practice game. He returned to the Hotel Normandie alone, anxious to make up with Pamela.

As he entered the suite, he heard strange noises coming from the bedroom. Surprised he opened the door and froze, paralyzed by what he saw. A huge black man, completely stripped, lay on his bed, and Lady Pam, also naked, was on her knees on the bed, her head reclining over the man's torso, her mouth making strange sucking noises.

The man was too busy moaning and grunting and Her Ladyship too concentrated on her work to notice Ash's entrance. So he just stood there for a while, too shocked by the disgusting scene to react.

Finally he screamed: "Get out of here, both of you!"

It was an awkward moment for the couple in bed. The man, who, judging by the sounds he was making, was obviously in the midst of a tremendous climax, raised his head and, seeing Ash, tried painfully to lift himself from the bed. But he could not do so without risking emasculation, for Pam had him solidly between her teeth. Pam was in no better position. She could not move her head, nor could she answer Ash, for it's notoriously bad manners to speak with your mouth full. So she just waved at Ash as if telling him to wait.

In barely a minute, without ever losing her composure, the lady stepped down from the bed. Walking up to Ash she said, "I'm sorry, lovey. But I didn't expect you so soon."

"I should say you didn't," Ash snapped back. "You disgust me! You're a tramp!"

"Don't take it so seriously," Pam laughed.

"This doesn't mean a thing. I was just bored and wanted some diversion."

"Some diversion!" he retorted. "Now, if you please, you and your boyfriend get out of here!"

"You Americans are so silly," she giggled. "There's no reason to act so angry. If you want, I'll never see him again." She tried to kiss him, but he turned away. He stormed out of the room and headed downstairs where he ordered the concierge to reserve another suite for him and to have the valet remove all his clothes to his new rooms.

He didn't hear from Pamela again and fortunately the gossip columns hadn't gotten a whiff of the scandal. He had almost forgotten it entirely when it was time to leave.

Two days before they were to return home, after their last victorious match against the Cowdray Park team, the Wildcats were invited to a dinner dance at the home of the Duke and Duchess of Wilshire on Hill Street, just a step away from Berkeley Square.

The house, which had been left to the duke by his wealthy American mother, was one of the most elegant in London. The entrance hall opened into the large high-ceilinged drawing room. The walls were the color of pale salmon and displayed on them were portraits of eight generations of Wilshires. Most of the furniture had been removed to allow room for dancing and a small, five-piece orchestra had been set up on a platform at the end of the room.

In the adjoining dining room a sumptuous buffet had been laid with salmon, caviar, roast beef, pheasant from the Wilshire country house, stuffed artichokes, boiled leeks and candied carrots.

The duke was a big, jolly fellow with a pink complexion and pronounced jowls. "Porchy" was best known as a big game hunter, and perhaps his greatest prize was the duchess. Jean Wilshire was a former Copa Girl, still stunning. Tonight her red hair was swept up and she was wearing a long bubble-skirted Balmain green brocade. At her throat was an emerald necklace that had once belonged to the Empress Josephine.

They greeted each of the more than two hundred guests as they arrived. The Duke and Duchess of Marlborough, the Duke of Bedford, the Duke and Duchess of Sutherland, the Earl of Warwick, Sir Laurence Olivier and Vivian Leigh, the Maharaja and Maharani of Jaipur, Stavros Niarchos, the Greek shipping magnate, and Alexander Korda, the film producer, were among those who arrived early.

Ash and his Wildcats came in a group and they bowed to Their Graces as one man. Manolo took the opportunity to peer down the decolletage of the well-endowed duchess. Impressed by what he saw, he resolved to find a way to become more intimate with the voluptuous lady.

He got his chance after dinner when the guests converged on the drawing room and the band began to play. He invited the duchess to dance. As the orchestra played "Let Me Go Lover," he pressed himself against her.

"You're so strong, Senor Chavez," she giggled.

"And you're so beautiful, my lady," he whispered in her ear. "Too beautiful not to be made love to."

"Do you think so?" she said coquettishly.

"I don't think so, I know so." He grinned, showing his magnificent, white teeth.

The music changed to "The Tennessee Waltz," and before Lady Wilshire fully realized what was happening, he had waltzed her out of the room and upstairs to the first empty room. It was a masculine room, adorned with African hunting trophies and gun cases and still reeking of the aroma of good cigars. But Manolo paid no heed. All he saw was the big Tudor four-poster in the middle of the room.

Silently and quickly he undressed the willing duchess, threw her on the bed, then stripped down himself. From the drawing room they could hear that the music had changed. The orchestra was playing "Hernando's Hideaway."

"Ah, a tango," Manolo exclaimed as he pounded on top of her. "It is so beautiful to make love to a tango."

There was no question that the duchess could tango beautifully. Then the tempo of the music changed again and the partners changed position. Manolo moved on his back and the duchess impaled herself on his shaft.

As she gripped him she began to chant, "I'm coming! I'm coming!"

At that moment the duke entered the room.

"Jean!" he bellowed. "What are you doing here? Who's that fellow below and what's he doing in my room?"

It was an awkward moment. The duchess, coming to the end of her orgasm, looked at her husband with a bewildered expression. She was hardly in a position to explain, so it remained for her companion to speak.

"It's me, Manolo Chavez, Your Grace," he said cordially. "Pardon me if I don't get up."

"Well . . . well . . . well." The duke was at a loss for words. "Guess I'll have to find another w.c."

"Please use ours," Manolo insisted.

"Yes, Porchy, dear, please do," Jean Wilshire said, having finally freed herself from the Argentine.

In full dignity the duke entered his bathroom. A few minutes later he recrossed the room. "Jean," he said as he reached the door. "Please see your guest out." He nodded curtly to Chavez.

Manolo looked at his departing host with admiration. "It's when I see things like that," he said, "that I know there'll always be an England!"

The duke found Ash chatting with Niarchos and Korda and pulled him aside. "Have a complaint about one of your teammates, Mr. Young," he said brusquely. "Martini's the name or something of the sort. Tall, dark, Spanish-looking chap."

"Manolo Chavez," Ash smiled. "What's he done this time?"

"Let it remain among us gentlemen, but I found him in my bedroom with my wife. In my house, Mr. Young! Bad show! It's simply *not done!*"

"I'm terribly sorry," an embarrassed Ash said. "We'll leave at once." He ran upstairs to the duke's bedroom and knocked on the heavy, oak door several times. There was no answer, so he simply walked in.

He was greeted by the sight of Manolo Chavez humping the duchess doggy fashion.

"Shove it in all the way," Her Ladyship was screaming. "Yes, like this, harder, harder!"

"*Sí, querida puta,* take it all," Manolo encouraged her. "*Sí,* move your ass, duchess."

Ash was so embarrassed he wanted to run and hide. Instead he coughed.

"Is that you again, Your Grace?" Manolo asked, not even turning his head or slackening his tempo. "We'll be through in a second."

"It's not the duke," Ash snapped. "You damn fool! What are you trying to do, fuck yourself into the grave? The duke's furious. He wants you out now."

A livid Ash waited outside the door as Chavez said his goodbyes to the duchess. When he joined his friend he was smiling.

"*Qué pasa hombre?*" he asked cheerfully. "It's not nice to interrupt a friend when he's making love. Especially to a lady with tits like that." He held out his hands from his chest, then exploded in laughter.

"Stop it, you fool!" Ash ordered. He was fed up with the Argentine and his antics. "Let's get out of here before they throw us out."

"Take it easy, captain, I'm coming. I'm sorry we don't have time to give the duke my thanks and compliments. Her Ladyship's a great piece of ass!"

*　　　*　　　*

The next morning in his suite at Claridge's, Ash received a call from the Hon. Maj. Robert Towers, President of the Hurlingham Club, the ruling body of polo in England. He wanted to see him about a problem concerning one of his teammates. Ash guessed immediately that Porchy Wilshire had been at work.

He offered the major a drink and poured one for himself.

"Sorry to trouble you, Mr. Young," Towers said as he sat heavily in the armchair. He lifted his glass of whiskey and water to his host. "Here's to you."

"You're not troubling me at all," Ash

assured him. He was impatient for the man to get to the point of his visit.

"It's that Argentine fellow on your team," Towers began.

"I regret what happened last night and I apologized to the duke."

"Oh, I'm not talking about Porchy Wilshire," the major laughed. "Porchy has the longest horns in the realm. Last time Jean was caught with the chauffeur. Can you imagine? The chauffeur! But one can't blame her too much. The woman's a nymphomaniac and poor Porchy hasn't been able to get it up for years."

Ash was not about to shed a tear for either of them.

"No, your boy Chavez has got himself involved in a *real* bloody mess," the major went on. "Lost twenty thousand pounds at the Eagle Club and left without paying. Just scribbled a note to charge it to the Wildcats."

"That sonofabitch," Ash muttered between his teeth. Nevertheless he would have to do something if he wanted to be invited back inside the stately homes of England. The British took their gambling debts seriously. "Have the manager see me."

On that note the good major left.

The manager of the Eagle Club dropped in on Young that same afternoon and Ash presented him with a check for ten thousand pounds.

"But that's only half of what Senor Chavez lost," he protested.

"Maybe, but it's twice as much as he's worth to me." Ash smiled maliciously. "What do you usually do when people refuse to pay?"

"We teach them a lesson they won't forget."

"Since I paid for half," Ash said, rising from his chair to see the man out. "Why don't you teach him half a lesson?"

*   *   *

A few hours before the Wildcats were to leave from Heathrow Airport, Ash was notified that his star player had met with an accident. He had run into three leather boys who had sent him to the hospital with a broken nose and broken arm. Ash did not send flowers. Nor did he send flowers to Lady Pamela.

His experiences with women, especially Lady Pamela, had left a bitter taste in his mouth, and had only confirmed his belief that all women were no good. They were just whores, no matter what their background, unless they were religious fanatics like his mother. Teresa Martinez, Jean Wilshire, Pamela Winship, what was the difference, except that one was a poor chicana and the others titled ladies. Yes, Manolo Chavez was right. Fuck them and leave them.

When it came time to marry he'd pick one who could be useful, someone rich and prominent, who could be a hostess and do his bidding. Love—that was just a silly word.

9

New York, N.Y.
January 1956

Shortly after New Year's Day, Ash Young returned to New York. In those few months in Houston since his return from Europe, he had convinced himself that he needed more than a polo mallet to become part of high society. Managing the Wildcats had taken more time and energy than running all his other businesses, and it had cost him a fortune. On the plus side, of course, there was the visit to the shah and the fact that it had opened many doors in the right places. Polo had served its purpose but unlike Yankee Doodle, Ash Young was not coming to town on a pony.

He took his usual suite at the Pierre and it was there one morning that he had the pleasure of seeing his name in print.

He had taken to reading the *Journal-American* and he turned quickly to the society page where "Cholly Knickerbocker Observes" took up two page-long columns. He had started reading the syndicated column in Houston knowing that what the columnist decreed in matters social was the law. So he read with special interest what Cholly had to say this day.

The subject was Old Guard society. Cholly contended that in today's world there was no place anymore for a static, monolithic society. In modern America there was only room for a society of achievement, a meritocracy where a man's worth was counted not by his origins but his achievements. Ash agreed wholeheartedly.

Instead of the Four Hundred, Cholly continued, there ought to be the Four Thousand, honoring the Americans who had achieved prominence in such fields as science, the arts, business, politics and sports. That didn't mean that there wouldn't always be a group of special people, celebrities who made news and kept the gossip columns going. This conglomeration of old and new names, mostly moneyed and sometimes colorful people who frequented the smart spots and made news, had been labeled Cafe Society, but today Cholly proclaimed a new title, the Jet Set, that frantic, often amusing, always interesting combination of big names and big money that travels from one corner of the Earth to the other in search of fun and frolic, always partying, always in the latest fashion, always in the columns.

To his surprise, Ash saw that he was included in the column, in an item about "that polo-playing playboy who has abandoned Houston for New York." He winced at the term playboy. He didn't like that at all. He wanted to become known, it was true, but known in the right way, as a man of substance and achievement.

He approached that task as he would any business opportunity. If it was a question of buying into society, he would buy right at the top. If it was a question of the right home or wife, he could buy those too.

He started with the home first.

He knew exactly where he wanted to live. Only Fifth Avenue and only between 79th and 60th Streets would be acceptable to a man in his position. He would be entertaining his European friends now, the Duke and Duchess of Windsor, Palm Beach's Loel and Gloria Guinness, the Viscomte and Viscomtess de Ribes of Paris, the Gianni Agnellis of Italy and of course the shah. For them he wanted only the best.

He found the apartment on Fifth Avenue and 70th Street, a twenty-room penthouse with a view of Central Park. Once the board of the building was assured that he was neither a Jew nor an entertainer he had the privilege of paying five hundred thousand dollars cash for it.

Phil Stewart recommended Etienne Florin, the stylish Frenchman, for the job of decorator. Ash and Monsieur Florin, a small, dapper man with a thin moustache and continental manner, ransacked Paris, London and the best auction houses in New York for the furniture from which various Louis and Marie Antoinette or Mesdames de Pompadour and du Barry had once held forth.

When it was finished, the apartment was a monument to grandeur. At a mirrored entrance hall stood a Louis XV carved and gilded console. Beyond it, the large square formal drawing room had a parquet floor taken from a Versailles chateau. The walls were painted sky blue, and two Louis XVI sofas covered in blue Venetian silk faced each other before a white marble Louis XVI mantel. Above the fireplace hung a Rubens Madonna and on either side were Caffieri sconces. The Isphahan floral rug was three hundred years old and one of the Louis XVI armchairs was supposedly once used in the chateau of Madame de Pompadour.

Although he was committed to fine French furniture, Ash Young's taste in art was becoming eclectic and the apartment gradually filled with fine paintings. The walls were hung with a Tiziano Madonna, a Botticelli Venus, two Vermeers, and four Picassos of the blue period.

Like other collectors before him, he became consumed with a desire to possess beautiful things. He wanted to surround himself with perfection and he could afford it. Besides, collecting was a way of meeting the right people, people of taste and culture.

Those people began to take him seriously when they realized he was not just buying *objets* by the yard. He wondered wryly what his father and mother would think of his growing reputation as a collector. His father would have sneered at anything that didn't make money and his mother would have railed against storing up worldly goods. Neither of them would have understood about loving beauty for its own sake. Sometimes he thought about Teresa Martinez. She would have understood, but that was not enough.

He took great pride in his collection of tiny gold and enamel snuff boxes. Many were encrusted with diamonds and rubies and emeralds and sapphires and he displayed them on a marble table in the drawing room. Among them was the charming enamel box from his new friend, the shah.

There were also Chinese jades and porcelain from the Ming dynasty on display in vitrines throughout the apartment and silver candelabra designed by Roitters for Catherine the Great in the formal dining room. He was a modern prince and he would surround himself with the relics of kings and queens who had gone before him.

*   *   *

Once Ash had established himself in his palace it was time to choose a consort. She would have to have impeccable social credentials to make up for his own lack of same, she would have to be beautiful and she would have to have the makings of a great hostess.

That season he was invited to the best parties. Everyone wanted to meet the young empire builder who still had time to lead a formidable polo team and amass a fine collection of Old Masters and moderns.

The girls at these parties had names like Vanderbilt, Whitney and Guest, names for Ash to conjure with, and they seemed to spend their lives on an endless round of parties, beginning the season in the fall in New York, moving south to Palm Beach when the weather grew chilly, and returning in the spring in time to join their friends for the summer in Southampton. In between there were excursions to Paris and Cuba.

He had met some of the girls before, when he was at Princeton, but then he had been shy and immersed in planning revenge on his father. Now they approached him. He was a glamorous polo-playing tycoon and they couldn't get enough of him.

Even though his eyes had been opened wide by titled English ladies, especially one of them, he still was not prepared for the ease with which they went to bed. It seemed that, to these girls, making love was as natural as eating or drinking. They were undressing him before the first kiss.

Sometimes, in bed with one of them, he would find himself thinking of Teresa. She had been no worse than these girls, probably a lot better. But then his heart would harden again. These girls were completely open, but she had lied. She had made a fool of him and for that he would never forgive her.

As much as he liked the society girls, none of them was quite what he had in mind for a wife. Then Phil Stewart introduced him to Eleanor "Cookie" Hollingsworth.

"You'll love Cookie," Phil told him. "Everybody does."

Ash knew all about the Hollingsworths. They were strictly Old Guard society, easily placing in the top twenty of the mythical Four Hundred. Constance Hollingsworth was a Pierrepont by birth and Alfred, through his mother, had the blood of the Rhinelanders in his veins. They easily looked down on the Astors and Vanderbilts as upstarts.

The Hollingsworth fortune began with the

famous Comstock lode in Colorado and by 1956 included extensive interests in uranium mines in the United States and diamond mines in South Africa. Alfred Hollingsworth was a man of immense influence and prestige, an advisor to President Eisenhower and a possible future ambassador to Great Britain. He was a man very much like the man Ash wanted to be.

Ash also knew a bit about Cookie Hollingsworth, who was being hailed in the society pages as the Brenda Frazier of the 1950s. He had seen her occasionally at parties, although they had never been introduced, and he remembered a pretty, fresh-faced girl with short, blond hair and a ready smile, always surrounded by an entourage of admirers.

Cookie Hollingsworth's New York was a small town bounded by the East River and Fifth Avenue, stretching as far south as B. Altman's on 34th Street and as far north as the Metropolitan Museum of Art on 81st. She would no sooner have considered a trip to Greenwich Village than she would a trip to Harlem.

Her day began at eleven when she would dress for lunch with friends at the Colony; from there she went shopping at The Tailored Woman or Hattie Carnegie or De Pinna. Later she would go home to prepare for the nightly round of charity balls, most of which seemed to be at the Waldorf.

Phil Stewart set up the date and Ash took Cookie to the Valentine's Day Ball at the Waldorf, held to benefit an American Indian charity. The huge Grand Ballroom was decorated with Indian symbols and thirty-five members of Arizona Indian tribes did traditional dances and songs for the guests. There was also a more conventional orchestra. Ash was impressed as he looked around the room and saw people like Basil Goulandris, Sen. John Kennedy, Jessie Donahue and Sonny Whitney. He was moving in the right circles now.

Later, they went dancing at El Morocco. But that, he soon realized, was a mistake. As soon as they sat down at their zebra-striped banquette, Cookie became the center of attention. A steady stream of people passed by the table with a continuous, "Hi, Cookie."

"Will you come to my party, Cookie? Oh you must!"

"Where have you been, Cookie?"

"You look great, Cookie!"

Mostly they simply ignored Ash, who was growing steadily more annoyed. Only occasionally would he get a polite nod or a lukewarm greeting.

"Cookie," he said during a brief lull. "Are you sure you're not running for office?"

She laughed. "I just love people."

He soon learned the truth, though. It wasn't people she loved but the acclaim, the publicity, the feeling of being important and instantly recognized. He understood because he thirsted for it too. He began to realize that by marrying Cookie he could share that acclaim, that recognition. He wanted Cookie Hollingsworth for his bride.

The fact that Cookie was promiscuous didn't bother him at all. He was not in love with her the way he'd been with Teresa. This was a business deal and he was going into it with his eyes open. The end would justify the means. The end was to have a rich, beautiful and socially connected wife and he would do anything to get her, pay any price.

*   *   *

At home in her bedroom, Cookie Hollingsworth was confiding her own thoughts about Ash Young to her sister Jessica.

"I don't understand," she said as she dressed. "We've gone out four times already and he sends me flowers every day and he still hasn't made a move."

Jessica, who was two years younger than Cookie, had been reading about the wedding of Grace Kelly and Prince Ranier III in Monaco and was trying to imagine what it would be like to marry a prince. Although she had to admit that Cookie's new Texas beau was much better looking than the prince.

"Maybe he's just shy," she offered. She was twenty years old and knew a lot about being shy.

"Don't be ridiculous. He's a Texan. There are no shy Texans!" Cookie began to rub Royal Jelly vigorously into her face as she sat before the vanity mirror. "Gee, I hope he's not queer!"

Jessica giggled. "There's only one way to find out."

"Yeah," Cookie agreed. "And if he doesn't make his move tonight, I will."

Jessica helped her sister into the blue organza strapless and watched with awe as she left on the arm of the handsome, gray-eyed Texan.

*   *   *

The occasion was the sixth Annual Evening in Paris Ball, an international event that brought out the cream of the Jet Set and, incidentally, raised money for several Franco-American charities.

The ball had begun in 1951 as part of the observance of the two thousandth birthday of Paris, but it was such a success that they decided to make it an annual affair.

That night the Grand Ballroom had been transformed into a forest of thirty-foot chestnut trees in full blossom and hung with hundreds of lanterns. On stage was an electronically controlled fountain. In the audience were more than a thousand guests and Ash was pleased to see that he and Cookie had been seated with the Baron de Gunzburg, Baron Eric Rothschild and Mr. and Mrs. Nicholas Goulandris.

At midnight the entertainment began with a fashion show. Eight Dior mannequins presented the spring collection as they entered through the parted streams of the fountain. Later a cabaret troupe from the Paris Lido and Jane Powell, Brigitte Bardot and Maurice Chevalier entertained.

The dinner itself was in the grand French manner, beginning with a cold, spicy Senegalaise, followed by sole cooked in white wine. The *plat de resistance* was small filet mignons cooked in bacon, served with creamed spinach and tender baby carrots. Desert was *profiteroles au chocolat*. All of this was accompanied by eighteen varieties of champagne and fifteen different French wines that flowed as freely as the fountain on stage.

They danced until five in the morning, although Ash began to get a bit uneasy when Cookie started licking his ear on the dance floor. He suggested they leave and to his surprise she readily agreed. He led her downstairs to his waiting limousine.

In keeping with his new way of life, Ash had

acquired a chauffeur, James, and a long, black Bentley. No sooner had the Bentley started to move along Park Avenue than Cookie was unzipping his trousers and fumbling for his penis. He tried to push her away but she was like a child searching for a tit. He would not raise his voice because of the chauffeur.

"Can't you wait, Cookie?" he whispered hoarsely. "We'll be at my place in five minutes."

But Cookie had lowered her head and was incommunicado.

All this time, James' eyes never left the road, but Ash watched with relief as the window between master and chauffeur rose discreetly, cutting off James from Cookie's noisy ministrations. He made a mental note to give the man a raise.

He had just begun to respond to Cookie's efforts when James announced that they were home. He zipped hurriedly, but to his great embarrassment he still had to walk by the doorman, porter and elevator operator with a telltale bulge in his pants.

Once inside his apartment, Cookie instinctively pulled him in the direction of the bedroom, holding his hand in hers and undressing herself with her free hand. She was down to her brassiere, stockings and garter belt when he took over.

He finally managed to get her out of the

apartment before she killed him, and alone he watched the dawn break and smoked a cigar. He had picked up the Davidoff habit on the Wildcats tour and arranged to have a box flown to him every other week. He savored the cigar as he considered his decision.

The evening had been a revelation. Besides the right social connections, Cookie Hollingsworth had turned out to be an all-around sexual performer. She was equipped with everything he wanted in his next acquisition.

That afternoon he called Cookie, and over drinks at the Ritz Bar he proposed.

*   *   *

The following night he came to dinner at the Hollingsworths' Park Avenue apartment. In contrast to the museum quality of his own penthouse, the Hollingsworth home had the unpretentious comfort of old money. A uniformed maid took his hat and coat and showed him into the large, sunny drawing room. The walls were painted buff and the windows were hung with heavy, yellow damask. There was a deep green wall-to-wall carpet and a carrara fireplace dominated one wall. At the opposite side was a large Sheraton breakfront bookcase. The Hollingsworths, Mr. and Mrs., Cookie and her younger brother and sister, Alfred Jr. and Jessica, were arrayed along the twin yellow, damask sofas that sat in front of the fireplace. There was a large bouquet of creamy, white peonies in the Ming vase on the low coffee table between the sofas.

Hollingsworth rose to shake Ash's hand, a tall, gray-haired man with pale blue eyes and an urbane manner. Mrs. Hollingsworth had a windblown look. He had heard that she was an avid gardener and immediately complimented her on the peonies. She flushed with pleasure. It turned out that both Hollingsworth *père* and *fils*, a somber blond, eighteen-year-old, had attended Choate and that broke the ice a little. He hardly noticed Jessica except that she was a shy, mousy girl who seemed to vanish into the woodwork.

To tell the truth, both Alfred and Constance Hollingsworth were delighted and relieved that their darling Cookie was engaged. She was beginning to worry them. Too many men, too much publicity about her escapades, her romances, her spending. It was time she settled down. At least this Texan had money of his own and he was intelligent and cultivated. They heaved twin sighs of relief that Cookie had not fallen for one of her playboys and welcomed Ashley Rodman Young into the fold.

The Hollingsworths had a country place in Darien, Connecticut and a few weeks later Ash was invited up for the weekend. Cookie insisted on driving him up because she had a brand new

Packard, beige with a two-tone streak, and she wanted to open it up on the highway. It was all a game to Cookie, a game to get the car up to 120 mph and a game to outdistance the police who came after her.

Sunday night, after a weekend of partying, they returned to New York. As the radio blared, Ash watched with alarm as the speedometer climbed past 130, but Cookie was oblivious to his nervousness. She just kept singing along with the radio, loudly crooning "Don't Be Cruel" with occasional sidelong glances at Ash. She didn't even see the huge Fruehauf truck loaded with shiny new Pontiacs ahead of them. She didn't even notice that it had stopped until it was too late.

He saw the crash coming and in a burst of self-preservation he opened the door. The impact of the hit threw him from the Packard and he rolled along the embankment as the front of the shiny, new car folded like an accordion under the truck, neatly severing poor Cookie's lovely, blond head from her body.

Cookie's funeral was an imposing affair that cost as much as her debut. Unfortunately, Ash was confined to Lenox Hill Hospital with two broken legs and lacerations and was unable to attend. His heart had not been broken, because his heart had never been committed in this affair, only his head. But he was bitterly disappointed to lose the girl and all she represented.

That spring, the Jet Set went into mourning for their favorite debutante and, in the midst of all the grief, poor Ash was almost forgotten. He sat in his private room, filled with expensive flower arrangements, but his only visitors were Tom Patterson, who had flown up from Houston to update him on the business, and Jessica Hollingsworth. Then Tom flew home to Houston and his new bride, Mary Eaton, and Ash's only caller was Jessica. The rest of the party people who had surrounded Cookie faded away. Their connection had been to Cookie, not to him.

Jessica was not as pretty or as sexy as her sister. She was thinner and more frail where Cookie had been robust and full of life. Her hair was brown, her eyes a nondescript blue, and although her features resembled Cookie's, her face was a bit too pinched to be really pretty.

But she visited him every day, sitting by his bed and chatting away about the funeral, the news about Cookie's friends, anything to chase away the ennui. She brought him books and candy and plants.

One of the books she brought him was Machiavelli's *The Prince* which he hadn't read since Princeton. It had been almost ten years and he read it now with the eyes of a seasoned businessman.

Machiavelli's inspiration was Cesare Borgia,

one of the two bastard children of Pope
Alexander VI, the Spaniard who went down in
history as one of the most nefarious and
debauched men to sit on St. Peter's throne.
History and legend charged Borgia and his
sister Lucrezia with incest, torture and poison-
ing. Most of these stories were rumors spread at
the time by the Italian clergy who despised the
Spanish pope and his progeny.

Machiavelli was a contemporary of Borgia
and not interested in rumors but facts. He
considered Borgia an excellent ruler. Ruthless
but efficient because, Machiavelli expounded,
"the end justifies the means."

Ash found himself reading all this with new
insight. It amused him that shy little Jessica
gave him such a cynical, sophisticated book and
he teased her about it on her next visit.

She blushed, and with a little color in her
face she looked almost pretty. "Oh, I don't
think of you as cynical," she assured him. "But
you're such a natural leader and so strong. I
admire that."

He looked at Cookie's little sister with new
interest. She wasn't as pretty or as lively as
poor Cookie, but that would make her all the
more easy to train. And she was cut from the
same cloth. She was a Hollingsworth with all
that meant.

He took her hand and held it, smiling at her.

She smiled back shyly. Machiavelli was right, the end would justify the means.

*　　*　　*

Once they had recovered from the shock of the tragedy, Alfred and Constance Hollingsworth were almost as relieved to marry off Jessica as they had been Cookie. She was so shy and mousy she had always been overshadowed by her sister. Maybe now, they hoped, she would come into her own.

So, six months after Cookie's funeral, on September 16, 1956, Jessica Hollingsworth of New York and Darien was married to Ashley Young of New York and Houston.

Hollingsworth spent two hundred thousand dollars on the wedding. The bride wore an antique white peau de soie gown trimmed with Alençon lace and a veil of French tulle. She carried a bouquet of phaleonopis orchids and stephanotis. The designer Francois La Griffou turned most of the ground floor of the Hollingsworths' Darien mansion into a reproduction of the Royal Pavillion at Versailles. The ballroom itself was a virtual forest of twenty thousand dollars worth of pink roses.

The nearly one thousand guests included the Duke and Duchess of Windsor, the Maharaja and Maharani of Jaipur, Clark Gable, Marlene

Dietrich, Joan Crawford, Charles Boyer and Bing Crosby, who sang "True Love" for the bride. Even Manolo Chavez turned up. The rest of the guest list was assorted Astors, Vanderbilts, Whitneys, Harrimans, Huttons, Donahues and Fords, all dancing to the alternating bands of Meyer Davis and Lester Lanin.

Eight hundred magnums of champagne and countless gallons of scotch, vodka and gin were poured. The buffet tables groaned under the weight of Iranian caviar (a special gift from Ash's friend the shah), Maine lobsters, Scotch salmon and French patés.

As the newlyweds left that night for a honeymoon in Havana, Ash was quite confident that he was beginning the start of a most satisfactory life.

Part Three

10

Houston, Texas
May 1955

Teresa Martinez woke up in the Houston Medical Center with an ashen-faced Mary and Tom beside her bed. Tom had come to the apartment to deliver Ash's check and when she didn't answer the door or the telephone he had asked the doorman to let him in. They had to break down the door. They found her in the bathroom, in the tub, the water pink with her blood. They rushed her to the hospital where they pumped life back into her.

They were just in time, Tom told her. Another four minutes and she would have died. But inside, Teresa knew, she was already dead.

She sent them away and refused to see anyone else. She spent the days in bed or listlessly walking the hospital hall, dark circles under her eyes, bandages on her wrists. She was so wrapped up in her own misery that she hardly noticed that one of the young interns had taken to stopping by her room every day after his rounds.

Bill Wilkerson was a tall young man with a square jaw, bushy red hair and thick eyebrows that shaded warm brown eyes. His fierce appearance hid a gentle nature that made him one of the most popular doctors in the hospital.

He was interested in all his patients, but most of all he was intrigued by the beautiful Miss Martinez. He couldn't understand why a young girl like that would want to kill herself. Fortunately, her friends had brought her into the Center in time and she would be ready to go home soon. Physically ready, at least, but he wondered about her mental state.

At first he told himself that his visits were part of the therapy. After all, he couldn't send her home in this depressed condition. Then he found himself looking forward to their sessions together, he doing most of the talking, about his plans for a clinic in the barrio, his love of medicine.

On her part, Teresa at first resented Wilkerson's visits. She wasn't his personal case and he was part of the system that had thwarted her one desire: to die. Then, in spite of herself, she began to warm to the gentle giant. She admired his dedication to his work and she came to appreciate his visits. She even looked forward to them.

That summer, "The Yellow Rose of Texas" was popular, and one afternoon he brought her a bouquet of yellow roses. To his surprise and delight she actually smiled.

"What are these for?" she asked as she held them.

"You'll be going home tomorrow, Teresa," he said gently. "That's something to celebrate."

She turned away from him and stared out the window. She didn't feel much like celebrating.

"If you'd like," he continued. "I can drive you home, make sure you're settled in."

She smiled again. "That's very nice, Doctor, but you don't have to."

"Please, I want to."

So she allowed him to take her home. She doubted that she had the energy or will to go back there on her own.

The young doctor was surprised at the elegant apartment house where she lived. He was even more surprised at the apartment which Teresa had almost finished decorating when Ash jilted her.

"I think you should go right to bed and rest," he said.

"No," she insisted. She might be depressed, but she hadn't forgotten her mother's lessons in hospitality.

"You're in my home and I have to play

hostess. Sit down and I'll make you some coffee.''

Wilkerson sat down on the blue velvet sofa and looked around the room as he waited. The apartment had him more puzzled than ever. Teresa Martinez didn't work and he was pretty sure there was no boyfriend. Certainly no man had ever turned up at the hospital.

She brought in the coffee service on a silver tray that had been part of her wedding purchases and put it on the low coffee table in front of him. She sat across from him and, as she leaned back in the familiar chair and looked around the comfortable apartment, it hit her all over again. She was home, a part of her life was over and she was completely alone in the world. She began to cry.

Wilkerson leaped to his feet and held her. Blindly she clutched his chest, crying into his arms.

"Teresa, what's wrong?" he begged. "Please tell me."

"No, I can't."

"C'mon, Teresa," he insisted. "Whatever it is, it will hurt less if you share it."

He brought her back down to the sofa and the story that she had pent up for weeks began to pour out. She told him about the White Horse, Sam Rosen, and finally her love affair with Ash Young. She told him about the wedding they had planned, her pregnancy and Ash's phone call in a tearful flow of words.

Wilkerson listened in silence. When she finished he took her in his arms. "Teresa," he stammered. "Will you marry me?"

He had been rehearsing a much better, more convincing speech for several days, but suddenly, when he looked at her dark brown eyes, those were the only words he could get out. When he realized that she was staring at him, he began to fear that he had gone too far.

"I'm sorry," he whispered, looking down at the rug.

"You don't have to apologize, Bill," she said, understanding his kindness and embarrassment. "I'm the one who should apologize. But how can I marry you? I don't love you and I'm expecting another man's child."

"Of course you don't love me!" he said with an awkward smile. "How could you love this face. But you'll get used to it. Right now you need me and your child needs a father."

Teresa could feel her eyes fill with tears as a wave of gratitude and tenderness swept over her. Bill didn't look ugly or clumsy to her at all. He was kind and generous and he would make a good father. Maybe of all the men she had known, he would be the best.

She leaned over and put her arms around his neck and kissed him.

They were married a few weeks later; Teresa's daughter, Christina, was born the following September.

11

Houston, Texas
July 1977

Christina Wilkerson had inherited her mother's dark good looks but it was her father, Dr. Wilkerson, who taught her to be loving and compassionate.

Other girls might have more clothes or live in fancier houses, but they didn't have a father like hers encouraging them along. Since the first grade, dark-haired Christina had proven to be an alert, bright student, bringing home good marks and getting all the leads in the school plays and making her father proud as a peacock. When he visited the hospital, every nurse on duty had to listen to Dr. Wilkerson's stories about Christina's latest triumphs in school and to admire the newest snapshot of her.

He wanted Teresa to enjoy her daughter too, but in spite of a brief rally after Christina's birth she seemed to have lost all interest in her daughter, her husband or life in general. She rarely left the small, tidy apartment they shared above his clinic in the barrio. He and Christina tried to keep liquor out of the house but she always seemed to manage to sneak it in and hide it. Her lovely, olive skin was now puffy, her voluptuous figure heavy and shapeless under housecoats, and she spent most of her days with a drink in her hand, staring glassy-eyed at the television screen in the darkened living room while he was at the clinic or hospital and Christina was at school.

When Teresa was in her cups she would start to warn Christina about men.

"They're no good, Christina," she would insist. "Watch out, never trust them."

Christina would always answer the same way. "What about Dad?" To her he was the finest man in the world.

Teresa would not be dissuaded. "He's an exception but don't be fooled. Never trust a man."

Christina's friends and teachers were puzzled when she turned down dates and party invitations to stay home but the truth was that she was afraid to leave her mother alone. With Dad working until late at night, someone had to keep an eye on her. Besides, someone had to

177

cook and clean for the three of them and poor Mother certainly wasn't up to it.

She finished high school in three years and started in a pre-med course at the University of Texas. She had decided to follow in her father's footsteps.

The summer after her freshman year all that changed. Her father began to complain of persistent colds and coughing. Sometimes he was too weak to make his rounds. When Christina was home she could hear him coughing late into the night.

Dr. Jennings, a family friend, had explained to both Bill and Christina that Teresa was slowly destroying herself with drink. He diagnosed her trouble as cirrhosis of the liver and warned that the liver could give out at any time unless she cut out alcohol. One night he dropped in to have a look at her. As Bill went to get Teresa, the older doctor turned to Christina.

"I really came to see you," he said. "There's something you should know."

"Yes, Dr. Jennings?" Christina could not imagine what it was.

"It's your father, Christina. He's a very sick man. He has lung cancer."

Her first thought was, *Why couldn't it have been Mother?* Why Dad, who loved life so much and had brought happiness to so many? Without asking, she knew that her father did not have long to live.

12

New York, N.Y.
July 1957

Stephanie Hollingsworth Young was born on July 17, 1957 in New York Center's Presbyterian Hospital. Presbyterian is not quite as chic as Doctor's or Flower Fifth, but it's the best endowed and best equipped and offers the finest medical care in the world. Ash Young was not interested in chic when it came to health and hospitals, he wanted the best and he could afford it.

She was born just a few weeks after Hurricane Audrey devastated a good portion of east Texas and Louisiana, including most of Rodman farm, but that wasn't how Ash always remembered the day.

July 17 was the day he closed the deal on Belvedere.

*   *   *

He had heard that Burt Harris, the Wall Street broker, was in trouble. The price of Harris & Co. stock had plummeted, and Harris had been forced to put his splendid Palm Beach mansion on the market. Ash had always disliked Harris, whom he regarded as weak and a good argument for inheritance taxes. All he had ever done was inherit a fortune from his hard-working father and manage to run it and the family brokerage into the ground. Liz Harris was different. He respected her as one of the most gifted hostesses in society, a perennial fixture on the Best Dressed list. It was too bad that Jessica wasn't more like her.

In spite of his wife's talents as a hostess, however, in July of 1957 Burt Harris was desperately in need of cash. He was asking two million dollars for Belvedere, but few people could raise that kind of money in a hurry. Ash Young could, but he had no intention of letting a weak-willed fool like Harris come out ahead in any business deal with him. With Tom Patterson running most of the operations of the Young Co. he rarely got a chance anymore to beat an adversary. The old juices started flowing at the prospect of outwitting Burt Harris.

He called at his Wall Street office late in June. Harris was a pale, weak-looking blond man with watery blue eyes. He tried to put up a brave front but Ash and everyone else on the Street knew that his back was to the wall. Ash got straight to the point.

"I'd like to buy Belvedere, Burt, as is, with everything included." He handed Harris a Morgan Guaranty check for one million dollars.

Harris looked at the check, puzzled, while Ash eyed him with distaste. He had no respect for someone who was as bad a businessman as Burt Harris.

"Ash," Harris began, his watery blue eyes even more watery with confusion. "I'm asking two million dollars just for the mansion. With the antiques and paintings we've collected over the years it's worth at least half a million more."

Ash smiled. Without any pressure the fool had already come down half a million. But it was still not enough. He leaned across the desk and stared directly at Harris.

"Look, Burt, you need cash and I've got it. I'm offering you a million dollars and you can cash that check today."

"But . . . but," Harris began to sputter as Ash rose abruptly.

181

"In that case," he said coldly. "I'm sorry to have wasted your time."

"Well, now wait," Harris said faintly. "Let's talk."

Ash closed the deal a few days later, the day his daughter was born. For one million dollars cash he bought out Burt Harris lock, stock and Aubusson carpets.

He boasted about the deal to his friends at the Brook Club where he had just become a member thanks to Alfred Hollingsworth.

"Liz Harris had the finest taste in Palm Beach," he laughed. "And for a million dollars I bought her taste."

*   *   *

Ash Young's approach to child rearing was much the same as his approach to buying a house, and when it became clear that there would be no more children he poured everything into Stephanie. She was to be raised as a princess and he would spare no expense to do it.

When she was a baby, it was easy. He and Jessica and Stephanie and her nurse shuttled between New York and Palm Beach with side trips to visit his old polo buddies in Europe. In those days, Stephanie was a cute, blond baby with a lively and friendly disposition. Sometimes, it was true, she could turn into a little hellion and throw a tantrum, but at least it showed she had some spunk. She must have gotten that from him, because Jessica didn't seem to have much.

When Stephanie was only five years old she was trying to learn to ride a two-wheeler that Ash had brought to Palm Beach from F.A.O. Schwarz in New York. He stood by as she tried to ride it. Time after time she struggled to mount the bike, but every time she failed, the bike fell over, she fell to the ground. She wanted to stop, but Ash wouldn't let her. Soon she was scratched and bleeding, her face covered with tears, but Ash wouldn't let her give up.

"Try it again, get back on," he demanded.

What had started out as a welcome present became an instrument of torture as her father made her try over and over again to stay on the bike.

Finally, after several hours she was able to stay on long enough to ride around the marble patio of the swimming pool. Ash beamed as he watched her. He had taught her a valuable lesson: never give up.

Unfortunately, when she grew up, the only thing Stephanie seemed able to apply this to was men, as time after time, no matter how disastrous the last relationship, she eagerly got back up for the next one.

As she came into her teens, Ash began to worry. She was a beautiful girl but she was lazy and undisciplined. Not stupid, though. When one of her teachers at the Hewitt School complained about her work, she snapped at her, "What do I care? I'm richer than you."

He couldn't understand it. He had given her the best money could buy: the best schools, clothes, dancing and riding lessons (at least she'd inherited his skill with horses) and now she was flunking out of Hewitt's.

He blamed Jessica. The woman was simply no match for her daughter. She couldn't discipline Stephanie, couldn't seem to control her. The solution was boarding school. Although he had hated every minute at Choate himself, this would be different. He chose Foxhall, one of the most exclusive finishing schools in the East, because Stephanie was his only daughter and he wanted the best for her.

He arranged a meeting for himself and Stephanie in the office of Mona Hampshire, Foxhall's headmistress. She was a plain woman in her late forties and she arched a blond eyebrow when she saw the transcript of Stephanie's grades at Hewitt. The eyebrow went back down again when she saw Ash's check for ten thousand dollars. The contribution would be highly appreciated by the Board of Trustees. She could hardly turn the girl away because she had a few problems at Hewitt. Besides, the rigid discipline of Foxhall was probably just what she needed.

Stephanie hated the school from the moment she arrived. She would have run away but it was nestled in the woods of Virginia and she wouldn't have had the slightest idea where to go. She hated the bare rooms, the curfew, the military uniforms and the drilling. They had to rise every morning to the sound of a trumpet and make their own beds regulation style.

And she was lonely. She didn't like the girls who seemed so full of themselves and so pleased to be members of such a fashionable school. They were nothing but rotten sneaks and if they thought they could stick their noses up in the air because they were rich, she had news for them: She was richer than them all!

She finally made one friend. Tall, stocky Linda was the only one who didn't seem to mind having Stephanie on her field hockey team. After the games Linda was always nice about how badly Stephanie had played. Then one night, as she lay in bed in her room, Stephanie felt something next to her. She jumped and was about to scream when a hand went over her mouth. A square, calloused hand, but still a girl's hand.

"Shhh," Linda whispered. "It's only me."

She relaxed a little. Maybe Linda had to tell her something.

"Let me in," she whispered and Stephanie obediently moved over and raised the blanket so that Linda could cuddle beside her. "That feels nice, doesn't it?"

Stephanie had to agree that it did, although she got a little worried when Linda began to grope for her breasts. They had been warned against that kind of thing by Miss Hampshire but it felt good and it was nice to have someone look out for you.

Besides Linda, the only thing she liked about Foxhall was the horses. She had first learned to ride at Grandpa's house in Darien and she had been allowed to bring her Morgan, Bonnie, down with her to Foxhall. At riding, at least, she was a star. She collected more blue ribbons than any other girl at the school. Within a year she had become captain of the riding team and gradually she had less time for Linda. With all the trophies she brought to Foxhall, Miss Hampshire found it easy to overlook her appalling marks and she made more friends among the girls.

The girls had started passing around well-worn paperback copies of *Lady Chatterly's Lover* and *Tropic of Cancer* and she recognized some of the things in the books as things she and Linda had done together, but Linda had become so jealous of her riding prowess and her new friends that she hardly spoke to her any more.

She wanted to know about sex with boys. But where was she going to find boys in this jail? Then she realized that they were right under her nose, or at least under Bonnie's nose. The stables.

She began to spend more time than ever at

the stables. One groom in particular caught her eye. He had black, curly hair, Irish blue eyes with dark, fringed lashes and broad, strong shoulders. His name was Tim Kelly. The way he grinned at her sometimes, as though he could read her thoughts, made her hot.

Kelly found the kid amusing. He found all these little rich girls amusing. He recognized the look on her face, too. Sooner or later he would be inside her wet little pants.

One warm spring afternoon she brought Bonnie into the stable after a workout. Tim was working in the tack room and he looked up, smiled and walked toward her.

"Here, allow me," he said as he helped her climb off Bonnie.

She could very well manage to get down by herself, but this time she slipped and fell into his arms. Pressing her body next to his she could smell the clean crispness of his denim workshirt and the sweat of his body. Mixed together they sent a wave of desire over her that made her slightly dizzy. She opened her mouth to him while her body went limp in his arms.

"Not now, Miss Young," he said, smiling as he pulled away.

"When?"

He had taken the reins from her and was leading Bonnie to the stable.

"I guess everyone will be at the game tonight," he said indifferently. "Me, I don't care much about basketball."

"Oh, neither do I," she insisted, following close behind him.

"Then why don't you come here tonight, during the game? No one will miss you."

She was thrilled. Of course she would come.

That night Stephanie dressed with special care. Thank God they didn't have to wear those stupid uniforms during the games. Instead, she dressed in her tightest Levis and a big, loose, striped man's shirt. She sprayed herself all over with patchouli and decided to forget underpants. That would probably really freak out Miss Hampshire but it just made the whole thing more dangerous and exciting.

That night was the annual basketball game between Foxhall and Middleburg and the teachers and the girls were too busy cheering to notice that Stephanie Young never returned from her foray to the ladies' room at halftime.

It was dark outside and she had only the moonlight to guide her to the stable where Tim was waiting. By the time she got there she was dripping with sweat. Ice Blue Secret didn't hold up under pressure, that was for sure. Then she saw Tim.

He was sitting on the fence outside the tack room. He grinned at her and she could feel her knees go weak. Silently he took her hand and led her to an empty stall.

He had thrown down a red plaid blanket on the straw. He sat down first and then took her hand and showed her where to sit beside him. The stable was totally quiet except for the occasional snort or kick of one of the horses. Pungent smells of raw wood, fresh hay, leather and manure filled the air. He began to slowly unbutton her shirt, caressing her breasts. Her nipples hardened under his touch. He moved his head down and sucked them, then pulled away.

"Take off your clothes," he ordered.

Obediently, she removed the Levis and watched as he stripped off his clothes. He wasn't wearing any underwear either. She also noticed that his penis was much larger than she had expected and she wondered whether he would be able to get it inside her. He began to gently push her head down to meet it.

"Suck it, Stephanie."

She took it in her mouth, opening wide. She was afraid she would choke but she sucked diligently and she began to actually enjoy the sensation of it pulsating against her throat. Suddenly he pushed her head away. He lay back and with his strong arms he lifted her and eased her on top of him. She cried out as he entered her, but he quickly put his hand over her mouth. The last thing he wanted was to frighten the horses.

Encouraged, she began to move rhythmically, faster. It was a little like riding a horse and with that thought she increased her motion from a trot to a gallop until she felt herself giving way. He gripped her hips and moved with her and suddenly she could feel him about to come. They clutched each other tightly as she screamed. Then it was over. Tired and damp she clung to him. She wanted to stay there with him for the rest of her life, she told him. If they wanted her off they would have to kill her first.

"Shh," he warned as he held her. "You'll have the whole school down here."

"I love you, Tim," she whispered.

"Whoa. Wait a minute, kid."

"Don't worry, Tim," she insisted. "I'll support you. I'll just tell my mom and dad."

He laughed, then shook his head. "Stephanie, darlin', you're a nice kid and a great fuck, but you're only sixteen. You've got a lot to learn about life. Stable hands and heiresses don't mix."

They were so involved in their discussion that they never heard the sound of approaching footsteps. The first thing they knew, they were surrounded by what seemed like fifty blazing searchlights, but was actually only four flashlights held by Miss Hampshire, the loyal Linda and two teachers. Suddenly Miss Hampshire was barking out orders in every direction.

"Kelly, you're fired. Be out of here tonight."

"Stephanie, I'm ashamed of you. You're a disgrace to Foxhall and your father."

13

Houston, Texas
November 1977

Bill Wilkerson died on Thanksgiving Day. The doctors at Houston Medical Center had assured Christina and her mother that nothing more could be done and they might as well take him home to die. Christina had cooked a turkey dinner for the three of them while Teresa sat beside him on the bed, holding his hand. Even though he couldn't eat much, tears came to his eyes when his daughter brought in the turkey.

"My girls," he said weakly. That night he died.

Teresa had stayed dry during the last months of his illness but now she began to drink again in earnest. And Christina didn't have the heart to stop her.

It wasn't fair, she thought. Her father, a gentle, humble doctor who had never hurt a soul, who had done only good for others, ending like that. Rotting inside, crying out at night from the pain.

But she wasn't going to have time to brood. With Dad gone, everything had changed. She dropped out of the university to work at the Ramsey Agency, the best and busiest modeling agency in Houston. But she still was not going to make enough for the two of them.

A few months after her father's death, one of the largest advertising agencies in New York, Hildebrandt, Goodson & Hill, came down to Houston to shoot a commercial for furs against the background of the Astrodome. It was an important account and John Bender, an agency vice president, had come down to supervise. He was there the day Christina walked off the set.

"Rudy," she shouted at the photographer, a short, lithe man in a red T-shirt. "You do your job and I'll do mine."

"What's the trouble here?" Bender asked. He was a tall, blond man in a tan poplin suit. He wore horn-rimmed glasses and highly polished brown oxfords.

She turned to him. Most of these executives didn't know any more about their products than the photographers but it was worth a shot.

"Rudy here is the best photographer in Houston," she said. "I can't argue with that.

But he wants me to leap around in these fur coats. It's so 1950s Avedon."

Bender thought the girl had a point and he told Rudy so. "After all, Rudy, we're not selling action wear, we're selling luxury."

A little mollified, Rudy went back to shooting it Christina's way. Bender, impressed with the tall, dark model's attitude, suggested they have a drink after the shooting.

"Have you ever thought about coming to New York?" he asked over drinks at the Galleria. "A girl with your looks is wasting herself in Houston."

"Well, I have heard from a scout for Jean Casardi," she admitted. Only yesterday the scout had stopped in at the agency and given her his card.

Bender laughed. "Casardi has Eileen Ford and Wilhelmina in a dither. They're both threatening to sue him for poaching their models."

"Did he?"

"It's a free country, Christina. The girls go with whomever treats them best," Bender said. "And Jean has a way with women."

She gave him a guarded look. If she went to New York it would be strictly for the money and she told Bender that.

"Don't worry, we're talking about a legitimate operation. Seriously, I can highly recommend Casardi."

She began to reconsider the scout's offer. She could go to New York and, once settled with jobs assured, she could bring her mother up to join her.

Two weeks later, she packed her book and bags and was on her way to New York.

*   *   *

Christina went directly from JFK airport to the Casardi office and sat nervously looking around the room as Casardi himself examined her book.

The "book" to a model is just like the stethoscope to a doctor or the racquet to a tennis player. Without it she might as well go roller skating. The book is the sum total of her career. In it she keeps all the best photographs that have been taken of her, all the magazine covers, editorial layouts and ads in which she had been featured. For a new model, getting an impressive book together is the primary goal. The most beautiful girl in the world is just another pretty face without pictures demonstrating how she projects on camera.

Casardi sat behind a large, black-lacquered Parsons table. The rest of the furniture in the office was upholstered in shades of dark brown and the walls were tan Ultrasuede. The rug on the floor was a sepia color. The room would have seemed dark but it was brightened by the hundreds of beautiful faces exposed on the walls—the faces of the top Paris and New York girls, the stars of the Casardi agency.

Some of the girls in Houston who occasionally worked in New York had come back with stories about how brutal agency people could be. But Jean Casardi seemed like a gentleman. He was a lean, darkly handsome Frenchman of about thirty who favored Cardin suits and brightly colored silk shirts which he wore tieless and open at the throat. His soft, brown eyes radiated wit and competence and Christina realized that was probably one of the reasons he was attracting so many girls from the other agencies.

When he was finished with the book he looked up at her and smiled. It was a warm, friendly smile and she relaxed immediately.

"How long have you been working at Ramsey's?" he asked.

"Nearly half a year."

"Good experience," he acknowledged. "But Houston and New York are two different places. These pictures, for example, just won't do."

"Are they that bad?" All she could think about was what new photographs were going to cost. She had come to New York to make money, not to spend it.

"Oh, there's nothing wrong with you," he said quickly. "It's just that the photographers here work differently and you'll need a more sophisticated book." He started pressing buttons on his phone. "I'll get Barbara in here, she can take over."

She had heard about Barbara Sawyer, Casardi's head booker and right hand woman. She had been warned by the girls in Houston that while Jean was the businessman who dealt with the clients, the terrible Barbara Sawyer had the power of life and death over the models.

"Jean, Paris just called and they can't find rooms for the ten girls arriving at Orly," she said, breezing in. "And I have five girls coming in from Milan in twenty minutes, so I don't have much time for you."

Barbara Sawyer was a tall woman in her late thirties. She had been a cover girl herself and she was still stunning. Her dark, short, curly hair framed her face, her makeup was carefully applied and she was wearing a smart red linen suit. Christina made a mental note to ask her how she made up her eyes. She looked harried, but later Christina would learn that she always did.

"I know you're busy, Barbara," Jean soothed her. "But I want you to meet Christina Wilkerson. She just arrived from Houston."

Barbara gave Christina a hard, speculative look. She was already taking inventory of Christina's height (5'9"), weight (120 pounds, she would have to lose 10), measurements (35-

24-33) and coloring (black hair, olive skin and terrific green eyes).

"Stand up," she ordered.

Obediently, Christina stood up.

"Now walk around the room."

Christina walked toward her, then away, toward the door and back again to Casardi's desk.

"OK honey, you can sit down now," Barbara said as she smiled at Casardi. "She'll do."

"I thought you'd like her." He grinned and handed her Christina's book. "But these will have to go."

She scanned the book quickly, occasionally making a clucking noise or holding up one of the pictures for Casardi to see. They seemed to have some code between them, communicating while hardly talking at all.

When she was finished with the book she handed it back to Christina.

"Let's forget about these," she said briskly. "But if you can start today I'll send you to some proper photographers for some test shots."

It was going to happen, Christina realized with relief. She had been hired by Casardi and she was on her way. She followed Barbara Sawyer to her office down the hall. It wasn't as large as Casardi's but it was bright and cheerful. The walls were painted apple green and the sofa and two chairs were white wicker with cushions of yellow and green flowered chintz. Barbara's huge, white wicker desk was crowded with papers and the wall next to her was completely covered with corkboard which in turn was almost completely covered with photographs, cartoons, magazine covers and old pieces of jewelry, campaign buttons and postcards.

"Look at this," Barbara sighed loudly as she picked up a stack of small, pink papers from the top of her phone. "Gone five minutes and I have ten messages." She pointed toward the sofa. "Sit down honey and we'll work out the rest. Do you have a place to stay?"

"Well, not yet." All she had was one suitcase, Casardi's address and her savings of three hundred dollars.

Barbara hollered to her secretary who was sitting outside the door. "Get Melinda Parsons on the phone." She turned back to Christina. "You'll like Melinda and she needs a roommate." She scribbled the address on a note pad and handed it to Christina.

It was all settled before Christina left to meet Melinda at her apartment on East 69th Street. For one hundred seventy-five dollars a month she had a roommate. She also had a diet, a schedule and a contract with Jean Casardi.

14

New York, N.Y.
January 1978

"Is this what they taught you at Foxhall, Stephanie?" Alex Mercati asked. "To rape an innocent man?"

Alex and Stephanie were in the top-floor bedroom of his townhouse on East 65th Street and the morning sun was pouring through the skylight above them.

At thirty-four the publisher of the influential *Reporter* was still almost boyishly handsome, with smiling, blue eyes, dark, curly hair and a lean, wiry body.

"It wasn't so bad, was it Alex?" she teased, rubbing a tanned leg against him. He put his arm around her protectively.

"It was great, Stephanie, just great. But you

don't have to do this. I'd like you anyway."
Somehow he felt a little guilty making love to
Stephanie. She seemed to cling so desperately
and if the stories he had been hearing were
true, Ash Young's little girl was heading for big
trouble. Now she was retrieving a joint from
her Hermés bag.

"You don't know what it's been like cooped
up in that bin for three months," she pouted as
she lit it. "Just because I got caught fucking my
shrink. It was no big deal. It doesn't make me
crazy, does it?"

"No, Stephanie, it doesn't make you crazy,"
he assured her. "But this is going to make me
late. I've got a magazine to put out."

He stood up and headed for the shower. He
had a busy day ahead, once he got rid of the
blond, beautiful but emotionally tiring Stephanie Young.

Be a diplomat, handle it carefully. That was
what his grandfather would have said, if he
were still around. But Count Dmitri Mercati,
Ambassador Plenipotentiary of Czar Nicholas
II of all the Russias, had died in 1917 at the
hands of the Bolsheviks. All his diplomatic
training had not saved him from being skinned
alive and thrown in a salt bath by his torturers.

The widowed Countess Mercati and her
young son, Basil, managed to escape to Italy.
Perhaps she chose Venice because that was
where Dmitri's father had been born. He had

only left Italy to serve Czar Paul I, so it was fitting that now the Mercatis should return.

This generation of Mercatis was broke, but the countess managed to support herself and her son in comfort until 1922 when Mussolini came to power. The jaunty countess took one look at the black shirts and left with her son for America.

Basil Mercati grew up to be a journalist, one of the star reporters on William Randolph Hearst's *Journal-American*. Maybe it was writing or maybe it was the fact that his White Russian mother had instilled in him the same horror of communism as the Chief, but only a few months after joining the paper he was a fixture and his controversial column ran untouched in one hundred Hearst papers around the country.

Basil married a young New Yorker of impeccable lineage, Pauline Stuyvesant, and from this love match of the bluest bloods, Alex Mercati was born. He was a product of his class, educated at Buckley, Choate and Harvard where he graduated magna cum laude in 1962. After a two year hitch as a "technical advisor" in Vietnam he returned home just in time to get word that Basil and Pauline had died in a plane crash.

His father had not been a rich man but he had been a good and honest journalist and he left a lot of friends. With his modest inheritance, Alex started up a news magazine. In 1966, no one believed that the world needed another news magazine, but through a combination of excellent reporting, lively arts coverage and some controversial stands on everything from Vietnam to rock and roll, *The Reporter* quickly became one of the must-reads for every informed person, and Alex Mercati became one of the most important opinion makers in the country, courted by power brokers and would-be power brokers.

He had also earned a reputation as a sexual athlete, but so far he had managed to remain free of any entanglements.

One of those power brokers courting him vigorously was Ashley Rodman Young. Alex was quite sure that Young's invitation to come down to Palm Beach in a few weeks came partly because of the cover story on him in the latest issue of *The Reporter* and partly because Young wanted to impress his other guests with his access to the media.

Well, he could use a weekend in the warmth and sun of Palm Beach. Now he had to think about who he would bring to share it.

Certainly not Ash Young's lovely, blond daughter. Young was a strange cold fish, but nothing about him was stranger than his icy, distant treatment of Stephanie.

Finished with his shower and his thoughts, Alex came back into the bedroom to dress.

"You still here?" he teased. Stephanie was still on the bed. "What are you going to do today?"

"Oh, I guess I'll have lunch with Grandma at The Colony Club," Stephanie sighed. "Then maybe we'll go to see *Star Wars*."

"What happened to your psychiatrist?" he asked as he began to button the blue oxford cloth shirt.

She giggled. "Daddy found out he was paying him a hundred dollars an hour to fuck me."

She came over to Alex and began to knot his tie. "If you married me, it would make everything so simple."

"I couldn't afford you," Alex laughed. "I hear you run through a thousand dollars a day."

"Oh, you've been listening to Daddy," she shrugged. "I can't help it if I like to buy my friends presents."

"Will you be at Garrett's party tonight?"

She pouted. "No, Grandma's having a dinner party and I promised to be there. They've been so nice about making Daddy take me out of the bin, I have to."

He kissed her on the cheek.

"Take care of yourself, Stephanie."

15

New York, N.Y.
February 1978

"Yes, Mother, I'm careful. Yes, Mother, we lock the doors. No, Mother, Mr. Casardi is a nice man and he's never tried to take advantage of me." Christina put down the phone with relief and smiled at her new roommate.

"Mothers," she said sadly. "I think mine is getting daffy. She talks sometimes like my father's still alive."

"They're all alike, love," Melinda said cheerfully. "Thank God mine is in London. Otherwise she'd be calling me every night, too."

At five foot seven, Melinda Parsons was smaller than most fashion models but her slim, boyish figure and thick mane of red hair had made her a great favorite with the junior magazines like *Mademoiselle* and *Glamour*. If it was not for Melinda, Christina was sure, she never would have been able to follow the regimen Barbara Sawyer had given her. But together they stuck to the diet, avoided everything white, did not drink and went to bed at nine o'clock. Little by little she was acquiring the sleek, finished look of a sophisticated model.

In spite of the regimen, Melinda managed to fit in a number of boyfriends and she couldn't understand how Christina could go night after night without a man.

"If I don't make love once a day, I just can't concentrate," she confided. "It's great for the nerves, you know. You're not a virgin are you?" Melinda pressed.

"No. Houston caught up to the 20th century a few years ago."

"I've heard about those Texas men. Did you ever have a real cowboy?"

"No, just a nice Texas medical student." And that was all she wanted to tell Melinda. She'd gladly lost her virginity to a fellow freshman at the University of Texas. There had been two men since then: a professor at school, and another student, but none of her experiences had been especially wonderful. It had been almost a year since she'd even kissed a man. Sometimes she wondered if she might be frigid. But that was hardly a subject she wanted to discuss with Melinda.

"Oh God," Melinda exclaimed suddenly. "I really put my foot in it this time."

"What do you mean?"

"I forgot—with your father dying and all, you've probably had a lot more on your mind than having fun."

"Thanks, Melinda." Christina smiled. "Just give me a little time. As soon as I get some bookings, I'll show you that I can be fun too."

*   *   *

One of the first places the Casardi agency sent her to was Tommy Dexter's studio.

"He's an up and coming photographer," Barbara assured her. "And he wants to test some new faces for a big cosmetics account. He's being very secretive and won't tell me any more than that. It's an open call, so expect other girls."

Christina didn't mind going on a look-see like this because Dexter, like other young photographers who were just getting started, had a reciprocal arrangement with the modeling agencies. They would send him new girls to be tested and in return he would give the models free prints for their books. The photographers and the girls both got good-looking samples to impress potential clients.

She took a taxi down to his studio which was in a loft in an industrial building in Soho. Labelle and Diana Ross tapes were playing so loudly she could hear them in the street and they made Dexter's studio very easy to find.

The photographer turned out to be a thin, agitated young man with long, black hair he wore pulled back in a pony tail. He was dressed in a white shirt and white, pleated pants. The shirt was open almost to the waist and she noticed that he had a tiny, silver spoon on a silver chain around his neck.

Dexter took one look at Christina and instructed his assistant, a sleek, dark girl called Ondine, to call the agency.

"Don't bother to send anyone else, Barbara," he said into the phone while grinning at Christina. "This girl is exactly what we're looking for."

For the next three days, from eight in the morning until eleven at night, Tommy Dexter shot Christina in every conceivable pose and costume. He probably would have kept her all night except he wanted her to get eight hours of sleep. He couldn't shoot a girl with bags under her eyes, no matter how beautiful she was otherwise.

"Okay," Dexter said on the third day. "Now take off your clothes."

There was nothing in her contract with Casardi about nude modeling and she told the photographer so.

"Relax, baby," he said. "If my client's spending six million dollars on a marketing campaign he has a right to know what you look like all over."

She took her clothes off, after all, Ondine was there, and she stood in front of the seamless white background paper. Dexter didn't even seem to notice her body as he positioned her and barked out commands, alternating with his own form of verbal encouragement, mostly obscene.

In spite of all the talk, though, he never touched her. Gradually she relaxed and even started to enjoy the shooting.

*   *   *

A few days later, Dexter called her to come downtown and pick up her pictures. They were sensational, he said. She was going to love them.

When she arrived at the studio, she was a little surprised that it was so quiet. No more Labelle and Diana Ross tapes blaring and Ondine was gone. Dexter wasn't wearing a shirt and she noticed how tan his chest was. He was still wearing his silver chain with the spoon. The lights were out and there were candles burning in glass holders on the floor.

"Sit down," he told her and handed her the pictures. While she looked them over he brought a tray of paté and brie and a bottle of chablis and placed it on the floor.

The photographs were great and Christina told him so as she sipped a glass of the wine. A few of them were a bit too daring and sexy for her taste, but if that was what his client wanted, who was she to argue?

He brought out a small silver box and slipped the silver spoon off the chain. When he opened the box she saw that it was full of white powder and she watched as he scooped a tiny bit of it. He kept one finger against one nostril and bringing the spoon up to the other, inhaled deeply. He did the same thing again with the other nostril.

"Want some?" he asked when he had finished.

"No thanks," she said. "The wine is enough." In fact she wasn't used to it and was already starting to feel a little lightheaded.

"Sure you won't try it?"

"No," she said, turning back to the photographs. "They're wonderful, Tommy," she said sincerely. "You're an artist. May I have copies?"

"Sure, baby," he said as he put his arm around her. "But aren't you going to thank me?"

She turned so that the kiss he had intended became a mere peck on the cheek. When he tried to kiss her on the mouth she stood up, knocking over the wine. Dexter jumped up after her.

"Sorry, I have to go," she said.

"Oh, no, you don't," he said, grabbing her by the waist and pulling her close to him. She could feel his hardness and struggled to break out of his grip. He only laughed, holding her tighter, his mouth pressed on hers.

"Let me go or I'll scream," she said.

"Not when you take this in your mouth," he answered as he pushed her to the floor. He unzipped his trousers, releasing his erect cock.

She stared at it in panic as he grabbed her head by the hair and pressed her face up against it.

"No one wants to hurt you, you silly bitch," he sneered. "Once you take this in your mouth you'll love it."

Slowly she relaxed, opening her mouth and allowing his fat cock to fill it.

"Good, baby," he encouraged her. "Now suck it hard."

She waited, fighting the urge to gag, until he released his grip on her hair and wrist. His hands moved to her shoulders as he muttered, "That's it, baby, that's it."

She saw her chance and clamped down hard. He screamed in pain and stumbled away as Christina quickly rose to her feet. He was doubled over and clutching his bloody cock. Blood was all over his white trousers.

"Bitch! You've killed me!" he whined. "I'm bleeding to death!"

But Christina had already grabbed her purse and coat and was running down the stairs. Once outside in the cold February air, she leaned against the wall of the building and struggled to catch her breath. She saw her face in a shop window and realized that there was blood on her chin. She wanted to cry, but suddenly she felt a wave of nausea. She turned to the curb, piled high with snow, and began to vomit into the gutter.

*   *   *

"I don't understand, love," Melinda said mildly as she polished her nails and listened to the Eagles singing about Hotel California. "All he wanted was a little blow job. And you did say the pictures were great. It's been three weeks for God's sake, I'm sure he's healed."

Christina leaned back in her chair. She was trying to select the best photographs for her new book from the hundreds that had been taken by young photographers she had seen in the weeks since her experience with Tommy Dexter. But none of them were as good as the ones she had left at his loft.

At first she had really been afraid that she had emasculated the poor photographer but Melinda, who seemed to know all about men, assured her that it was unlikely.

She and Melinda were coming from two different directions when it came to men. The redhead had often told her that the idea was to use the man before he used you. Christina saw it differently.

"I don't care about Tommy Dexter or his pictures," she said firmly. "What bothers me is that Barbara Sawyer seems to think that somehow I'm to blame for what happened."

She began to pick up the pictures and put them into neat stacks. The telephone rang and Melinda picked it up. She chatted for a few minutes and handed it to Christina.

"It's for you, love," she said. "Barbara."

She was relieved that Barbara was calling. It meant that she wasn't going to hold the Dexter incident against her.

"Hello, honey," Barbara said. "I just got a call from Roberta Rubin, the marketing director for Eve Cosmetics. Apparently she's seen your pictures and wants to talk to you."

"How could she see my pictures?" Christina was puzzled. "I'm just working on my new book now."

"I'd like to know, too, honey," Barbara said peevishly. "I wouldn't like to think you're showing those awful Ramsey shots around."

"Oh, no, definitely not."

"Then don't worry about it, just show up at the Eve office for your nine o'clock appointment with Miss Rubin and get lots of sleep tonight."

16

New York, N.Y.
February 1978

The Eve Cosmetics offices were in the Young Building at Fifth Avenue and 52nd Street. As Christina sat in the dimly lit waiting room she read the Young Co. annual report and learned that Eve had just been acquired by Ashley Young. She turned to the latest copy of *The Reporter* and read how Ash Young and the Young Co. planned to revitalize the foundering firm. According to *The Reporter*, Young took an active role in reorganizing companies he acquired and he made a practice of turning them around. This time he had brought in the dynamic Roberta Rubin to become marketing director of Eve.

"Miss Rubin will see you now," the secretary told Christina and led her down the dark corridor to Miss Rubin's office. It was a corner office with a sweeping view of downtown New York. Every couch, chair, and other piece of furniture in the room was stainless steel or black leather. Miss Rubin sat on a black leather Eames chair behind a huge stainless steel desk.

She remained seated when Christina entered the room, but indicated that she should sit in one of the leather chairs.

Miss Rubin was a woman in her early forties with blond hair pulled back in a sleek chignon and wearing a light beige, tailored wool suit and crisp, white silk blouse. Her desk was clear except for about six large photos, and as Christina came closer she recognized them as Tommy Dexter's.

"Where did you get those?" she stuttered.

Miss Rubin sat down in her chair, leaned back and laughed. "From Tommy Dexter, of course. He knows I like a beautiful body." She lit a cigarette in a long, white ivory holder.

"But . . . but," Christina stammered. She was totally confused.

"Don't worry," Miss Rubin said. "Tommy told me all about your last encounter. He'll be out of commission awhile, but he'll recover. Unfortunately." She laughed again. "Tommy is a pig, like most men, but has excellent taste and he was right about you. You're the girl we've been looking for."

Looking for for what, Christina wondered, but she was too awed by the deep voice of Miss Rubin to interrupt her.

"Briefly, we're looking for a new face for our campaign to revitalize the image of the Eve girl. We want a fresh contemporary type and you're it."

Christina could hardly believe what she was hearing.

"Beginning tomorrow," Miss Rubin continued. "We'll test you for three days for print and television. You'll get one thousand dollars a day whether or not we end up using you. If you're selected as the Eve girl we'll sign you to an exclusive contract."

She sounded like a general explaining his battle plan, but Christina hardly heard anything she said. All she knew was that she was being considered as the Eve girl. And of course she was going to get it. Nobody could stop her now.

The following day, when she arrived for the first shooting, a small batallion of people descended on her. Jeanette, the manicurist, applied paper patches to her nails to strengthen them; Shima, the Japanese hairdresser, used a blow dryer and round hairbrush to shape her long, black hair; Ingrid, the makeup artist, checked to make sure her face was not shiny under the lights.

This sort of thing continued for three days

as, under the attentive supervision of Miss Rubin, Christina was photographed, videotaped and interviewed. There were three photographers, Tommy Dexter among them. She kept her distance from him all during the three days of testing, but when the time came to leave he sought her out.

"I'm sorry, Christina," he said.

"I'm sorry, too, Tommy," she answered with a smile.

They would never be friends, but at least the ice was broken between them.

*   *   *

It was another two days before Roberta Rubin called her at home with the results of the tests.

"I've got good news, Christina," she barked. "You've passed the tests with flying colors. I just called Jean Casardi and we're sitting down to work out the terms of your contract tomorrow."

"Miss Rubin," she said happily. "I can't thank you enough for this chance."

"Please, call me Roberta," she answered. "And you can thank me tomorrow. We'll have dinner together and celebrate."

The next morning, she was back in Roberta Rubin's stainless steel office with Jean Casardi to work out the details of the contract.

Casardi was not pleased with the document

that had been drafted by Eve lawyers. It called for Christina to work exclusively for Eve for two years at one hundred twenty-five thousand dollars a year. He immediately objected to the exclusivity.

"It's a hell of a contract for an unknown girl," Roberta insisted.

"Lauren Hutton's getting twice as much from Revlon," he said. "And Margaux Hemingway got one million from Faberge."

"That was paid out over five years and she was a name," Roberta countered. "And Hutton's an established model. We're taking a chance on this girl."

It went on like that, but after hours of haggling it was agreed in principle, subject to Mr. Young's final approval, that the exclusivity clause would be eliminated. Miss Wilkerson would receive one hundred thousand dollars the first year and one hundred twenty-five thousand dollars the second. She couldn't accept work for any other cosmetic product or for any other company that might be a competitor to Eve, but she was free to take other work.

Casardi was pleased with the arrangement. He explained to Christina that he was calculating on her becoming one of New York's leading models within the year. They were going to raise her rate to two thousand dollars a day as soon as the Eve campaign broke.

Everything seemed perfect. All there was left

to wait for was Ash Young's approval of the final contract.

*   *   *

That night Roberta and Christina celebrated at Pearl's. The tiny Chinese restaurant on West 46th Street was in the heart of the diamond district but it had become a popular watering hole for Seventh Avenue fashion types and Fifth Avenue retailers. Roberta was a frequent patron, but like everyone else she had to wait for a table; Pearl did not believe in reservations or credit cards.

They began with champagne at the bar while they were waiting, then more champagne as they worked their way through lemon chicken and still more champagne for dessert.

Later, as they walked home along Madison Avenue, Christina almost slipped on the curb. Roberta grabbed her arm and held it for just a second too long. It made Christina uncomfortable. Still, when Roberta invited her up to her apartment for a nightcap, she could hardly refuse her new boss. She went.

Like her office, Roberta Rubin's apartment was modern and hard edged. The two women sat on a low, black leather couch and finished another bottle of champagne as Roberta regaled Christina with stories about the cosmetics business.

By now Christina was feeling a little dizzy

and when she stood up to leave she stumbled. Roberta grabbed her by the arms.

"You better go lie down," Roberta warned. "You can't go out on the street like this." She led her into the bedroom and Christina passed out on the black silk coverlet on Roberta's brass bed.

Sometime during the night she had a dream. Someone was making love to her. Gentle hands were touching her lips and someone's tongue was leaving a moist trail all over her body. She was floating. Now other lips were on hers. She awoke with a start as she climaxed.

"What's the matter, honey?" Roberta whispered. "Wasn't it beautiful?" She was beside Christina and her blond hair was loose and around her shoulders. She, like Christina, was naked.

Christina panicked as she realized what had happened. Her head was splitting with a champagne hangover and she had gone to bed with Roberta Rubin. Disgusted, she leaped out of bed and began to gather up her clothes.

"Where are you going?" Roberta was also a little hungover but she certainly hadn't expected the girl to behave this way. She grabbed Christina's arm as she headed for the door.

"Let me go, Roberta," she said, shaking herself free. "You're disgusting."

"Don't think you can get away from me, Christina," she screamed back. "You're mine now, do you understand?"

Tearfully, Christina slammed the door.

*   *   *

It was almost ten in the morning when she returned to the apartment. Melinda was making coffee and began pummelling her with questions about where she had spent the night. But Christina didn't want to talk. She headed straight for the bathroom where she stayed under the shower for a very long time.

You're mine, Roberta had screamed at her. Did she really believe that she would ever allow her to touch her again? But she knew that she hadn't heard the last of Roberta. Damn. Why couldn't she have waited until the contract was signed?

She couldn't sit home and worry, though. That would be the worst thing. Besides, Roberta might have been right. If she was not interested in men, maybe she was a lesbian. For the first time since coming to New York, she wanted to go out, to party, to meet men.

"Listen, Melinda," she said as the redhead poured coffee for the two of them. "I'm really in the mood to party now. The tests are over and I can enjoy myself. How about tonight?"

"Super!" Melinda agreed. "There's a party tonight at Paul Garrett's. He's always after me to bring my pretty friends. You're going to have a ball!"

Part Four

17

New York, N.Y.
February 1978

At Paul Garrett's townhouse on Gracie Square there were indeed plenty of men—AC and DC. Garrett was gay, so naturally the place was full of members of that great fraternity, but there was also the other kind, the old-fashioned type who still enjoy women. In this category were Stanley Morris, ex-All-American and currently a reporter at the *New York Times,* and Alex Mercati, publisher of *The Reporter.*

Morris and Mercati were introduced by their host to Melinda and Christina and as naturally as two and two makes four they all decided after a while to go out on the town. It also happened naturally that the two combinations that formed were Stanley and Melinda and Alex and Christina.

They ended up at El Morocco where the host, Jeff Jones, received them like lost brothers and sisters. They drank, they danced and thoroughly enjoyed themselves.

For a while, at least, Christina was able to push the dark thoughts of Roberta Rubin from her mind. She found Alex Mercati very attractive, loaded with charm and intelligence, and the sexiest man she had met in her life.

For his part, Mercati was sure that he had never met a young woman as beautiful or as exciting as Christina Wilkerson.

Morris and Melinda were not doing badly either. The ruggedly handsome reporter was all over the redhead and at one point he practically lifted her in his arms and carried her into the misty night.

Alex and Christina were in no such rush to go. They were much too busy looking into each other's eyes. They were the last to leave the club, when the waiters had already cleared all the tables and were waiting impatiently to close.

Outside, in spite of the winter's chill in the air, they walked back to Christina's apartment holding hands. When they reached her building he kissed her gently on the lips. He had no wish to press his advantage and besides, she had already promised that they would meet again the next evening.

* * *

As Christina was drifting off to sleep, Melinda was with Stanley Morris at his apartment on Sutton Place. At first he had been charming; they had shared a few more drinks and necked a bit on the huge, beige, suede sofa that faced his view of the East River.

He began to undress her so slowly and teasingly that she wanted to scream. When he had got down to her bra and panties she whispered, "Excuse me, love," and slipped into the bathroom. She quickly inserted her diaphragm (Melinda would not use the pill—it made her gain weight—but she was always prepared) and came back.

He was waiting for her in the bedroom, dressed in the weirdest outfit she had ever seen. He was naked except for a black leather mask, black leather boots and a black belt around his waist, a section of which was wrapped around his crotch and supported his upright cock. He was holding a black whip in his hand and when he saw her he screamed.

"Kneel, you bitch!"

"What is this, Stan, a joke?" she laughed.

His fist caught her in the eye and she

staggered. Again he hit her and sent her sprawling on the carpet.

"Kneel, you whore!" he screamed even louder and the nasty whistle of the whip missed her by inches.

Terrified, she obeyed. He cracked the whip once more and this time it hit her on the face. She cried in pain as blood oozed from her cheek. She turned away only to have him crack it again and again on her naked back and buttocks.

As she writhed in pain on the carpet, begging him to stop, he advanced towards her. With the toe of his boot, he pushed her and forced her to turn over so that now she was on her back staring up at him. He began to masturbate, then he came, his whole body trembling, spurting all over her. When she tried to wriggle away, he placed a booted foot on her chest and pressed harder. The hot sperm washed over her face.

She lay there, numb with fear, not daring to move until he stepped away, sat on the bed and took off his mask. His expression and voice were back to normal as he spoke to her casually.

"Why don't you put your clothes back on, Melinda?"

She was bleeding and her jaw ached, but she just grabbed her clothes, put on her coat and walked quickly to the door. She turned for just a second. He was sitting there on the bed as if nothing had happened, still naked, with his boots on and the whip in his hand. He blew her a kiss.

"Call me soon, Melinda, I'd love to see you again."

*   *   *

"I can't believe it," a shocked Christina said as Melinda recounted the story of that night. Melinda was a mess, her lips swollen and bloody, one eye half closed, her red hair disheveled and matted with blood.

"The man is dangerous and you should call the police."

Melinda shook her head. "What's the use? He's a powerful guy and can make a lot of trouble for me. Besides, I doubt anyone would believe me. He's probably done this to other girls and nothing ever happened."

"That's exactly why we should do something," Christina insisted. "Maybe Barbara and Jean can help."

"Oh, God, no," Melinda cried. "They think I'm wacky enough without knowing about this. I just want to forget it ever happened."

Suddenly Christina realized that there was someone else they could turn to. She had only known him a few hours, but she sensed that Alex Mercati would understand. First she put Melinda to bed and then she dialed his number.

His sleepy voice answered on the second

ring. "Christina, it's you," he said, sounding sleepy but pleased. "I was just dreaming about you."

She told him what had happened to Melinda. Suddenly he was wide awake.

"I've heard that Morris is a strange guy, but I never thought he was that kinky," he said. "Are you sure Melinda won't go to the police?"

"She's afraid of the publicity," Christina explained. "But she's a mess. She's going to have to see a doctor tomorrow and she's not going to be able to work until those bruises heal."

"I'll see what I can do," he said cryptically. "And I'll see you tomorrow night."

18

New York, N.Y.
February 1978

When he bought the townhouse on East 65th Street, Alex Mercati conveniently arranged to have the editorial offices of *The Reporter* on the ground floor. The other three stories were his private living quarters. That way he could wake up to the morning sun streaming through the skylight of his top-floor bedroom and descend the mahogany staircase to his office where he could make an early start on the day.

He was at his desk as usual at nine a.m. in spite of the late night at El Morocco. The office was in the rear of the building and faced a small garden, mostly covered with snow this morning. The only bit of color came from a fat blue jay who was breakfasting at a feeder hanging from a leafless cherry tree.

Alex turned away from the window and looked over his calendar. He noticed with annoyance that he had committed himself to two dates for that night. Christina Wilkerson and Stephanie Young.

Stephanie was a good kid, but too crazy and unpredictable. The last thing he wanted was to get involved with the madcap daughter of Ashley Young.

Actually, next to a madcap heiress, the least likely woman he would be involved with was a model. As a class he didn't like them. They were usually stupid, vain and indifferent to anything outside themselves. But this Christina Wilkerson seemed to be an exception. She was smart and reasonably unaware of her beauty and sexuality.

No doubt about it, Christina was the one he was going to see tonight. He might even ask her to come down to Palm Beach. But enough of planning his evening, he had other, pressing business to take care of.

*　　　*　　　*

Morris was waiting for him that afternoon at the bar of Charley O's in Rockefeller Center, and he had the look of a man who expected to be offered a job.

They shook hands and Alex ordered a Cutty Sark on the rocks for himself and a vodka martini for Morris. He still found it hard to reconcile the serious, fastidious young journalist in the navy blue Armani suit with the sadistic brute Melinda Parsons had described.

He had known Morris casually for several years, well enough for the occasional favor, tennis date or night on the town. He never dreamed when he suggested that Melinda and Christina join them for a jaunt to El Morocco that he was involving the pretty redhead with a sadist. For that reason most of all he felt he had to make it up to her.

He had met Morris' kind before and he should have recognized the signs. Very proper, impeccably heterosexual, polite, almost too reserved with women. Then suddenly such a man would snap and the poor girl unlucky enough to be with him was the next victim.

He didn't waste time with small talk. After the briefest of preliminaries he got straight to the point.

"I talked to Melinda Parsons this morning."

Morris said nothing. He sipped his martini slowly but Alex noticed that the hand that held his cigarette was trembling. Two could play the waiting game and he just watched until Morris finally spoke.

"I don't know what you're talking about, Alex. Should that mean something to me?"

"Look, Morris, if it were up to me, Melinda Parsons would have called the police immediately."

"Why should she? We just had some innocent fun. And she didn't mind a bit." But he looked relieved.

"Some fun! She's all bloodied and bruised," Alex snapped. "She didn't call the cops because she's afraid of the publicity. But I told her to send all the doctor bills to you. She won't be able to work for a few weeks and I want that taken care of, too."

"Who are you, her manager?" Morris' tone was surly. As long as the police were not involved, he felt confident.

"No, I'm her friend," Alex said coolly. "The story isn't even interesting enough for me to run in *The Reporter*, but I'm sure your mother wouldn't be pleased and it would no doubt cost you your job at the *Times!*"

That was different. Morris' income was subsidized by his socially ambitious mother. He suddenly saw his carefully cultivated reputation as a man about town about to crumble. His hands shook more than ever.

"OK, OK," he muttered. "But don't think it's over between you and me."

"I'm sure it isn't," Alex said as he left Morris alone at the crowded bar.

* * *

Back at his office, he picked up the phone ringing on his private line. It was Stephanie.

"Hi, Alex," she said breezily. "We have a date tonight. When are you picking me up?"

"I'm sorry, Stephanie," he said, feeling like a heel. "Something's come up. I've got to write a last minute editorial, and it's got to be done tonight."

"Ooooh," she said. "Can't we just have a quick bite? We can go home early."

She sounded so disappointed that he felt thoroughly ashamed of himself. But he had made up his mind.

"No, really. I can't, Stephanie. I'll never finish otherwise."

"Suppose I let you alone, I'll just come and watch you. When you're finished we could spend the night together."

"No, Stephanie, not tonight. I'll call you tomorrow."

"Oh, Alex, otherwise all I'll do is sit in bed and read a book," she pouted.

"It'll do you good," he laughed.

"Fuck you, Alex," Stephanie yelled and slammed down the phone so hard that a buzz rang in his ear for several minutes afterward.

19

New York, N.Y.
February 1978

Stephanie Young couldn't believe it. After Alex cancelled their date, she had gotten that boring Jimmy Bacon to take her to dinner at "21." Now, here they were at Regine's and that bastard was sitting at a table on the other side of the dance floor engrossed in conversation with a striking brunette. So that was the piece he was working on. Some piece.

James Bacon III was handsome, wealthy and well born but he was just too Boston, too square and too unsexy for her. Just the kind of man her father would love to see her with. He was a total bore, but he had been available at the last minute and it was better than staying home.

"Jimmy, I want a double Dewar's," she said.

She wanted to get very drunk. She hardly looked at Bacon but continued to stare at Mercati. He was so wrapped up in the dark bitch he hadn't even noticed her. She ought to walk over and spit in his face but instead she swallowed the scotch and asked Jimmy for another.

"Aw, Stephie," Bacon whined. "Don't you want to dance?"

"No, Jimmy, not now." She tried to hide her rage at Mercati, while Jimmy obediently ordered another double Dewar's. Suddenly a deep masculine voice spoke out next to them.

"If it isn't Jimmy Bacon!"

Stephanie and Jimmy looked up to see a roguish, ruddy-faced man of indeterminate age grinning at them as he stood over the table. The face was vaguely familiar.

"Stephanie, meet Teddy McElroy," Jimmy shouted over the blare of the music.

Now she recognized him. Teddy McElroy, sometime actor, occasional playboy and frequent adventurer had most recently been in the headlines when his wife, the sixtyish Beatrice Carhart, had thrown him out of their River House apartment. The story around town was that after three weeks of married life she had found him in bed with a chambermaid.

"I'm here with my agent," Teddy said, indicating a distant table where a portly, balding man sat between two heavily made-up blondes in dresses cut down to their nipples. "Why don't you join us?"

Jimmy started to decline, but Stephanie cut him off. "We'd love to," she snapped, smiling brightly at McElroy. His blue eyes reminded her of Tim Kelly's and just because Alex Mercati had disappointed her was no reason not to climb back on the bike.

The sound of "I Will Survive" blared across the room and Teddy asked her to dance. She leaped up and followed him onto the tiny, mirrored dance floor. It was exhilarating to move to the loud, pounding disco beat, moving close to McElroy, teasing him.

Then the music became slower and, as they listened to "Rumours," she relaxed in his arms and he playfully kissed her ear. Over his shoulder she could see that they were next to Alex and the dark-haired girl. He smiled at her and she disengaged herself from Teddy McElroy's grip.

"Fancy seeing you here," she said, looking at the dark girl. "Is this your piece?"

Alex smoothly ignored that and introduced her to Christina Wilkerson.

It only made Stephanie more furious. He was caught in a lie and he wasn't even embarrassed or apologetic, the son of a bitch.

"Nice meeting you, Christina," she said, glaring at Alex. Then she buried her head back in McElroy's arms and he smoothly led her away.

McElroy was pleased to have the blond girl to himself. She was a good looking chick and as he sorted out the name in his mind he remembered reading in the gossip columns that she was the daughter of the fabulously wealthy Ashley Young. Yes, quite a good looking chick.

*   *   *

Christina sensed that Alex was embarrassed by the encounter with the blond girl and when he suggested that they go somewhere else for some breakfast she agreed. They ended up at the Brasserie, a twenty-four hour cafe in the Seagram's Building. It was after two and the place was almost empty. Over eggs benedict he informed her that the Morris matter had been taken care of.

"I'll have to call Melinda," she said, getting up from the table. "That's fabulous news."

When she came back there was a look of consternation on her face.

"Is something wrong?" he asked as she sat down.

"Melinda got a bunch of roses from Stan Morris tonight after I left with you," she said.

"That's nice," he said coolly.

"Tucked inside the flowers there was a check

237

for five thousand dollars," she continued. "You knew all about it, didn't you?"

Alex shrugged. "All in a day's work."

She sipped her coffee. There was so much she had to learn about this man.

"Who was the blond girl at Regine's?" she asked. The girl had looked as though she wanted to kill.

"Who, Stephanie?" he hesitated. "Just a poor little rich girl with a father and mother who have too much money and not enough time for their daughter. And that's all she is to me."

"Did you say her name was Young?"

"Yes, her father's a friend, well, a business associate, really. I don't think anyone's a friend of Ash Young."

Christina frowned. "You mean the tycoon from Houston? That Ash Young?"

"Yes," Alex acknowledged.

"He's my new boss," she said, telling him about the Eve Girl campaign, but skipping over the nightmarish incident with Roberta Rubin. "So it's all just waiting for his final approval," she concluded.

"What did you think of Roberta Rubin?" Alex asked.

Christina looked at him quizzically, then told him the rest of the story. It was a relief to share it with someone.

"Be careful, Christina," he warned when she

finished. "Roberta Rubin's a vindictive woman. I'm sure you haven't heard the last of her."

She shook her head. "I've met so many awful people here, Alex. Roberta, Tommy Dexter, Stanley Morris—"

Alex took her hand. "You must have met someone decent, Christina."

"Yes," she said thoughtfully. "There's Melinda. And Jean and Barbara."

"Anyone else?" He looked hurt.

She laughed. "Oh, I think so. I've only known you two days, but I feel as though I've known you forever."

Alex paid for breakfast and they walked out into the snowy night. There was a cab waiting and they headed uptown.

Christina stared out the window. "So this is winter in New York?" she said.

"That's right," Alex agreed. "I just realized all this snow must be new to you."

"Yes," Christina said. "Growing up in Houston I saw a little but nothing like this. And my mother is Mexican, you know, so I don't think I've got the blood for a cold climate."

"I've got a great idea, Christina," he said. "Ash Young's invited me down to his house in Palm Beach next weekend. Why don't you come with me?"

She hesitated. She was crazy about Alex but she wasn't sure about going off for a weekend with him so soon. If there was one thing she had learned since coming to New York it was that she had to be careful.

"The house is a showplace," Alex went on. "And Young is a celebrity collector, so you never know who'll turn up at dinner."

"Will Stephanie Young be there?" She was sure that Stephanie wouldn't welcome her visit.

Alex laughed. "That's highly unlikely. Young's cut her out of his life. She spends most of her time with her grandparents now."

"I don't know, Alex," she demurred.

"Besides, I think it would be a good idea for Young to meet you, just in case Roberta Rubin has something up her sleeve."

"Oh, Alex," she laughed. "You think of everything. Of course I'll come."

They had reached her building. He stepped out and walked with her to the door. "Will I see you tomorrow, Christina?"

"Tomorrow night and every night."

Part Five

20

Las Vegas, Nevada
March 1978

If Christina was concerned about bumping into a jealous Stephanie Young at Belvedere, she need not have worried. For the next day Stephanie was awakening in the arms of her new husband, Teddy McElroy, in their suite at Caesar's Palace in Las Vegas.

She lay naked on the bed, lazily stretching her hand across his hairy chest. They had arrived only hours before, after a brief visit to a twenty-four hour wedding chapel on the strip.

She vaguely remembered leaving Regine's after muttering something about a headache to a crestfallen Jimmy Bacon. Teddy would take her home, she insisted. Poor Jimmy was left with the agent, the check and two dizzy blondes who waved unhappily at the departing Teddy. From there they had gone to his suite at the Sherry-Netherlands and made love all night.

"Baby," Teddy suggested in the morning. "Let's fly to Vegas and get married."

She liked that idea. She had gone off with Teddy to make Alex Mercati jealous but marrying him would totally freak out Daddy. She pictured the look on his face when he got the news and almost wished she could be there.

She found herself wondering what her father would think of the honeymoon suite. The room was large and decorated with the kind of fake French antiques he hated. She and Teddy had spent the night in a king-sized bed beneath a mural of a fire, flames lapping around the headboard. The rest of the walls were covered with red-and-white-striped paper and hung with framed drawings of Roman temples. In one corner was a small well-stocked bar, and at the end of the room sliding glass doors led to a small terrace. The floor was covered with red wall-to-wall shag carpeting.

The suite was already filled with flowers, baskets of fruit and champagne, compliments of the management and McElroy's friends in town. So this was what it was going to be like, married to a celebrity. She padded about quietly so as not to wake her sleeping husband and examined the gifts. Two of the flower baskets were addressed to her and she opened the cards carefully.

The first was from Tony Torelli, the singer, and said: "Welcome. Expect you and Teddy as my guests for dinner tonight after the show."

So she was going to meet the famous singer!

The other card was from someone named Carlo Gallenzo. She had never heard of him but he wanted Teddy and her to come to his house for a swim and lunch.

It was going to take awhile to get to know all her new husband's friends.

*   *   *

Teddy McElroy watched his new bride from the bed as she ordered breakfast from room service. The long, tanned legs, the firm, little ass, the tawny hair that barely covered her voluptuous breasts, the small muff of blond pubic hair surrounded by a provocative little triangle of white skin preserved by the tiniest of bikinis. And she was the daughter of Ashley Young. He hardly knew which pleased him more, the body or the bankroll. Meeting and marrying her had changed all the prospects in his life in a matter of a few hours. It had been a lucky break.

The painful truth was that he was broke. Beatrice had thrown him out at the worst possible time, his career was going nowhere and his investments had soured. Worse, he was in debt to the casinos. He owed the Alhambra alone one hundred twenty-five thousand dollars. He had latched onto Stephanie like a drowning man.

"Have you called your father?" he asked as Stephanie put down the phone.

She looked at him. "No, I was waiting for you."

"I don't want your father to find out about us on the late news, he'll be furious," he snapped. "Get him on the phone."

"You don't know Daddy," she said as she prepared a pitcher of Bloody Marys at the bar. "He'll be furious anyway."

But she obediently placed a person-to-person call to Ashley Young in Palm Beach. In minutes he was on the line.

"What's up, sister?" he barked.

Stephanie winced. She hated it when he called her that. Why couldn't he call her daughter?

"What are you doing in Las Vegas?" he asked.

She looked across the room for support from Teddy. He smiled at her encouragingly.

"I was married today, Daddy."

After a moment of silence, "Against whom?"

"Daddy, stop joking."

"I'm not joking," he said coolly. "Who's the unlucky guy?"

"Teddy McElroy, he's a wond—"

"I know who he is." He cut her off. "You don't have to explain. Put him on the line."

Stephanie handed the phone to Teddy, who took it eagerly.

"Hello, Mr. Young," he said, winking at Stephanie. "It's great to meet you."

"I can't say the same."

Teddy was startled. "Why say that, Mr. Young? I love Stephanie and I think I can make her happy."

"I don't give a damn what you think," Ash hissed. "She's made her bed, let her lie in it. But I warn you, McElroy, I know all about you. You'll never get a penny from the Youngs. Stephanie doesn't have it and I won't give it to you. You can tell my daughter that I'll talk to her again when she's ready to divorce you. Good day."

When McElroy hung up the phone, his face was white with anger and creeping fear. The man had insulted him, which was bad enough, but if he couldn't raise the one hundred twenty-five thousand dollars he owed the Alhambra through Stephanie, he didn't know how he was going to do it.

"I told you Daddy wouldn't be pleased," she giggled as she sipped her Bloody Mary. "But don't worry, Teddy. I'm married to you now. He can't do anything to us."

He wanted to hit the silly bitch, but he couldn't show his anger. He had to think. Suddenly an idea flashed in his mind. He was

247

married to one of America's richest heiresses. No one needed to know that she had been cut off without a penny.

He jumped off the bed and began to search through his jacket, starting slowly and then becoming more and more frantic.

"What are you looking for, Teddy?"

"I can't find my wallet," he said with irritation.

They searched the entire suite, but no wallet. In spite of his searching, Teddy knew there was none to be found because he had hidden it too well.

"This is awful. It'll take a week to replace my credit cards, and my checkbook's in New York," he said. Then he turned to Stephanie. "Have you got any cash?"

She went to her purse and counted out some bills. "I have eight hundred dollars," she said helpfully. "And this," she waved her checkbook.

"How much is in there?" He was struggling not to sound too frantic.

"It must be nearly five thousand dollars," she yawned. That Bloody Mary had made her sleepy again. "Mom and Daddy gave me three thousand dollars each last week. Daddy says it's a gift so it's tax free."

"Would you mind, darling, if we used it? It's only until I replace my credit cards."

"Oh, I know what a hassle that can be," she

said. "I have bonds in New York and every time I want to cash some it's a big production."

"Bonds?" His ears pricked up. "How much in bonds?"

"I'm not sure," she said. "Does fifty thousand dollars sound right?"

Fifty thousand dollars sounded just right, but he said nothing. "I didn't realize I was marrying such a rich broad," he lied.

"Teddy, what's mine is yours." She signed a blank check and handed it to him. "You just fill in what you need, honey, I'm going back to sleep." She lay down on the bed and closed her eyes.

As Teddy sipped a Bloody Mary and reviewed his options, he watched her. She was lying on her stomach, face down on the sheets, like a big, golden angel and all his for the taking.

He rose from the bed quietly and went into the bathroom. He found the iron ring in his shaving kit. He wanted to introduce her to a little trick he had learned in Japan.

Noiselessly he returned to the bed and eased himself next to her. He began to kiss her; then, moving along her stomach and lifting her thighs, he began to explore her sex with his tongue. She moaned with pleasure in her sleep and he could feel himself begin to harden.

He slipped the ring over his balls until it was tight against his body, then he forced his semi-erect cock through it. Cutting off the flow of blood, the ring gave him a longer, harder erection.

She was fully awake now, loudly encouraging him harder, harder as he pumped into her. She quickly came but he never slackened his tempo and she came again and again until her whole body shuddered and she slowly sank back into an exhausted sleep.

He slipped the ring off his exhausted cock and reached across the bedside table for one of her cigarettes. He lit it and leaned back, looking at the contented form of his sleeping beauty.

"Well, my dear bride," he murmured. "You see what you get for five grand."

21

Palm Beach, Florida
March 1978

Ashley Young had sent his car and driver to meet Alex and Christina at the Palm Beach airport Saturday morning. Now they were speeding along Ocean Avenue past the luxurious villas and mansions of Palm Beach stalwarts like Rose Kennedy, Winston Guest and Charles Wrightsman. No wonder they called the palm-tree-lined boulevard the Avenue of the Rich.

Belvedere was obscured by a six-foot stucco wall surrounding the two acre property. James the driver stopped in front of a high iron gate flanked by two stone lions, jumped out to open the gate and returned to the car. As they passed through the entrance the gate closed automatically behind them.

"We'll be approaching Belvedere from the rear," Alex explained. "All Palm Beach mansions face the ocean."

The limousine moved smoothly down the three-hundred-foot driveway lined with tall palm trees and flanked by two acres of verdant lawns. Then Belvedere came into view.

Christina recognized it from magazine pictures, but in real life it was even more impressive: a three-story Spanish-style villa designed by the renowned architect Addison Mizener.

"It's beautiful, isn't it?" Alex said, reading her thoughts.

"Yes, everything about it is perfect."

"It ought to be. Ash Young is known to go into a rage if there are tire marks in the driveway," Alex laughed. "Wait until you meet him."

Inside the house, the entrance hall was lined with dark green marble. The stately August met them at the door and led them through a small gallery, where four Renoirs were on display, and upstairs to meet their host.

Young was behind his desk deep in conversation with another man, but they both rose when they saw Christina. Young extended his hand when Alex introduced them. He was a good-looking man of medium height in a navy blazer and ascot and white slacks. His gray eyes were the color of steel.

"What a coincidence," he said. "I was looking at some pictures of you before I left New York."

For one awful minute Christina thought only of the Tommy Dexter photographs. Then she realized he was referring to the Eve test shots.

"I expect we'll be doing some business when I'm back in New York next week," he continued.

"I hope so, Mr. Young," she said.

"This is my associate, Tom Patterson," Ash added, indicating the other man who greeted them cordially.

"If you're conducting business, we don't want to disturb you," Alex offered.

"Not at all," Ash said, his tone turning sour. "I just got the news that my idiot daughter married Teddy McElroy in Las Vegas yesterday. Tom and I are moving fast to make sure the bastard doesn't get a dime. Excuse my language, Miss Wilkerson."

Christina smiled and August led the two of them to their rooms. When they were gone, the two older men resumed their work.

"A spendthrift trust is what we want," Ash said briskly. "We'll limit her to thirty thousand dollars a year. Are you listening?"

"Hm?" Patterson looked up. "I'm sorry, Ash. I was thinking about that girl with Mercati. She looks familiar, somehow, like I've seen her before."

"He said she's from Houston. You probably have," Ash snapped. "Now we've got work to do. Neither McElroy nor Stephanie is going to get a dime from me!"

That was Ash Young, Patterson thought sadly, a cold-blooded money machine. He had no interest in people unless they could do something for him. With this disastrous marriage Stephanie had ceased to be useful to him, therefore he was cutting her off.

"As far as I'm concerned, I've put an X over her name," Ash continued. "I couldn't care less what happens to her now as long as she doesn't drag my name through the mud."

"Well, this should take care of that," Patterson said, then added hopefully, "Maybe the marriage will even work out."

"She'd be better off if we committed her, but the Hollingsworths would never stand for it. The best I can do is set up an idiot's trust. She'll have a roof over her head, but after that my responsibility ends."

*　　*　　*

While Young and Patterson were discussing their business, the discreet August led Alex and Christina to separate but adjoining rooms. Christina's was a small, feminine room with pale blue walls and a blue flowered rug on the floor. There were sliding glass doors that looked out on Belvedere's three hundred and fifty feet of ocean front. Between beach and house she could see the huge swimming pool surrounded by a marble patio and beyond it, several marble steps below, the clay tennis courts.

She turned away and began to unpack. Before she left New York, Melinda had insisted on taking her to Bendel's to pick out a suitable evening dress. The one they had decided on was a tight-fitting green silk that matched her eyes. It was long and bare at one shoulder and slit up the side to show a lot of leg. As she hung it up she was glad that Melinda had talked her into buying it.

She thought about Ashley Young, her host and soon-to-be employer. He was a handsome man, far handsomer than newspaper photos showed, but those cold, gray eyes were frightening. They were as hard as steel. She wouldn't want to be at the mercy of such a man. Neither as a wife, and far less as a daughter. She thought with sympathy about Stephanie. She smiled to herself. Mama ought to meet Mr. Young. He was exactly the kind of man she was always warning her about.

*   *   *

Ash Young did not usually linger in his bath. Wasted time was wasted money. But this evening he soaked in the black marble tub, trying to relax and calm the excitement he felt. His fury at Stephanie had almost subsided, even though she had pulled this marriage stunt on the eve of an important dinner party. There was something else on his mind. He couldn't stop thinking about the beautiful, dark girl he had just met.

Infatuation, if that was what it was, was an unusual emotion for him. Except for that interlude with Teresa Martinez so many years ago in Houston, he had been more content to pursue money and power than women.

The prospect of putting over a big deal, or crushing a competitor, always excited him more than the sight of the most erotic woman. He had long ago lost interest in Jessica and when he needed sex at all he could pay for it. He was surprised therefore to find himself getting so excited just thinking about that Texas girl.

He stepped out of the tub and dried himself briskly, then examined himself in the full-length mirror. He was in excellent shape for fifty. The daily swims and twice weekly treatments from Dr. Reinhardt were working. He had the body of a man twenty years younger and that gray hair just made him look more distinguished. In his well-cut, black dinner jacket with shiny black silk lapels, tailored for him by Caraceni of Milan, and the cream silk shirt buttoned with tiny diamond studs, he couldn't help admitting that he looked quite handsome. Yes, tonight at dinner he would have a chat with the dark girl.

*   *   *

He found Jessica awaiting their guests in the drawing room. She was seated on one of the Louis XVI bergeres upholstered in pale mauve Venetian silk and she was wearing the new white crepe Givenchy and emerald necklace as he had instructed. He gave her a brush of a kiss on the cheek.

He moved away from her and surveyed the drawing room with satisfaction. Any small changes he had made since purchasing it from Liz Harris almost twenty-one years before had been for the better.

It was a room of imperial proportions. On one side, three sliding glass doors looked out on the beach and gardens. The floor of Carrara was covered with a blue Savonnerie carpet and there was a fire burning in the fireplace under a yellow marble Louis XV mantel. A huge pair of blackamoor torchères guarded each side.

At the other end of the room was a doorway leading to the formal dining room. It was flanked by two huge, mirrored glass vitrines in which he displayed his collection of French and Meissen porcelain.

Yes, he told himself, he was a man who had everything.

*   *   *

Alex called for Christina at eight-fifteen. She could tell from his expression that she looked good and taking his arm she followed him downstairs to the drawing room where Young's guests were already assembling. As house guests they did not go through the routine of exchanging greetings with their host but as soon as they entered the room conversation ceased. All heads turned in Christina's direction.

Even Ash Young felt his pulse quicken when he saw the dark-haired girl with Mercati. He could have stared at her all night, but unfortunately, Stavros Pateras had just made his disorderly appearance.

The Greek shipping tycoon, a small, dark man with a large nose and an even larger ego, was already half drunk. His elegant wife, Sophie, stood by quietly as if nothing was wrong.

"Keep an eye on him, Jessica," Ash warned. "You know how he gets when he's this way." The golden Greek was liable to act in the crudest manner, insulting the men and grabbing at the women.

Alex and Christina made some small talk with Jessica Young, complimenting her on her new jewels. Alex judged from the vague smile and bemused attitude that she was well dosed with Valium tonight. It was probably the only way she could manage to be the perfect hostess Ash wanted, mingling with the guests, easily exchanging polite and meaningless words with them, always wearing the same set smile.

*　　*　　*

Ash sought them out and as he approached, Jessica excused herself to move on.

"I hope you're enjoying yourself Miss Wilkerson," he said. "Would you like some champagne?"

"Yes, thank you," she said.

In a minute, a second butler had appeared with a tray of three tulip-shaped glasses. Ash's crystal was so heavily leaded it could be bent with two fingers at the stem without breaking. He firmly believed that fine wine simply did not taste the same in ordinary stemware.

"What's this I hear about Yamani and King Kalid deserting the dollar?" Alex asked as he sipped the champagne. "The rumor in New York is that they're going to diversify into marks and Swiss francs."

"If they do, it'll be because those horses' asses in Washington have driven the dollar into the ground," Ash said bitterly. "Soon we'll be dealing in peanuts." He looked around the room. "Here's Yamani himself, you can ask him what he's up to."

The powerful, dark-skinned Arab was not tall but he was obviously a man who was comfortable wielding the power of OPEC. He wore a Saville Row suit and was charm itself.

"I'm sorry to miss Mr. Kissinger on this trip," he confided as he sipped Chivas on the rocks.

It amused Alex that the Arabs who drank no alcohol at home loved their fine scotch whiskey when abroad. It was even funnier that they who so mistrusted the Jews considered a German Jew to be America's most enlightened creator of foreign policy.

Their chat was cut short when August announced that dinner was about to be served in the dining room.

The room, also known as the Bird Room, had dark green walls hung with framed prints of rare birds, but it was dominated by a huge Rousseau painting that depicted hundreds of multicolored parrots peering at each other in a jungle. Several niches in the walls held Jessica Young's collection of Meissen birds and her glazed eyes actually lit up when a guest asked about them. She eagerly identified every species.

The twenty guests were seated at a dining table in the style of Louis XV, specially built so that it could be made longer or shorter, according to the number of guests, without affecting the design of the piece.

Alex noticed with displeasure that he was seated between two aging society hostesses, each of whom had had so many face and breast lifts that their navels were now beauty marks on their chins. He could see poor Christina fending off the lusty Pateras across the table.

He read the tiny dinner menu perched on a miniature easel in front of each setting. Dinner would begin with caviar and blinis which he adored, followed by vichysoisse. The main course would be *carré d'agneau,* which was fine because he liked the way Ash's French chef prepared lamb, pink and not overcooked. What followed was routine, salad, cheeses, and a strawberry mousse for desert.

On the other side of the table, Christina was enjoying the dinner far less than Alex. She could not believe the things the awful Pateras was whispering in her ear as he pressed his knee against hers and occasionally gave her a friendly little pinch under the table. She fended him off as best she could but when his hand reached dangerously high on her thigh she dug her nails into it. To her surprise he just laughed.

"I'd much rather feel those sharp nails on my back," he said lasciviously. "When you're under me in bed."

"You'll have to spend a few of your millions to learn some manners first," she whispered, furious but anxious to avoid a scene.

Pateras only laughed harder. "I like your spirit," he said thickly. "The flash of your green eyes excites me even more."

She realized that Sophie Pateras was watching her closely. "I sympathize with you, child," her dark eyes seemed to say. "But there's nothing I can do about it."

Mercifully, at that moment Jessica Young rose from the table, a signal to the guests that dinner was over. As they followed her back into the drawing room, the drunken Pateras clutched Christina's arm, but Alex rushed to her side, pushing him away.

"Sorry, Stavros," he said. "But I have something to tell Miss Wilkerson."

Pateras grunted and moved away as Christina sighed with relief.

"Thanks, Alex, that man is impossible."

"I know, he thinks he's a Greek god, but he's only a goddamn Greek."

She laughed. "Do you know he propositioned me?"

"I'm not surprised," Alex replied. "You'd be amazed at how many women end up in bed with that baboon. All because of his money."

"Why does a man like Ash Young even allow Pateras into his home?"

Alex shrugged. "There are the tankers, of

course, but they also have a kind of running rivalry over art and fine furniture."

"Oh, really?" It was hard for Christina to imagine a man less likely to appreciate fine art than Stavros Pateras.

"Young always outbids on the furniture and Pateras gets the paintings," Alex added. "Although without Jessica or an appraiser next to him I don't think Ash would know the difference between a Limoge bowl and a Sevres chamber pot."

"I'm sorry for what happened at dinner, Miss Wilkerson," Ash said as he joined them. "I should have known better than to have Stavros Pateras seated next to a beautiful young woman."

"You're not responsible for your guests' behavior, Mr. Young," she smiled.

"It's generous of you to say that, but in this house I'm responsible for everything. It won't happen again, I promise you." He moved on to his other guests, but not before Alex and Christina both noticed the look in his gray eyes.

"What have you done to the old man?" Alex whispered. "I've never seen Ash Young so infatuated."

"Oh, really?" She watched as he moved among the other guests.

263

"Are you a witch, Christina?" he said. "That you can bewitch all men?"

She turned to smile at him. "Of course. I'm Circe, the temptress. Men fall in love with me and I turn them into pigs!"

"Oink, oink," he grunted and they both exploded in laughter.

Later, as the party dwindled down, Alex and Christina took leave of their hosts and walked upstairs together. They paused at the door to her room.

"I had a wonderful time tonight, Alex," she said. "I want to thank you for asking me down."

"Is that all?" he asked.

She kissed him and he took her in his arms and held her. "Good night, Alex." She left him at the door.

*　　*　　*

Christina woke the next morning to sunlight streaming through the glass doors and the sound of the bedside telephone ringing.

"Hello?" she said, her voice still groggy from sleep.

"Christina! What are you doing in Palm Beach?" Her mother sounded on the verge of hysteria.

"Calm down, Mama," she said. She was

struggling to wake up and clear her thoughts. She couldn't understand why her mother was so upset or why she was even calling at all. It wasn't even seven o'clock in Houston.

"I couldn't sleep," her mother rattled on. "I had a feeling you were in danger, Christina. I called Melinda and she gave me the number. What are you doing in Ash Young's house?"

"Don't worry, Mama," Christina said patiently. "I didn't want to tell you until it was final, but it looks like I'll be working for Mr. Young." She explained about the Eve Girl contract and all that it would mean for the two of them. To her shock, her mother did not sound pleased at all.

"I want you to come home, Christina. Getting involved with Ashley Young will only bring you trouble."

"Really, Mama, you read too many gossip columns," Christina said. She was becoming irritated. "You don't even know Mr. Young."

"No," her mother said faintly. "I guess I never knew him at all."

"He may not be the nicest man in the world, but he's not a monster," Christina continued. "Besides, I'm here with Alex. He'll look out for me."

Her mother did not sound convinced. "Be careful, Christina," she rambled on.

"I will, Mama," she promised. "And I'll call you when I get home tonight."

*   *   *

Her mother's surprise phone call had left Christina deeply disturbed. She sounded worse than ever and she wondered if she had done the right thing leaving her alone in Houston. Still, if she was going to make enough money to support the two of them, she had no choice. And once she signed the Eve contract she could bring Mama up to New York and get her to start rebuilding her life.

She wanted to take a walk and think, and she dressed hurriedly in linen trousers and a loose silk shirt. The beach looked deserted and she could be alone to concentrate. She had to think about her mother and Alex and about her new boss, Ashley Young.

She walked along the secluded beach, listening to the crash of the surf. The air was damp and salty and in a few minutes she was quite far from the house. She looked back and could see it surrounded by the early morning fog. She rolled up her trousers and walked barefoot in the wet sand.

The water was inviting. A swim in the ocean would do her good. Refresh her body and her mind. Slowly, she removed her shirt and trousers, slipped off her panties and left them in a neat pile in a grove of palm trees. No one else in the house would be up for hours and she had the beach to herself.

She ran into the cold, foamy surf. Bill Wilkerson had taught her to swim in the gulf and she was an excellent swimmer, despite the strong waves of the Atlantic. Ten minutes later, refreshed, she ran back to the grove for her clothes.

"Here, I brought you this," a man's voice said and she turned to see Ash Young standing in the grove with a thick, white towel in his hand. He had been hidden by the trees as she approached and now she realized she was completely naked. She wondered how long he had been watching her.

"I saw you dive into the ocean from my window, Christina," he said, smiling. "So I thought you'd need this."

Overnight she had gone from Miss Wilkerson to Christina, she noticed as she took the towel. "That's very nice of you, Ash, but now if you don't mind, I'll put my clothes back on."

"Please do," he laughed. "I'll turn around while you dress."

It was absurd.

Ash was surprised himself that he had come to the palm grove, but something about the girl drew him like a magnet. She was going back to

New York with Mercati but he had to see her again. As they walked back toward the house he approached her about it.

"You know, Christina, if you're going to be the new Eve girl, we'll be thrown together quite a bit," he said. "Socially as well as for business purposes."

"Certainly, Ash," she agreed. "I'd be happy to see you and Mrs. Young any time."

"You don't understand," his tone hardened slightly. "I want to see you alone."

Suddenly, Christina started to regret coming down to Palm Beach. Maybe in her efforts to get around Roberta Rubin she had only made more trouble for herself. But she was not going to encourage Ashley Young just because he could make her the Eve girl.

"It's not my style to go out with married men," she said.

"Not even a man who can control your future?" he said, gray eyes hardening.

"It's true I want to be the Eve girl more than anything else in the world," she admitted. "But not that way."

"I see," he smiled.

She was not sure what the smile meant. She had either just been very smart or very stupid.

"I had a wonderful time here, Ash," she assured him. "And I hope I will see you in New York."

"Oh, you will," he said. "You will."

22

Las Vegas, Nevada
March 1978

Tony Torelli's maroon Rolls Royce called for
the McElroys at one that afternoon and
delivered them at Carlo Gallenzo's mansion a
few minutes later. The house was on a crest
overlooking the Alhambra golf course. It was a
large house, all white and gold inside and white
marble outside, including the swimming pool.
It reproduced the gaudy and sumptuous taste
of the Alhambra, one of the most luxurious
hotels in Las Vegas. In fact, the house belonged
to the corporation controlling the hotel. Who
controlled the corporation was not so clear.

They found their host emerging from the
pool. He was a big man in his middle fifties with
a strong, Roman face and a winning smile. His

thick but muscular body was still dripping wet but he embraced Torelli, crumpling his elegant white linen suit. Then, laughing at the good joke on his friend, he turned to the McElroys, shaking hands with Teddy and gallantly kissing Stephanie's hand.

Don Gallenzo called to another man, a stocky, dark man in casual golf clothes who had been sitting in a lawn chair at the end of the pool. He was introduced as his associate, Renny, shook hands with Teddy and Stephanie, then returned to his chair. Teddy whispered that Renny was Gallenzo's bodyguard and pointed out the outline of his gun and holster underneath the loose-fitting blue shirt. On the rare occasion when he took his eyes off Gallenzo he was scanning the rolling, green lawn. Behind him two Knerps speakers blared out the strains of Verdi's *Aida*.

"*Bellissima!*" Gallenzo exclaimed to Stephanie. "Raffaello could not have painted a greater beauty."

Stephanie giggled, delighted with the compliment but confused because she only knew one Raffaello and he was her hairdresser.

Gallenzo turned back to Torelli to exchange a few words in Italian. There was obviously a special relationship between the two men, visible in the almost conspiratorial way they spoke to each other.

The older man was the Padrino, the *capo de*

tutti capi. His empire of business, vice and gambling reached all the way from lower Manhattan to Los Angeles, from Seattle to the Bahamas. The younger man was one of America's favorite singers, a friend of presidents, a lover of Hollywood's most glamorous women, a man who could command any fee, no matter how astronomical, for an appearance.

They continued their discussion while Teddy and Stephanie went into the pool house to change into their bathing suits, but when they reemerged all conversation ceased. Both men's eyes gravitated to the girl. She was wearing a tiny, white fishnet bikini that revealed her body in all its splendor.

"Divina," Gallenzo muttered. "A body and a face to launch a thousand ships." He considered himself a man of culture and good taste whose appreciation ranged from art and literature to beautiful women. *"Bella come un fiore,"* he added with a poetic touch. "As beautiful as a flower." Unlike most of his cohorts, who spoke a little dialect mixed with bad English, Gallenzo had schooled himself in the Italian of Dante and Boccaccio.

Torelli merely nodded. He couldn't match the older man's vast vocabulary in either language, so he remained silent.

Stephanie had dived into the pool and was swimming with the grace of a mermaid. Teddy, temporarily forgotten, was also splashing around but he could have drowned and no one would have noticed.

After a while, she emerged from the pool like a goddess emerging from the sea. She stretched out on a lounge next to Gallenzo and Torelli. For one full minute no one spoke, but Teddy was aware that both men would have given anything to bed his wife at that moment.

The spell was broken when Marco, Gallenzo's major domo, appeared to announce that luncheon would be served on the patio. They helped themselves to a buffet loaded with antipasto, veal parmigiana and fettuccine and ate by the pool in their bathing suits. As they ate and drank, Carlo Gallenzo noticed with pleasure that the girl had a hearty appetite. To him that was a sign of a hearty appetite for sex. He wondered idly how long the rapidly disintigrating Teddy McElroy was going to be able to keep his lusty, young bride satisfied.

By the time Marco returned with espresso and cigars for the men and Stephanie excused herself to change her clothes, he had made up his mind. He would extend McElroy the credit he wanted. He was probably not worth the risk, but the girl was entrancing and he had been hooked. McElroy had won himself a reprieve.

His old debt would be extended by two weeks and he would get an additional credit line of one hundred thousand dollars at the Alhambra casino. But there would be no more extensions after that.

Unfortunately, Teddy McElroy's problem was not money. Teddy McElroy was simply a fool. In his mind it was all quite clear. Now that he was back in everyone's good graces—Gallenzo's, Torelli's, the Alhambra's—he was hot, he could feel it. And with one hundred thousand dollars to play with, he could pyramid it into a fortune. He would repay his debts and get back to work on his career.

Besides being a fool, Teddy was also a loser. He tried everything, blackjack, roulette, écarté and chemin de fer. The first night he lost ten thousand dollars. The second he doubled his antes, trying to recoup the previous night's losses, and he lost twice as much. He won a few thousand on the third night, but then everything went bad again and by the tenth night he had blown every penny of the one hundred thousand dollar credit line. No more, he was told, and this time they were no longer smiling.

*   *   *

Stephanie Young McElroy had also stopped smiling. She was supposed to be on her honeymoon and her husband spent all his time in the casinos. She had seen all the shows, Tom Jones at Caesars, Ann-Margaret at the Hilton, Helen

Reddy at the MGM-Grand, but she was tired of going alone.

Worse, he hadn't made love to her in ten days. By the time he got into bed at six in the morning after gambling all night he was usually too drunk or too depressed about losing to do anything but pass out. Finally one afternoon as he lay in bed she confronted him.

"Teddy, look at me," she cried. "Have you forgotten I exist?"

"I'm looking at you, I know you exist," he said, struggling to talk. His tongue was heavy and his head felt like a balloon.

"What kind of honeymoon is it when the husband spends all his time gambling and never touches his wife?"

"You know I love you, honey," he mumbled. "I was just carried away a bit." He was in no mood to argue. Now that he was cut off at the Alhambra he was in a hell of a lot of trouble. Even in his hung-over condition he was trying desperately to scheme a way out of it.

Fortunately, Stephanie's tirade was cut short by a call from Tony Torelli. He was to bring Teddy to see Gallenzo again, this time alone. Something he couldn't discuss on the phone. That left Teddy more nervous than ever.

Teddy dressed in a hurry and waited nervously for Torelli to arrive. When he did he greeted Stephanie with a warm smile but the look he gave Teddy was cold.

"We have to hurry, Teddy," was all he said. "They're waiting for us at the Alhambra."

A crestfallen McElroy followed him out of the room.

*   *   *

The door to the suite at the Alhambra was opened by a sallow-faced, sinister-looking type who gave Tony a half smile of recognition and led them silently to the living room. Teddy was so nervous that his knees began to buckle under him as a gargantuan man greeted them.

"*Como'sta,* goombah," the giant said in a harsh, raspy voice as he embraced Torelli, lifting the slight singer like a rag doll.

"I'm fine, Angelo," Torelli said when he recovered his breath. "This is Teddy Mc-Elroy."

"Any friend of Tony's is a friend of mine," Angelo said, taking Teddy's hand.

Teddy winced. The handshake felt like huge pliers crushing bone. So this was Angelo Barboza, the enforcer. He had heard too many stories about "The Butcher" not to know who he was.

"Well, now that the two of you have met, I'll leave you alone," Torelli offered. "I know you've got lots to talk about." With a wave of his hand he left the room.

"Please don't go," Teddy called after him, but the Butcher had already closed the door.

"Just sit down, Ted, I gotta talk to you," the Butcher said. "You wanna drink?"

"Whiskey, please." Teddy sank into one of the soft chairs as the Butcher poured two fingers of Jameson's and handed it to him.

"Now, Teddy boy," he rasped. "You and me has to discuss some financing."

"Yes," Teddy said weakly. At least he was beginning to feel the warm glow of the whiskey.

"You owe the Alhambra two hundred twenty-five thousand dollars. Dat's a lot of moolah. Got any plans how you're gonna pay it?"

"Not exactly," Teddy admitted. "But Don Gallenzo can guarantee for me."

"The Don did you a favor. He put you on the arm for a lot of money. But this is business. You gotta pay up in one week. So we tell you how to do it."

Teddy pulled out his silk handkerchief and began to mop his brow.

"You're lucky, Ted," Barboza continued. "Your father-in-law's a rich guy."

"He'll never pay a dime," Teddy said bitterly.

"Oh, yes, he will," Barboza assured him. "'Cause you got something he wants."

"What's that?" He desperately craved another drink but he was afraid to ask for it.

"You're married to his daughter, pal,"

Barboza smiled. "And you're gonna tell him that for two hundred twenty-five thousand dollars you'll divorce her."

"No way," Teddy said, surprising even himself with the force of his objection. But he was not anxious to divorce his golden goose. Besides, Ash Young would never go for it. He told Barboza as much.

"That's your job, pal," Barboza answered. "You conned the Don this long, you can con that guy outta two hundred twenty-five thousand grand. Think about it."

"I need another drink," Teddy gasped.

"Sure, pal," Barboza said affably and he turned to the bar. As his attention was diverted, Teddy began to move slowly, quietly toward the door, but just as he reached it, Barboza caught his reflection in the mirror over the bar. He dashed across the room, grabbing Teddy by his collar, turning him around and dealing a glancing blow to his kidneys. Teddy moaned and fell to his knees as Barboza gripped his arms and twisted them behind his back.

"Please, Angelo," Teddy begged. "I gotta talk to Gallenzo."

"He don't wanna talk to you 'til you pay what you owe, pal," Barboza answered, tightening his grip.

"Give me a break," Teddy pleaded.

"I'm just doin' what I'm told, pal," Barboza

grunted. Then, like a bored gorilla, he released him and allowed him to stand. He knew as well as Teddy that he had no place to go.

"Wise up, McElroy," he added. "No broad's worth the aggravation."

Teddy wasn't listening. He was too busy trying to decide which hurt him more, his kidneys or his arms. If this was the way the boys treated him when they wanted something, he didn't look forward to disappointing them.

"OK," he said huskily. His throat felt dry and sore. "Can I get that drink now?"

Barboza shook his head. "No time. You gotta leave for New York tomorrow. You come back with the money, you get all the drinks you want."

"What happens if Young doesn't bite?"

"That's your problem, pal," Barboza's face twisted in a grimace meant to be a smile. "I just want the money."

"And if I can't get it?"

"Then you better pray, pal, 'cause you're one dead fish."

*　　*　　*

Dead fish don't swim, but as Teddy McElroy left the Alhambra he decided that he still had a lot of swimming to do. There was no way Ashley Young was going to buy a divorce, no matter how much he hated him, but there might be another way out.

He recalled that Stephanie had once mentioned bonds in a bank in New York. A scheme began to form in his mind and by the time he returned to their suite he was sure of exactly what he was going to do. He was the old Teddy again. A winner.

Stephanie was in the bedroom, watching television and still pouting. He ignored it.

"Stephanie, honey, I'm sorry for the way I've behaved," he said contritely. "I've been a fool. Here I am, married to the most beautiful girl in the world and what do I do but leave her alone all night. I'd deserve it if you threw me out."

"Well," Stephanie answered, a bit soothed. "I'm glad that you admit it."

"I just hope you can forgive me," he insisted. "And I promise, I'm through with gambling."

"Really?"

He sat beside her on the bed. "Sure, I've just been at loose ends, waiting for the right deal to come along," he improvised. "And now it has."

"Tell me about it," she said, her curiosity aroused.

"I'm part of a consortium, honey, that's a group of partners, and we're putting together one of the biggest gold deals in history." He noticed with pleasure that she was listening. "It's a five million dollar package, divided by five partners, and we each stand to make a fifty percent profit. With the dollar going down and gold going up there's no way we can lose. Each of us has to put down fifty grand in cash, though."

"What's wrong with that?" she asked.

"Well, unfortunately, most of my capital is tied up in a picture I'm co-producing and in my land deal in the Fiji Islands. But I'm flying to New York tomorrow to arrange a loan."

Stephanie brightened. "Teddy, I have some bonds in New York. Maybe you could use them if your bank doesn't come through fast enough."

"I wouldn't want to do that, Stephanie. But I appreciate the offer." He took her in his arms and kissed her. "If I do need your bonds I'd only take them as a guarantee. I wouldn't even cash them."

*   *   *

That night they skipped dinner and the casinos. When Teddy left for New York in the morning, he had a letter from his wife authorizing her bank to give him her bonds.

*   *   *

In a way, the gold deal sounded so great that Teddy regretted that it did not exist. On the other hand, a horse named Starlight did and she was running in the third race at Santa Anita on

Sunday, three days away, and paying 5 to 1. Not that he was putting all his eggs in one basket. He would put down forty thousand dollars from the bonds on the horse and spread the rest around on the Colts-Jets game and some crap games in New York. He was feeling lucky, and by the time the weekend was over and it was time to return to Vegas he would have enough to pay the Butcher, not to mention Stephanie. Yes, Teddy could see it all before him, as he had seen so many other schemes in his life.

23

Las Vegas, Nevada

The same day that Teddy McElroy took off for New York, Carlo Gallenzo invited Stephanie for lunch at his villa. This time there were no other guests and he could ask her a question that had puzzled him for weeks.

"Stephanie," he began gently. "Please don't take offense at what I'm going to say, but tell me, why did you marry Teddy?"

The question surprised her and she thought before answering. "Because I fell in love with him." But she realized that was not the exact truth. "No," she added. "It happened so fast, I probably did it on an impulse."

She wondered if Carlo had ever been lonely or frightened and if he would understand someone who was. She was afraid to be alone, that was why she had married Teddy McElroy in a twenty-four hour wedding chapel and that was why she was still here. It was like her father taught her, she had to keep climbing back on the bike.

"I see," Carlo was saying. "And now that you're married, you're happy?"

"You're getting very personal today, Carlo, aren't you?"

"Stephanie, if you want me to stop I will," he said gently. "But I'm asking these questions because I care about you. I'm concerned."

"All right then, to answer your question, I don't know," she said. "Since we've been here Teddy's changed. All that gambling and drinking—it's driving me crazy."

"That's what I wanted to talk to you about," said Gallenzo. "Because your husband is in serious trouble."

"What sort of trouble?"

"Well, to begin with, he owes the Alhambra two hundred twenty-five thousand dollars."

"Oh, he can afford it," she said lightly. "Teddy made lots in the movies and he has all kinds of investments."

"No, Stephanie. Your husband is broke. He is also a liar and a fortune hunter."

Stephanie stared at Gallenzo. She was shocked, though at the same time she knew that what he said was true. She had been a fool to marry a man she hardly knew, a man she had picked up in a discotheque. And now she couldn't even turn to Alex or her father.

"I suppose some of it is my fault," he said gently. "I kept extending his credit because I thought he might leave and I wouldn't see you anymore."

She reached for his thick, square hand and squeezed it. "I'm glad I stayed," she said.

"*Cara,* nothing will happen to you, I assure you," he said. "Unfortunately, I'll be out of town for a few days. I'll be back Tuesday and when your husband returns we'll see what happens. But whatever happens I doubt you'll want to stay with him."

She didn't answer.

"If you need anything or you need to get in touch with me, just call me at La Cantina. Remember, you're here under my protection," he continued. "Stephanie, I care for you. *Ti voglio bene.*"

"I care for you too, Carlo."

He took her hand and kissed it.

* * *

Gallenzo was not anxious to leave Las Vegas or Stephanie, but there were important matters to attend to. The whole underworld was in a state of turmoil. A wind of war was blowing from New York, where boss was being pitted against boss and new armies of thugs were being recruited by opposing families. They were bringing young Sicilians in through Canada and Mexico, old country Mafiosi recruited for just one purpose: to bring back respect and honor to La Cosa Nostra.

Don Gallenzo had no objection to a reflowering of old country traditions and respect, but as boss of all bosses he could not allow a new bloodletting to take place. The future of La Cosa Nostra was in danger and that was why he had summoned the *capi* to La Cantina, the exclusive Southern California resort near Palm Springs.

*   *   *

The night Gallenzo left, Tony Torelli made his move. He had been waiting for a chance at Stephanie McElroy ever since the afternoon he saw her beside Gallenzo's pool in that white bikini. Teddy McElroy must be a fool to leave his lusty, new bride alone in Las Vegas, and as for Carlo, Torelli convinced himself that he was actually doing his *padrone* a favor. The new Mrs. McElroy was not going to sit up in that suite at Caesar's forever. At least with him she would be in excellent hands.

When Stephanie accepted Torelli's invitation to dinner, she assumed they were going someplace like Dome of the Sea or the Bachanalle. But as he took her back to his suite at the Alhambra, he explained that it was hard for him to eat in any of the restaurants in Vegas because the fans kept bothering him. Instead, they would have privacy and comfort, alone together.

When they arrived at his suite the table had already been set on the terrace and from it they could see the bright neon skyline of Las Vegas. A waiter brought out chateaubriand and tomatoes and roquefort salad. While they polished it off with a dark red burgundy, Torelli told Stephanie about the ups and downs of his career.

"I owe everything to the Don," he said. "Everyone said I was washed up ten years ago, but he brought me here, he gave me a second chance."

"He's really an exceptional man, isn't he?" Stephanie agreed.

"Yeah," Tony said. "I'd play here for nothing, but fortunately," he grinned. "I bring in the high rollers, so I get plenty."

The waiter had reappeared with a chocolate and coffee mousse and Grand Marnier and *espresso*. As he served it, Stephanie stood up.

"I almost forgot," she said, pulling a clumsily wrapped package from her purse.

Tony unwrapped it. Inside was a gold cigarette case. It must have easily cost five thousand dollars. "Hey, kid, you didn't have to do this." He was genuinely embarrassed. He would have been even more embarrassed had he known that Stephanie hadn't yet paid for it—just charged it at the Van Cleef jewelry shop downstairs. Even when he was down and out he didn't take expensive gifts from women and, unlike her husband, he could afford his own cigarette case.

"You've been so nice to Teddy and me," she insisted. "I want you to have it. I've got plenty of money." She leaned over to kiss him and he took her hand and kissed it. He held her hand and stared at her over the candles.

"You're very beautiful, Stephanie," he said at last. "You shouldn't be alone." He stood up and came to her side of the table. He began to kiss her neck. She turned and looked up at him. She had made a mistake to rush into marriage with Teddy. Tony Torelli was the kind of man she needed. Strong, forceful. He took her hand again and gently pulled her back inside the suite. He led her to his bedroom, a huge room with red walls and a red shag rug and a red silk cover on the huge bed.

He opened the tie of her dress. It flew open and underneath she was wearing nothing. He began to nibble on her neck and caress her breasts as the dress fell to the floor.

It had been three weeks since Teddy had made love to her but she forgot all about him. He was in New York and she was here. With Tony. And Tony really cared about her, she could tell.

He lowered her onto the bed and turned her on her stomach. "I'm going to give you a special treatment, baby," he whispered hoarsely. Like Greeks and Arabs, Sicilians are very fond of the *culo* and he had been thinking about her firm, pink *culo* since that first afternoon at Gallenzo's. He parted her legs, placing a knee between them and pressing it hard against her. Next he lifted her by the waist, raising her to her knees and caressing her breasts as he penetrated her deeply from behind.

She screamed in pain and tried to resist, but he continued, relentlessly. At first it was like being raped, but gradually her pain turned to pleasure, then ecstasy as she climaxed with a violence she had never felt before.

* * *

It was seven in the morning when Stephanie returned to Caesar's but the lobby was still crowded with tourists and gamblers and the casino was as noisy as ever. Her phone was ringing when she came into the suite.

"Stephanie?" her father's voice was brusque. "McElroy was just here."

"What?" She was still groggy from the session with Tony.

"Sister, you really know how to pick them," he went on. "He offered to divorce you for a quarter of a million. I told him I wouldn't give him a quarter. I could have him arrested for bigamy, you know. He married you without ever divorcing Beatrice Carhart!"

Stephanie sat down on the bed. "Are you kidding, Daddy?" she asked. She was incredulous.

"Of course not. Beatrice told me herself the decree hasn't been granted yet. You're still a free woman."

"Where's Teddy now?"

"He ran out of here when I threatened to call the cops."

She was stunned. First, Carlo Gallenzo told her that her husband was a liar and now her father was saying that Teddy was willing to divorce her, forget all the lies he had told her about loving her, for a quarter of a million dollars.

"Oh, there's something else," her father went on, his voice heavy with sarcasm. He sounded as though he was telling a good story, but he always did find other people's stupidity amusing. "Your beloved forged your signature and tried to cash your bonds. Fortunately, the bank called me. So that makes two felonies he's committed."

"What can I say, Daddy?" she sighed. "That I really know how to pick them?"

"Don't say anything, sister," he snapped. "Just get lost."

*　　　*　　　*

Stephanie put the phone down. There was a bitter taste in her mouth, the same way she felt

289

every time she spoke with her father. Of course he was right about Teddy McElroy. But he was wrong about everything else, about the way he treated her, had always treated her. He was wrong as a father, wrong as a man.

She had to talk to someone. She quickly dialed Tony at the Alhambra. The hotel operator told her that Mr. Torelli had left Las Vegas just an hour ago.

"Checked out?" she cried. She had only been with him a few hours ago. He must have left his suite right after she did. "What about tonight's show?"

"Sammy Davis Jr. is replacing Mr. Torelli," the operator said.

Stephanie put the phone back down. She just couldn't believe it. Last night he had made love to her, possessed her, now he was gone without a word of goodbye.

She looked out the sliding glass windows toward the sky. It was full of clouds. They seemed to be closing in on her everywhere. She shivered and threw herself on the bed.

She lay there for an hour, maybe more. Then the phone rang again. It was Carlo. At least he would understand.

"I called you several times last night," he said, his tone cold. "But there was no answer."

"I had dinner with Tony; I guess I stayed out a little late."

"I know."

Suddenly she knew also. She knew why Torelli's show had been cancelled and why he had left so abruptly.

"Carlo," she said childishly. "I have something to tell you. I'm not married."

"What do you mean?"

"Daddy called this morning to tell me Teddy's not even divorced from Mrs. Carhart."

"Congratulations, *cara*," he said with more warmth.

"Imagine, being congratulated for not being married," she said wistfully. "Oh, Carlo I miss you. I need you here. When Teddy comes back it's going to be such a mess."

"Don't worry about him, Stephanie," he assured her. "I'll be back tomorrow."

"I'll be waiting."

* * *

It was the afternoon of the following day that Teddy McElroy returned from his New York adventure, defeated but still undaunted. He had no particular idea how to extricate himself from the mess he was in but he had every intention of surviving and he knew that the safest place for that was near his beautiful bride.

He was sure Young would by now have informed Stephanie of what had happened. She would be angry, of course, but he would take

291

her in his arms, tell her that he was forced to do it, and then make love to her, perhaps using the ring trick once more on her, and the little nympho would forgive him.

Then he would send her to plead with Gallenzo, if necessary even let her go to bed with the Don, and everything would be fixed.

But things didn't turn out exactly as planned. He made a cheerful entrance with a, "Hi, darling, have you missed me?" And he went over to kiss her, but she turned away.

"Daddy called yesterday. He told me everything."

So Ash Young moved fast, as he had expected. "I was forced to do it, Stephanie," he pleaded. "Or they would kill me. But don't worry." He took a pistol from his coat and slammed it on the table.

"Who would kill you? I don't believe a word of it. It's just like your story about the gold," she screamed.

"No, it's true, I swear. The Butcher said he'd kill me unless I paid back the money I lost. He forced me to see your father about it."

Stephanie stared at him. He had changed so much in the three weeks they had been together. The strain of his gambling problems was getting to him. His eyes were red, he was unshaven and his suit looked like he had slept in it. She wondered how she could have ever believed that this man could make her happy.

"The Butcher, who's that?" she asked.

"He's Gallenzo's executioner."

"You're lying, Carlo is a gentleman. He'd never do a thing like that. And you lied about being divorced from that old woman and you lied about everything else. You even stole from me. Now I hope you go to jail."

That made him lose control.

"You little bitch!" he yelled as he slapped her across the face so hard she fell to the floor.

She was up in a second and threw herself at him screaming. All the anger that had been building for weeks came out as she clawed and kicked like a hellcat. Then she saw the gun and grabbed it. But Teddy was faster. Before she could point it at him, he caught her with a punch on the jaw. She collapsed like a rag doll as everything around her went black. That was the last thing she remembered.

24

New York, N.Y.

Christina came back from her triumphant
Palm Beach weekend to shattering news. On
Monday morning Barbara Sawyer called.
Sounding even more agitated than usual, she
urged Christina to come to the Casardi office
right away.

"What's going on love?" a sleepy eyed
Melinda asked as she poured them both black
coffee.

"I don't know, Melinda," but somehow she
knew it was not good news. "The Eve contract
was ready to sign when I left, and now it sounds
like everything is up in the air."

"Maybe you should have been nicer to Ash
Young," Melinda teased.

A concerned Jean Casardi and Barbara
Sawyer were waiting for her in his office.

"I just heard from a friend of mine at Eve that they're talking to their lawyers about backing out of the contract," Jean told her. "They're hinting about problems with your reputation."

Christina was stunned. All she could do was stare at Casardi.

"That's not all," Barbara added. "The *Vogue* cover and the *Harper's Bazaar* assignment have both been cancelled."

That was an even worse blow. The covers would have established her as a major new model and doubled her fee.

"I don't understand," Christina said weakly.

"To bring it to a point," Barbara said, "the whole ugly Tommy Dexter story is all over the trade. *Women's Wear Daily* has a blind item about it this morning."

"But I don't understand. Tommy apologized. We're friends. He even took the test shots for the Eve campaign." *That was it*, she realized. Roberta Rubin was behind it. She was the only other person who knew about the Tommy Dexter incident.

"Frankly, Christina," Casardi said. "Your entire career is in jeopardy. You'd better get this straightened out."

Christina went home to the apartment in a deep depression. Her whole world was collapsing. The Eve contract meant that she could bring her mother to New York and look after her. She just couldn't lose it because of a lecherous photographer and a libidinous lesbian who wouldn't take no for an answer.

The telephone was ringing as she came in the door. She picked it up, not really wanting to talk to anyone, not even Alex Mercati.

"Christina?"

It was Ash Young. Exactly what she needed to make the day complete, a call from a lusting tycoon. Maybe Melinda was right and he was behind the latest developments.

"Yes, Ash, how are you?" she said evenly.

"I'm very well, thank you," he answered in clipped tones. "But I'd like to see you as soon as possible."

"I'm afraid I'm very busy now," she said, although it looked like she was going to have a lot of free time on her hands soon. Besides, she had already made it clear to him that she was not interested in a married man.

"This is a business matter, Christina," he said brusquely. "It concerns the Eve campaign. I expect you in my office at two o'clock sharp."

As she prepared for the meeting she wondered if tangling with Ashley Young was going to be any more pleasant than tangling with Roberta Rubin.

*   *   *

Ash had been surprised when his marketing director told him that perhaps they should reconsider signing Christina Wilkerson. He knew enough about Roberta Rubin's habits to smell a rat.

Young's office in the Young building was furnished in the best of British antiques. Most of the floor-to-ceiling mahogany bookcases, the hunting prints, the comfortable red leather sofa and the dark green leather wing chairs had been taken from the country home of the impoverished Earl of Cassel. And Young worked at the very same ornately carved desk where the Earl's ancestor plotted restoring Charles II to the Crown.

Christina Wilkerson sat in front of him in one of the wing chairs. She was wearing a gray suit softened by the white silk blouse that tied in a bow at her neck. Her black hair was pulled loosely back, tied with a green ribbon. Her green eyes were angry. She had just finished telling Ash her side of the Rubin-Dexter episode, most of which came as no surprise.

The Young Company carefully researched all its top executives, and some disturbing rumors about Roberta had reached him in the past. Still, she was the driving force behind the revitalization of Eve. The whole Eve Girl campaign had been her idea, and as long as she kept out of trouble he could not care less if she fucked men, women or dogs.

"Well, you've had quite an introduction to New York," he said.

297

Christina disliked the paternal tone in his voice, but she concentrated on what it would mean to be the Eve Girl—with money that would bring her mother to New York, giving her some real care. She smiled back at Ash.

"I hope you've learned your lesson, Christina. You're living in a jungle and you'll have to be tough to survive." He turned to his intercom and instructed his secretary to bring in Roberta Rubin. When the blond executive arrived, she was obviously surprised to find Christina in Ash's office.

"Now Miss Rubin," he said. "I understand that you and Miss Wilkerson had a misunderstanding. But I've warned you that we can't let your personal life interfere with Eve cosmetics, can we?"

Roberta Rubin glared at her, her face white with rage.

"I don't know what she's talking about," she said.

"It doesn't matter," Ash announced. "But I want you to stop harassing her. Withdraw the insinuations and the contracts will be signed immediately."

"Is that all?" Roberta obviously knew when she had been beaten.

"Yes, thank you." Ash dismissed her.

She left the room quickly and they were alone again.

"Thank you," Christina said.

He smiled at her, his gray eyes warming slightly. "Just remember that you owe me," he said. "Now I'd like you to be my guest at dinner tomorrow night. We'll celebrate your becoming the Eve Girl."

Before Christina could think of an excuse, he had summoned his secretary and she was being escorted to the elevator. Ash Young was certainly a man of action.

That night, over dinner in a secluded corner at L'Aiglon, Christina confided the details of her meeting to Alex Mercati.

"I'm impressed with you, Christina," he said. "You handled that very well. But I have to warn you that you're playing with fire when you go up against the Roberta Rubins and the Ash Youngs of the world."

"I'll be careful," she smiled.

Later he took her home to his townhouse for a nightcap. He brought her up to his bedroom and they lay on his bed, sipping Courvoisier and staring up at the skylight. The March sky was dark and almost starless. Gently he took her in his arms and kissed her as his hand moved over her breast. She trembled slightly. "I love you, Christina," he whispered. In the dim light he began to undress her. When she was naked he hastily undressed himself, then returned to her and began to kiss her on the mouth, the ears, the neck. He was moving down her body, kissing her stomach, then her thighs.

Instinctively, she reached for him and began to caress him as he moved on top of her. He lifted her and together they began to move, completely, passionately, wondrously.

*   *   *

"Congratulations, Miss Wilkerson, and welcome to the family," Ash Young said the following morning as he handed Christina a check for ten thousand dollars, the first installment on her contract. A grim Roberta Rubin and the jubilant Jean Casardi and Barbara Sawyer stood by in the all white conference room as she signed the two year contract to represent Eve Cosmetics as the Eve Girl.

Still flushed from her night with Alex, Christina smiled graciously and accepted their good wishes. Roberta opened the conference room door and a retinue of sales people entered, along with a trio of white jacketed waiters bearing bottles of champagne. They all raised a toast to the new Eve Girl.

Ash led her through the crowd, introducing her to the executives she would be working with. One of the first was Herb Daley, the pudgy, balding head of promotion.

"I'd like to see you tomorrow, Miss Wilkerson," he said. "I'll need your curriculum vitae and any other pertinent data to send to the press."

"There's not much to tell about me, Mr. Daley, but I'll be happy to make up any story you want."

He chuckled and picked up another glass of champagne from a passing waiter. "That won't be necessary, Miss Wilkerson. We'll find a few interesting things to say, I'm sure."

She was beginning to realize that she could play this role to the hilt. She had signed the contract and she would live up to the fine print. But there was nothing in it that said she had to go to bed with Ash Young or any of his lecherous executives, up to and including Herb Daley and Roberta Rubin.

That night Ash Young's chauffeur, a black man in a black uniform, picked Christina up in a black limousine and delivered her to "21." Ash—impeccably dressed as usual—was waiting in the mahogany panelled reception room. His gray eyes were unsmiling, austere, almost grim. He greeted her with a handshake, still baffling her about the purpose of the dinner. Supposedly it was to celebrate the contract, but she suspected there was going to be more.

The head waiter led them directly to the corner round table. It could accommodate eight people, but Ash sat there even when he was alone.

Since turning fifty, he had become obsessed with his health. Except for the lavish dinners he consumed when entertaining at Belvedere or Fifth Avenue, he stuck to the rigid diet that Dr. Reinhardt gave him: broiled filet of sole, plain spinach, no dessert, and plain tea.

"I'm keeping a close check on my chloresterol," Ash explained.

As Christina polished off her filet Rossini, baked potato and arugula salad, he gave her an exact calorie count for each dish. He winced every time she sipped her glass of bordeaux. Just for spite, she ordered strawberries and cream for dessert.

"I have an investment in you now," he warned. "I don't want to see the Eve girl fall apart."

So that was it. He seemed to think that by signing that contract she had become as much his possession as one of his Louis XVI fauteuils.

"You don't smoke, do you, Christina?" he asked.

"I don't like the taste."

"Good, there's nothing I hate more than a woman who smells like cigarette smoke," he said. "I gave it up fourteen years ago when the Surgeon General's report came out and I've never regretted it."

"Tell me, Ash, do you have any vices, any weaknesses?" she asked, laughing.

"Of course, I have my weak points," he said severely. "But I try not to show them."

There was no question that Ash Young was a distinguished looking—even handsome—man, but there was something about the coldness in those gray eyes that made her uncomfortable.

"Just remember, Christina," he continued. "You're going to represent Eve. Your face will be on television and magazines all over the country. You'll be smiling from a thousand posters. I want to take special care of you."

"Personally or professionally?"

"Both." More than an affirmation, it sounded like a command.

"I thought you were a happily married man."

"A man can be married, Christina, and still be attracted to another woman," Ash confirmed, though he considered himself above that sort of thing—until now.

"True. But for a single girl to get involved with a married man is stupid and can only lead to trouble," she said. "And how would Mrs. Young feel?"

"Let me worry about that," he snapped.

"Don't you love your wife?"

He hesitated. "I like Jessica, but I don't love her."

"Have you ever loved anyone Ash?"

He *seemed* to be thinking about the answer

to that one, too. But he evaded it. "That's an unfair question."

"I don't think so," she insisted. "If I'm to consider a relationship with a man, I have a right to know what kind of man he is."

"What kind of man do you think I am?"

She pondered a few seconds. "I think you're smart and cool. But I don't think your heart rules your head. I don't think you've ever loved."

He smiled. "But I'm in love with you."

"I doubt that, Ash. You may think you are, but love doesn't come easy to a man like you. Have you ever loved another woman?"

"I was in love once," he said, his tone subdued. "With a girl as beautiful as you. But she turned out to be a tramp," he added defiantly. "It was a long time ago."

"What ever happened to her?"

"I don't know, and I don't care."

"Did she hurt you? Was she unfaithful to you?"

"You should have been a lawyer, Christina," he said with irritation. "No, I don't think she was unfaithful to me. But I found out what she did before she met me. She was a waitress in a pick-up joint and slept with all sorts of guys."

"Poor Ash," she shook her head. "No wonder you want to know about me. You should dig into my shady past."

"Do you have a past, Christina?"

"My past is very ordinary, Ash. I had a mother and father who loved each other and me. I grew up in Houston, and if my father hadn't died last fall I probably wouldn't even be here."

"I'm sorry about your father, Christina, but I'm glad you're here. It's been a long time since I've met anyone as exciting as you."

"What is it you want, Ash?" Christina asked. "For me to be your mistress?"

"I didn't say that," he protested.

"Do you want to marry me?"

"Perhaps."

"Knowing so little about me?"

"No matter what the past, Christina."

"That's big of you," she mocked. "But you just let me know what Mrs. Young has to say about all this and then we can have dinner again."

She rose from the table, shook his hand and left the restaurant.

*   *   *

Alex Mercati would have been pleased to know how little Christina was enjoying dinner. He had been expecting to take her out for a celebration of the contract, but when he called at the last minute, she told him she was dining with Ash Young.

He did not like the sound of that. He had seen

the way Young looked at Christina at Belvedere, and he recognized that look. He was in love with Christina Wilkerson himself. Now, to his dismay, he had to admit that he was feeling intense jealousy.

No, he told himself. Christina was too smart to fall for someone like Ash Young. He stared at the clock on his desk. It was eleven. Perhaps if he was right she could be home by now. He decided to call.

She picked up the phone on the second ring.

"How was your evening with the boss?" He tried to sound casual.

"Fine, Alex. But he doesn't take no for an answer. It's obvious that most of the time he gets his own way."

"I hope not this time."

"No," she laughed. "Not this time."

"Well, then, how about coming over here?"

"Not tonight, Alex. I don't know why, but I feel nervous and bushed," she said. "Wish me luck with the shooting tomorrow and a big kiss to you."

"Good night, Christina. I love you."

"I love you too," she answered.

Part Six

25

Las Vegas, Nevada

The suicide of actor-playboy Teddy McElroy made national news. According to the police report, he shot himself and died instantly, sometime between five and seven p.m. A hotel detective, summoned by other hotel guests who had heard the sound of gunshots in the McElroy suite, found him lying in a pool of blood, the gun still in his hand. The reason for the suicide was unclear, although it was known that the actor had career problems and huge gambling debts.

The real mystery was the abrupt disappearance of McElroy's bride, the madcap heiress, Stephanie Young. As reporters were quick to discover, the couple was never legally married and McElroy was in fact a bigamist.

Miss Young's father issued a statement to the press:

"I don't know why Mr. McElroy shot himself, but it was not soon enough. I had the displeasure of meeting him only once, when he came to see me about my daughter. I threw him out. Why my daughter ever became mixed up with this adventurer is the mystery of today's youth. Some take drugs, some become terrorists. It seems my daughter marries swindlers."

While reporters searched for the missing bride, she was safely ensconced in Carlo Gallenzo's mansion. He had advised his good friend, Captain John Oberdorfer of the Las Vegas Police Department, that Stephanie had been his guest during the hours when McElroy shot himself. She would, of course, be available to talk to him whenever he wished, but he wanted to shield her from the press. Therefore, her whereabouts must be kept secret.

Stephanie spent most of the time beside Carlo's pool, lying in the sun. She was still in shock. She could recall the awful fight with Teddy, but after that she could remember nothing. Carlo had explained that he and his bodyguard, Renny, had heard her fighting with Teddy, then the sound of the gun. By the time they managed to break into the suite, they found her unconscious beside her husband's body. There was no doubt, Gallenzo assured her, that he had killed himself.

That part just didn't make sense to Stephanie and she thought about it over and over as she lay by the pool. If Teddy wanted to die, he would have let her shoot him when they were struggling. Besides, he wasn't the type to take his own life. He always believed he would get out of whatever fix he was in. The whole idea of suicide just wasn't like Teddy.

But if he didn't kill himself, who killed him? She was absolutely sure she had not. But the more she thought about it, the more she began to see that it could have only been Carlo. He had saved her from Teddy. He did it because he loved her, she was sure of that.

It was exciting to think that a man could love her enough to kill for her.

In the next few weeks another mystery developed. Here she was, living in Carlo's house, eternally grateful to him because he had rescued her from a madman, and Carlo didn't take advantage of it. He was obviously attracted to her, but his attitude remained courtly and distant.

She wistfully remembered a novel she had read at Foxhall about the lords of old who had the right to take the brides of their subjects on the first night. Not that this was her first night, but living in his house she was sort of like a subject of Carlo's and she somewhat regretted that he did not enforce his *droit du seigneur*.

Well, if he was not going to make the first move, it was up to her. One night, after she and Carlo had both retired to their respective bedrooms, she decided to act.

She took out the transparent peach silk dressing gown she had bought when she first married Teddy. Unfortunately, she never had a chance to wear it. Now she was glad she had saved it. As she put it on she noticed that it showed every curve. If this did not do it, nothing would.

Paolo, the night guard, was seated at the end of the hall and she passed him on her way to Carlo's room. He winked and she winked back. She was now so used to Carlo's guards that they were like part of the furniture.

She knocked gently on Carlo's door.

"Come in," he said.

He was sitting up in bed, reading, but he put aside the book and smiled when he saw her. He too had been waiting for this moment.

"Carlo," she said softly. "I'm all on edge tonight. I hope you don't mind my coming to talk to you. I just can't fall asleep."

Their eyes locked for an instant as she stood over the bed. He raised his strong arms and pulled her down onto the bed. Their mouths met for a long hungry kiss. His large square hands roamed her body and he quickly loosened the robe. It slipped to the floor.

He brought her to him. *"Ti amo,"* he whispered. *"Cara."*

* * *

Stephanie and Carlo had barely begun their affair when he had to leave for another meeting at La Cantina. He had summoned the heads of crime families from all over the United States, and the plush California spa was bursting with activity when he arrived.

The atmosphere was almost festive, but Gallenzo's reason for calling the meeting was serious. Salvatore Patriarca, the don from New Jersey, was challenging Gallenzo's leadership. Ordinarily, that wouldn't have worried him because Patriarca was a brainless bully, but he was being advised by Phil Fox. The former accountant was as smart as his name indicated and he had a lot of influence with the other bosses who resented Gallenzo's authority.

The first day's meeting confirmed Gallenzo's worst suspicions. Patriarca took exception to everything he proposed and Fox suggested mellifluously that he should perhaps take a little vacation to Italy to escape the heat from the IRS and the FBI. They all knew that was a polite way of suggesting he hand over control to Patriarca.

But what really alarmed Gallenzo was the realization that many of the other men seemed to be leaning toward Patriarca. Counting heads at the conference table one afternoon Gallenzo felt sure of only two men: Frank Magliocco and Vito Fiumara. Well, he still had three days.

For the next two days he used all his resources to battle Patriarca at the meetings and to do some lobbying on the golf course, in the steambath and by the pool. He cajoled, promised and threatened. By the time the convention was over and they were all ready to return to their home grounds, he thought he had the situation pretty well in hand. Only "Punchy" Gennaro, the Louisiana delegate, and Massachusetts's Lou Puzzangara, still leaned toward Patriarca. Gallenzo would have to take care of them later.

He flew back to Las Vegas that night, satisfied with the work he had accomplished at La Cantina. Had he known the names of two of the passengers on the next plane, he might have been less lighthearted. Joe Bruccola and Vincent Accaro, two of Patriarca's hit men, landed in Vegas exactly two hours after Gallenzo. A car met them at the airport and carried them, not to one of the plush hotels on the strip, but to a small hotel nearby. They didn't plan to stay in town long.

Stephanie was waiting for Carlo in the doorway when he arrived home. She was wearing a blue silk caftan that clung to her body and was slit to reveal her long tanned legs. She squealed with delight when she unwrapped the present he had brought her, a diamond necklace, and insisted he put it on her.

"I missed you, *amore mio*," he whispered as he touched her neck.

"I missed you too, Carlo."

During the three days he had been gone she had found time to think. She was not a reflective person, but she knew that she cared for him in a deeper and more meaningful way than she had ever cared for anyone before. With Carlo she felt safe and loved, feelings she had rarely known.

They had dinner by the terrace, but they hardly touched their food. They were too busy holding hands, touching each other, exchanging small kisses and looking into each other's eyes.

When Marco noticed that his master hadn't finished his *espresso*, he shook his head in wonder. But Carlo and Stephanie were already walking hand in hand toward his room upstairs.

The moon was full that night, bathing Carlo's room in a silver light.

"*Bambina mia*," he muttered as he kissed her again. "I want every part of you."

"I love you, Carlo," she answered.

They made love hungrily, their need sharpened by three days of separation. So consumed were they by their passion that they did not hear the strangers enter the house—until there was a crashing at the door. The room was suddenly lit by the fire of machine guns, their bullets tearing into Carlo's back.

They must have thought Stephanie was dead too because, in a last convulsive reflex, Carlo's head bounced against hers, covering her face with blood and knocking her unconscious.

The police, called by a terrified cook who had been awakened by the sound of gunfire, found them as they were, Carlo's body on top of Stephanie. She was rushed to Las Vegas hospital. They found Marco lying in the kitchen: he had been strangled with a thin wire that had cut deep into his throat. Gallenzo's two bodyguards, Paolo and Renny, had mysteriously disappeared.

Stephanie's condition actually was not that serious. One bullet had grazed her head, another had gone through Gallenzo's body and spent itself near her hip and a third had broken her tibia. Otherwise, she was in a state of shock. And to the despair of the Las Vegas police, she couldn't recall much of what had happened or give any description, except that there were two men and they had mean eyes.

A few days later, FBI Special Agent Victor Procaci arrived in Las Vegas to interrogate the girl. At twenty-nine, Procaci was a tall, handsome man with black curly hair and large dark brown eyes. He was a native New Yorker who had grown up in a Brooklyn neighborhood where the three career paths for young men led to crime, the Church, or the police. Vic Procaci became an FBI agent.

After graduating from St. John's Law School and a hitch in Vietnam, he joined the Justice Department's investigative arm in 1972 and was immediately sent to the intensive twelve week training program at Quantico, Virginia. In the five years since then, he had been promoted to Special Agent with the Organized Crime Section.

He had nothing against La Cosa Nostra's gambling operations, but he hated the fact that most of the profits went to fund narcotics, prostitution and shylocks. Most of all, he hated the bad name it gave Italian Americans, most of whom were as honest and hardworking as his own family. He wanted to destroy people like Patriarca, wipe them from the face of the earth. That was what had brought him to Las Vegas. He was quite sure that somehow Patriarca was involved in the Gallenzo hit.

With his manner and warmth, Procaci had been able to overcome one of the Bureau's major problems: friction between the Bureau and local U.S. attorneys who resented an outsider intruding on their investigations. Procaci was a guy they could trust.

It was this same natural warmth that Stephanie Young responded to as she looked up at the handsome young agent from her hospital bed. She was pale and haggard from her ordeal, but to Procaci she looked like a pink and gold angel. The room itself was a bare hospital cubicle, but it was filled with flowers from Stephanie's grandparents and friends—none from her father and mother, however.

"Hello, Mr. Procaci," she said in that breathless finishing school voice. "That nice policeman outside told me you were coming."

"Good," he said gently as he seated himself beside her bed. "Do you know why I'm here?"

"Not really," she giggled and her blue eyes twinkled mischievously. She was still groggy from medication, but she could tell this young FBI agent was very sexy. She was beginning to feel better already.

"I'm with the Organized Crime Section of the Bureau," he explained. "And my job is to investigate and collect evidence so that the Justice Department can indict and prosecute."

He knew he sounded like he was talking to a child, but this girl, in spite of the wild stories he had heard, still seemed like a child. He wondered how she ever got mixed up with Carlo Gallenzo.

"Do you live here?" she asked, her mind wandering already.

"No, I work out of the New York field office," he said. "But I travel all over the country when I'm on a case. Right now I want to get the men who killed your friend Gallenzo—and the man who ordered the hit."

"Oh, I hope you do!" she said. Her eyes

welled up with tears. "They had no right to do that!"

"I need your help, Miss Young," Procaci continued. "I want you to think about it even though I know it hurts." He brought out some black and white glossy photographs and spread them out on the bed. They were mug shots and candids of Salvatore Patriarca, Phil Fox and several hired guns they were known to use, including Joe Bruccola and Vinnie Accaro. He already knew that Bruccola and Accaro had been in Vegas the night Gallenzo was murdered. "Do you recognize any of these men?" he asked.

She stared at the photographs, but it was no use. She shook her head.

He hid his disappointment and smiled as he stood up. "Thank you anyway, Miss Young. You rest well now and I'll be visiting you again soon."

"I hope so!" she smiled back.

Outside in the hall, Procaci nodded at the two Las Vegas uniformed policemen guarding Stephanie's door and returned to the parking lot. He was worried. Whoever had killed Gallenzo didn't know that she couldn't identify them and they were going to be back to finish the job. The underworld didn't believe in leaving a dangerous witness alive. Sooner or later she would have to leave the hospital and when she did she would be an easy target.

Lou Owsley, an agent with the local FBI

office, was waiting for Procaci in his car. He was going to drive Procaci back to the airport.

"How did it go?" he asked immediately.

"Not well," Vic admitted. "It's like you said, she doesn't remember a thing."

"The word on the Strip is that Sal Patriarca commissioned the Gallenzo hit," Owsley said as he headed for the road.

"I know," Vic said. "Boy, I'd like to nail that son of a bitch. At least Gallenzo was a man of some honor, but Patriarca is a bloodthirsty pig. It would be a pleasure to see him in jail."

They continued to discuss the case and their non-existent leads until they reached the airport.

"You know the kid's parents never came out here?" Owsley remarked. "Never called or anything. They've just abandoned her."

"No kidding?" Vic said. No matter how wild her escapades in the last few months the kid had almost died. He wondered what her famous father was like, but he would know soon enough. He was going to need Mr. Young's help whether he liked it or not.

Back in New York, Vic made an appointment to call on Ashley Young. When he arrived, he was shown into the library where Young was waiting for him at a heavy, carved mahogany conference table. Young was flanked by two lawyers, intense men in conservative pin-striped suits who never spoke to Vic but occasionally made notes on yellow legal pads and showed them to Young.

"I don't see how I can help you," Young finally said. "I only know about my daughter from what I read in the papers."

"Did you know that she's in a hospital in Las Vegas?" Vic snapped. He had taken an immediate dislike to this man.

"I've had no news from Stephanie for some time," he said coldly. "I don't like the company she keeps."

"I don't think you realize that your daughter's life is in danger," Vic went on, laying out the story of Gallenzo's murder and explaining that the killers could not afford to let Stephanie live.

"What do you want me to do about it?" Ash snapped.

"I don't want her released from the hospital. If she's free to move around there's no way we can protect her."

"Then put her in jail, that's the safest place."

"Mr. Young, your daughter hasn't committed any crime," Vic said. He was beginning to get angry. "I suggest you place her in a clinic where we can have her watched."

"She should be committed," Ash said icily. Someplace where she could no longer embarrass him with her escapades.

Vic ignored the remark and continued. "I

know a small clinic outside Los Angeles. I believe the doctor in charge will cooperate with us. Your daughter will be safe. But I need your authorization for her to be admitted."

"All right," Young said. "I'll give you the authorization. You have one month. After that, I'll decide where she should go."

Procaci was relieved to leave Ash Young's office. Compared to him the wise guys were not so bad after all.

A few days later Stephanie Young entered the exclusive private clinic run by Dr. Herbert Rankow, who specialized in rest cures and postoperative depressions. It was a large colonial-style mansion situated on three acres in Beverly Hills, hidden protectively behind tall privet hedges.

Stephanie had put all her trust in her new protector. In a strange new way she was excited to be the center of such danger.

Vic leaked the story that she was recovering at the Rankow clinic, hinting broadly that she had recovered enough to give a full description of the killers of Carlo Gallenzo. The *Herald* published a photograph showing the location of her room, a large one on the ground floor, facing the swimming pool. It was the most exposed room in the clinic.

Half a dozen new interns appeared, but if someone had looked closely they might have observed that their white tunics were bulging from the hardware they wore underneath. They were FBI and Los Angeles police working together.

All this was of great interest to Joe Bruccola and Vinnie Accaro. For one thing, their employer was not happy that a witness had escaped. For another, he refused to pay up until the job was done. And as far as he was concerned the job was to eliminate both Gallenzo and his paramour.

For three days the two men parked by the side of the road, a few yards from the gates to the Rankow clinic, getting the nighttime rhythm of the place and deciding when and where to make their move. On the third day, when the City of Los Angeles sanitation truck appeared at two in the morning for its daily pickup, they were ready. It pulled up to the gate and the driver spoke into the intercom. Within seconds, the truck was passing through, Bruccola and Accaro, gripping the back, sailing in along with it. As the truck neared the kitchen wing, they leaped off and moved quickly toward the west wing where, according to the *Herald,* Miss Stephanie Young was staying.

"I'm telling you, it's a piece of cake," Bruccola insisted as they moved through the damp grass toward the rear of the building. The room they wanted had French doors that opened onto a flagstone terrace. The white cotton curtains moved slightly in the gentle evening breeze. They moved closer, hiding behind a clump of pink azaleas as they neared the room.

"Look at that," Accaro whispered. Most of the room was dark but they could make out a blond woman sitting up in bed watching television. Her face was illuminated by the light of the screen.

"Jesus," Bruccola said with disappointment. "What a dog."

"Yeah," Accaro agreed. "I thought Gallenzo had some taste."

They drew their guns and moved across the patio and into the room. But no sooner had they passed through the doorway then a voice shouted at them.

"Drop your guns, raise your hands or you're dead," came the order. "Against the wall, you know the procedure."

Stunned, the two men lifted their hands above their heads and stared at the big blonde pointing a gun at them from the bed.

"Nice to see you guys," she growled as she removed her wig.

"Volinsky!" Accaro gasped. The blonde was bald and he recognized her—or him, rather.

"We been waitin' for you," Sergeant Volinsky smiled. He stepped out of the bed and with his free hand began to remove the generous falsies from beneath his frilly bed jacket.

"I always knew you were queer, Volinsky,"

Bruccola spat, but the sergeant's ham fist caught him in the jaw and sent him sprawling.

"Joey, baby, that's no way to treat a lady!" Volinsky rubbed his knuckles, then took out his handcuffs and moved to link Bruccola to the bed. "I got a guy here for you named Procaci," he added. "He's dying to meet you."

Volinsky turned to the door that opened to the hallway and shouted. "Hey, you guys, I got our pals."

In the split second that his back was turned, Accaro dropped to his knees and removed the small pistol he kept tied to his calf. But as he lifted it, the two agents summoned by Volinsky stormed into the room, guns drawn. At the sight of Accaro's gun they fired, killing him instantly. He crumpled to the floor and his lifeless hand released his gun. It hit the floor, firing, ironically hitting Bruccola.

At that moment, Procaci appeared in the doorway. "Shit," he thundered. "You've killed my two witnesses."

26

New York, N.Y.
June 1978

Teresa Wilkerson was proud of her beautiful daughter, the new Eve girl. With her first check, Christina had insisted on bringing her up from Houston to New York. She arranged for her mother to attend the Smathers Institute for a few weeks where she was detoxified and counselled about her drinking. She made up her mind to straighten out her life. After all, Christina was a celebrity now, she had to make her proud, too. It was a matter of life or death.

To celebrate her release from Smathers and the new little apartment she had found, Christina and Alex were taking her to dinner at Gino's on Lexington Avenue near Bloomingdale's. The unpretentious restaurant was noisy and crowded but Alex assured them the food and the service were impeccable.

He ordered for them all, *spaghetti al segreto* with Gino's special sauce, followed by *cotolette alla Milanese,* sauteed breaded veal chops, and sauteed peas with prosciutto. In deference to Mrs. Wilkerson, he did not order any wine.

"I haven't had such a good meal in years," Teresa said. "But I must have put on at least five pounds."

"You're wrong, Mom," Christina said. "Now that you've stopped drinking, you can eat normally and you won't put on any weight."

"That's true, Mrs. Wilkerson," Alex added. "Italian food isn't half as fattening as people think. That's if you eat like the Italians do. This meal is a lot less fattening than an American meal of steak with French fries and a rich dessert."

"But I've always heard that Italian women were like us Mexican women. After the first child they get fat and sloppy," Teresa said.

Christina looked at her mother with sympathy. "Mama, you're going to take care of yourself now and in no time you'll be slim and beautiful again."

"And I already have a long line of gentlemen waiting to meet you when that happens," Alex added.

"Oh, dear," Teresa laughed and for the first time Christina noticed a small sparkle of life in her mother. And Alex had brought it out.

*   *   *

Ashley Young had been coming to Max Reinhardt twice weekly for six years and the little Viennese doctor could always tell when he was in a foul humor. He was certainly in one this afternoon and Reinhardt did what he could to bring him out of it.

Reinhardt owed a great deal to Ash Young. He had fled Austria during the war and had been struggling in New York until he met the Houston millionaire. He was keenly interested in rejuvenation, Young told him, and he had heard through a friend about this obscure doctor who claimed to have found the elixir of perennial youth. Young visited his modest offices on the Upper West Side and eagerly listened as Reinhardt explained that he had a formula that could restore human cells and thus prolong the life and vitality of a human being.

But the American Medical Association, he complained, refused to recognize him or his theory and he had no funds to continue his research and thus prove the validity of his claims.

Ash listened and the words were like music

to his ears. He proposed to finance the doctor's research. In the meantime he became his leading patient. He had even insisted that Reinhardt move to these glamorous offices in the Young Building just so he could conveniently get his twice-weekly shots.

Reinhardt was correct. Ash was in a foul mood. That idiot Stephanie seemed to be moving from one scandal to another. Now it was shootouts with the FBI and mobsters. He would gladly have her committed, were it not for the Hollingsworths. They seemed to dote on her no matter what she did.

And the arrangement with Christina Wilkerson was not going according to plan either. The girl was a cool customer. Not giving a damn about most people, he could usually handle them as he wished. But there was something about this girl. He had to have her. Her indifference had him on the defensive, a position he did not enjoy at all.

The problem, he decided, was Jessica. She had failed in raising Stephanie, now she was standing in the way of his affair with Christina. There had to be a separation. Surely, then, the girl would fall into line. He would tell her he would marry her as soon as he was free. Then he could have her and once she was his he could decide whether she was worth the price he would have to pay to let Jessica go.

His mental strategizing was suddenly interrupted by the little doctor who signaled that he should follow him into his office.

"What is it, doctor?" Ash insisted. He was alarmed by the doctor's somber mien.

"Nothing to worry about," the doctor tried to reassure him. "There's some irregularity in the heartbeat, but I'll give you some digitalis for that. I'm going to run some more tests, but meanwhile I want you to avoid stress and stick to that diet I gave you."

"Yes, yes, of course," Young said impatiently. "But what about my heart?"

"We'll do our best with what we have," Reinhardt assured him.

27

New York, N.Y.
June 1978

Alfred and Constance Hollingsworth did not
believe for one minute that their only grand-
daughter was crazy, no matter what her father
tried to tell them. She was just like poor Cookie,
high spirited, perhaps, but what she needed was
love and affection and they were going to give it
to her. They decided to have a dinner party at
their Park Avenue apartment to celebrate her
return to New York.

Like Ash Young, the Hollingsworths entertained in the grand manner. But to them it
came naturally and they relaxed and enjoyed
themselves as their twenty guests sipped
champagne and nibbled Beluga caviar before
dinner. As a result, even Stavros Pateras, who

was negotiating a tanker deal with Hollingsworth, kept his drinking to a minimum.

He noticed Stephanie immediately. She was
wearing a short, pink silk Halston and her face
showed none of the strain of the past few
months. In fact, she looked ravishing.

On her part, Stephanie was delighted to find
that she was seated between Pateras and Prince
Selim of Saudi Arabia. She already knew the
Greek from Palm Beach days, but the tall,
handsome young Arab would be a new con-
quest.

Pateras cornered her as she walked into the
dining room. "You will have dinner with me
tomorrow?" he whispered.

It was more a command than an invitation,
but she agreed. Especially when he hinted at his
upcoming cruise of the Greek islands and the
Turkish coast.

So much for tomorrow. Tonight she would
have the Arab. Prince Selim was one of the
forty-two grandsons of the late King Ibn Saud
by his myriad wives. He bore little resemblance
to the conventional picture of Arabs as crude,
coarse, swarthy men in flowing robes. Selim
was tall with large, dark brown eyes and black
hair. His suits were made for him in London,
his shoes in Milan and his shirts in Paris. His
manner was impeccable and, having travelled
all over the world, he was a sophisticated,
knowledgable young man. As they talked

during dinner, Stephanie felt herself falling in love once again.

Immediately after dinner, Stephanie and the young prince headed for Studio 54. As usual there was a crowd outside the huge discotheque on West 54th Street. Most of them would be there all night, begging to get in. But Marc, the gatekeeper, recognized Selim and Stephanie immediately and if he was surprised to see the Arab prince and the golden heiress together, he did not show it.

They walked through the crowd, past a mirrored hall lined with silver trees and into the multileveled main room. It was almost totally dark except for the dance floor and Selim and Stephanie bypassed the low, velvet banquettes and headed for the crowded floor. On a raised platform nearby, a thin young man worked behind an elaborate control panel that an airline pilot might envy. He waved at Selim and Stephanie as they went by.

The music was not just choice but loud, and between the multicolor flashing of the light show and the noise of the mass of popper-sniffing, leather-clad men, elegantly dressed women, and unidentified dancing objects, Stephanie and Selim hardly talked.

As a completely naked blond man danced by alone, Selim grabbed her arm.

"Let's get out of here," he whispered in her ear. "We'll go to Le Club."

Le Club, situated on the east side of the city, had a more selective and traditional atmosphere than Studio and was open to members only. They headed immediately for the large high-ceilinged room in the rear, where the walls were orange-pink and one wall was almost completely covered with a handsome Flemish tapestry depicting some feudal lord at the hunt. On the other side was a large fireplace over which hung hunting trophies of some of the members and musical instruments.

After dancing for several hours, they sat on one of the dark green love seats in front of the fire. Selim put his arm around her. She looked up at him and smiled. His soft brown eyes made her think of Carlo.

"Shall we go back to my place?" he whispered. "For a drink?"

She did not hesitate. She was ready to try again.

*   *   *

"Actually, Stephanie, as a good Moslem, I don't drink at all," Selim confessed when they were inside his Olympic Towers suite.

Stephanie was looking around for a chair to sit on, but Selim's apartment was decorated in the new minimal style and instead of furniture it consisted of various platforms and levels covered in black industrial carpeting. The walls, too, were black, but the windows presented a beautiful view of the spires of St. Patrick's Cathedral next door. Looking at the tall spires, Stephanie remembered Selim.

"It's all right, Selim," she smiled. "I'm not thirsty." With a flick of her hand the pink silk Halston fell to the floor revealing her as nature made her.

"Allah be praised," he sighed, staring at her.

"Let me help you," she said eagerly. Otherwise, she was afraid, he might stand there all night. She expertly unzipped his tight trousers as he hurriedly slipped out of the rest of his clothes. Free, he grabbed her by the shoulders and laid her down on the carpet.

He moved over her and without further ado he impaled her as his Saracen ancestors had impaled Christian maidens four centuries ago.

As Stephanie climaxed for the second time, it occurred to her that life in a harem might not be so bad. But, finally, exhausted, she had to beg Selim to stop. She fell asleep in his arms.

When she woke up in bed with Selim, Stephanie was convinced that she was in love again. She told him so.

"Unfortunately, Stephanie, I'm leaving this morning to return to Saudi Arabia, but you'll hear from me, I promise."

"Maybe I could visit you," she offered.

"I wish it could be so, but it cannot," he sighed. "My country is very strange. A woman alone would not be permitted to enter Saudi Arabia."

She was astonished. "You're kidding!"

"No, I'm not Stephanie. In my country I become a very different man than I am now," he said solemnly. "I don't drink, I don't mix with women. We live by the laws of Islam and our king is a most religious man."

"But what's wrong with my visiting you?" she insisted. "I'm not married and neither are you. So what's the fuss about?"

"You don't understand," he said, shaking his head. "Unless we were married under Islamic law, you and I could not even see each other."

"But how could we get married if we can't see each other?" Stephanie was beginning to regret not paying more attention when they covered the Arabs at Foxhall.

"Our marriages are arranged by our families," Selim explained. "We seldom marry foreign women and then only if they convert to Islam."

"I wouldn't mind that," Stephanie retorted. After one night with Selim she was sure she could be happy with him under any circumstances.

"I couldn't see you leading the life of an Arab woman," he said, smiling. "Confined to your home, wrapped up in a *chador* when you go out," he touched her cheek and brushed away the tear that was rolling down it. "We'll meet in other places, Stephanie. New York, London, Paris. If I could, I would never go home, but I have no choice."

"Okay, sweet prince." She put her arms around his neck and drew him to her for a long kiss. "Come back soon, though."

*   *   *

But Stephanie's father had taught her well, and she was ready to bounce back again that very night when she kept her date with Pateras.

Stavros Pateras was twenty years older than Selim and in contrast he was a methodical man who planned every move he made well in advance. As a small, scrawny boy just beginning to assemble his merchant fleet, he had seduced and won the hand of Sophie Lyras, the beautiful daughter of Andreas Lyras, one of the richest of the Greek sea lords. Since then he had slept with duchesses, countesses and some of the most beautiful women in the world. He almost never failed to get a woman he wanted, not because he was sexy, but because he was rich. To Stavros Pateras, most women were whores and he knew the price of their favors.

Now he wanted Stephanie Young, the beautiful daughter of his rival, Ash Young. It would be a delightful way to humiliate a man he intensely disliked. He would make his daughter his mistress.

Pateras noticed with interest that Stephanie did not wear any real jewelry and he had heard that despite his great wealth Ash Young was quite stingy with his daughter. He decided that Miss Young would enjoy a present.

That night he took her to dinner at La Caravelle. He was a frequent customer and so they were seated at the red velvet banquette by the pillar in the main room. The light green walls were decorated with murals of Parisian scenes and a small vase of dark red roses was at their table.

Stephanie ordered squabs à la russe, served in a sauce of tomatoes and shallots, and Stavros polished off a filet de boeuf en croute. As they drained the last of the Bordeaux-Medoc he spoke.

"Close your eyes, Stephanie," he ordered.

She did as she was told.

"Now give me your hand."

She held out a small white hand. She could feel him putting something on her wrist. It felt like a handcuff.

"Now you can look," he commanded.

"Stavros, it's simply beautiful," she said, staring at the diamond and ruby bracelet as it glowed in the soft light of the restaurant.

"A small token of my admiration for you," he said. "It suits you perfectly."

Stephanie was thrilled. Through the rest of dinner and later as they danced at Le Club she clung to him. It had been so long since anyone had given her a present, especially one as beautiful as this bracelet. She had been wrong about Selim, she realized. Stavros was the one, he would take care of her. He was a little crude, and he was married, but he was generous and powerful and he would take care of her.

He took her back to his suite at the Carlyle where they made love until dawn. Like Carlo, he surprised her that a man his age could be such a vigorous lover.

Later as she dressed, he took her by the arm. "I want you to be ready to fly with me to Paris tomorrow," he said.

"Paris?" She looked surprised. Then she smiled. "Of course, tomorrow."

28

New York, N.Y.
June 1978

Ash and Jessica were at dinner, alone in the dining room of their Fifth Avenue apartment. They faced each other across the long Louis XIV table, seated on matching gilded chairs that the antiquary had assured Ash once held the derriere of the Roi Soleil himself. The walls were hung with red damask and a Lalique chandelier gave light from overhead. Two candles burned in silver holders on the table.

Ash watched his wife closely. She was a little more relaxed than usual. The anti-depressants her doctor had prescribed seemed to be working. It was a good time to bring up the separation.

Reasonably and gently he explained why it

was for the best. "We'll have time to reflect on our marriage," he put it. To his surprise she began to cry.

"Why now, all of a sudden, Ash?" she asked.

"It's better for you, Jessica." He eyed her with distaste. "You're still a good looking woman. You can start to make a life for yourself."

Inside, in spite of the Valium, she was reeling. He had ignored her for years, now suddenly he wanted to cut her out of his life.

"It's too late, Ash," she said, filling her wineglass. Her hand was trembling. "I know what I look like. I'm dried up. That can happen to a woman who's not loved, who's never been loved."

Ash never lost his composure. "You're too hard on yourself, Jessica," he said coolly. "I may have neglected you the last few years, but I've always cared for you."

She laughed bitterly. "You never cared about anyone but yourself. And now you want to throw me out like an old rag! I know what you're after. It's that Eve girl. Well, you've ruined my life, but you won't ruin hers. You're stuck with me."

He was actually surprised. Jessica hadn't shown this much spirit in years. He had never expected her to put up such a fight. And she knew about Christina which meant she was not so dumb after all. He realized with annoyance that she would not be easy to get rid of. For the moment the wisest course was a quick retreat.

"Perhaps I was too hasty, Jessica," he said. "You're probably right. Why should we separate after so many years together?"

"I think you're just trying to humor me," she said glumly, staring at the half-empty wineglass. "But it's too late for me to start over. I only wish I had the strength to do it."

"Let's not talk about it anymore," he said, filling both their glasses. He raised his in a silent toast to her. "The subject is closed."

*   *   *

Ash considered the Jessica problem for several days. It was not only that Jessica would not hear of a separation. It would not do to lock horns with her father. Alfred Hollingsworth was still a powerful man.

The idea for a solution came one night as he gazed at Jessica's glassy eyes.

The woman was already a pill addict. Pills to go to sleep, pills to wake up, pills to quiet her nerves, pills to lose weight. All he had to do was to see that she increased the dosage, slowly but surely.

It was a dangerous plan, but in emergencies he had learned that one must often apply dangerous and even deadly measures.

Ash raised the subject on his next visit to Dr. Reinhardt.

"Mr. Young, what you're asking me to do is most unusual," the doctor said. He took off his gold-rimmed glasses and began to clean them with his handkerchief. "Pills, twice the usual strength, would have to be specially made. You can't find them in a pharmacy."

"That's why I want you to do it, doctor," Ash said amiably.

"But it would be against the law, Mr. Young." The little Austrian's accent became more pronounced the more nervous he became.

"Don't worry, doctor, no one is going to be harmed."

"May I ask why you need them?"

"I just want them," Ash snapped. "That's all."

Reinhardt shrugged. They both knew that he needed money for his research. And the money was forthcoming only as long as he cooperated with Ash Young.

"All right, Mr. Young," he sighed. "But I'm not responsible for the consequences."

"I want them tomorrow, the latest," Ash ordered. "Good day."

29

New York, N.Y.
June 1978

It had been several weeks since Vic Procaci had heard from Stephanie Young. She had never returned to the Rankow Clinic as she was supposed to and he was worried about her. Although Accaro and Bruccola were gone, her life might still be in danger.

Maybe he was just kidding himself. He liked Stephanie a lot. She was sort of a space cadet, but underneath the brittle veneer was a very insecure girl who had surprised him with her courage and fortitude. She had bounced back from that terrible experience with Gallenzo in Las Vegas; that kind of trauma could have destroyed the strongest mind. She cooperated bravely in nailing Accaro and Bruccola. Yes, she was something special.

He tried reaching her at her parents' apartment, but all he got from Ash Young was a curt expression of disinterest and a suggestion that he try the Hollingsworths. The grandparents told him she was in Paris visiting Mr. and Mrs. Stavros Pateras and gave him the phone number.

"The shipping tycoon?" he asked. He was not used to moving in those circles and thought maybe it would be better to forget the whole thing. But no, he wanted to reach the girl. He dialed Pateras' home in Paris, glancing at his desk clock. It was eleven in the morning, which would make it four in the afternoon in Paris.

He paused to consider what he would do if the person who picked up the phone spoke to him in French since his own was limited to *merci beaucoup* and *couchez avec,* but to his relief a very English voice answered. The butler, no doubt. He asked for Miss Stephanie Young in his most official manner.

"Who is calling, please?" the English voice was noncommittal.

"Mr. Procaci of the Federal Bureau of Investigation, calling from New York."

"I will see, sir. Please wait a moment."

As he waited, he flipped through the latest copy of *The Reporter* magazine. A new series of ads caught his eye. He did not usually look at women's cosmetics ads, but the new girl in the Eve ads was a knockout. The color pictures were especially striking because they captured her green eyes.

"Vic, how in the world did you find me?" Stephanie chirped happily as she came on the line.

"It's my job, finding people," he said. "But your grandfather helped. He told me you're staying with Pateras and his wife."

She giggled. "Not exactly."

"What do you mean?"

"My grandparents would never have let me come to Paris alone, Vic, so I told them Sophie Pateras was here."

"And she's not?"

She giggled again. "I don't think it would be much fun for her here." Then she tried to change the subject. "What about you, sweetie? How are you?"

"I'm fine," he answered. "But it's you I'm concerned about. You were supposed to come back to the clinic, remember?"

"Give me a break, Vic," she sighed. "I couldn't stand it anymore."

"Stephanie, that's not the point," he said patiently. "We could watch over you there. When you travel around the world we can't do anything. Remember, you're still in danger."

"Vic, don't worry. Nobody will harm me

here," she assured him. "Pateras is so afraid of kidnapping that we have bodyguards day and night."

He decided not to mention that Carlo Gallenzo's guards hadn't done him much good. He didn't want to upset her when she sounded so happy. If she was with a man as rich and powerful as Pateras, perhaps she was safe. So she was happy and safe. Then why was he so miserable?

30

New York, N.Y.
July 1978

Jessica Young struggled to get out of bed. She was having trouble moving her legs and she felt dizzy and desperately tired, but she could not sleep because that only meant falling into the nightmares that had come to fill her dreams. In them she fell headlong into a bottomless pit and her screams echoed in her brain.

She took two of the new red pills Ash had obtained for her and poured some water from the silver carafe beside her bed. Today, especially, she had to look sharp. George Vanderfelt, the curator of Versailles, was coming to lunch. She did not feel very sharp now, though, and she sank back in the pillows, waiting, praying, for the pills to take effect.

At last she began to feel a spurt of new energy shoot into her and she managed to rise and move into the bathroom. She bathed in the pink marble tub and dried herself quickly. Next she began to work on her face. She labored with the makeup and brushes to paint her face into a ritual mask that hid the ravages of time and pain. She brushed her light brown hair back into a sleek French twist, but when she finished and faced herself in the mirror she saw a frustrated and unhappy woman.

Charlotte, her maid, was waiting in the bedroom. She had laid out the brown Chanel suit she had bought last season in Paris. She looked concerned when she saw her mistress.

"Madame," she insisted. "You are not well, please let me call a doctor." She had been watching Jessica's condition deteriorate for weeks and she could bear it no longer.

"No!" Jessica answered. "Mr. Young is taking care of me."

It was already twelve-thirty. All she needed now was her vodka martini and she would be ready to face Vanderfelt and Ash in the library.

A butler brought the drink on a silver tray and informed her that Mr. Young wished her to join him in the library in ten minutes. As soon as he was gone, she reached for another of Ash's pills. She swallowed it and lay on the bed smoking a cigarette, but her hand trembled so that she had to put it down. She needed the drink, but her hands were shaking too much to pick it up off the tray. She could hear Charlotte singing a French song to herself as she cleaned up after Jessica in the bathroom. She wanted to call to her, but the words would not come.

She realized she would not be able to make it down to the library unless she had that drink. Ash would be furious. He would never forgive her if she was not there to greet Vanderfelt. They had already contributed so much to the restoration, it had become his pet project.

She made one last effort to reach for the glass, but she only knocked it off the tray, spilling it on her suit. She slipped off the peach silk cover of the bed and sank to the floor, her whole body shaking.

Charlotte heard her fall and came running into the room. She lifted her back on the bed and quickly summoned Mr. Young.

"Put her to bed," he ordered when he came into the room. "And give her another red pill."

"But Monsieur Young," the little maid protested. "I think it is the pills that are making madame ill."

He turned on her angrily. "Do as I say, Charlotte, or you'll be out of a job."

He turned and walked back to the library to inform Vanderfelt that his wife was indisposed. Unfortunately, she would not be able to join them for lunch. Nevertheless, the two men enjoyed their meal and discussed the progress of the restoration.

"I'm about to leave for the Middle East and Iran, George," Ash said as he concluded lunch by writing a twenty-five thousand dollar check toward the restoration of the landmark. "Perhaps I can get my friend the shah to come up with a donation."

"I understand the Pahlevi Foundation's got plenty to spend," Vanderfelt said as his eyes lit up. "And the empress herself is a great collector of French antiques."

"Yes, she's a great asset to him," Ash mused. He could not help comparing what a problem Jessica was for him. What he needed was someone like the empress, someone like Christina Wilkerson.

The shah had quickly divorced his first wife, Soraya, when he felt she was no longer useful to him and could not give him an heir. Too bad he couldn't just as easily dismiss Jessica. But, one way or another, she had to go.

31

New York, N.Y.
July 1978

In the two months since her release from
Smathers, Teresa Wilkerson had been in full
control of herself. The puffiness around her
face had disappeared and her figure was
starting to take shape again. She was even
managing to attend AA meetings. Christina
kept her company as much as her work and
Alex allowed, but when Teresa was alone she
seemed happy enough cooking for herself in
the cozy, little apartment and watching her
favorite soap operas on television. She spent
most of her time on the scrapbooks she had
begun to keep for Christina. Not just the Eve
girl campaign and other ads but the magazine
stories and photos of her dates with Alex
Mercati.

"Alex seems like a nice man," she said to Christina over lunch one afternoon. She had prepared it for them in her tiny, new kitchen.

"Nice and intelligent," Christina added.

"As nice as Ash Young?"

Christina was surprised. She was never sure how closely her mother followed her career or how much she knew about her boss.

"It's strictly a business relationship with Ash Young, Mama. He's cool and has a brain like a computer," Christina said. "But I don't see how any woman could ever love him. He's so domineering, so selfish and totally heartless."

"I've been reading about his daughter in the columns and magazines," Teresa offered. "She's certainly led a wild life."

"That should tell you what kind of man he is," Christina snapped. "I met Stephanie Young one night at Regine's. She's a beautiful girl who's so desperate for love she'll take it from anyone."

They finished their lunch in silence, but afterward Christina brought out an envelope.

"You've been dry for two months now, Mama. I want you to celebrate." She handed her the envelope.

Teresa opened it. It was a gift certificate for a day of beauty at Elizabeth Arden.

"Oh, Christina," her mother squealed with pleasure.

"It's time you started taking better care of

yourself. You can't go on the way you have," Christina warned. "Get yourself back in shape and you'll have a new life."

"You sound so convincing, Christina," Teresa said. "I almost believe it. But look at me, can I ever be beautiful again?"

"It's up to you, Mama," Christina said. "Now, will you be all right while I'm away with Alex?"

"Sure, honey, you go to Southampton with your friend," Teresa smiled. "And I'll go to Elizabeth Arden and get beautiful. The Cashes upstairs have invited me to dinner tomorrow. Won't they be surprised."

"Good," Christina said, kissing her mother goodbye. "I'll call you from Southampton."

* * *

Christina was relieved to have the weekend free for Alex. Between the Eve shootings, her mother, and his deadlines they had had too little time alone together.

"I bought this house the first year *The Reporter* went into the black," Alex said as they pulled up to the small cottage on the Southampton dunes. "This house dates from when this whole area was a British colony."

They approached the doorway along a walk lined with pots of red geraniums. Christina looked around.

"Which way is the ocean?" she asked.

"Follow me," he said as he unlocked the yellow door and they walked into the deserted house. The rooms were large and barely furnished. The polished hardwood floors were covered with a few braided rugs and there was an empty fireplace at the end of the living room. They moved quickly toward the rear of the house. There a huge redwood deck had been added and they stood there looking out at the Atlantic.

"Oh, Alex," she gasped. "It's beautiful." She was awed by the power of the blue waves as they crashed against the beach.

"I forgot you've probably never seen this before," he said.

"No, I haven't," she said. "I grew up on the gulf, which is big, but nothing like this." And the Gulf of Mexico had been full of oil tankers and wells, whereas this water was clean and the air was fresh and salty.

"You should see it in the winter, when all the tourists and summer people are gone," he said. "But my favorite time is after a hurricane."

"I want to take a swim," she said. "Where do I change?"

They both changed quickly and went swimming in the surf. It was their weekend and they planned to make every minute count.

They did, too. When they weren't making love, they were playing tennis or biking around the small village a few miles away from his house. To Christina's surprise, Alex turned out to be a marvelous cook. He taught her how to select and prepare a lobster and on Saturday night he cooked an elaborate Italian dinner which the two of them shared by candlelight on the deck.

The only minor flaw was that she was unable to reach her mother on the telephone.

"You know, Christina," he said as they sipped their wine, "these three days with you have been the happiest of my life."

She took his hand. "I love you, Alex."

"Then why don't you marry me?"

"What?" She was taken by surprise. But they had known each other for five months and it did seem as though it had been forever.

"Well?" he persisted. "Is it such a terrible idea?"

"No, it's just that I hadn't thought about it," she admitted. "To tell you the truth, Alex, I never thought I'd marry anyone."

"You're joking! The way you look?" he laughed. "That's why I've got to move fast."

"What about my mother, Alex? She's getting better, but I've still got to stand by her."

"Christina, the way you take care of your mother is only one of the things I love about you. If you marry me, she'll always be welcome in our home."

She smiled. "I'm sorry you never got to meet

my father, Alex. Everyone liked him. He was a doctor who devoted his whole life to helping people." She hesitated, thinking of Bill Wilkerson's last, painful days. "I don't know why he couldn't help Mama, but he used to tell me to be patient with her and someday I'd understand."

"What about me, Christina? How patient do I have to be?"

"Give me some time, Alex. We're in July now, why don't we say that I'll be able to decide by Christmas. Right now, between Mama and the Eve campaign, I hardly have time to think."

"Just so long as you don't run off with Ash Young," he teased.

She laughed. "Never, Alex, never in a million years."

* * *

Teresa Wilkerson's weekend started off equally well. As she sat under the dryer at Arden's, she read the *New York Times*. There was a front page story about the return of Ash Young from a business trip to the Middle East and his comments on OPEC and the oil crisis. There was a photograph, too, and he had hardly aged at all. The hair was a little grayer, but he was as handsome as ever.

"The West had better brace for another rise in oil prices," he told the *Times*. "All the OPEC members but Saudi Arabia are pushing for an increase."

So he still had the same quick temper. It frightened her sometimes that Christina had the same temper. She was a lot like Ash in many ways. The same brilliance, the same drive, but at least she had the softening influence of Bill Wilkerson. Marrying him had been the smartest thing she had ever done.

She looked back at the photograph of Ash. It disturbed her that he was calling Christina and working so closely with her. They both knew that he got what he wanted. But his own daughter? No, it was time he knew the truth about Christina. He had a beautiful, successful daughter and he ought to know it.

By the time the hairdresser and masseuse and manicurist and facialist had finished with her, she felt almost as good as she had twenty years ago. She took one last look in the mirror. They had rinsed the beginnings of gray out of her thick, black hair and the makeup emphasized her high cheekbones and dark brown eyes. She was wearing the beige suit that had been a present from Christina. It fit her well and now that she had lost weight she did not look bad at all. She would pay a surprise call on Ash Young. For old times' sake.

*　　*　　*

Ash Young was in the library when a maid brought him word that a Mrs. Martinez was there to see him.

"I have no such appointment," he snapped, then looked up to see the dark-haired woman standing in the doorway. He knew her instantly, but twenty years had done nothing to change his feelings. He swore silently. The damned maid. If August had been there, this would never have happened.

"What are you doing here?" he asked, his voice icy.

"I just wanted to see you again, Ash." She was embarrassed. Now that she was here, in his apartment, she was nervous and insecure again. It was like being in some fabulous palace or museum. It made her feel small and insignificant.

"I'm sorry," he replied. "But I've nothing to say to you now or ever."

"We're two mature people now, Ash," she protested, as tears started to fill her eyes. "Can't we at least talk for the sake of what went between us?"

"I don't like to remember my mistakes," he snapped. He had no wish to prolong this unpleasant situation. He rang for the maid.

"Please leave."

In seconds, the maid reappeared.

"Please show this lady out," he commanded.

Teresa followed the girl mechanically. Oblivious to the intense July heat, she walked all the way back to her apartment as if in a trance, stopping only to pick up a bottle of bourbon. Once home, she threw herself on the bed and broke into sobs. She had wasted her life over a man totally unworthy of the love she had given him. She thought of Bill Wilkerson who had more love in his little finger than Ash Young would ever know. And she had treated Bill so badly, neglecting him and Christina to drink all day and dream about what life would have been like with Ash Young.

After an hour she was all cried out. She rose from the bed and changed from her new suit to a housecoat. Then she took the bourbon and a glass and sat down at her writing desk. She poured herself a glass, took pen in hand and began to scribble a note to Ash.

By the time she finished the letter she had finished the bottle. She was not used to so much liquor anymore and between that and the heat and the painful scene at Ash's apartment, she was exhausted. She folded the letter into an envelope and stuck it in her pocket, then lay down on the bed. In a few minutes she was asleep.

It was in the middle of the night that she woke up with a start. Her bedroom window was open and a slight breeze rustled the curtains but did nothing to relieve the oppressive heat. She felt as though an enormous weight was on her chest; she couldn't breathe and her body was wet with sweat. A wave of nausea overwhelmed her and she wanted to vomit. She staggered to the bathroom, but as she stood over the sink, nothing would come. Instead, a stabbing pain shot through her right side as if her insides were being torn apart, and to her horror she began to vomit blood. After a few minutes the vomiting stopped, but the pain continued. She gripped the cold sides of the sink as she tried to stand. Suddenly another flash of pain pierced her body and she surrendered herself to it.

*　　*　　*

It was one o'clock Monday morning before Christina and Alex emerged from the Midtown Tunnel and back into New York City. Christina was beginning to be concerned because she had been unable to reach her mother all weekend and she suggested they stop by her apartment in spite of the late hour.

They rang from downstairs, but there was no answer. The doorman said that he had not seen Mrs. Wilkerson since Friday night.

"It was around six when she came in," he said. "And she didn't go out again."

"That's very strange," Christina said. "I called her last night and there was no answer. Could you possibly have missed her if she went out?"

"Not likely, miss, but it could have happened

when I was in the john. I'm a fast operator, though," he said with a grin. "But in that case I should have seen her when she came back."

Christina and Alex looked at each other. Then she remembered Teresa's Saturday dinner date with the Cashes upstairs. The doorman rang their apartment for her.

"I'm sorry to disturb you, Mrs. Cash," Christina said as she took the doorman's phone. "But I can't reach my mother. Have you seen her?"

Mrs. Cash was obviously not pleased to be disturbed. It was now almost two.

"Well, she was supposed to come to dinner on Saturday night," the Boston accent came back with irritation. "But she never showed up. Didn't even call to apologize."

"I'm sure she'll explain, Mrs. Cash," Christina replied curtly. "Good night."

She replaced the phone and turned to Alex. Now she was really worried. "Alex, we have to get inside Mama's place. Maybe she's sick in there."

Alex turned to the doorman. "Do you have a passkey for Mrs. Wilkerson's apartment?"

"I'd have to advise the manager," he said. "But he's asleep."

"I don't give a damn what he's doing. You go call him and tell him to come right down," Alex commanded. "Or I'll get him down here myself."

Ten minutes later, a sleepy manager was listening to Alex explain that they had to get inside Mrs. Wilkerson's apartment immediately. He nodded and led them to the elevator. At the apartment door they banged loudly but there was no answer. He used the passkey.

As soon as they entered the apartment they knew something was wrong. From the doorway they could see the light in the bathroom. They ran toward it.

She was lying on the tile floor in a pool of blood, her housecoat soaked in blood. Christina turned away, and then she saw the pulpy mass in the sink. It looked like raw liver.

Alex moved quickly to grab Christina before she collapsed. He led her to a chair in the living room and held her there.

"God, how awful," she sobbed, burying her head in his arms. "What happened to her? She's dead, isn't she?"

"Yes, Christina, your mother is dead," he said gently. "Perhaps you better go home now, darling. I'll stay here until the doctor and the police come."

"Police?"

"I'm sorry, Christina. It's routine. But there's no need for you to be here, I'll take care of it."

"I'll go home, Alex," she said calmly. "But I want to say goodbye to Mama."

She went back into the room. She wanted to

be alone just a few minutes with her mother.
Perhaps Teresa would find the peace she had
not had on Earth. She touched her mother's
hair and wiped the pink foam from her lips. It
was the least she could do. Alex would not let
her move the body. She stood up to leave. Then
she saw the letter in her pocket. She gently took
it out. To her surprise, it was addressed to Ash
Young. She opened it and as she read it her jaw
tightened.

"Dear Ash,
   "I'm glad I had the nerve to visit you today. After all these painful years in which
I continued to love you and suffer from
our being apart, I finally realized that I
was in love with a man of my dreams, not
the real Ash Young.
   "Today, you showed yourself for what
you really are. Someone without a drop of
human kindness. Of course, I should have
known that. You never once, in all these
years, bothered to inquire about your
child. I know you probably don't even care
to know, but you have a lovely daughter, a
girl you should be proud of. I wanted to
talk to you about her, but you never gave
me a chance. You threw me out like some
beggar.
   "I never did you any harm, Ash, except
perhaps to love you too much. But you

have hurt me terribly. Still, I'm not sure which of us is the worse for it, me for being reduced to what I am today, or you for what you are, a man with a stone in place of his heart.''

Christina read the note over twice, then folded it again and put it in her purse. Now she understood everything about her mother, except how she could have ever loved Ash Young.

"Don't worry, Mama," she muttered. "He'll pay for this, I swear it."

32

New York, N.Y.
July 1978

Ash was enjoying dinner in his apartment, but he was lost in thought. It had been three days since that surprise visit from Teresa Martinez. Why suddenly, after all these years, had she come to see him? He certainly did not regret rushing her out the door like a dismissed maid, but it disturbed him. He could not concentrate on his work. He kept recalling how she had looked years ago in Houston. Those few months with her had been the happiest in his life, the only time when he enjoyed someone simply for what she was. But the happiness was built on a lie and Teresa Martinez had turned out to be like everyone else, willing to sell herself for a price.

It would be interesting to know what

Christina Wilkerson's price was. He had not found it yet, but he would. She had the same dark good looks of Teresa Martinez all over again, but the similarity ended there. Twenty years ago Teresa was a malleable, docile chicana. Christina Wilkerson was a modern American girl with a mind of her own. She was not going to be easy to tame, but tame her he would or his name was not Ashley Rodman Young.

He had already taken care of Jessica. She had made a brave effort to dress for dinner, but as he looked at her across the table he could see that she was thinner than ever and her skin had an unhealthy pallor. There were dark shadows under her eyes. She barely ate and seemed to have difficulty speaking. The ravages of Dr. Reinhardt's pills were evident.

"Are you all right, dear?" he asked with concern.

"Much better, Ash," she assured him. "I'm sure that I'll be up and about soon."

"Of course you will. But be sure to take your medicine. It's important that you sleep well."

She excused herself before coffee was served. She could hardly sit up and Charlotte had to help her make it to the bedroom.

"Good night, Ash," she said sadly. "I'm sorry if I spoiled your dinner."

"Sleep well, Jessica. Rest, that's what you need."

No, he assured himself. It wouldn't be long now.

*   *   *

Teresa Wilkerson's funeral on Tuesday morning was as pathetic as her death. Only Christina, Melinda Parsons and Alex Mercati attended the Mass of the Resurrection in the small Catholic church. At the cemetery the priest read a short prayer before the earth covered her forever. Christina turned away from the grave and grasped Alex's arm for support as they returned to Manhattan.

She had read and reread Teresa's letter. She had cried over it, trying to visualize the humiliation and suffering of her mother. Now she understood everything. All the years she had resented her mother for her drunkenness, the way Papa told her someday she would understand. Now she understood it all.

When the three mourners returned to Christina's apartment, there was another letter waiting for her.

"Dear Christina,

"When I called this morning, I learned that your mother had passed away. Please accept my condolences and feel free to ask anything of me that might alleviate your loss. Remember that I am here, that I want

368

to see you the moment you feel composed, and that I have to talk seriously about matters that may change your entire life.

"I'll be calling you Wednesday morning. Perhaps the two of us can have a quiet dinner together and talk.

"Yours,
"Ash"

Every time she reread that letter, an incredible bitterness and cold hatred filled her soul to such an extent that things that should have counted, such as her love for Alex or her successful new career, did not matter anymore. It was obvious from Ash's letter that he didn't realize that the mother she had just buried was Teresa Martinez, and that pleased her. Now, all she could think about was how she was going to make him pay for killing her mother. Because he had killed her as surely as if he had carved out her heart with a knife or taken a gun and blasted the life out of her. That grisly picture of her mother lying in a pool of blood, her liver lying in the bathroom sink, would remain forever in her mind.

So many things now became clear. The way Teresa had withdrawn into a shell while she was growing up. The special way that Bill Wilkerson had loved her.

Now Ash Young wanted to talk to her "seriously about matters that might change her entire life." Before it had been amusing to be pursued by a famous tycoon. He was a bastard, of course, but he meant nothing to her. Now her feelings had changed. Now she truly hated him.

She was his daughter, after all, and she was somehow going to use that to destroy him.

33

New York, N.Y.
July 1978

The next time Ash Young called to offer his condolences, he also asked to see her, but not at his office. She suggested that they meet for a drink at the bar of the Regency Hotel. It was not one of Alex's favorite spots and she was anxious to keep the rendezvous strictly secret.

"What's the matter, Christina," Young teased when he arrived at the dimly lit bar. "Are you afraid someone will see us?"

"To tell you the truth," she admitted. "I don't want anyone to know."

The waiter brought their drinks, a vodka martini for Ash, a glass of white wine for Christina.

"Are you afraid your friend Mercati will hear about it?" he persisted.

Christina sipped the cold wine thoughtfully. "Him, among others. But there are other reasons. You seem to have trouble remembering that you're married."

"I've already told you, Christina, I'm arranging a divorce!" There was impatience in his voice.

"Fine," she smiled. "When that happens there'll be no problem."

He could feel himself getting angry, but he struggled to control it. Reinhardt had warned him not to get unduly excited. It could be bad for his heart.

"Jessica has already agreed to a divorce," he lied. "But it will take a little time and, in the meantime, I want to see you. This is no fling, Christina. I want to marry you."

"Isn't this awfully hasty, Ash?"

"I know what I want," he said. "And when I make a decision, I see no need to delay implementing it."

"You make it sound like I'm a tanker deal or some kind of acquisition."

He smiled. "In some ways you are." She was going to be his consort, his empress.

"But Ash," she laughed. "You know so little about me, about my past. I'm not a society girl."

"I don't give a damn about your background, Christina. The wife of Ash Young will be accepted anywhere. I want you, that's enough."

Christina ran her finger around the rim of

the wineglass. "You know, Ash, you haven't even asked me if I want to marry you."

He seemed taken aback for a second. That possibility had not occurred to him.

"First of all, I don't love you," she continued. "And you haven't done anything to make me love you."

Ironically, the more she resisted and taunted him, the more he wanted her. Perhaps there was someone else.

"Are you in love with Mercati?" he asked.

She smiled. "That's my secret and I don't have to answer." She stood up. "And now I have to go. Thank you for the drink and the proposal." She was up and out before he could say anything else.

He remained at the table and ordered another vodka martini. This was not going to be easy, but he would get her. The girl was more ambitious than she appeared to be, but what really disturbed him was the relationship with Mercati. Just from the way she said Mercati's name he could tell she was sleeping with him. The thought of them making love disturbed him and, to his surprise, he felt a surge of rage. Somehow he had to get the publisher out of the way and soon.

34

New York, N.Y.
July 1978

Alex Mercati accepted Ash Young's invitation to lunch at "21" with mixed feelings. He
had always found the man intriguing, which
was why he had covered him so extensively in
The Reporter. At the same time, he was well
aware of the way the tycoon was pursuing
Christina. At first, they had both laughed about
it, but since her mother's death a change had
come over her. Lately, there was a wall between
them, and he suspected that the wall had
something to do with Ash Young.

But Ash Young did not suggest lunch
without a reason and Alex waited with interest
to learn what the purpose of this meeting was.
When the waiter brought their coffee, Ash
began to make his pitch.

"I suppose you've been following the mess in Teheran," he said, lighting one of his long Davidoff cigars.

"Yes, I have," Alex acknowledged. *The Reporter* had recently published a whole series on Iranian dissidents.

"Those fools in Washington deserve an A for Asses for the way they've meddled there," Ash went on.

"You met with the shah when you were just in Iran, didn't you?" Alex asked. "What does he say?"

"He and his ministers are deeply concerned about the ambiguous game our government is playing, Alex. We use Iran as a military base and listening post against the Soviet Union and we pat the shah on the back for being our ally, and at the same time we undermine him by accusing him of oppression and torture."

Alex smiled. "You're not claiming that SAVAK treats dissidents with kid gloves, are you?"

"Of course not, Alex," Ash said impatiently. "But in three-quarters of the world they use strong methods with the opposition. And Iran is not a democracy. It's a backward country with millions of illiterates."

"We do have a habit of treating our allies worse than our enemies," Alex agreed. "But the shah's arrogance and his constant pressing for oil price increases have hardly won him new friends here."

"I know, I know," Ash admitted. "But the fact is that Iran holds the key to stability in the Middle East. It's our barrier against communism."

"So far, Ash, you're not telling me anything I don't know."

"Alex," Ash lowered his voice as it took on an intimate tone. "You're an influential publisher. If people like you don't make this understood, we're going to lose Iran. The next government could plunge the whole country into chaos. We need Iran's oil and we need our bases there."

Alex nodded. Now he understood what Ash was getting at. "Are you asking me to do some lobbying for the shah?"

"Unofficially, of course," Ash added hastily.

Alex considered the idea. The truth was that with *The Reporter* doing so well, he barely had time to consider anything else. On the other hand, he had always been intrigued by diplomacy, perhaps it was in his genes. He was fascinated by the prospect of playing a role in foreign affairs. He did not particularly care for the shah, he was despotic and arrogant, but he was a friend of the United States, for better or worse. A hostile press and the naivete of the new president should not be allowed to undermine that.

"The shah's no saint," Ash acknowledged. "But he's improved Iran's economy and per capita income. He's built schools and hospitals and he's trying to transfer an illiterate, feudal country into a modern industrial power."

"But how stable is the government?" Alex asked. "I've been hearing about power cuts and food shortages and demonstrations against the shah. The word is that anyone who can afford it is sending their assets abroad."

"Believe me, Alex, the shah is firmly entrenched. He's got more than a half million troops," Ash said. "Probably one of the best-equipped armies in the world. He's completely secure."

"I don't know, Ash," Alex shook his head. "There are 180,000 mullahs and they've never forgiven him for taking their land and giving it to the peasants."

"He's suppressed other revolts. Remember Mossadegh?" Ash said emphatically. "The shah had to leave the country, but he returned stronger than ever."

As Ash continued to talk, Alex considered the offer. The shah was a fascinating figure and, no matter what Ash said, he was in serious trouble. As far as Alex could tell, four disparate groups had united in their opposition to him: the mullahs, the bazaar, the middle class and the Marxists.

The shah had not just confiscated the mullahs' lands, he had redistributed them to the peasants without any concrete program, so they were not terribly better off either. Meanwhile he failed to show the proper respect for Islam and was never seen inside a mosque.

The bazaar, the businessmen centered mainly in the vegetable markets, were not known as the "drawers of knives" for nothing. They had been the center of cash power in Iran for centuries and resented being cut out of the industrial process, especially when they saw what they considered their proper cut going to the Pahlevis and their foundation. The middle class, meanwhile, was frustrated by the corruption and repression. The Marxists were simply behaving like Marxists.

He had stopped listening to Ash until he realized he was talking about money.

"Iran Air has a five hundred thousand dollar a year contract with Lansing & Lewis, the New York public relations firm," he was saying. "You can be paid a consultant's fee of one hundred fifty thousand dollars out of that. Or, if you prefer, the fee can be sent directly from Iran to a numbered account in a Swiss bank that you designate."

"Hold it right there, Ash," Alex said quickly. "If I do agree to do this, it would be as a favor to the country. I don't need the money and I don't want it."

Ash shook his head. "I wish it were that simple, Alex. But you know how business is done in the Middle East. The handshake deal doesn't exist. Money has to change hands for them to trust you."

Alex shrugged. He still did not like the idea but it would be an easy matter to sign over the money to some charity, when and if it ever appeared. Still, there was another complication.

"If money's involved, won't I have to register with the Justice Department?" he asked. "How can my work be confidential if I have to register?"

Ash waved his hands. "All taken care of. Lansing & Lewis is registered with Justice and you'll be considered a consultant to them."

Alex had to admit the deal intrigued him. Perhaps eventually it would lead to a major story for *The Reporter*.

"Just who would I be dealing with in Iran?" he asked.

"You would meet first with Hoveyda, then the shah himself."

Alex's interest sharpened. Amir Abbas Hoveyda had a reputation for brilliance and honesty. He was so clean that he had been forced to resign as prime minister almost a year ago and was now minister of the court.

"I thought he was out of favor with the shah," he said.

"Some," Ash admitted. "But the shah still respects his advice, even if he doesn't always take it."

"How soon would they want to meet me?" Alex asked.

"The shah is on vacation this month," Ash answered. "He's on the Caspian Sea with King Constantine and King Hussein." He obviously relished discussing royalty so casually, even ex-royals like the former King of Greece.

"Assuming that I'm interested, Ash," Alex said, "*The Reporter* still comes first, and if this thing got out it could hurt it. I wouldn't want to be accused of influence peddling."

"You can be assured of total discretion on the part of the Iranians," Ash insisted. "And the same goes for Lansing & Lewis."

As they left "21," Alex had just about made up his mind. He agreed to give Ash his answer in a few days.

Ash watched him disappear into a taxi. He walked back to the Young Building with a rare smile. Mercati had taken the bait and would soon be at his mercy.

*   *   *

That night, Alex discussed Ash Young's offer with Christina.

"The whole thing sounds very exciting," she agreed. "But I can't understand the need for all the secrecy. I just have a strange feeling about it, Alex. Please be careful, whatever you do."

"Don't worry, Christina, I intend to be," he

assured her. "But what about you? Will you be all right in the Bahamas?"

As part of her new role as the Eve girl, Christina had been invited to give a brief speech to the Young Co. executives at their annual conference at Paradise Island. Alex had been helping her with the speech, supplying *The Reporter*'s files on the career of Ash Young, the growth of the Young Co. and the recent acquisition of Eve Cosmetics.

"I'm sorry I won't be there to hear it," he said. "But while you're down there, I'll be in Teheran."

"Don't worry about me, Alex. I'm a big girl and I can take care of myself."

"Just remember I'll miss you and I love you. And when I get back, I'm taking you away from all this for a few days. We'll fly to Marbella, on the coast of Spain, just you and me."

"I'd like that, Alex," she said sadly. But she wondered if they could ever really be alone again. The specter of Ash Young seemed to have settled permanently between them.

35

Nassau, The Bahamas
August 1978

Paradise Island is part of the Bahamas, situated across from Nassau Harbor, with a view of the clear, blue water surrounding it. Most of the Eve staff, even Roberta Rubin, were billetted at the posh Ocean Club, but Ash Young had insisted that the new Eve girl be a guest at the private home he had leased.

Christina came down a few days early for some shootings and she plunged into the work with new enthusiasm. Phil Mason, the art director, and Mel Sheldon, the photographer, were easy to work with. No pressures, no angles, just people trying to do a good job. They shot her dancing on the white beach in flowing, transparent robes, and sitting on the black volcanic rocks while gentle waves licked at her feet. They took pictures of her running after a ball on the tennis court, on the golf course trying hopelessly to sink a putt, astride a black horse cavorting on the white beach and drifting through the elaborate formal gardens of the Ocean Club.

Exhausted from the day of work, they decided to skip the casino and have a simple dinner at the club. It was ten-thirty when she said good night to the two men and headed for Ash Young's villa near Nassau Yacht Haven.

Christina advised the smiling houseboy that she wanted to be awakened at seven, and hurried upstairs to bed.

Her room had sliding glass doors that led to a balcony and a view of Nassau Harbor. Once inside, she opened the doors and undressed quickly. It was a balmy night and the scent of night-blooming cereus was heavy in the air. She slipped on a green silk kimono and stood at the rail enjoying her solitude. She watched the moon's reflection covering everything with a silvery patina. The moon truly was the "sovereign mistress of melancholy." Suddenly she missed Alex terribly.

"Forgive me if I intrude," a voice called nearby.

Startled, she turned to see Ash Young standing on the adjoining balcony.

"My God! You scared me!" she said. "What are you doing here?"

"I was just admiring a beautiful woman lost in her thoughts," he said amiably.

The kimono had fallen open and she realized he was staring at her breasts. She pulled it closed. He moved closer to join her on her side of the balcony.

How she hated him, as she looked into his cold gray eyes. She moved to go back into her room but he grabbed her wrist and held it tightly.

"Please leave, Ash, or I'll scream for your servants."

"There's no need for that," he said, releasing her and reluctantly moving back toward his side of the balcony. The girl was impossible but every time she rejected him he only became more desperate to have her. And have her he would!

* * *

The next morning Christina was irritated and upset. She had barely slept and she was anxious to give a good speech. Fortunately, the lack of sleep did not show in her face.

She dressed with great care in a white linen suit she had bought especially for this. Her black hair was pulled back and tied with a red ribbon. This was going to be the unveiling of another side of Christina Wilkerson and it had to be perfect.

Ash greeted her at breakfast as if nothing had

happened and he led her through the crowd, introducing her to the Young Co. executives. When he came to Tom Patterson, he introduced her as a fellow Houstonian.

"Yes, Miss Wilkerson, I think we've met," he said politely.

"Of course, at Belvedere in February."

He was puzzled. Somehow he still had the feeling he had met her before that. There was something so familiar about her, but he still could not place it.

At last it was time for Christina to give her speech.

"Almost fifty years ago," she began, "a man named Drew Young struck oil in Kilgore, Texas. That was the beginning of the Young Co. But it took his son, Ashley Rodman Young, to build it, over the last twenty-five years, into one of the largest conglomerates in the world."

She went on, enumerating the impact of each acquisition from those early tankers to Eve cosmetics. Ash found some of it news even to him. Tom Patterson leaned over and whispered in his ear.

"All that beauty and she's got brains, too."

Yes, he reflected, as he listened. But he was beginning to think that her price might not be so high after all. Just different. He could offer her a chance to learn more about the business. Groom her for better things. It would be interesting to see if she bit.

"And so," Christina concluded. "As we approach the golden anniversary of the Young Co., it is now a multinational business. And we look forward to the same kind of growth in the next fifty years."

Enthusiastic applause filled the room as Ash rose to take Christina's arm.

"Let's talk business," he whispered as he led her out of the room. Her place on the stage had already been taken by a young head of the Nevada-based Young Tool and Die Co. and the assembled executives watched wistfully as the beautiful Christina left.

As Ash and Christina sipped drinks by the pool, he made his proposition. He wanted Christina to be the spokeswoman for the Eve girl, representing the company not just in advertising, but on television and in newspaper and magazine interviews. She would be more than a beautiful, nameless face. Her personality, her intelligence and warmth would define the Eve girl for the 1980s.

"I'll talk to Casardi and Roberta when we get back about renegotiating the contract," Ash said briskly. "I hope you understand that for the next several months you'll be travelling around the world. There'll be no time for friends . . . or other relationships."

She knew he was talking about Alex. If she accepted this deal, she would have to ask Alex to wait. She just was not sure he would.

"The payoff, of course," Ash continued,

"will be that in time we'll bring you into the business end. It'll be an opportunity for you to learn on the line." He smiled. "You wouldn't be the first beautiful woman to become president of a company."

"That's very exciting," she said calmly. Inside she was hysterical. She was beginning to see how she could have her revenge. It was a plan that would so neatly accomplish the goal that it could only have come from Ash Young, or Ash Young's bastard daughter.

The only thing holding her back was Alex. She could not have him and her revenge, too. She would have to choose.

36

Teheran, Iran
August 1978

A gust of the hot August sirocco engulfed Alex Mercati as he emerged from the plane at the Mehrabad airport. The small, dark man in the black suit who greeted him identified himself as Amin Athar of the Iranian Foreign Office.

During the forty-minute drive to the Royal Teheran Hilton, Athar informed Alex that an appointment had been arranged for the next morning in Hoveyda's office, but in the meantime he would be glad to show him around the city.

"I've been instructed to see that you have a pleasant and enjoyable time while you're with us," Athar told him.

"That's very kind," Alex answered.

"Tonight you might enjoy some company?" Athar continued in a conspiratorial tone.

"Thank you, but please don't put yourself out," Alex said. "I can fend for myself." He stared out the window at the dusty scenery. The view improved a little as they approached the city.

Teheran sat on a plateau four thousand feet up, and as they neared it from the west, they had a magnificent view of the steep and snowy Elbiez Mountain range to the north and the strikingly beautiful specter of Mt. Damavahd, the dormant volcano now covered with snow.

Teheran itself was considered the most polluted city in the world. It was a city of four and a half million people, four million of whom lived in the slums to the south. The northern section of the city was westernized with skyscrapers and wide but crowded boulevards. Farther out to the south and west were the new factories that were part of the shah's industrial program. In spite of the broad, new streets and tall buildings, there was a bleak and unfinished quality about it all.

They turned right on Shah Reza Boulevard and landed in the middle of one of Teheran's famous traffic jams. While they sat, Athar pointed out Shahyad Square, site of the huge arch the shah erected in 1971 to commemorate twenty-five hundred years of monarchy.

As the traffic began to move again, Athar renewed his offer to entertain Alex.

"We have very beautiful women in Teheran, Mr. Mercati," he continued. "Perhaps you would like to meet some. The minister of the court doesn't believe that a man can appreciate a new country if he is not in the company of a woman."

"Mr. Hoveyda is a very perceptive man," Alex answered noncommittally.

Athar dropped him at the Hilton and promised to return at eight o'clock.

Athar had obviously taken Alex's answers for an agreement, for when he returned that night he brought two beautiful young women. He introduced the tall golden blonde as Miss Inga and the petite brunette as Mademoiselle Janine. Over drinks at the hotel bar, they told Alex that they were models and had been in Teheran a few months.

After a few drinks, Athar offered to drive them to a local restaurant he recommended highly. The four of them piled into Athar's car, but when they arrived, Alex realized that he did not plan to join them. He insisted he come along.

"No, sir," the dark man said, smiling. "I'm sorry, but I'll be here in the morning to take you to the meeting with Minister Hoveyda. I wish you a pleasant evening."

After Athar was gone, Inga and Janine seemed to relax. The restaurant specialized in Iranian dishes and over a meal of chelo kebab, unleavened bread and the uniquely flavorful Persian rice, they explained that they had arrived in Teheran a week apart, but their stories were similar. They confided that they had been working for a good model agency in Paris, but the work was unsteady and so they occasionally did some jobs on the side for Madame Claude, Paris' most famous madam.

One day Mme. Claude approached them with an interesting proposition: a trip to Teheran as guests of Shah Mohammed Reza Pahlevi and a check for fifty thousand francs for services rendered.

Their evening was preceded by a candlelight dinner with caviar and champagne in the private suite the shah reserved for such encounters. A small string quartet would play behind a discreet velvet curtain and a short dance with His Majesty would end with a waltz from the drawing room to the bedroom.

In between engagements with the shah, Janine and Inga ran into each other in the lobby of their hotel and resumed a friendship begun in Paris. When the time came to go home and the prime minister's office invited them to stay, they agreed.

For five thousand francs a week and all expenses, they were expected to be at the disposal of the shah's guests. If they could gather some interesting pieces of intelligence they were to report them to the Foreign Office.

They soon learned that there were at least a dozen other beautiful young women of all nationalities similarly employed.

For dessert, the three of them selected from twelve varieties of Persian melons, and in a mood of expansiveness, Alex invited Inga and Janine back up to his suite.

The Foreign Office had thoughtfully stocked Alex's suite with champagne and a king-sized bed. There was no string quartet, but Janine had brought a cassette player and some American disco tapes and they danced to them.

"Would you like to hear something funny?" Janine asked as she began to replace a tape.

"What's that?" Alex was having such a good time he was ready for anything.

Janine put in a new cassette and the room filled with the sound of a man giving some kind of speech. His voice was straining and he was obviously overwrought. The girls began to giggle as the man continued his indecipherable message.

"Would you like to fuck to this?" Inga asked. "It just gets better and better."

"Who is it?" Alex asked.

"Oh, some crazy fanatic who wants everyone in Iran to go back to speaking Farsi and wearing chadors and drinking tea instead of champagne," Inga said.

"The shah threw him out, of course," Janine added. "And he's in Paris now. Can you imagine someone like that in Paris?" She laughed.

"Where did you get the tapes?" Alex had heard about these taped messages from the exiled Ayatollah Khomeni but he had understood they were being suppressed.

"Oh, they smuggle them in," Inga said casually. "We got this from Janine's maid."

"Do you want to hear more?" Janine asked.

"No," he said emphatically. "Turn it off."

The strange man's ranting had reminded him of another curious figure who seemed so ridiculous in the old newsreel footage that showed him wildly orating to his people, but who nonetheless had managed to galvanize an entire nation and threaten the future of the free world. He somehow suspected that the last thing they should be doing was laughing at the man.

He could see the girls were disappointed that he did not share their amusement. He decided to make it up to them in another way.

If it was Mr. Hoveyda's intent to bring him to the meeting in a weakened condition, then he succeeded, because Inga and Janine performed all sorts of delicious sexual tortures on him, making love to him together and separately until he had not an ounce of strength left and had to beg for mercy. At the end of the extraordinary performance he still could not tell which of the two had pleased him more, and during the love sessions he was only able to tell them apart by the blond or black hair on his face.

"So now, ladies," Alex said as they relaxed in bed together. "What will you report to the Foreign Office about me?"

"*Tres simple*," smiled Janine. "We tell zem you are terrific fuck!"

"Ja, ja, me too," added Inga. And all three burst into laughter.

*   *   *

Amir Abbas Hoveyda, former prime minister of His Imperial Majesty's government, and currently minister at court, bowed deeply as Alex entered his office.

"I hope your first night in Iran was a pleasant one," he said with a smile.

He was a dark man in his fifties. His large forehead receding into total baldness, the thick eyebrows surmounting deep black eyes, the long straight nose and the thin mouth gave an impression of intelligence and severity. The moment he smiled, a smile that revealed teeth discolored by tobacco, the warmth of his personality emerged. He carried a silver-tipped cane and there was a small pink orchid in his lapel.

"Perhaps too pleasant, Your Excellency," Alex smiled back.

"I'm happy to see that Athar arranged things nicely," Hoveyda nodded. "But now for the purpose of your visit. Do you understand what we have in mind?"

"I think I do, sir."

"The United States concerns us. You're our strongest ally and we depend on you, just as you depend on us," he said gravely. "We are offended when we read unfavorable articles in your press and when some of your congress-men criticize us."

"That's the nature of the United States, Mr. Hoveyda," Alex said politely.

"I realize that, of course, and I'm a great admirer of your country, Mr. Mercati," Hoveyda assured him. "But, unfortunately, this sort of thing plays right into the hands of elements that are trying to subvert the monarchy and this government. We have to stop the lies about us."

"I understand," Alex said. He realized it was inappropriate to mention the rumors he had heard only that morning about rioting in Esfahan, but he decided to bring up the disturbing tapes.

"I heard one of Khomeini's speeches last night," he said. "Even without understanding Farsi I have to admit it was a rabble rouser."

"Ah," Hoveyda nodded. "You've heard the cassettes already."

Alex nodded.

"Ruhollah Khomeini is of no consequence," Hoveyda said with a dismissive gesture. "He and his people are sending in tens of thousands of those cassettes, it's true, but the Ayatollah is safely neutralized in exile at Neuphe le Chateau."

"You sound awfully convincing," Alex said.

Hoveyda smiled. "We have eleven nuclear reactors on order with France. They will do whatever we tell them to do to him." He looked up and nodded as a manservant came in with a tray of tea. The servant poured cups for Hoveyda and Alex and then departed.

Hoveyda sipped the hot drink and continued. "A man like you, Mr. Mercati, an influential publisher with many friends in high places, can also do much to help us."

Alex sipped the sweet tea. He wanted to make it clear to Hoveyda that although he was interested in supporting the positive aspects of the regime, he had no intentions of becoming its mouthpiece.

"I can contact some of my colleagues and give them the facts as I see them," he agreed. "But you must understand that what I can do through *The Reporter* is limited. If it were ever known that I had an arrangement with you, I would be compromised and both of us would be hurt, no matter how just the cause."

"I understand that, Mr. Mercati. Discretion and secrecy are a primary consideration in the agreement."

"That's good, Your Excellency," he agreed. "But I also believe that your government must take certain measures for this arrangement to work, such as drawing the reins in on SAVAK and ending the torture of prisoners."

Hoveyda shrugged. "There have been excesses, of course. But they've been highly exaggerated by the American press," he emphasized. "You Americans do not understand us. We are not a democracy, not yet."

"I'm not asking you to change your form of government, Mr. Hoveyda, but just to consider public opinion."

"The question is in His Majesty's hands," Hoveyda said with a gesture of his hands. "But all your suggestions will be given due consideration."

"I understand, Your Excellency, but I can only be of help if I'm in a position to offer advice that will be heeded."

Hoveyda smiled and rose. The interview was at an end. "Perhaps you can share those thoughts with His Majesty," he said as he showed Alex to the door. "He will be expecting you at the palace at five this afternoon."

*   *   *

A government limousine picked Alex up at a quarter to five and carried him, with a motorcycle escort, to the Niavaran Palace nearby. The tall ironwork doors swung open,

letting the limousine into a heavily guarded
courtyard. The shah's elite imperial guard were
immaculate in their navy blue uniforms with
turquoise blue scarfs, gleaming black boots and
white laces. Nearby he could see the barracks
and watchtowers.

The limousine stopped and a young captain
asked to see Alex's briefcase. He presented it,
the officer examined it with surprising thor-
oughness, then signalled the driver to move on.
They proceeded another two hundred yards,
past beautifully manicured gardens of cypress
pine, roses, mimosa and weeping willows, and
stopped in front of the entrance to the
Niavaran Palace.

The palace was a large whitewashed stucco
building of undistinguished style. Alex walked
briskly up the fifteen steps to the doorway
where he was met by an Iranian in tails, the
shah's chief of protocol. They shook hands and
he led him inside.

The interior was somewhat more impressive.
The walls were decorated with traditional
Persian mirror work and frescoes depicting
great moments in Persian history. The ceilings
were set with glittering mirror work. There
were only a few European antiques, and from
what Alex could see they were of indifferent
quality.

The marble floors in colored patterns were
covered here and there with Shiraz rugs and
maroon and rich purples and blues. Perhaps in

his quest for glory, the shah had made a tactical mistake, Alex mused, for the press had apparently glorified his palaces far more than they deserved.

They entered a small, tiled anteroom. The other men waiting all appeared to be military officers. They wore uniforms elaborately trimmed in gold braid and heavy with medals and were called in to see the shah one at a time.

They had no sooner seated themselves on imitation Louis XVI chairs when a tall blond woman with dark eyes entered the room.

"Your Majesty," his escort said, bowing deeply.

Alex rose quickly as the empress approached him. "You're Mr. Mercati," she said graciously. She spoke with a slight French accent. "I'm happy to meet you. I enjoy reading *The Reporter*."

"Your Majesty is too kind," he answered. So this was Farah Diba, the third wife of the shah and his empress for twenty years. He wondered for a moment how she occupied herself when her husband was busy entertaining the models. She did not look like a woman who would be happy at home knitting.

"My husband will see you in a few minutes," she said. "I hope we meet again soon." She gave him her hand and he bowed and kissed it.

Moments later he was summoned before the shah.

The shah wore the uniform of a general of

the army, full of gold braid and decorations, but in spite of the impressive uniform he looked far less hard and intimidating than his photographs. He was working at a large black lacquer and ormolu Louis XV desk. Behind the desk was a collection of photographs, most of heads of state, some of the Pahlevi family and, prominently displayed, a photograph of Farah's predecessor, Soraya.

The shah put aside the papers he had been reading and removed his reading glasses as Alex approached the desk. He noticed the shah was wearing a gold wedding ring.

"Ah, Mr. Mercati, please sit down." He indicated one of the chairs. "Mr. Hoveyda has informed me of the conversation he had with you. We are pleased that you will help us with our problems with the American media."

A manservant silently appeared with a tray of tea and *nabat*, a crystallized sugar candy, and disappeared just as quietly.

"I will do my best, Your Majesty," Alex said. "Most right-thinking people in the United States believe that you and your country are of vital importance to the West."

The shah shook his head. "Then why do they complain about our buying arms? Don't they know that our strong army is the biggest deterrent against Soviet Russia?"

He got up and started to pace the room. With his hands behind his back, he reminded Alex of paintings of Napoleon.

"They complain about increases in oil prices," the shah continued. "But what do they do about conserving energy? We are building a new country. In a few years Iran will be one of the major powers in the world. They had better heed us."

Alex was about to reply, but the shah seemed to be in another world. He had begun a long, involved story of how he had survived the 1949 assassination attempt when an assassin posing as a news photographer had fired five shots at close range. Two bullets had grazed the shah's body, two missed, the fifth ripped through his cheek and upper lip. In spite of that, the young ruler walked calmly away and drove himself to the hospital as his guards wrestled with and finally killed the gunman. Immediately after treatment he made a broadcast to the nation to prove his wounds were slight. His courage in the face of near-death had done much to establish him in the hearts of his countrymen.

Then the shah switched gears again and began to talk about waste and corruption in the government.

"I have fifteen hundred helicopters," he laughed bitterly. "And only three hundred pilots in the whole country. So what? Every society has a certain amount of corruption."

Alex remained silent. The shah was agitated and it was better not to say anything than to say something wrong. He had heard rumors that the shah was lately incapable of concentrating.

He would lose his train of thought in the middle of a sentence, then sit in dumb silence for minutes before picking up an altogether different subject. Now he was seeing it for himself.

Finally the shah relaxed and sat down again.

"How long do you plan to stay with us, Mr. Mercati?" he asked in a more even tone.

"If everything is in order, I may go back tomorrow, Your Majesty," he answered. "I do have a magazine to put out."

"In that case I hope you have an enjoyable trip and I wish you success in this enterprise." He rose and offered his hand to Alex who shook it and left.

That afternoon, August 23, a huge and mysterious fire destroyed the Teheran vegetable market. Two weeks later, martial law was declared in Iran.

37

New York, N.Y.
August 1978

Alex Mercati rushed from JFK to his home, deposited his bags and headed straight for Christina's. In spite of his fling with Inga and Janine, she had never been far from his thoughts. If anything, his experiences with other women only made him appreciate her more. But to his surprise, she didn't look quite as happy to see him when he appeared at her door.

"Is something wrong, Christina?" he asked with concern. "Did anything happen at Paradise Island?"

She shook her head. "Nothing unusual. Ash tried to get in my room, the speech was a success and Mel and Phil got some good shots for the Eve campaign."

He didn't like the way she was talking. A hard

edge had crept into her voice that he had not noticed before. And it wasn't like her to be so flippant and he told her so.

"If you don't like it, you don't have to stay," she shot back.

He let that go. "Tell me about Paradise Island," he asked.

She loosened up a bit then and recounted everything that had happened. The speech they had worked on together had been a success, she told him, so successful in fact that Young was expanding her role as the Eve girl. He was going to give her an opportunity to learn the business and she would be travelling all over the world to promote the product.

"That's great," Alex said, trying to sound enthusiastic although he was deeply suspicious of Young's motives. He worried about Christina. She was still unspoiled, even naive, and he didn't want her taken advantage of. Also, the idea of travelling so much sounded like it was going to mean long separations for them and he didn't like that at all. Still, he didn't want to spoil her big break.

"You'll have to get a lot of rest in Marbella," he added. "So when we come back you can throw yourself into this."

There was an awkward pause and then Christina spoke.

"I won't be going to Marbella," she said nervously. "At least, not now."

"What? But we planned this—"

"I know we did," she replied. "But something's come up."

"Yeah," he said angrily. "And it's called Ash Young."

"That's not true! I'm only going to Paris on a promotional trip," she replied.

He relented. "I don't understand, Christina. You're going to be my wife. You don't need to work for Young anymore. You yourself told me you have nothing but contempt for him."

"And that's all I'll ever have," she answered.

"Then get away from him. You know he's only taking you to Paris so he can make love to you. He wants you, Christina, and he thinks if he can't get you in New York, you'll be more vulnerable in Paris."

She longed to tell him that she wanted only three things in life: she wanted Alex to love her, she wanted to destroy her father, Ashley Young, and she wanted to get the Young fortune that was rightfully hers. She wanted to confide that this Paris trip was a way of getting closer to Ash Young, to somehow see if there was a way she could have her revenge, but there was no way she could. Someday, perhaps, she could tell Alex everything, but not now.

As she sat there silently, Alex watched her. An awful cloud of suspicion was beginning to form in his mind and the more he tried to push it away, the more persistently it stayed.

Maybe Christina was not going to Paris as reluctantly as she claimed.

"What really happened in Paradise Island, Christina?" he demanded.

"What do you mean?"

"Why this sudden need to be close to Young? When I left, you loathed the guy and now suddenly he's become your mentor, he's taking you to Paris, and all our plans are off."

"So you think there's something going between Ash and me?"

"I didn't say that," he added hastily.

"But you're thinking it," she replied. "I can see it in your eyes, Alex. You don't trust me."

"How can I trust you when you've changed this way?"

"If you think I've changed, perhaps you'd better stop seeing me," she said coolly. "You seem to have the wrong idea about me."

He shook his head as he rose to leave. He still couldn't believe that the woman he loved was behaving so callously. He turned at the door and tried once more to get through to her.

"I love you, Christina," he insisted. "And I know you're hiding something. Won't you share it with me?"

"I think we've said all we have to say," she answered.

When he was gone, she turned away from the door, ran to her room and collapsed on the bed in tears.

Part Seven

38

Paris
September 1978

Christina Wilkerson had never been more
lonely in her life. At least during the two weeks
spent shooting the new Eve commercials she
had been too busy to think about Alex or Ash
Young or what she was going to do. Now the
shooting was over and everyone had returned
to New York, everyone that is but Ashley
Young and Christina.

She smiled at the thought of the buzz that
probably caused among the Eve staffers. At
least it would give them something to talk about
on the long flight home. Of course, Roberta
Rubin had suspected that she and Ash were
having an affair for months. Poor Roberta
would probably be surprised to learn that Ash

had not gotten very far at all. Not that he hadn't tried. He had even arranged for her to have the suite next to his at the Ritz and fresh flowers arrived from him every day. He probably would have been on the set every day, too, but unfortunately world affairs had intervened.

The shah's government was in serious trouble, and most of Ash's time was taken up with the crisis, so while he was in meetings all day, Christina wandered about Paris.

Ash insisted that the city had lost its charm, but to her it was the most beautiful place she had ever seen, with the exception of the lobby of the Ritz which was usually crowded with noisy Arabs and their families.

She shopped at the elegant boutiques on the Avenue Victor Hugo and the Faubourg St. Honor and the Ritz concierge arranged seats for her at the fashion houses of St. Laurent and Chloe. At Fauchon on the Place de la Madeleine she picked out chocolates for Barbara Sawyer and Jean Casardi, and at Dior she bought a sexy dressing gown for Melinda. Most of all she enjoyed just walking through the elegant streets, gazing at the windows and the ancient buildings. Sometimes she wondered what it would be like to share it all with Alex, then she caught herself and remembered that that was all over.

She discovered the Louvre and went back

many times, wandering from the Greek and Roman antiquities to the Egyptian art brought back to Paris by Napoleon. There were magnificent paintings by Titian and Rembrandt. Each day she explored a different section of the huge building. The day she was in the Medici Gallery, marvelling at the twenty Rubens portraits of Maria de Medici, she met Franco Rizzoni.

She was staring at the painting of the marriage of Maria de Medici and Henry de Navarre. It was a huge work with about fifty noblemen, ladies in waiting, clergy, pages and cherubs floating about. In spite of Rubens' romantic touch, it was obviously not a love match. The bride and groom looked at each other warily, she delicate but somewhat snobbish, he large and crude.

Christina was so intent on imagining the story behind the painting that she hardly noticed the handsome blond man next to her until their shoulders bumped. Suddenly he was speaking in a torrent of apologetic French. She shook her head.

"Je suis Américaine," she said uncertainly. It was one of the few phrases she had picked up and she had not had a chance to use it.

The man smiled and his blue eyes glittered mischievously. He was wearing a well-tailored gray suit and red silk tie.

411

"Ah, mademoiselle, forgive me," he said in excellent English touched with an Italian accent. He asked if she was a student.

No, Christina shook her head, explaining that she was a tourist.

He smiled more broadly. So was he! How delightful! He introduced himself as Franco Rizzoni and explained that he owned an art gallery in Rome. Then he asked her to lunch. She hesitated, but Rizzoni went into a small speech about how awful the Salon de Thé was at the Louvre. She could not possibly be planning to eat there.

She went along with her new friend to a café near the Palais Royal where they shared croque-monsieurs, the French version of the ham sandwich, and white wine. Rizzoni gave her a history of Maria de Medici's marriage to Henry and how she brought civilization, that is, Italian design, taste and style, to the French court.

Christina listened intently, delighted with her opinionated new friend. The hours flew and it was not until the street began to fill with homebound Parisians that she realized it was after five. Ash was probably already furious. They were supposed to dine together at eight.

"Excuse me, Franco," she said with reluctance. "I'm late, but thank you for everything." She rose from the table.

"Can't I see you again?" he pleaded as he

hastily scattered some franc notes on the table and the *garçon* just as hastily cleared them away.

Christina agreed and gave him her room number at the Ritz. For the first time since arriving in Paris she began to think she could be happy again.

*   *   *

That evening she dined with Ash at La Tour d'Argent, one of the finest, oldest and most expensive restaurants in France. The owner, Claude Terrail, a tall, lean man with the profile of a hawk and the manners of a Casanova, was equally famous as a restauranteur and a womanizer. He gave Christina an appreciative look and led them on a quick tour of the cave where he stored his great wines. There he selected an old, dusty bottle of Chateau Rothschild to go with the *spécialité de la maison, le canard pressé*.

The pressed duck had a strong and unusual taste but Christina hardly noticed. She was captivated by the view of Notre Dame from the dining room's large, circular window. It was all so lovely: the city, the dinner, everything. Only she was with the wrong man. She ought to be with Alex Mercati, sharing this with him, instead of sitting across from a man she despised.

Sometimes her thoughts wandered and she found herself hoping that she would hear from Rizzoni again. At least he promised to be amusing company.

Ash was irritated that her mind was obviously not on him. He began to talk about the problems of the day, the negotiations with Iran and other negotiations with OPEC. She nodded politely but without interest.

Suddenly they heard a coarse and all too familiar voice calling to them.

"What a surprise, I didn't know you were in Paris, Ash, and in what charming company!"

Ash winced. He had not come to Paris to have Stavros Pateras at the next table, but there he was and heading toward them.

"You've met Miss Wilkerson, I believe," Ash said, hardly troubling to hide his annoyance.

"Of course, I remember the beautiful young lady from Texas who was my dinner partner in Palm Beach," he said as he took her hand and kissed it. "Indeed, I'm delighted the two of you are here. I'm giving a dinner party Tuesday night and I'd be most pleased if the two of you would come."

"We'd love to," Christina said without giving Ash a chance to refuse. Anything to avoid spending another night alone in his company.

"I'm so glad," Pateras smiled. "Because I

know someone who'll be most happily surprised to see you. Until Tuesday."

*   *   *

The next morning, to Christina's delight, Rizzoni called just after Ash had left. He invited her to tour the Musée de Jeu de Paume. The tiny museum was a revelation. Pictures she had seen in prints all her life, works by Lautrec and Degas and Monet and Van Gogh were all there. Only they were the brilliant originals. Franco seemed to know the story behind each painting, which model was which painter's mistress, who had married well and who had led a tragic life. Something about his wide knowledge and sophistication reminded her of Alex, but where Alex was serious, Franco seemed to live for a good time. But there were so many things about Alex that no one else could possibly replace, she reminded herself. The point was to get on with her life.

The sadness showed on her face, for Franco suddenly looked concerned. He insisted they leave the museum for some fresh air. A few minutes later, as they walked along the Place Concorde, he stopped at a small newsstand. Although she could still only read a few words of French, she could make out some of the headlines, most of which concerned the shah and his troubles. There were some English

language magazines, too; *Time, Newsweek* and
The Reporter. Rizzoni scooped up them all, then
began flipping through them. She was puzzled
until he came to what he wanted. He showed
her a two-page ad for the Eve girl. He had
recognized her.

Yes, she admitted, it was she.

But these ads, they are a disgrace, Franco
insisted angrily, they did no justice to her real
beauty.

She started to laugh. It was the first time she
had laughed since leaving New York. Franco
might not be Alex, but he was going to be very
good for her morale.

*   *   *

That night she and Ash attended a party in
the back room of Maxim's. More than a
hundred people crowded in, the women in long
gowns of velvet and taffeta, the men in black
tie. To her pleasure and Ash's dismay, Franco
Rizzoni emerged from the revelers to greet
them.

So this was the Italian Christina had
described meeting at the Louvre. The appearance of the handsome, young gallery owner
disturbed him more than he cared to admit.
When Christina mentioned him, he had hoped
that the man was a mere gigolo who would soon
learn that she had no money of her own. But he
had checked on his credentials and Rizzoni was

exactly what he claimed to be: a successful art dealer from Rome on a visit to Paris that was part business but mostly pleasure.

He was not pleased about this development at all. Christina had kept him at a distance for weeks, but he had expected that once the Eve staff had gone and there were no witnesses she would relax. But it had not happened. Instead he had been so tied up with this Iran fiasco that he had left her to her own devices, which seemed to include Rizzoni.

He watched uneasily as Rizzoni embraced Christina. The way he held her hand a little too long and the way he looked at her. So that was the way it was. She would not make love with him, but this gigolo could get anything he wanted.

The small band played until dawn and Christina danced with Rizzoni. He was delightful company, witty and even if he was a compulsive flirt it didn't mean a thing. To him it was as natural as breathing. She sensed that she had made a good friend. But as she looked back at the table, she saw Ash glaring at them, his face contorted with hatred.

*   *   *

When in Paris, Stavros Pateras lived in a fourteen-room greystone house in the elegant 7th *arrondisement*, and in spite of his crudity, or perhaps because of it, he managed to assemble quite a cross section of European society for his parties. In Paris, as in the rest of the world, money talks.

The English butler led Ash and Christina into the drawing room and they saw Stephanie. She rushed to greet them, dressed in violet taffeta St. Laurent and looking ravishing. She gave her father a perfunctory peck on the cheek and turned immediately to Christina.

"You and I have met before," she said, smiling. She was anxious to prove that she was no longer the spoiled child she had been at Regine's.

"Yes, but only for a fleeting moment," Christina acknowledged.

Ash himself was in a cold fury. So this was the surprise Pateras had waiting for him. His daughter was living with the Greek. As if he didn't know the girl was a fool, Pateras had to rub his face in it. He resisted his natural reflex to leave. His only choice was to remain, pretending he was unaware of Pateras' malicious coup.

He followed silently as Stephanie led them to their host. Pateras had obviously put away a great deal of champagne.

"Shall I call you Daddy?" He laughed and, to Ash's chagrin, several of the guests nearby joined.

"The only one you can call Daddy is the devil himself," he muttered under his breath.

But Stavros Pateras had good ears. "Of course, the devil," he nodded. "An extraordinary personage. So often invoked and so little appreciated."

"Let them be, Christina," Stephanie suggested as she pulled her away. "I want to hear about you and Alex Mercati. I thought you two were an item."

Christina sighed. It was still hard to believe that she had severed her relationship with Alex.

"We were both too involved in our careers, I guess," she lied. She wanted to change the subject. "What about you, what are you doing with Stavros Pateras?"

Stephanie shrugged. "He takes care of me. He treats me like a princess, his chauffeur takes me anywhere I want to go and we're out every night. We practically live at Regine's and Club 7."

"Where's his wife when all this is going on?"

"When I ask, he just says she's in Greece."

"Are you happy, Stephanie?"

The girl looked at her, her blue eyes shining with intensity. "No, Christina, I'm not. I thought at first that Stavros was like Carlo, that he loved me and he'd take care of me. But now I think he only wants me because of my father. You saw the way he was gloating just now. I'm just another possession he outbid my father for."

Christina put her hand on the girl's shoulder. She understood her completely and she longed to tell her about the father they shared. But not yet.

"Everyone needs someone who loves them," she said softly.

Stephanie smiled a little. "That's why I can't understand how you could drop someone like Alex. Unless, of course, he dropped you." She looked at Christina expectantly.

"That's more like it," Christina lied.

Stephanie looked pleased. Now they had something in common. "He did the same to me," she sighed. "We're two of Alex Mercati's dropouts."

*   *   *

The idea of Rizzoni as a rival had stimulated Ash, and as a man who knew nothing of love, he was far more stimulated by jealousy than affection. When they returned to the Ritz later that night, Christina realized that he would not be as easily put off as before.

He insisted on seeing her to her suite, and as he moved to kiss her good night, he pushed his way into her room.

"Please, Ash," she said softly. "I thought we had an understanding."

"I thought so, too, Christina," he said softly. She wondered if it was the same voice he had used with her mother so many years ago. "But you seem to be finding amusements elsewhere."

She knew he meant Rizzoni.

"Really, that's ridiculous," she snapped. "Franco is just a friend."

He ignored that and pulled her toward him. He began to kiss her, fondling her breasts through the sheer dress. She tried to push him away but he clung to her. His touch became more intense and suddenly he was pulling at her dress. A strange, morbid pleasure invaded her as she found her body responding in spite of her hatred of the man.

"Yes, Christina," he whispered hoarsely. "You do like it, don't you?"

Suddenly a feeling of disgust swept over her. This was her father. How dare he?

He had forced her down on the settee and was caressing her thighs. She renewed her resistance but it did no good. Then suddenly Ash pulled away, his face a terrible pale color. He stood up and began to rifle through the pockets of his dinner jacket.

"Ash, are you all right?" It was a strange question to address to a man who was in the process of raping her, but she was concerned about the awful pallor in his face.

He had found what he wanted. "Water," he barked and she ran to the small refrigerator for a bottle of Perrier and brought it back to him

421

just as he dropped a small gold pillbox back into his pocket. But too late, she had seen him take out the pills.

"I apologize for my behavior, Christina," he said grandly when he had finished swallowing the water. "Good night."

Christina watched him leave and locked the door behind him. She was more disturbed than ever.

*　　　*　　　*

The following morning her wake-up call came with a message. The Ritz operator informed her that Mr. Young was expecting her for breakfast in his suite. When she arrived, he was on the terrace overlooking the Place Vendome, but such a view was wasted on him as he was buried in a stack of morning papers that included the *International Herald Tribune*, *Le Monde* and the *London Times*.

"What's the news, Ash?" she asked as she seated herself on the terrace. She had decided that it was best to pretend that nothing had happened.

A room service waiter poured espresso for her and placed a warm croissant on her Limoge dish. As soon as he was gone, Ash spoke.

"Jessica is dead."

The cold detachment in his voice shocked her.

"I don't have all the details yet," he

continued casually. "But it seems she took too many sleeping pills."

"She killed herself?" Christina remembered the one and only time she had met Jessica Young. It was at Belvedere. She recalled a sad, thin woman, eager to please, who only lit up when asked about her collection of Meissen birds. Poor Jessica. She started out life so differently from Teresa Martinez and yet they both ended up very much the same, courtesy of Ashley Young.

"Really, Christina," he said. "It's the best thing that could have happened."

He was dismissing his wife of twenty-four years as easily as he had dismissed her mother.

"Ash," she said. "She was your wife and you talk as if she was some intruder you had to get rid of."

"Calm down, Christina. It was nothing like that," he said coolly. "Jessica was hooked on pills. Pills to sleep, to get up, to diet, anything to avoid reality. They were too much for her heart."

"How is Stephanie taking this?" she asked.

"She's fine," he said, barely interested. "She's on her way back to New York now. We'll leave for New York tonight. Tom Patterson is taking care of the funeral arrangements now."

"You have no compassion for anyone, do you, Ash?" she marvelled.

"Look, Christina," he said with irritation.

He was beginning to lose patience. "If you want to go into mourning for my wife, I don't mind."

Of course. Now she understood why the death seemed to please him. The last obstacle to their affair had been removed. She almost envied Jessica Young. At least she was free now. Her own ordeal was just beginning.

39

New York, N.Y.
September 1978

The service for Jessica Hollingsworth Young at Frank Campbell's was crowded with friends and colleagues of the Youngs' and Hollingsworths'. Ash arrived wearing a dark suit and a gray expression and he moved quickly to the end of the room where Jessica's coffin lay surrounded by huge bouquets of fall flowers. He paused for one last kiss.

Poor Jessica looked small and pitiful. Her pale, pinched face was covered with more makeup than she had ever worn in her life.

He turned away and moved on to the Hollingsworths who were seated on a couch nearby. Jessica's mother was sobbing quietly as Stephanie held her arm. Mr. Hollingsworth stood by impassively and when Ash offered him his hand the older man ignored it, looking through his son-in-law as if he did not see him at all.

Embarrassed, Ash withdrew his hand. He started to say something, then thought better of it. With a curt nod he walked out of the stuffy room.

Out in the street, he took a deep breath of the early autumn air. He was furious. Hollingsworth had no right to humiliate him so publicly. They obviously blamed him for Jessica's death. Well, they could blame him all they wanted, there was no way they were ever going to go farther than idle speculation.

The special pills were a matter strictly between him and Dr. Reinhardt.

His next step, in fact, was to visit Reinhardt. The sudden attack he had experienced at the Ritz had not only come at an inconvenient time, it had frightened him more than he cared to admit. It was not just that the sudden pains had been so excruciating. He felt genuine anger at being unable to control them.

Damn. With his money and power, he should not have to suffer that kind of thing. He was going to tell Reinhardt that, and if the old doctor couldn't do something about it he'd get himself another boy.

40

New York, N.Y.
September 1978

Vic Procaci's small, tidy studio apartment was at 14th Street and First Avenue, just a few subway stops from his roots in Brooklyn and close to the midtown office of the FBI. This morning he was awakened there by the insistent buzz of the downstairs intercom.

"Hello," he said sleepily. "Who is it?"

"It's me, Stephanie Young," the giggling voice said. "I'm here in your lobby and I'm coming right up."

Moments later, the young agent let Stephanie into his apartment. She was dressed in black which only emphasized her pink and white complexion and pale blond hair.

"I'm home for my mother's funeral," she

said brightly. "And you told me to look you up when I got to town."

"I'm sorry about your mother, I read about it in the papers."

"Don't be sorry, Vic," she said. "Daddy made her life miserable. She stopped living a long time ago."

"How's Pateras?"

She made a face. "That pig! I wouldn't go back if he gave me all his money."

"Why did you go with him in the first place?"

"You know me, Vic. Anything for a good time. I guess I was just bored and I didn't want to go back to that awful clinic," she pouted. "Besides, Paris was exciting for a while and Stavros gave me everything I wanted."

"Did you go to bed with him?" He could not bear the idea of her with Pateras.

"Of course, silly," she laughed, then noticed the hurt look on his face. "But it was terrible. When he drinks he's just a pig."

"I guess you didn't part friends."

"No. When I got the news about Mother, I just took all my things and left for the airport. I guess I'll stay with my grandparents for a while. But I'm here now."

She got up from the sofa and walked over to him. She sat in his lap and put an arm around his shoulder. "Poor Vic, always working. Don't you ever have any fun?" She kissed him on the lips and, taking his hand, guided it under her blouse.

He was still not fully awake, but he'd learned a few things in Brooklyn that even the lusty Greeks did not know. He reacted quickly, caressing her nipples, and as they hardened so did he. Quickly he undressed her and then himself. Her soft blondness melted in his strong embrace.

Later, they showered together in his tiny bathroom.

"At least I didn't make the trip for nothing," she giggled as he took a thick towel and began to dry her like a child.

"You're crazy, Stephanie," he shook his head. "But beautiful."

"Then why don't we spend a few days together," she said eagerly. "We'll have a good time."

"I wish I could," his voice was patient. "But I'm still working on the Gallenzo case. I'm so beat at the end of the day I could never take care of you."

"You didn't do so badly this morning," she teased.

"So they call me One Time Procaci," he said as he tucked in his shirt.

Stephanie pointed to his open fly.

"That's me all right," he laughed. "A closed mind and an open fly. But I've got to get to work. And as for you, I don't want to hear that you've run off again with some fucking millionaire."

"I'm through with the big money," she grinned. "All I want now is a nice young man with a big cock and a small brain who makes love to me once before breakfast, once after dinner and on Sunday afternoons."

"Gee, Stephanie," he shook his head, "that cuts me out. After dinner, I watch *Starsky & Hutch.*"

"Oh, we can watch, then make love."

"No way. After that comes Johnny Carson. By then, I'm too tired to do anything. Sorry Stephanie, but we're from different worlds."

"Don't be silly, Vic," she persisted. "I know a perfect way for us to make love and not miss your shows."

"Let me guess," he laughed. "OK, we'll try it again sometime." He kissed her on the lips, smacked her playfully on her bottom and closed the door on her. But when he left for his office uptown a few minutes later, he was whistling.

41

New York, N.Y.
October 1978

The elderly Viennese doctor shook his head gravely as he faced Ash Young and thought wistfully of the ancient tradition of slaying the messenger who brought bad news. If anyone resembled an ancient potentate it was his fabulous patron-patient Ashley Young, but it was he, humble Max Reinhardt, who was about to deliver some unpleasant news.

"You were quite right to consult me immediately, Mr. Young," he said. He was holding the results of Ash's latest EKG and laboratory tests.

Ash shifted restlessly in his chair. He just wanted the old faker to get on with it, find out what was wrong and prescribe something. That was what he was paying for.

"Now that we know the digitalis was only partially successful, we'll have to heighten the dosage. I have some other medication I want you to start taking as well. We don't want another experience like you had in Paris."

Ash relaxed. He had given Reinhardt an expurgated version of the night with Christina but the doctor's diagnosis matched his own. He had suffered a mild heart attack, a warning sign, but with Reinhardt's medication, careful diet and no stress it was nothing to be concerned about.

He would not have to fear an incident like the one that sent Nelson Rockefeller and other great men into lascivious history.

Nevertheless, he waited several weeks before seeing Christina again. He had to act as a bereaved husband. He kept in touch with her by phone. For one thing, he was more involved than ever in trying to straighten out the Pahlevi family investments. The damned Iran situation was totally out of hand. The shah had become a creature of his advisors and the empress had emerged as the true guiding power, something that impressed him considerably. After all, in spite of the shah's pretensions, his consort was merely the niece of a court dentist educated at rather conventional French schools. But she had grown in her role.

Yes, he was more convinced than ever that Christina Wilkerson could grow in the same way.

* * *

Tom Patterson struggled to hide his concern when Ash announced his plans to marry.

"I know what you're thinking, Tom," he said to his longtime confidante. "Middle-aged madness or something like that."

"Not at all," Patterson insisted. "It's just so sudden. Have you discussed it with the girl?"

"Not yet," Ash admitted. "I want to work out a settlement with you first. Just because I'm marrying her doesn't mean she's getting her hands on my money."

Patterson relaxed a little. That sounded more like the Ash he had known for thirty years.

"I want to draw up a contract, something with adequate compensation for her, and you might as well give it in steps so that it'll behoove her to stick it out."

Patterson left Young's office, struck with how little Ash had changed.

42

New York, N.Y.
November 1978

Ash waited almost a month before he invited Christina to dinner at his apartment. Christina had never been there before and she was impressed with the opulence, although the coldness and impersonal quality made her think of the Louvre.

They were served in the dining room, a far more formal room than that at Belvedere. The walls were hung with pale blue silk and the Louis XIV fauteuils were upholstered in slightly darker velvet. A huge silver epergne filled with gold and orange flowers dominated the center of the table, but it was hastily removed as Ash and Christina sat down. A uniformed maid and a butler moved in and out of the room unobtrusively serving the meal.

The dinner itself was relatively spartan, prepared according to the new regimen Dr. Reinhardt had issued. There were broiled lamb chops, spinach and baked squash. There was no wine and dessert was a melon. It was while Christina was finishing the melon that Ash issued his proposition.

"I want to marry you, Christina," he said.

She gulped the melon, hastily avoiding choking and stared at him.

"Don't be surprised," he said coolly. "It would be to your advantage. As my wife you would have a position of honor and I'm sure that you'll be far better at the job than my first wife was."

So, Christina thought. As with everything in his life, marriage was a business deal. He never mentioned love. Still, this was it, the break she had been waiting for.

"Of course I'll marry you," she heard herself saying and wondered if he could hear her heart beating wildly.

"Excellent," he said and rose and walked to an ornately gilded cabinet nearby. On it was a leather folder which he took up and opened. He handed the three-page document inside to Christina. "I'd like you to sign this."

To his surprise, she began to read it and as she did her eyebrows arched slightly. She frowned and continued reading with great concentration. When she was through she handed it back to him.

"This is a prenuptial agreement," she said. "I won't sign it."

"Why not?" he said. "It's for your own good, Christina. This way you'll have your own income and a nice sum, too."

"I already have an income as the Eve girl, Ash," she said firmly. "I don't need your money. I just don't care to sign it, that's all. If you don't trust me, you don't have to marry me."

"Please, Christina, don't be unreasonable," he insisted. "I'm involved in all sorts of corporations and I'm sure you don't want to get mixed up in all those business matters. This agreement clarifies exactly where you stand. It's a protection for you."

It irritated her that he thought she was stupid or naive enough to believe him. "Why go through all this, Ash?" she said in a voice heavy with sarcasm. "When you've had enough of me, all you have to do is give me some sleeping pills."

It was a wild remark but he glared at her for a minute, wondering how much she knew. But it was impossible, there was no way she could know how close to the mark she was.

"That remark is in terrible taste, Christina," he said.

"Maybe, but so is this agreement. You're the one who wants to get married, Ash. Either take me for better or worse or we can forget it."

He scrutinized her closely. He had to admire her. She had poise and tremendous self-control. But he was still the smarter of the two. Even if she didn't sign the agreement he could deal with her if the need arose. It was better not to make an issue of it now.

"Very well," he shrugged. "Forget about the agreement then. It doesn't really matter."

The ease with which he accepted her refusal only convinced her that he had made up his mind to have her. That was the most important thing to him now, and to her too. Just as he was driven by the need for possession, she was driven by the thirst for revenge. She would have the Young empire.

"We can be married this weekend in Paris. The mayor is a friend of mine and his staff can make the arrangements."

"No!" she said firmly.

"What?" He was surprised at the vehemence in her voice.

"I just mean that it's too soon, Ash. What will the Hollingsworths think? And Stephanie?"

"I don't give a damn what anyone thinks. If I want to marry you, I'll damn well marry you."

Yes, Christina thought to herself. You damn well will. But when she did speak, it was to ask him to wait at least a decent six months from Jessica's death. Reluctantly, he agreed. That would give them both time to plan. He reached over to seal their pact with a kiss but she pulled away.

"Now what's wrong?" he said starchily.

"Nothing, Ash," she answered. "It's just that I thought you understood how I feel. I want everything to wait until we're married."

"Very well," he said. There was no use in getting excited. He had achieved the main goal. He would have this beautiful creature as his wife. He sent Christina home with his chauffeur and went to bed satisfied.

*　　*　　*

If Tom Patterson was surprised when Ashley Young announced that he was going to marry Christina Wilkerson without any prenuptial agreement, he did not show it. Long experience had taught him that it was useless to argue once his employer had decided on an acquisition. And somehow this marriage seemed to be another acquisition.

Besides, there was really nothing to worry about. Ash was in excellent health, as far as he knew. Stephanie was provided for, if not generously so. If Ash wanted to marry a beautiful young Texan, it was entirely his business. And as for any intentions Miss Wilkerson might have of getting her lacquered fingernails on Ash Young's fortune, he was quite sure Ash could handle himself.

43

Marbella, Spain
December 1978

Waking suddenly, Alex Mercati jumped out of bed and opened the curtains that had kept his room at the Marbella Club in almost total darkness. The morning sun reflected on the Mediterranean was almost blinding.

Marbella, the plush resort on the Costa del Sol, was Spain's answer to the Cote d'Azur and the Costa Smeralda, and the Marbella Club was its heart. The series of whitewashed stucco cottages with the red clay tile roofs typical of Andalusia did not even look like a hotel but a succession of small villas hidden among lush gardens of bougainvillaea, oleander and hibiscus.

"For God's sake, close those curtains," a

feminine voice groaned from the bed he had just abandoned.

He obliged, leaving them open a crack so that a ray of sun shone on a firm pair of buttocks, marked by a small white V against the deeply tanned body. The indelible mark of the bikini.

Princess Vicky von Holstein, his companion, was the golden-haired wife of His Serene Highness Prince Otto von Holstein of Austria, a jovial, engaging fellow who enjoyed shooting, skiing, golfing, eating and the pleasures of the flesh. He was a pillar of Marbella society and a longtime friend of Alex.

The princess, the former Vicky Marsh, had been a movie starlet of sorts before she met the prince. Born in a small North Carolina town, she used her sexy body and provocative face to full advantage through two marriages, one to a movie cameraman, the other to a Hollywood publicist, and innumerable affairs. After stints in New York and Hollywood, where she reached star status only in the boudoir, she settled in London where she made a few porno films and became known as the best cocksucker in the realm. It was in London that she met Prince Otto, who never recovered from their first encounter and promptly asked her to marry him.

The prince was fond of telling his buddies that he had never met a woman who could equal Vicky in bed. He did such a good public relations job for his wife that sooner or later they were all moved to test his claim.

Otto was generous in everything and he had insisted that his despondent friend join him in Marbella. He and Vicky welcomed Alex with a large dinner party at Regine's, the resort's most elegant watering hole, to which they had invited an assortment of the most beautiful women in Marbella, all of whom seemed eager to boost his spirits.

Since dinner on the Costa del Sol seldom started before midnight, it was five in the morning before Alex, bushed after the long flight from New York, the elaborate dinner and the strenuous dancing, was finally free to retire. It was a relief to sink into his bed at the Club.

Then there was a knock at his door.

Wearily he wrapped a towel around his waist, got up to open the door and to his amazement found himself face to face with the princess.

"Mind if I come in?" she drawled as she pushed her way past him. "I didn't think it would be very hospitable of me to let you spend your first night alone." She sat on his bed and smiled up at him.

"But what about Otto?" he asked.

"Oh, don't worry about the prince," she shrugged. "I gave him a couple of sleeping pills and he's snoring already."

"But . . . but . . ." he started to object but she had made up her mind.

She pulled the towel from his waist and was already on her knees licking at his manhood. There was little he could do but rise to the occasion. She pushed him on the bed and quickly loosened her own robe. She was naked underneath, the tanned body still as good as when it starred in *The Seduction of Cynthia* and *Fanny Hill 1960*. She moved on top of him, amply demonstrating that all her husband's claims were justified. She was still probably the best lay on the Costa del Sol.

But that had been seven hours ago and now that he had awakened with her beside him, he was disgusted. Disgusted with her and with himself. His friend Otto did not deserve this. But then he did not deserve what he had gotten from Christina.

*　　*　　*

Vicky was the first. After her came Clara, the wife of a Spanish sherry millionaire, then Ludmilla, a voluptuous Yugoslav recently divorced from an Italian baron, followed by Pupette, a chic French widow, and Helga, a stunning Berliner who was engaged to a German industrialist, and Britt, a tall Swede who liked to make love after playing tennis. There were others, a different one every night, his for the choosing. But it was always the same story. He did not make love to them, he fucked them. And the moment it was over, he never wanted to see them again.

He found himself thinking of Christina constantly, the perfume and softness of her skin, the way she purred in his arms after they made love, like a contented kitten, the way she whispered "I love you" in his ear.

Sometimes he thought of going back, calling her, apologizing for his jealousy. Then someone was kind enough to show him an item in the *International Herald Tribune.* The Eve girl and the tycoon were going to be married. So he had been right about her. It didn't matter.

The days in Marbella were all the same. Bright sunshine, white beaches, parties, women. They gave him no relief. Only in concentrating on winning a difficult tennis match or a keen golf game could he forget for a moment. But only for a moment.

On Christmas morning he shook himself free from the arms of Marisa, the Eurasian wife of a British financier and jumped into his swimming trunks. He slipped on a robe and walked quickly to the deserted beach. The sea was agitated but he went to the end of the jetty and dived in.

He swam for a long time without looking back and when he finally turned he realized he was dangerously far from shore. He was fighting a current. He was a strong swimmer but after a while he knew it was bringing him further and further adrift. He could feel himself tiring.

He was not going to make it, but he was calm and felt strangely at peace. He was alone with the blue sky and the blue sea. He let himself float as the shore drifted further and further away. He wondered if Christina would cry when she learned he was dead.

Suddenly he heard the faint noise of a motor and saw a bright red speedboat approaching. It was manned by a dark young man and pulling a beautiful blond girl on water skis. He waved an arm and shouted. They saw him and came to an abrupt stop.

"Could you give me a lift?" he called. "I've lost my way."

44

New York, N.Y.
January 1979

Stephanie Young spent New Year's Day
moving in with her new boyfriend. Jonathan
Jones was as far removed from Teddy McElroy
and Carlo Gallenzo and Stavros Pateras as she
could get. He was a musician and she had met
him in a coffee shop in the East Village. At last
she had something to keep her really occupied.
She was going to help Jonathan and his band
become famous.

Jonathan had everything. He was young,
which already separated him from most of the
men she had known, and he was slender and
different-looking with his long hair and short
beard and talented. True, he wasn't as rich or as
famous as the other men in her life. In fact, as

far as money went he was probably even poorer than Tim Kelly, the groom at Foxhall. But that didn't matter. She would always have an income. Even her father could not stop that.

Only maybe the income would not be enough. Because unfortunately, Jonathan had one tiny flaw. He seemed to be a junkie. It was only a few weeks into their relationship before she realized exactly how important drugs were to him. She had grown up around pills, so the fact that he took a lot of ups and downs at first meant nothing to her. And everyone she knew smoked marijuana, so that was nothing new.

So it was a few weeks before she actually noticed the scars on Jonathan's arms. When she asked him about them, he insisted they were old tracks, that he had beaten his habit and was starting a new life. She liked that. It was nice to think that the two of them were starting over together.

Then one afternoon she returned to their apartment early and found him shooting up, a dirty scarf tied around his arm and him practically incoherent, worse than her mother when she was really stoned.

Even worse was the fact that they were hardly ever alone. The guys from the band all seemed to be living in the tiny apartment and bringing their girlfriends over. She tried to make the apartment look nice, but it was a losing battle. She usually ended up getting high with Jonathan and forgetting about the whole thing.

Only, lately, Jonathan had begun nagging her about money. The band wasn't working and they needed new equipment, he insisted. Couldn't she ask her father for bread? That was a laugh. He didn't seem to understand that her father was the last person she could ask. And even Grandmother and Grandfather Hollingsworth were angry with her for moving in with Jonathan. They were not likely to make it easier for her. No, there was not going to be any more money than the regular one thousand-dollar check every month from her trust. And by the time Jonathan got through with that, there wasn't even enough left for food.

Still, to celebrate their first month together, one of the guys from the band brought home some wine and really heavy Thai stick and, as they smoked it, he explained to Stephanie how they were going to make a really big score, with her help.

45

New York, N.Y.
January 1979

"It's all so exciting," Melinda Parsons was saying. She and Christina were sitting in the tiny living room of the apartment they wouldn't be sharing much longer. It was one of the rare nights lately when they were both home together. "Remember when I helped you pick out a gown to take to Palm Beach and how nervous you were? Whoever thought you'd end up marrying Ashley Young?"

Who indeed? Christina shrugged.

"Really, Christina, I don't understand you," Melinda said irritably.

Christina had changed since her mother's death. She seemed cooler, more distant. But she hadn't changed totally and that was what really worried Melinda. It was just not like her friend to contemplate marriage with a man she obviously cared nothing about. She had tried to talk to her about it, but Christina made it clear that the subject was off limits.

There were so many strange things going on, Melinda thought. Alex Mercati was totally out of the picture and this Italian was calling all the time. Christina tried to play it down, but it was obvious that Franco Rizzoni was crazy about her. She seemed to be the main reason he had come to New York. On the other hand, the engaged couple spent hardly any time together. Christina insisted she wanted it that way. Ash Young was off in Morocco or something with the shah and Christina was here supposedly making plans for their wedding. Though she didn't seem too interested.

"What did you say, Melinda?" her friend asked idly.

"I just think it's funny that the two of you aren't in Palm Beach. I'd give anything to be someplace warm and sunny."

"I told you, I don't want to go back there until it's really all mine." Although she could have added that it was already all hers, by right of birth. "Besides, we're both too busy."

The phone rang and Christina answered. It was Stephanie Young.

"When did you get back to New York?" she asked. It seemed like a lifetime since they met in Paris.

"After Mother's funeral I just never went

back to Pateras," Stephanie explained. "Oh, I've got lots to tell you, Christina. Can we have lunch? Alone?"

"I think I can manage," Christina said. "Where should we meet?"

"I don't care. Just a quiet place where we can talk."

"What about P.J. Clarke's? That's so noisy nobody will be able to hear us."

"Sold. I'll meet you there at one o'clock."

*　　　*　　　*

P.J. Clarke's at 55th and Third Avenue is an old-fashioned saloon that has maintained its own kind of gritty integrity in spite of the fact that its bar was more often crowded these days with young advertising executives than Irish working men. Christina found Stephanie at a table in the back room. There was a tall, slim, unkempt young man with her. Christina did not like the look of him at all.

"I thought you said to come alone?" she asked as she sat down.

"Oh, Jonathan was just leaving," Stephanie explained. "But I wanted you to meet him. Jonathan, this is my friend—and future step-mother—Christina Wilkerson."

Jones merely nodded and stood up. Christina noticed that his eyes were glassy. He was extremely thin and his tight, faded blue jeans and long brown hair did not look terribly clean. He waved a tattooed hand at the two women and left the restaurant.

"Where did you find him?" Christina could not help asking.

"Isn't he wonderful?" Stephanie said. "Knowing him has changed my whole life."

Over spinach salads and glasses of chablis, Stephanie brought Christina up to date on her latest adventures.

"But what happened?" Christina asked. "When I saw you in Paris, Pateras had you swimming in luxury."

"Well . . ." Stephanie searched for the words. "I left Stavros after I saw you. Jonathan has shown me that money doesn't mean anything."

"What does he do for a living?" In spite of herself, Christina felt like a concerned parent. She was not pleased with the way Stephanie looked, pale and tired, and she was certainly not impressed with Jonathan Jones.

"He's a musician," Stephanie said uneasily. "And a very talented one. But he's out of a job right now and we're broke. I even sold the jewelry that Stavros gave me, but we're broke again."

"How much do you need?"

"Five hundred dollars," Stephanie said. "But I'll pay you back as soon as Jonathan gets a gig."

Christina was convinced there was probably a very good reason why Jonathan needed so much money and she was pretty sure she knew what it was.

"Stephanie," she said gently. "This musician friend of yours. Is he on some kind of drugs? Is that why you need the money?"

She shrugged. "All musicians do dope. It inspires them."

"So that's it." Christina took a deep breath. "Listen to me, Stephanie. I can't give you money to help you and your boyfriend destroy yourselves. Especially when I see what it's doing to you."

In truth, Christina felt nothing but pity for the girl. They were sisters after all and perhaps if she had been raised by Ash Young instead of Bill Wilkerson she too would have grown up this hungry and desperate for love. She reached across the table and gently laid her hand on Stephanie's shoulder.

"You've been in love before, Stephanie, remember?" She almost envied her ability to forget the other men. If only she could forget Alex Mercati as easily.

"I've never loved anyone the way I love Jonathan," Stephanie insisted. "No man, not even Carlo, made me feel like he does."

"All right," Christina sighed and opened her purse. She took out five hundred-dollar bills and handed them to Stephanie. "You're in luck. I just cashed a check," she said as she handed the money to the girl. "But you have to promise to stay in touch with me. If you need more, just call me."

"You're a great girl, Christina," Stephanie smiled as she dropped the money into her purse. "I won't forget this. You know, I'm dying to ask you a question."

Christina braced herself. She had an idea what was coming. "Ask away, Stephanie."

"Why are you marrying my father?"

It would have been interesting to see Stephanie's reaction to the truth: that she was marrying Ash Young because she hoped somehow to destroy him and to claim the Young empire that was hers by all rights. Surely if there was one person alive who knew first hand what a bastard Ash Young was it was Stephanie. But she could not bring herself to confide in anyone. Not yet. Instead, she tried to answer casually.

"Oh, your father is a rich and powerful man."

Stephanie shook her head. "That's not it. You're not a social climber and you're not a gold digger. There's got to be something else."

Not even Stephanie considered that anyone might be marrying her father for love.

"Maybe you're right, Stephanie," she acknowledged. "Maybe someday you'll know the real reason."

"OK, Christina. Keep your secret. But whatever it is, I'm on your side." She lit a cigarette. "You know, I ran into Alex Mercati the other day."

"You saw Alex?" Christina was jolted. "What did he say?"

"He told me that he never expected you to turn out to be a scheming gold digger. I think you really hurt him. He can't believe you're marrying Daddy."

"I don't blame him," Christina said sadly. "I guess I treated him badly."

"But why? Every girl in New York was after him and you broke his heart."

"I love him."

"That doesn't make sense."

"Stephanie, someday you'll know the whole story and you'll understand. Not now."

Stephanie sighed. "I don't think I'll ever understand, but just remember I'm on your side. By the way, when is my wonderful father coming back from Morocco?"

"Next week," Christina answered as they rose and left the crowded, noisy restaurant. On the street, they kissed and Stephanie patted her purse.

"Thank you, Christina. For everything."

46

New York, N.Y.
February 1979

Ash Young returned from Morocco to find his beautiful apartment in a shambles, overrun with policemen and the normally unflappable August distraught and heavily bandaged. Burglars had entered sometime during the night, the poor man explained, and stolen innumerable objects. Missing were the priceless collection of jeweled snuffboxes, the fifteen lapis lazuli elephants, the heavy gold plates, the Fabergé boxes and his own jewelry.

That was not the worst of it. The vandals had destroyed what they couldn't take. Glass vitrines were shattered, sofas and Louis XVI armchairs covered with Venetian silk had been ripped apart. Tapestries and paintings had been sliced with knives, walls spray painted with obscenities and someone had even shat on one of the Iranian carpets that had been a gift from the shah.

Ash was livid. He demanded to know how the vandals could have entered the apartment, past the sophisticated alarm system, past the doorman and building staff.

The police told him that the doorman had been found tied up like a salami with tape around his mouth and over his eyes. He had been felled by a karate chop on the back of the neck after a stranger, a scruffy-looking fellow with long hair, had asked for the Young apartment. The servants had all been out except for August, who bore the wounds of his losing battle.

Two things were certain, the police told Ash. The robbers must have come with a truck—it was the only way they could have carried away so much—and they must have been well-informed about the layout of the apartment and the movements of the household.

Ash sank back in one of the ruined bergeres, took out some of the new medication prescribed by Reinhardt and quickly gulped two pills. He was stunned by the awful toll of the damage. Four of the paintings were a total loss. The Titian, fortunately, had only one neat slice across it and could be restored. The El Greco, which had been smeared with obscene remarks in lipstick, presented no serious problem. More serious was the damage to the tapestries and carpets. There was no way to salvage the mutilated silks and brocades on most of the furniture.

All in all, between what had been stolen and what had been destroyed, he figured that his loss was close to two million dollars. Who, he wondered, could hate him so much? Like the Shah, he seemed to have enemies everywhere.

47

New York, N.Y.
February 1979

It was two o'clock and Christina had a nasty feeling of apprehension. Franco had never shown up for their one o'clock lunch date at Grenouille. Impeccable, punctual Franco, who liked to say he was the only Roman who was always on time. It was simply not like him to be late.

She had called the Waldorf but there was no answer in his suite, so she decided to walk to the hotel. Something was definitely wrong. Franco would never stand her up like this.

Snow was falling as she hit Park Avenue and she could hear the ambulance siren wailing. Traffic in front of the hotel was tied up and a small crowd had grouped near the entrance. A tall policeman was trying to hold them back.

"Officer," she said, tugging on his sleeve. "Please, what's going on?"

"Some junkie freaked out upstairs and came out the window stark naked. You don't wanna look, miss, it's not too pretty," he cautioned her as the attendants wheeled a covered body on a stretcher into the waiting ambulance. He went back to pushing the crowd and exhorting them to keep moving.

Christina walked blindly through the plush lobby and toward the elevator. The feeling of anxiety deepened. She pushed the button for the twelfth floor and when the doors opened she saw the hall was crowded with policemen, reporters and photographers.

"Mac, you're a wop," one photographer was shouting down the hall to one of the policemen. "How do you spell the guy's name?"

A tall, young policeman shouted back, "R-I-Z-Z-O-N-I."

Christina never even stepped out of the elevator. She just let the doors close again and as it descended she sank to the floor. When the doors opened again, she walked like a zombie through the lobby and back out to Park Avenue. The crowd had thinned and the ambulance had disappeared.

She needed to walk awhile, to clear her head and sort out what had happened. Franco was just not the type to kill himself and he was certainly no junkie, no one who would fly out a window while high on drugs. He was just a good-looking playboy who never tired of the chase. Even though she wasn't interested in becoming one of his conquests, she had become very fond of him. Now he was dead.

None of it made any sense.

*   *   *

Ash Young sat by the telephone in the restored library of the Fifth Avenue apartment stroking one of the jeweled snuffboxes that the robbers had overlooked as he tried to concentrate on the *Times*. Today's story announced that that weak-willed fool Shahpur Bahktiar had allowed Khomeini to return to Iran. The army had of course immediately declared itself neutral, in effect withdrawing their support. Bahktiar had fled to Paris and Khomeini assumed power. The story disturbed him but he could not focus on it. He was waiting for an important call and it was already fifteen minutes late.

The idiots. It was a simple matter and it had all been planned in detail. They were being paid one hundred thousand dollars to get rid of a useless Italian gigolo, a parasite. It could not go wrong. He wanted the thing settled before he left for Riyadh. He didn't want it hanging over his head while he was dealing with the Arabs.

The sound of the phone interrupted his thoughts. He lifted the receiver on his private line.

"The package was dropped," the low voice whispered.

So everything had worked according to plan. It always did when it was his plan. He had paid the appropriate price and the job had been done. He smiled thinly. Now he could concentrate on his reading.

*　　*　　*

After walking ten blocks, Christina decided on what she had to do. She stopped at a corner pay phone and dialed Alex Mercati's number.

His secretary came on the line and told her that he was in a meeting. It was clear from the tone of her voice that she had not forgiven Christina for jilting her boss.

"Please, Jean, tell him it's most important that I see him," she insisted.

"I'm sorry, Miss Wilkerson, but Mr. Mercati has an extremely busy schedule and can't be disturbed."

"I know how busy he can be, Jean, but you know I wouldn't insist unless I had to."

"All right, Miss Wilkerson, I'll try. Please hold the line."

After staying on hold for nearly five minutes Christina had almost run out of change when Jean came back on to announce that Alex could see her.

Ten minutes later, Christina was ushered into Alex's office in the 65th Street townhouse where they had once been so happy together. He stood up and smiled tightly.

"What can I do for you?" he asked, his tone icy.

"Alex, I know how difficult this is," she said as she seated herself in an armchair. "But you're the only person I could turn to."

"What about your fiancé?" he said sarcastically. "You're marrying a very powerful man, can't he help you?"

"You don't understand," she insisted. "Ash is insanely jealous. If he knew I was meeting another man—"

Somehow that hurt him even more, but he listened patiently as Christina described meeting Rizzoni in Paris, how they had become fast friends, Ash's jealous scenes, and finally, the awful scene she had just left.

"Did you . . . love . . . this guy?" he asked gently.

"Oh, no," she said. "Franco was a friend. We had fun together. He lived for a good time. That's why I can't believe that he'd kill himself. I've got to find out what happened."

"All right, Christina," Alex said. "I'll see what I can do."

*   *   *

Ash Young was slightly puzzled by Christina's reaction to the death of her friend. He had expected her to be upset, which she obviously was, but as they shared dinner at "21," she insisted that the Italian could not have possibly committed suicide. Well, it hardly mattered what she thought, there was nothing she could do about it. The important thing was that his rival was out of the way. Unfortunately, the detective that he had hired to follow Christina had informed him of an even more irritating development.

"Ah, Christina," he said coolly. "You're seeing your friend Mercati again, aren't you?"

"I don't see what that has to do with it, Ash," she answered.

"Oh, it has quite a bit to do with it, Christina," he smiled. "Since you're going to be my wife your reputation is important to me. I certainly wouldn't want your name linked with a man who may go to jail."

"What are you talking about?" She was thoroughly confused.

Ash toyed with the water glass as he savored the moment. "Didn't Alex discuss his trip to Teheran with you? Don't you know about his arrangement with the shah's government?"

"Of course, he told me everything," she snapped. "Including how you set it up for him." But she was beginning to feel nervous. She had always suspected that Ash was up to no good when he approached Alex about the Teheran trip.

"You know, Christina, point of view is crucial," he said slowly. "Take us, for example.

People in the room probably think one of two things. Either I'm a rich man who's bought himself a beautiful young mistress—and of course we would know how wrong that is—or there may even be a few romantics in the room who think that we're actually in love."

Christina listened in silence.

"You, of course, are in love, but you're still in love with your friend Mercati. I, who am not in love, want you and I'm willing to pay for you."

"You make me sound like a whore," she snapped.

He waved his hand in a gesture of dismissal. "Not at all, not at all. It's simply that everything and everyone has a price and I'm willing to pay it."

"If that's the way you feel, Ash," she said angrily. "You can consider the wedding off. I'm not for sale." She began to rise from the table.

"You'd better sit down, Christina," he said. "This concerns your friend Mercati."

She sat down.

"Several months ago, Alex Mercati entered into a secret contract with the Iranian government to improve the shah's image with the news media in the United States. He accepted a fee of one hundred fifty thousand dollars a year and never reported the fee or registered with the Justice Department."

He went on to describe how the revolutionary government was now anxious to expose all these so-called collaborators with the old regime. He reminded Christina of several similar incidents which had destroyed the career of a United States senator and a prominent journalist.

"But you told Alex that the registration was taken care of," Christina said. "And he never wanted the money, you know that."

"I'm afraid that what you and I know carries very little weight, Christina," Ash said. "Alex has made a lot of enemies and they'll enjoy printing this story."

"But it'll ruin him; it'll ruin *The Reporter*."

"Yes, I suppose it will."

Now she understood. He knew there was no question of love between them, but that would not stop him. But it was amusing to think that he believed he had to blackmail her to close the deal. She could end the whole charade simply by telling him now that she was his daughter, but no. Let him think that he had her. If it gave him pleasure to think that he was blackmailing her into the marriage, so be it. The point was that she was going to get her hands on the Young empire. And to do it she was willing to sacrifice even her love for Alex Mercati.

It did not occur to her that Young's own drive to have her had already cost Franco Rizzoni his life.

48

New York, N.Y.
February 1979

Mike Ryan, captain of the 23rd Precinct, had known Alex Mercati for more than ten years, and he had always appreciated the journalist's dedication to the facts. Nevertheless, he found his theory of the death of Franco Rizzoni just a little farfetched.

Ryan chewed on his unlit pipe as he always did in moments of deep thought. He had the results of the Rizzoni autopsy on his desk and it did show that Mercati was at least half right. There was something fishy about the death. Rizzoni had been dead to the world before he hit the pavement with enough heroin in his veins to knock out a horse. But the guy was definitely not an addict and the only puncture the medical examiner found was on the upper part of Rizzoni's right arm near the shoulder. There was no way the guy could have done it himself. But none of this proved that Ashley Young had anything to do with it, which was what Mercati seemed to suspect.

"It's an interesting idea, Alex," he acknowledged. "But what proof have you got?"

"None at this point," Alex admitted. "But logic tells you it was Young. He's insanely jealous of Chris—Miss Wilkerson."

"From what you told me, he has good reason," Ryan smiled. "Do you know her well?"

Alex squirmed uncomfortably before he replied. "Quite well."

"I don't mean to pry, Alex," Ryan said. "It's just that Miss Wilkerson could be imagining things and it's possible that she's influenced your thinking."

"She didn't imagine that Rizzoni was pushed out of the Waldorf," Mercati said.

"No," Ryan admitted, chewing on the pipe. "No, she didn't imagine that." He moved back to the desk to face Mercati. "I'll tell you what, Alex. I'll send a couple of detectives over there to nose around and we'll see if they can come up with something."

*   *   *

It took only three days for Ryan's men to come back to him with the first results of their investigation into the bizarre circumstances surrounding the death of Franco Rizzoni. One of the Waldorf maids had seen window washers entering the art dealer's room shortly before he leaped. By the time Rizzoni's body had hit the pavement, the two supposed window washers had disappeared down a back staircase and into the street.

The two had probably overpowered the young Italian, jammed the needle in his shoulder and thrown him into the street. It was definitely a professional job.

That fact made it even more interesting. The FBI was still investigating the Carlo Gallenzo murder and he had spoken several times with the young investigator on the case, Vic Procaci who was convinced that they were linked to Salvatore Patriarca and beyond that to some-one in New York. Perhaps there was a connection with this latest mob hit. He decided to give Procaci a call.

Part Eight

49

New York, N.Y.
April 1979

Antonio Costanza wiped the sauce from his heavy lips and belched happily. He had just finished the last bit of *penne all'arrabbiata* on his plate. The "angry pasta" in spicy tomato sauce was the specialty of Camillo, the Neapolitan restaurant in Brooklyn where he had agreed to meet with Vic Procaci.

They had been talking and eating for the last hour and Vic had put his problem before the older man. He wanted to know who had murdered Franco Rizzoni and more important who was behind it.

"It's a problem," the older man admitted, shaking his head. "The fucking papers saying the organization's mixed up in it." He drained his glass of red wine. "Carmine Turcone is the man you wanna talk to."

"Who's Carmine Turcone?"

Costanza tore a piece off an evil-looking cigar, stuffed it in his mouth and lit it, sending puffs of foul smoke in every direction.

"Turcone," he grunted, "is a *pezzo di merda* who's done some odd jobs for the Massilia family. The talk is that he hired the hit men."

"Nice guy, I imagine," Vic smiled.

"Sure, sure," Costanza laughed. "You couldn't meet any nicer."

"Where can I find him?" Vic was anxious to get to Turcone as quickly as possible.

Costanza stopped laughing long enough to tell him that the man he was looking for lived in a tenement on Ninth Avenue.

*　　*　　*

Costanza was right. Carmine Turcone turned out to look and smell like a piece of shit. Fat, greasy and bald with hairy arms and small pig eyes that shifted continuously, he was obviously intimidated when Vic told him he had been sent by Costanza.

The apartment itself was furnished with cast-off furniture and Vic sat gingerly on an upholstered chair that was spilling stuffing out onto the floor.

"Who paid you for the Rizzoni job, Carmine?" he asked, getting straight to the point.

"Rizzoni? Rizzoni?" the fat man said blankly. "I don't know what you're talking about."

He began to walk into the other room, but Vic grabbed him by the back of his soiled undershirt and turned him around.

"Listen, fatso," he said as he hit Turcone in the belly with a hard fist. Turcone fell like a sack of potatoes, contorting with pain and struggling to breathe.

"If you play ball with me, Carmine, you may survive. If you don't, I'll let Costanza handle you."

Painfully, Turcone got back on his feet and sank onto a dirty armchair. "Okay, I'll talk, but you're not going to like it."

"Don't waste my time," Vic snapped. "Who gave you the contract?"

The fat man smiled. "Jay Maloney."

Vic was stunned. "Maloney, the senator?"

"Ex-senator," Turcone corrected him.

After a long and brilliant career in the Senate, Jay Maloney had been implicated in a payoff scandal. Then he was defeated for re-election. And in the two years since, he established himself as a lobbyist for the oil industry.

"How much did he pay you?" Procaci demanded.

"Twenty-five grand up front," Turcone answered. "And twenty-five after the job was done."

"That's big money," Vic said. "What was your cut?"

Turcone shifted uneasily. "I gave ten thousand to each of the guys. Maloney and me split the rest."

"What other guys?"

"What are you trying to do to me, mister?" Turcone whined. "I tell you, I'm as good as dead."

"I'm waiting."

"Pete Marcuso and Danny Soriano," Turcone grunted.

"Never heard of them."

Turcone took out a dirty handkerchief and wiped the sweat from his brow. "They're new talent, soldiers in the Maggadino family. If Maggadino hears about this he'll cut off my balls."

"You just tell them I tried to beat the truth out of you and you never said a word," Vic said sarcastically. "Here, I'll make it look good."

He lifted his fist, smashing Turcone's fat nose and sending him sprawling on the floor. The fat man was still sitting there, bloody and whimpering, as Procaci stepped out onto the street.

Vic hailed a taxi and gave the address of the 23rd Precinct. He had to talk to Mike Ryan. His hunch had been right. The Rizzoni murder was a mob hit but, more than that, the order to kill must have come from the highest level.

He noticed the cabbie watching him through the rear-view mirror. Looking down, he saw that his white shirt was smeared with blood, Turcone's blood. He took out a handkerchief, but most of it had already dried.

He grinned at the driver. "I ran into a meat loaf."

*   *   *

The police captain listened in silence until Procaci finished Turcone's story, then rose from his desk and went to the window. He did not speak for a while, just chewed on his pipe and stared out at the street.

"Some fucking mess, Vic," he said, his back still turned. "What do you intend to do about it?"

"I'm not sure, Mike." They both knew that facing Maloney with Turcone's statement at this point would be useless. A cheap hood's word was worthless next to that of even a mildly tarnished United States senator.

50

New York, N.Y.
April 1979

Vic Procaci heard about the arrest of Jonathan Jones and his band on the eleven o'clock news. There was a brief film clip of four scruffy young men who, according to the commentator, had robbed the lavish Fifth Avenue apartment of oil millionaire and conglomerateer Ashley Rodman Young. Their East Village apartment contained a veritable arsenal of deadly weapons and living among them was the sick, incoherent daughter of Young himself.

Vic had only been half-listening as he prepared for bed. Now he sat down and listened carefully. Stephanie Young, suffering from malnutrition and drug intoxication, had been taken to St. Vincent's Hospital. A hospital spokesman said her condition was serious.

Next, several policemen were interviewed. They declared that many of the objects recently stolen from the Young apartment, along with a considerable supply of heroin and cocaine, had been found there.

Finally, Tom Patterson appeared on the screen to read a brief statement from Miss Young's father:

> I am pleased that the robbers have been apprehended and I hope that they will pay fully for their crime, which included not just stealing, but destroying priceless art treasures.

There was no comment about his daughter.

Vic switched off the television. He was stunned by the news that Stephanie was sick and in so much trouble. He had not heard from her in more than two months and now he understood why. He dressed quickly and hurried across town to St. Vincent's.

Christina was already at the hospital. In a few minutes, she realized that this was the young FBI agent Alex had told her about, but even in his distress Procaci avoided discussing the case with a non-professional. Together they waited almost an hour for news of Stephanie's condition.

"At least now I know what happened to Ash's apartment," Christina said. "She must have given her friends a plan of the whole building." She shook her head. "I don't understand. I told her I'd help her."

"I can understand that you feel betrayed, Miss Wilkerson," Vic said. "But it sounds like this was as much a crime of revenge as robbery."

"Please, call me Christina," she said. "And I think you're right."

A bespectacled young doctor approached them. "Miss Young can see you now," he said. "One at a time, please, she's still weak."

"You go ahead, Vic," Christina offered.

"Thank you," he said as he followed the young doctor to Stephanie's room.

She looked very small and helpless lying there in the bed. There were tubes attached to her arms and a respirator was nearby. She was almost as white as the hospital sheets, her long blond hair dirty and matted and dark hollows under her eyes. But she recognized him and managed to smile.

"Oh, Vic, I'm sorry I can't get up," she sighed.

The joke was a good sign and already he felt better. "I thought I told you to stay out of trouble," he said as he sat down next to the bed.

"Honey, you know me. I can't say no."

"What am I gonna do with you?"

"You shouldn't have let me go, Vic," she pouted. "You'd keep me out of trouble."

That was the truth. At least he loved her enough to come tearing over when he heard she was sick. There was still no sign of her father and the kid had almost died.

He knew how he felt about Stephanie and he couldn't dismiss her as just another bimbo he could fuck and forget. It was just that the kid had been involved with so many men. She'd gone to bed with him on the spur of the moment. For a traditional guy like himself it was hard to take. But the more he saw of the father, the more it became clear why the kid was this way. Jesus, the guy couldn't even get in a cab and come down and see her? She was his daughter for Christ's sake. No wonder she was throwing herself at one man after another.

He was probably crazy for what he was about to do, but he had to do it.

"Look, Stephanie," he began. "When you get out of here, I want you to stay with me. Someone has to look after you until you're back on your feet."

She looked at him warily. "And then you'll throw me out?"

"No," he shook his head. "Then I'm going to marry you."

"I don't think I heard that," she said, her voice almost a whisper.

"You heard it," he said firmly. "Only you'll

479

have to change your ways. No more trips to Las Vegas or Paris. No more drugs." He bent over and kissed her. "Now I'll send in Christina, then I want you to get some rest."

"I can't wait to tell her," she giggled happily. "You'll be surprised how fast I'm going to get out of here."

* * *

Ash Young listened stonily when Christina called from St. Vincent's to announce that Stephanie was going to recover and even marry again.

"It's no longer my concern," he said icily. "She's a tramp and a thief and a junkie. Now she's taken up with another gigolo."

"Vic Procaci is no gigolo," Christina assured him. "And he'll give her a lot of love. That's something I don't think she's had before."

"You see what being nice to her gets," he snapped. "She let her boyfriend nearly destroy my home. I've done everything I could for her, given her the best money could buy and she turns out like this."

"Did you ever give her love, Ash?"

He hung up.

51

New York, N.Y.
April 1979

Vic Procaci stayed at the hospital with Stephanie until almost dawn, then went home to catch a few hours of sleep. He woke up to the news that Carmine Turcone had been found sitting in his car in a Brooklyn parking lot, his hands and feet bound. He had been strangled, his tongue cut out and pinned to his chest. Exit one witness.

Things went downhill from there. When he arrived at the office, his supervisor informed him that he was being taken off the Gallenzo case.

"But why, chief?" he protested. "I told you only yesterday that we could wrap it up soon."

"There are no whys or whats, Vic," the

chief's voice was hard. "I have another assignment for you. Nick Carraway is replacing you as of now."

"What's the beef, sir?" Procaci exploded. "There must be a reason!"

His chief stared at him without sympathy. "You know the rules, Vic. No agent gets personally involved in a case."

So he knew about Stephanie already and she wasn't even out of the hospital. "It's not what you think, sir. I can exp—"

But the chief cut him off. "It's not what I think, Vic. It's what they think in Washington. This order comes from the top. There's no point in arguing." He rose from his chair to signify that the conversation was at an end.

Vic also stood up. Only one man was powerful enough to move so quickly and surely to cut off his investigation. It was useless to try to fight Ash Young at this level.

"OK, chief. Orders are orders," he said reluctantly. "But I don't like it and neither should you. Something in this case stinks to high heaven."

*　　*　　*

Mike Ryan listened to Procaci's story with interest. He had his own problems that morning.

"You ain't heard nothing yet," he assured

Procaci. "Two hours ago, I was told to forget all about the Rizzoni case. The medical examiner says he can't find any evidence of violence. He's classifying it as suicide and that's it."

Vic laughed bitterly. "They've covered everything. No witnesses, the investigation's stopped and we're all supposed to act like nothing happened. I could puke."

But his mind was already racing, thinking of something Turcone had hinted at when he mentioned the name of Jay Maloney. He'd given the impression that even the ex-Senator was not acting alone, that somewhere behind him someone else, someone very powerful, was pulling the strings. Someone, perhaps, who would be very anxious to use any pretext to remove Vic Procaci from the investigation.

"You know, Mike," Procaci said casually. "I think I'm going to have a chat with Maloney."

Ryan laughed. "I thought you were off the case?"

"Sure I am," Vic smiled. "Officially, I can't do a thing. But, unofficially, I can nail that bastard and whoever is behind him. And I have a pretty good idea who that is."

52

New York, N.Y.
April 1979

Alex Mercati sat in front of his typewriter, staring at the blank page. He was supposed to be writing a final obituary on Mohammed Reza Pahlevi's White Revolution. The shah was now in exile, poor Hoveyda still in jail.

To Alex it was a tragic story. A brilliant, energetic man with dazzling plans for bringing his country into an important role in the world, a man of great ideas, had failed because he could not follow through.

Perhaps his greatest tragedy was expressed in a catch phrase Alex had heard often when he visited Teheran in August. "Nobody dared to say a lie to Reza Shah," they would whisper. "No one dared say the truth to his son."

When the last drops of oil petered out at the end of the twentieth century, the Shahanshah, the King of Kings, would be at one with Ozymandias.

These thoughts had been floating through his head for nearly a half hour and still he had not written one word.

Every time a thought formed in his mind, it was replaced by a vision of Christina. One moment she was crying, the next she was laughing, then she was pleading with him to come and help her.

It had been weeks since he had heard from her and it was driving him crazy. He wanted to see her, to touch her, and the idea that she was alone with that monster made him crazy. She had warned him not to try to contact her because she was sure that Ash was having her watched. But he was beginning to fear that she was in real danger. He had to talk with her.

He buzzed his secretary.

"Jean, please get me Christina Wilkerson on the line. It's important."

Two minutes later, Jean was back on the intercom. "Miss Wilkerson isn't home, but I left messages with her answering service and the agency to call you."

"Thanks, Jean." He felt better already. He started his editorial and about an hour and twenty minutes later he completed the last sentence. Just then, Jean buzzed him to announce that Miss Wilkerson was on the line.

"I called as soon as I got your message," Christina said nervously. "Is something wrong?"

"I've got to see you," he said.

"But I told you, I think Ash is having me watched. Can't this wait until after the wedding?"

"No!" he was emphatic. That was exactly the point. He had to somehow talk her out of this marriage.

"But I'm getting married in two days."

"That's why I have to see you."

"All right, Alex," she relented. "We'll meet for one last goodbye. But we have to be careful."

She suggested that he drop by Orsini's the next day when she would be lunching with Melinda. No one would suspect such an accidental meeting. Alex agreed. It was the only way.

It had never occurred to either of them that his line was tapped.

*   *   *

The stocky, red-faced man who visited Ash Young in his office at the Young Building was Conrad Hoffer, probably the best wiretapper in the business. He had worked extensively for Central Intelligence and other government agencies. When a private individual required his services, the price was high because the work was highly illegal. The fee he charged Ash Young for tapping Christina Wilkerson's apartment and Alex Mercati's office was twenty-five thousand dollars.

He considered it worth the price. Now he knew for sure that his fiancée and Mercati were still seeing each other. His enemies were everywhere. His own daughter had destroyed his home and now his fiancée was still seeing her former lover. His heart racing, he groped anxiously for Reinhardt's pills.

53

New York, N.Y.
April 1979

As Alex walked into Orsini's, he felt his heart pounding. He had it bad, like a schoolboy on his first date. He walked up to the first floor and he saw them immediately. Or rather he saw Christina. He barely noticed Melinda.

He approached the corner table. "What are you two concocting together?" he said as casually as he could.

They both looked up and smiled.

"Hello, darling," Christina said. She was wearing a white linen suit and a green silk blouse that matched her eyes. Her black hair was loose around her shoulders. She was more beautiful than he remembered.

"I had to see you," he admitted. "May I sit down?"

"Yes, please join us," she agreed. Then, more softly, she whispered, "If someone is watching us, I guess this looks casual enough."

"Christina," he whispered back. "This can't go on. I don't know what's happening to you and I'm worried sick."

"What's happening is that tomorrow I'll be Mrs. Ashley Rodman Young," she said.

Melinda coughed delicately. "Perhaps I should leave the two of you alone," she suggested.

"Thanks, Melinda," Christina agreed. "This won't take long." She turned back to Alex.

"Christina, you can't go through with this," he said.

"It's a little late for that," she smiled sadly. "Ash has made all the arrangements. After the ceremony, we're flying to Belvedere."

There was an awkward pause. They were both recalling their own trip there together.

"Christina, you were right about Rizzoni," Alex said at last. "I've been working with Procaci and the police and we know now for sure that he was murdered. It was a professional job. And listen to this: someone is trying to squelch the investigation."

"But I told you, Franco wasn't like that at all, he'd be the last person to get involved with gangsters."

"He got involved with you, Christina."

A cold chill invaded her body and she began to see where he was leading.

"Do you mean to say that Ash had something to do with killing Franco?"

"Yes, Christina, that's exactly what I'm saying," he insisted. "You've got to call this marriage off."

"No!" she said. "I can't."

"What do you mean, you can't?" he continued, his tone changing from concern to anger. "How can you go through knowing that he might be a murderer?"

She struggled to control herself. Even now she could not bring herself to confide her secret, yet she was sure in her heart that Alex was right. Ash was quite capable of murder. "All I know, Alex, is that you don't want me to marry Ash Young and that you'd do anything to stop it."

"But you admitted that you think he's spying on you!"

"That doesn't make him a murderer."

"Oh, Christina, how can I make you understand what kind of man he really is?"

What kind of man Ash Young really is? She wanted to scream. If anyone knew the real Ash Young, it was she. But that was not going to stop her from marrying him.

"Suppose I told you that I know exactly what kind of man he is?" she said, and described how she had refused to sign the prenuptial agreement and her remark about the pills. "You should have seen the way he looked at me,

Alex. You know, I think he killed Jessica, too."

"But if you think he's a murderer," Alex said gravely. "How can you possibly go through with this marriage?"

Christina sighed. "Suppose I told you that I hate him more than any man I've ever known, that I'm only marrying him because I hope somehow to destroy him?"

"Christina, what are you talking about?"

She longed to tell him the story of her mother, but now was not the time. All she could say was that she had her reasons.

He decided to try another tack. "Suppose I could prove that he murdered Rizzoni? Would that change your mind?"

"Only if it meant he was going to jail," she said firmly. "I want to see him finally pay for something."

54

New York, N.Y.
April 1979

Christina's wedding day, the day Alex Mercati had convinced himself would never arrive, was here. While the woman he loved was marrying a man she admitted she loathed, he struggled to concentrate on putting out the magazine. Then he got Procaci's call.

"I guess you've seen the papers," Procaci said.

"Yes, I've got them in front of me," he answered. Jean had just brought them in. Both the *Post* and the *News* had stories on the wedding describing the fairy tale saga of the poor girl from Texas who had married her fabulously wealthy employer. At this very minute, the ceremony was being performed by State Supreme Court Justice Everett Ewebanks in Young's apartment, with Tom Patterson and Melinda Parsons as witnesses. Then the newlyweds would be on their way to Palm Beach.

"Well, all is not lost, pal," Procaci insisted. "I've had some breaks. Got time to see me?"

"All the time in the world," Alex tried to put some enthusiasm into his voice, but as far as he was concerned the battle had already been lost.

"I'm still here in Washington," Procaci said. "I've still a few things to straighten out, but I'll catch the first plane I can for New York and come to see you. It could be quite late, but I think you'll want to hear the latest developments."

"I'll be here," Alex said. "But will you give me a hint of what it's all about?"

"I'd better not on the phone," Vic replied. "But I can assure you, you'll be most interested."

It was 11:00 p.m. when Procaci finally reached Mercati's house. He looked bushed, but pleased. Even before Alex had finished fixing him a scotch and soda, he was describing the latest developments in the Rizzoni case.

"Before he was offed, that slime Turcone insisted he got paid by Jay Maloney," Procaci said. "But there was no way we could've used his word against Maloney's. Then I got an idea."

Gleefully, talking faster now as he relished his story, Procaci explained that he had called on Maloney in Washington.

"I told him we'd connected him to the Rizzoni hit and I gave him the impression that whoever he was working for had already talked to me and was blaming him for everything. It was a lie, but it worked. I told him that if he came clean he might get off easily. Otherwise he was in for life. Maloney broke down and admitted everything. I had a stenographer take down his entire deposition. Even wrote down the name of his boss. And guess who that is?"

Alex already knew: Ashley Rodman Young. He ran over to the phone. "I've got to call Christina," he shouted.

Procaci rushed to restrain him. "You're crazy if you do that, Alex. You'd alert the old man. Let the police handle it."

"But don't you see what can happen in the meantime, Vic?" Alex was almost hysterical. "Ashley Young has powerful connections. If you go to the police he'll probably hear that there is a warrant for his arrest and fly the coop, taking Christina along. Then, when he's out of the country, someone will take care of Maloney, and Young will return unscratched."

Procaci had to admit that Mercati had a point. Young's long reach had already shown itself when he and Captain Ryan had both been dropped out of the case and Rizzoni's death had been declared a suicide. "Okay," he said. "Let's you and I fly down to Palm Beach first thing in the morning. But no phone calls. Promise?"

"Promise," said Alex. "I'll just call the airline and reserve two seats."

Alex couldn't sleep that night.

55

Palm Beach, Florida
April 1979

The newlyweds flew down to Palm Beach in Mr. Young's own Lockheed jet. The dependable August had preceded them to prepare Belvedere for its new mistress, and he was waiting for them in the doorway as Young's limousine moved down the long driveway.

Christina recalled the first time she had approached the huge, white stucco mansion, sitting beside Alex on her way to meet the fabled Ashley Young. She smiled as she remembered Alex telling her that Ash went into a rage if there were tire marks in the drive.

As the footman brought her bags up to her room, she looked around at the marble stairs, the priceless antiques on display everywhere.

The house reflected her father's personality: perfectly furnished and decorated, but cold with nary a single corner where one could relax and throw up one's feet without fearing to spoil an irreplaceable *objet*.

She remembered how disturbed her mother had been when she learned she was at Belvedere. How she had gone for a swim and found Ash there on the empty beach, watching her.

It had all started here and now it would end here. She wished suddenly that she could turn the clock back and cancel all that had happened.

She and Ash had barely talked during the flight down, but now he explained to her that they had adjoining bedroom suites. Jessica's had been redecorated for her and Jessica's maid, Charlotte, was waiting to help her. Dinner would be served at eight. It would not be necessary to dress.

Her room turned out to be huge, with French doors that led to a flagstone terrace and a view of the Atlantic. The walls of the room were hung with royal blue silk that matched the coverings on the chairs and the bed. Jessica's Meissen had been removed and instead the open glass shelves were filled with Limoges.

There were two doors which Charlotte explained stiffly led to Mr. Young's bedroom and to Christina's private bath, a luxurious affair of pink marble with gold fixtures.

Christina watched the young maid as she drew her bath and removed the Marina Ferrari silk dress with delicate flower prints that she had recently purchased in New York. Soon she would have to have a long talk with the girl. But for tonight she was too tired. She could barely cope with the idea of dining with her new husband.

While Charlotte unpacked for her, Christina undressed and let herself sink into the perfumed bubbles of the pink, marble tub. So this is the luxury wealth gives you, she thought. How ironic. How many women would gladly trade places with her tonight? But were they willing to endure what she had in order to get here? Would they be able to continue to pay the price?

Christina struggled to push those thoughts from her mind. All this was hers. It belonged to her by right—blood right. Her mother had paid for it in her own blood, and by God she would have it.

It was almost eight o'clock when she stepped out of the tub and began to towel herself off. She derived more perverse pleasure knowing that the ever punctual Ash was probably already waiting for her downstairs. She didn't bother with make-up or jewelry and simply brushed her long dark hair back into a pony tail, tying it with a blue ribbon and heading for the downstairs terrace.

The flagstone terrace overlooked the large

gardens of Belvedere. A small table, covered with a flowered Porthault cloth, was set for two. It was all very beautiful and romantic: white and pink roses in a silver vase, golden plates and candles protected from the ocean breezes by glass covers. Beside the table a bottle of Crystal champagne waited on ice.

As Christina had expected, Ash was dressed for dinner. He wore a blue blazer and white gabardine pants. He had tied a blue and red silk scarf rakishly above the neck of his cream silk shirt. As August held a chair for her, Ash looked at her with concern.

"You seem disturbed, Christina."

"Just a slight headache," she answered. "But I'll be all right. I took two aspirins."

He waited in silence as August opened the champagne and poured it into two glasses. Then, with a nod Ash dismissed him and turned his attention back to Christina.

"I wouldn't want my beautiful bride to be sick on our wedding night," he said. "This is a night for celebration." And he raised his glass in a toast.

Christina sipped the champagne, thinking: "I toast to your ruin, you monster." She could only nibble at the grilled veal chop and salad that was served. She had a knot in her stomach from worrying over how to keep Ash at bay. He was looking at her as if to scrutinize her thoughts, and she had the sensation of his reading her mind very clearly.

After a while he spoke. "Is something worrying you, Christina? You shouldn't hold any secrets from your husband. First-night jitters perhaps?"

She did not answer and he did not insist. For the rest of the meal he talked about the new plane he intended to buy—to take them and a few selected friends on a trip around the world.

Finally, the awful moment that Christina was dreading arrived. As they walked upstairs Ash paused outside her bedroom. The time of truth had come. He would want to collect what he had paid for.

They paused in front of her bedroom door. Charlotte had left it open, but as Christina moved through, Ash pulled her toward him. He began to kiss her. She tried to pull away, a reflexive revulsion, but his grip held her tight.

"This is the moment I've been waiting for," he whispered hoarsely.

"But the servants," she protested.

"I've sent them all away. We're alone here."

Alone. At least there'd be no witnesses to her shame. She let him lead her inside her bedroom and to the bed. He began to caress her breast and his hand continued to explore her body. She closed her eyes, struggling to suppress her loathing and disgust. But she had no choice. This was the *via crucis* she had chosen for herself so that she might obtain her final vendetta.

No, Christina reflected bitterly. She had

forsaken the man she loved. She had set out to seduce her own father and she had more than succeeded. The man was literally mad about her. His entire empire would be hers on a silver platter. She could not lose it all now because she did not have the stomach for it, because the idea of this cold-blooded, incestuous union offended her morality. It was the price she had to pay to destroy this man.

No. She could not stop now, but neither would she totally surrender to him. She would never give him that satisfaction. One moan of pleasure from her and he would have won. Instead, she remained limp and silent as he finally gave up trying to arouse her and moved on top of her, entering her with desperate urgency. As he climaxed in a hoarse scream that was half rage and half a rattle of pain, she knew she had won. She smiled.

Yet even now, as they lay beside each other in silence, he seemed unaware of the depth of her hatred. But her failure to respond to his love-making had deeply disturbed him. He kissed her on the cheek, rose from the bed and with the words "Sleep well, dear," he left. As soon as he was gone she raced to the bathroom and ran the shower. She stood under the torrent of steamy water, as hot as she could bear, and struggled to scrub every last trace of Ash Young from her body while her mind plotted the next move.

In the morning, she promised herself, she would have a long talk with Charlotte.

*   *   *

The next day, the sun woke Christina at seven o'clock, but she waited until nine before ringing for her breakfast. As expected, it was Charlotte who brought her the tray of orange juice, warm croissants and coffee.

"Charlotte, please sit down," she said gently. "I have to ask you some questions."

The maid took a seat on a blue silk fauteuil and stared at her new, young mistress with serious brown eyes. She could not hide her resentment of the girl who had replaced her beloved mistress.

Christina seated herself on the opposite chair. "I want to ask you about Mrs. Young."

The brown eyes became even more somber and Charlotte seemed to tense up. "What about Madame Young?"

"I know that you hardly know me," Christina continued. "But you must trust me and answer my questions carefully."

"Yes, madame." She sensed that she could trust Christina completely.

"Why didn't you try to stop your mistress from taking all those pills?"

The brown eyes filled with tears. She had been waiting months for someone to ask her that. She pulled out a linen handkerchief and began to dab at her eyes as she answered.

"It was Monsieur Young. He said she had to take them." Charlotte began to cry. "I told him they made madame sick, but he would not believe me."

"He didn't believe you?" Christina's heart was beating wildly. So it was not just Rizzoni who was a victim.

"Monsieur Young said the doctors wanted madame to take those pills every morning and every night before bed," she started to sob. "It was so terrible, Madame could not eat, she was weak. . . ."

Christina came and put her arm around Charlotte, comforting her. She waited until the girl had composed herself before she resumed her questions.

"What about Mrs. Young, Charlotte? Did she ever talk about her health?"

"*Oui*, madame," Charlotte nodded. "She said she was afraid of dying. Oh, it was so sad." The tears began to pour again. "She was so good and kind, but she was afraid of Monsieur Young. She knew the pills were bad for her but she kept taking them because Monsieur insisted."

"Did you try to stop it, Charlotte?"

"Oh, yes, madame," she said. "I called a doctor once, but Monsieur Young heard me and he was furious. He told me that if I ever did it again he would fire me."

"Do you think you could tell this to the police?" Christina asked.

"Oh, yes, madame, if you believe me."

She needed time to think. She would have to call Alex and tell him that it didn't matter about Rizzoni, she had an eyewitness to another murder. But she would have to move quickly. She sent the little maid away and turned back to the room.

Ash was standing in his doorway.

"How long have you been there?" she said nervously.

"Long enough."

"You heard?"

"Yes."

"I'm leaving," she announced.

"No, you're not," he said as he grabbed her arm. "I paid a lot of money for you and you're not going anywhere."

She turned to look at him with disgust. "You think you can solve anything with money, don't you, Ash? But I'm going to get your money eventually anyway."

"You leave here and you'll never see a penny. I'll have the marriage annulled faster than you know."

"I don't think so," she said coolly.

He laughed. "Surely you're not going to take what the girl told you seriously, are you? They're the romantic ravings of a servant."

"And Alex? Is he imagining that you had Franco Rizzoni killed?"

His face turned the awful ashen color she had seen once before in Paris.

"I did it for you, Christina," he said, relaxing his grip. But he seemed to have difficulty getting the words out. "I had to have you."

It was awful and yet her first reaction was to laugh. She moved back on the bed and laughed so hard that tears spilled from her eyes. Her reaction only made him more furious.

"I don't think it's very funny," he said with a grimace as he struggled against the pain shooting through his right arm. "I thought we understood each other, Christina," he insisted. "I thought we had an agreement."

"How could I honor an agreement with a murderer?"

"I got rid of Jessica and Rizzoni for you, Christina. I loved you."

"The way you loved my mother?" she taunted.

"I never knew your mother."

"Oh no?" she demanded. "Look at me, Ash, look at me."

He stared at her, held by the rage in her eyes. Slowly, an awful transfiguration took place before him as the woman he'd hungered to possess became the image of the girl he'd once loved.

"*Teresa,*" he whispered.

"Yes, yes," Christina stormed. "Teresa, my mother, your victim. You do remember her, don't you? She never forgot you."

"Teresa was your mother? Then—"

"Yes, then I'm your daughter, Ash, or should I call you Father?"

"You knew that and you married me?" He could feel the pain spreading to his chest and there was no way to control it. He groped in the pocket of his jacket for the gold pillbox, but in his nervous state the box slipped onto the blue Aubusson carpet.

Downstairs, there was some kind of commotion. They could hear August arguing with someone, their voices rising, but Christina ignored them and strode toward the small gold box. Deftly, she stooped, grabbed it and tossed it out the open french doors.

Ash watched with dismay, clutching his side. The pain had become excruciating. His face had turned an awful blue color. If he could just get downstairs, August would help him. But it was too late. He could hardly see now and, blindly groping for support, he reached up to one of the glass shelves. To his horror, it gave way, bringing down glass, steel supports and priceless Limoges upon him.

The noise cut short the quarrel downstairs and suddenly August burst into the room, followed by Alex Mercati and Vic Procaci.

"Christina, are you all right?" he screamed.

She ran to his arms as he looked past her to the fallen body of Ash Young surrounded by shards of porcelain and glass. Some of the glass had cut him and blood was seeping onto the blue rug. August knelt beside the body, then rose and addressed his new mistress.

"I shall call an ambulance, madame," he intoned and tactfully left the room.

Alone with Alex and Vic, she poured out the whole story, about Ash and Teresa, about Jessica and about her own plan to destroy him. At last he understood what lay behind her strange behavior.

"Oh, my poor darling," he said as he listened to the mounting account of Young's horrors. "If only you'd told me. I'd never have let you go through with this alone."

Gently, he explained to her what Procaci had found out, how the murder of Rizzoni had been commissioned by Ashley Young.

"But how did a man like Ash ever get involved with gangsters?"

"At that level of corruption, they're all brothers," Vic said. "We even have evidence he leaned on Patriarca to exterminate Carlo Gallenzo. He was terrified that Stephanie was going to marry him."

Christina shook her head. "But he must have known she'd be with Carlo when it happened. She could have been killed, too."

"That was what he planned on."

"The whole story is incredible."

Alex took her hand. "Your father was an incredible man."

Epilogue

Palm Beach
December 1979

Ash Young lay in his hospital bed, his once vital body withered and shrunk from the idle months since his stroke. Deprived of the sun, his skin had faded to alabaster. Even his hair had whitened. When his eyes closed he looked like a corpse, and when they opened, a truer tragedy was apparent. The cold gray that had stared down so many rivals now blazed in the helpless body. But it was useless. Any message they bore was wasted on his attendants.

Ash was a feeble old man, at the mercy of round-the-clock nurses. There were four of them: Felice, stout and dark, would wake him for his morning wash and shave, and feed him breakfast. Martha, a gray-haired grandmotherly type, fed him lunch. The dinner shift was assumed by thin, red-haired Claire, until Helga came in at eight, stern faced, and put him to bed. And sometime between then and dawn, the round would begin again.

Once in a while, when the heavy window curtains were drawn wide, Ash could look out to the gardens of Spring Lake, the rest home to which his devoted young wife had committed him shortly after his stroke. But most of the time he was in darkness, while his bored attendants showed their preference for the large screen television that took up most of the rear wall.

It was Claire now. She had finished feeding him—a humiliating experience. After wiping the drippings from Ash's chin as though he were an infant, she piled the dishes neatly on a tray and summoned the orderly to remove them. The orderly joked with her for a few minutes, ignoring the pain-wracked gray eyes staring at them from the bed. But Claire cut the conversation short, dismissed the orderly, and turned her interest to the television screen.

It was time for Claire's favorite show, "The Nightly Magazine," and tonight's feature was especially important. The personality profile was on Christina Young. Claire leaned back in the armchair and stared at the screen.

Ash stared too. There was no escaping Christina's image. She was more beautiful than ever. Someone was talking—a narrator. The background looked so familiar, but Ash couldn't place it. He struggled with his tired, aching brain to make sense of what he was watching. Was it at Belvedere? Yes, Christina was now the mistress of Belvedere. From what Ash could see, little had changed. The same opulence prevailed. And yet, of course, everything had changed.

The off-camera narration described Christina: "The beautiful former model had been married only a few hours when her husband, international tycoon Ashley Young, was incapacitated by a paralyzing stroke," the newsman gushed. "Not since Christina Onassis took over her late father's shipping empire has so young a woman found herself at the helm of such a grand organization and in possession of such a fortune."

The film continued with a montage of Christina's doings: Christina with Tom Patterson, her right hand man, who was saying "Mr. Young could not have selected a better heir," Christina with her "favorite stepdaughter," and Stephanie telling an interviewer "Christina and I are just like sisters."

Ash's feeble heart raced with agitation. But the worst was yet to come, for soon the focus returned to Christina herself. She was joined in her drawing room by Alex Mercati, "her closest business advisor and good friend."

Ash's mouth twisted in a pitiful attempt to protest. But nurse Claire's attention was on the Christina Young story. She was totally enthralled with the Cinderella tale of the poor half-Chicana Texas girl, daughter of a ghetto doctor and a Mexican mother, who had parlayed her beauty and brains into a storybook marriage to one of the world's richest men. According to the narrator of this tale, tragedy entered the picture when her husband was felled by a devastating stroke. But Christina had survived that too, taking over the Young empire. Supported by her "good friend" Mercati and Tom Patterson, she had established herself as a fully capable replacement for her husband.

"Lies, lies," Ash struggled to scream, but it was hopeless. He tried to control his fury. He thought about what the doctor had said. Another stroke—even a mild one—would kill him. He wouldn't mind dying and ending this torture, but he had to resist that. He could not let that happen. Even in this helpless state, his withered shell of a body still stood between Christina and the man she really loved. He must hang on. He must.

Riveted to the television screen, Claire did not notice the warm tears beginning to flow from the cold gray eyes of Ashley Young.

EXCITING BESTSELLERS FROM ZEBRA

PLEASURE DOME (1134, $3.75)
by Judith Liederman
Though she posed as the perfect society wife, Laina Eastman was harboring a clandestine love. And within an empire of boundless opulence, throughout the decades following World War II, Laina's love would meet the challenges of fate . . .

HERITAGE (1100, $3.75)
by Lewis Orde
Beautiful innocent Leah and her two brothers were forced by the holocaust to flee their parents' home. A courageous immigrant family, each battled for love, power and their very lifeline—their HERITAGE.

FOUR SISTERS (1048, $3.75)
by James Fritzhand
From the ghettos of Moscow to the glamor and glitter of the Winter Palace, four elegant beauties are torn between love and sorrow, danger and desire—but will forever be bound together as FOUR SISTERS.

BYGONES (1030, $3.75)
by Frank Wilkinson
Once the extraordinary Gwyneth set eyes on the handsome aristocrat Benjamin Whisten, she was determined to foster the illicit love affair that would shape three generations—and win a remarkable woman an unforgettable dynasty!

THE LION'S WAY (900, $3.75)
by Lewis Orde
An all-consuming saga that spans four generations in the life of troubled and talented David, who struggles to rise above his immigrant heritage and rise to a world of glamour, fame and success!

Available wherever paperbacks are sold, or order direct from the Publisher. Send cover price plus 50¢ per copy for mailing and handling to Zebra Books, 475 Park Avenue South, New York, N.Y. 10016. DO NOT SEND CASH.

BESTSELLING ROMANCES BY JANELLE TAYLOR